# The
## *Story of*

Also available by *Marcia Preston*

THE BUTTERFLY HOUSE

# The
# *Story* of *Us*

## MARCIA PRESTON

MIRA

*MIRA is a registered trademark of Harlequin Enterprises Limited,
used under licence.*

*First published in Great Britain 2007
MIRA Books, Eton House, 18-24 Paradise Road,
Richmond, Surrey, TW9 1SR*

© Marcia Preston 2005

*First published in 2006 by Harlequin Enterprises Limited in USA
under the title The Piano Man.*

*ISBN: 978 0 7783 0138 7*

58-0707

*Printed in Great Britain
by Clays Ltd, St Ives plc*

## ACKNOWLEDGEMENTS

The idea for this story began with a television commercial for a local hospital. I am deeply grateful to Jim Lenhard, the heart recipient featured in the commercial, and his wife, Evelyn, who welcomed me into their home and talked about their experience. My sincere thanks and respect to Shirley Treanor, who was gracious and courageous in talking with me about her son Robert, the donor of Jim's new heart.

I'm grateful to friends Judy and John McNerney and the transplant support group at Integris Baptist Medical Centre in Oklahoma City; to Phil Van Satvern at the Oklahoma Organ Sharing Network; and to David Click, RN, Sandy Schimmel, Martha Clark Scala and her sister Margo Potheau, Sharon Williams, Charles Perry and Donna Ferrell. Special thanks to nurse Laura French, who works with transplant patients at the Nazia Zudhi Transplant Institute in Oklahoma City.

For their assistance with matters from music to real estate, San Antonio flora and fauna and NCAA recruiting, my thanks to Greg Heltman, general director of the Santa Fe Symphony and Chorus; Annabelle Kirkwood with Monte Vista Realty; RE/MAX realtor Marilyn Kennedy; Julie McGeehee at The University of Oklahoma; Joan Hall and E Shan Correa, writers and friends; Keith Gibson, genial nurseryman in San Antonio; Marcia Marsden, a Texas ornithologist; Eldon Matthews, retired long-haul trucker and fisherman.

On a personal level, thanks as always to my husband and research buddy, Paul; to Suzanne and Jeff; to my editor Miranda Stecyk and agent Elaine English.

This book is dedicated to all the families whose loved ones were organ donors, to their recipients and to everyone who has registered as a potential donor.

# Prologue

All weekend Nathan had the weird feeling he was watching himself in a video. On Friday when the Texas A&M University coaches showed the recruits through the athletic facilities—the weight rooms and training area, the practice field—Nathan saw it like a dream. Nothing felt quite real.

The student host assigned to him and his friend Kent toured them through the athletes' dormitory and cafeteria. Then Nathan asked to see the biology department. Kent had no idea about a major course of study, so he didn't care about anything on campus unless it was connected with sports. Kent and Nathan had played football together since they were small, and Kent was a first-rate defensive back. But his grades at Judson High were a factor. Today's coaches wanted recruits who could think as well as hit, players who wouldn't be put on academic probation. Kent was smart enough; he just didn't study. Only one school had recruited him so far. But Nathan, with his nearly perfect marks, had choices.

Their student host, Dejuan Sams, was a freshman with the team and a good student, as Nathan would be. A highly regarded player, Dejuan likely would replace the team's senior starter next year. Nathan liked Dejuan right away and did his best to pay attention, ask intelligent questions. But he couldn't shake this eerie feeling that he was just going through the motions. His mind had detached, as if some big decision were already made.

Maybe it was that Cajun shrimp he'd eaten at the buffet dinner last night. He'd never seen so much food. Great food. He'd thought Kent was going to kill himself.

Saturday was a game day, and the team always spent the night before at a local hotel, to cut down on distractions. The recruits got to stay there, too. This morning they were hanging out with the coaches, sitting in on the position meetings. It was an inside look at the program and Nathan liked what he saw.

He'd already visited the University of Texas in Austin, his other top choice. His mom had gone with him that time because she knew her way around the campus. Ages ago she'd attended the University of Texas for a year, before she dropped out to have him, her one and only. He knew his mom would like him to attend UT, but she hadn't tried to sway his decision. She'd be a big fan no matter where he ended up.

The UT visit was unofficial, which meant they'd looked around mostly on their own. This trip, an overnight visit with Kent along, was different. Nathan was seriously interested in attending A&M, and he'd wanted to get a feeling for living here on his own. "Neither of Kent's parents will come along, for sure," he'd told his mom. Kent was constantly at odds with his dad and didn't communicate much at all with his mother. So Nathan's mom had agreed, reluctantly, to let them make the drive from San Antonio to College Station alone.

Nathan was lucky in a thousand ways. Even without a dad at home, he had better parenting than most kids he knew. His mom trusted him absolutely. But she was a worrier; she couldn't help it. He knew she wouldn't relax until he got home.

At noon Dejuan handed them two tickets and turned them loose to enjoy the game. Nathan and Kent joined the seventy thousand people milling into the stadium in the sticky, late-September sunshine. Despite last night's feast, Kent's eyes lit up when he saw all the concession stands.

He grinned at Nathan, his freckles popping. "Serious junk food!"

Kent got in line. Nathan waited around while Kent armed himself with nachos, two hotdogs, a slice of pizza and a huge bottle of cola. Nathan's stomach still felt queasy. When he passed up the taco stand, Kent looked at him with alarm.

"You okay?"

"Sure. I'm just not hungry yet." He got a bottle of water and led Kent up the ramp.

The stadium was rocking. A&M prided itself on the loudest crowd in the Big 12 Conference, the confederation of universities that competed together every year. The stands were an ocean of twirling white bandanas. Nathan had come to a game here with his high school coach, and he'd watched dozens of times on TV. But during those games he hadn't pictured himself as part of the student body. Now he imagined running onto the field with the team, surfing on that gigantic wave of crowd noise. It was a great feeling.

Nathan and Kent joined the frenetic roar, whooping and shouting for every good play the entire first half of the game. At intermission, they watched the University's famous marching band perform on the field.

By the third quarter, A&M was already twenty-one points ahead. Kent's interest drifted to a cute girl on the cheerleader squad, on the sideline directly in front of them. The girl had a long, dark ponytail that made Nathan think of Lindsey, not for the first time that day.

Lindsey wasn't the cheerleader type, which was fine by him. She was a straight-A student, a little on the serious side, but Nathan could always make her laugh. Lindsey had what he thought of—but would never say aloud—as a *sense of nobility*. She had strong ethics, an unfailing sense of what was right and what was wrong. Nathan admired that, because he tended to see both sides of every issue, and sometimes that was a disadvantage. In government class, they'd had mock elections and he couldn't decide which presidential candidate he'd vote for because he saw things he did and didn't like on both sides.

Lindsey planned to major in journalism, and yesterday he'd picked up a listing of the university's journalism classes to take back to her. She was keeping her options open, but he sure hoped she'd go to college where he did. The possibility of going to separate universities hundreds of miles apart made Nathan's chest tight. Maybe he was too young to know if it would last, but he knew that besides his mom, Lindsey was the only person he'd ever loved.

He checked his watch. Lindsey probably wasn't home yet. She worked weekends at a community newspaper that she called a "rag," some kind of journalism slang. In all this noise, he couldn't have heard anything on the mobile phone anyway.

Nathan focused his attention on Sellkirk, the starting quarterback who was still in the game despite the lead. His palms itched. Sellkirk's passing arm wasn't the best in the league, but he had quick feet and patience with his passes. He wasn't much of a threat as a runner, though he could scramble when he had to. Nathan could run, and his arm was stronger. But Sellkirk's main strength was his leadership of the team.

That was key. Lots of guys had athletic ability and a good arm, but the quarterback had to rally the team, make them believe they could win. Nathan had done it at his high school in San Antonio. But could he do it as an incoming freshman among older teammates? The A&M coach had promised that Nathan could compete for the starting spot. Sellkirk had one more year of eligibility, and he wasn't good enough to get picked up early for the professional football league. As a senior, the starting slot was his to lose, but Nathan could tell the coach was open for a change. Nathan loved to compete, but in his strange mood today, a starting spot didn't seem nearly as important to him as it should have.

Kent finally caught the cheerleader's attention. "My name's Kent!" he yelled down to her. "What's your name?"

The girl smiled up at him with perfect white teeth. "Ashley. My boyfriend's on the team." She pointed. "Number 86."

"One of the meateaters. It figures!" Kent pantomimed choking himself. The girl laughed and fell into step with her teammates.

"You think she can't tell you're a high school kid?" Nathan said.

The home team scored again and the band belted out the school song. Kent filled his mouth with popcorn and didn't bother to stand up. "This is a slaughter. You ready?"

"Yeah. Let's get ahead of the traffic."

It was too late for that. Cars clogged every street leading to the main highway. Nathan inched his seven-year-old sport utility vehicle into the queue, and Kent turned up the radio and drummed the dashboard. With nothing to do but follow the bumper in front of them, Nathan let his mind wander. He thought about moving away from home next year.

He'd been doing that a lot lately, getting sentimental about his high school years, even about this old car that he would drive to college. He called it The Tank. The Ford Explorer was the first new vehicle his mom had ever owned, when her career in real estate began to take off. He had a picture of the two of them with the beat-up maroon Oldsmobile she'd driven before that. In the photo Claire was twenty and looked even younger, her hair long and straight, and he was a plump-faced baby, his eyes round and happy. Rather than put him in daycare when he was small, she took him with her to meet real estate clients. She said the clients would gush over the baby strapped to her back, and want to help her out. She'd called him her partner and secret weapon. Together they'd made her a marvel in the local real estate business.

He worried about leaving his mom alone next year. She needed more interests than just him and her job. She was only thirty-six, and he kept hoping she'd connect with a nice guy. But unless the guy wanted to buy a house, Nathan didn't know where she'd meet him.

What was up with all this nostalgia? Had to be that shrimp. His stomach didn't exactly hurt; he just felt uneasy.

The sun moved lower, piercing his eyes even with his sunglasses on. Carbon monoxide fumes wrinkled up from the road as the cars crawled forward. Nathan rolled up the windows and switched on the air conditioning. He looked forward to the cool fronts that swept through in October— that was the right weather for football.

After a while Nathan pulled out his mobile phone and turned down the radio, motioning to Kent to tone down the drums. He let the phone ring a long time but Lindsey didn't answer. She didn't carry a mobile and the Sanchez family had no recording machine. He laid the phone in the console and turned up the radio.

When they finally reached the main highway out of College Station, the traffic thinned and picked up speed. Kent dozed off with his head against the window, mouth hanging open. Soon they hit a four-lane stretch and Nathan checked his watch. Might be a good time to catch Mom in her office. Saturday was always a work day in the real estate business.

He waited while a huge truck whooshed past in the left lane, then pushed the auto dial. Claire answered on the second ring.

"Hi, Mom. What's happening?"

"Nothing but paperwork. I was hoping you'd call soon. Where are you?"

He heard the wariness in her voice. She disapproved of his talking on the phone while he was driving, never mind that real estate agents did it all the time.

"On twenty-one east of Bastrop. Don't worry; we're past the heavy traffic." Another monster truck pulling two trailers passed him at that moment, rocking the Explorer. Nathan locked his fist on the wheel and hoped Claire couldn't hear the roar.

"How was the visit?" she said.

"Great. We liked the athletic center and dorms. The athletic director was a little too slick, but the coaches were cool. Especially the quarterbacks' coach. I liked him a lot." Static crackled in his ear as the car passed under a set of power lines. "What?"

"I said what about the science department? Did you meet anybody there?"

"Professors weren't around on Friday afternoon. But I saw one of the labs and picked up a catalog that lists the courses. I'll have Mr. Stevens look at it and see what he thinks."

His physics teacher at the high school, a wiry-built guy in his mid-twenties with an electric brain, had become Nathan's advisor and friend. Only seven years separated their ages; it was almost like having a big brother.

"So how does Texas A&M compare with University of Texas?" she said.

"It's nice." He paused. "Bottom line is I don't know. I like both schools, and that's un-American. Then again, UT hasn't officially offered yet."

"They will. Besides, you can use your trust fund and go wherever you want."

The trust was a legacy from the grandparents he'd never met, his dad's rich parents who had given the money to Claire so she'd leave them alone when his dad split, before he was born. She hadn't touched a penny of the money, saving it for his college. He thought of it as Blood Money, and he preferred not to touch it either.

Kent woke up, yawned and belched.

"Kent says hi," Nathan told her and lost her next remark in the static. Kent was pointing to a road sign as they whizzed past.

"Damn. I think I just missed the split for Highway 21."

"Did you? Oh well, you can still skirt around the south of Austin and catch I-35 south."

"I know. It'll just take longer."

"Okay, hang up and drive. See you at home."

He signed off and checked the map folded open over the visor. Yep, he'd just added at least half an hour to the trip home. And he wanted to see Lindsey yet tonight.

By the time they hit I-35 south, the sun had set and they'd entered that odd nether-light between daylight and dusk. Kent was listening to rap music, which Nathan hated. He pushed in a Toby Keith CD, good old country stuff.

Pulling into the left lane to pass a van, Nathan caught a strange movement on the other side of the highway. Something black, about the size of a big dog, came streaking across the inside lane. It looked as if it had come out from under a big commercial truck, but in the fading light he wasn't sure. Had the truck hit a dog?

Nathan squinted. *"What the hell...?"*

Kent sat forward. "What?"

The black object hit the concrete road divider and leapt up, airborne. Coming at them like a rocket.

Nathan swore and stomped the brakes.

He tried to swerve, but another truck was riding his bumper and the van had sped up when he tried to pass. There was no place to go—and no time.

Kent screamed.

The impact was too loud to hear. Nathan felt its horrendous shock, glass shattering like an explosion of diamonds.

It was beautiful. So silent and slow.

Once again Nathan detached from his surroundings. He was floating. And this time he understood the decision that was already made.

His mother's face rose clearly before him. Lindsey's, too.

*Don't be sad,* he wanted to tell them. *I'm all right. It's peaceful here.*

He saw a brilliant white light, familiar and comforting. And beyond the light, somewhere in the infinite distance, he heard the strange, sweet music of a violin.

# Chapter One

*September 2005*

Claire O'Neal switched off the car radio with an impatient flick of her wrist. After two straight weeks of temperatures above a hundred degrees, the weatherman was heralding a cool front tomorrow.

*Don't count on it,* she thought. *Nothing in this world is predictable. Not even San Antonio heat.*

She parked her SUV in the driveway of the Spanish-style four-bedroom in Terrell Hills. It was 8:30 a.m. and the clients were due at nine. Claire gathered her clipboard and stepped out onto the driveway, her linen slacks sticking to her legs.

*Hotter than Hades, but at least it's humid,* Nathan joked. His voice was a constant presence in her head, frozen forever in the self-assurance of seventeen.

She opened the tailgate of the bronze Lexus and pulled out a cardboard box that held a coffee service and Southwest-style mugs. The sellers had vacated a week ago, and the aroma of coffee would give the empty house a homey atmosphere and help dispel the lingering scents of cleansers and former lives. She set her clipboard on top of the box and carried it up the sidewalk to the front door.

The house had curb appeal—a cream-colored stucco exterior and tile roof, with landscaping that was appropriate and understated. Live oak trees shaded the sidewalk on the quiet street. This property should be perfect for the clients.

The incline wasn't steep, but Claire was panting by the time she set the box down to unlock. When Nathan was alive, she used to jog with him every morning to keep herself in shape. Nowadays she worked sixty hours a week, and that didn't leave much time for exercise.

*What about midnight to three?* Nathan said. *You're awake then anyway.*

In the entryway she paused to catch her breath. She wanted to kick off her shoes and feel the cool Mexican tile beneath her feet, but instead she carried the box down a short hallway to the kitchen and set up the coffee ready to brew. With the box hidden beneath the sink, she carried her clipboard through the house, checking details.

The walls had been repainted, the almond-colored carpeting in the bedrooms freshly shampooed. Even the windows sparkled. Claire insisted on clean windows. Clients might not notice on a conscious level, but spotless windows gave a subtle impression of a well-maintained house. Such small details often sealed a sale.

In the family room, she stopped a moment and pictured herself and Nathan living here. It was a trick she'd learned when he was a baby. At first she'd done it as a fantasy, dreaming of the day they could live in a better house. Soon she learned that imagining it this way helped her understand which features to point out. This house had a game room Nathan would have loved. She could see him there shooting pool with Kent, watching football on TV.

Her nose burned and she turned away, walking briskly to the kitchen where she switched on the coffeemaker.

At nine on the dot, she answered the doorbell, smiling. Showing houses was her favorite part of the job. She liked helping people see possibilities in the rooms. The process of buying a house was an affirmation of the future, and Claire needed to see that look in people's eyes.

Mr. Johnson removed his wide-brimmed hat. He stood over six feet, with thick white hair and a melted-butter Texas drawl. "Mornin', Ms. O'Neal. Gonna be another scorcher."

Claire had never figured out why some native Texans acquired that Southern inflection more than others. "It sure is. But it's nice and cool in here. Come in. And please call me Claire."

Nanene Johnson was already scanning the tile floors and gleaming windows. "The house sure makes a good first impression," she said. Mrs. Johnson was quieter than her husband but there was strength in her eyes. Claire had known at their first meeting which one of them would make the final decision on a house.

"Isn't it lovely?" Claire said. "I'll give you a quick tour and then you can explore on your own." For a moment Claire was twenty years old again, with a baby harness tugging on her shoulders. Where was her partner, her secret weapon?

Later, the Johnsons accepted coffee and wandered off to re-visit the rooms and talk privately. Claire stood at the breakfast bar with her coffee mug and checked her electronic day runner. Her stomach tightened when she saw a notation for 3:00 p.m.——Dr. Reuben.

Just then something caught her eye and she glanced outdoors to the shaded patio. Her coffee cup stopped at her lips. Nathan was stretched out on a chaise lounge in the shade of the mes-quite trees.

A pleurisy-like pain pinched her chest. She called her visions *mirages*. She never knew when or where he might appear, but when he did, it stopped her breath. She squeezed her eyes shut, her heartbeat tripping.

*Not now. Please. Not while I'm working.* She forced two deep breaths, and when she looked again, he was gone.

Gradually the fist loosened in her chest. With a paper napkin, she blotted perspiration from her throat and forehead. In the half bath off the kitchen, she ran cold water over her wrists and looked at her face in the mirror. She looked scared, the professional veneer melted like wax. She set her teeth and pulled herself together one nerve at a time.

When the Johnsons rejoined her in the kitchen, they didn't seem to notice the dark half-moons below her eyes. Mr. John-son asked about plumbing and taxes and the neighborhood as-sociation, the kinds of questions serious buyers ask. Claire was grateful for questions that had factual answers.

It was after ten when she walked them to the door. "If you're seriously interested, you wouldn't want to wait too long to make an offer. It's such a nice property, I expect it will sell fast."

Mr. Johnson nodded. "We'll talk it over and call you this afternoon."

Claire cleaned up the coffee things and left them on the counter for the next showing. No sale was sure until the papers were signed.

Before leaving the house, she glanced again at the shaded patio. Nothing there but a pair of white-winged doves hunting for seeds.

Four cars prickled in the sun behind the offices of O'Neal Realty. Claire had moved her expanding business here five years ago, to a more visible location in a strip of retail businesses. She parked beside Janelle's white van and cracked the windows before getting out. The van's side mirror was beaded with water from a fresh car wash, which meant Janelle would be chauffeuring clients today.

Janelle was the sister Claire never had. They'd worked together for years, and Claire had wanted Janelle to be her partner when she bought out the agency. But Janelle had four kids. She didn't want the debt or the extra responsibility of a partnership. Most of all she didn't want to feel guilty when she took off for Little League games and piano recitals. "My work is not my life," she'd told Claire.

At that time, it wasn't Claire's life, either—Nathan was. And Nathan had convinced her to buy the agency on her own.

Claire let herself in the back door to her office and stashed her purse and papers in her desk. In the office up front, an open area divided by planters and half walls, only four agents were scattered among the dozen desks. It was Monday, when most of the agents took off after working the weekend. Of the four, everybody was on the phone except Irv Washington, whose desk sat nearest to the coffee bar.

She poured herself a cup. "Morning, Irv."

Irv gave her a smile and a salute. "Morning, boss."

Every agency was required by Texas law to have at least one agent with a broker's license. Until Claire earned her rating that spring, Irv Washington had been it. He could have hung out his own shingle and collected the agency percentage himself, but this was Irv's second career after twenty years in law enforcement. He seemed content to stay here and not be in charge. Claire felt lucky to have him.

"You show the one in Terrell Hills this morning?" he asked.

"Yes. It looks great inside, and I think the clients really liked it."

"The couple I'm showing around this afternoon might be interested, too. They like that location."

"I'll get you a key."

"Did you crank the air-conditioning?"

She gave him a thumbs-up. "Arctic minus one."

The coffee was stale. She poured it out and took a bottle of water from the fridge, carrying it with her to Janelle's desk by the front windows. Janelle was still on the phone and Claire dropped into a chair to wait.

A new picture of Janelle's kids sat on the desk. They were all in swimsuits and mugging for the camera—except for Kyle, who was a high schooler and much too cool for mugging. The twins, Danny and Jill, showed off nearly identical smiles. Callie was the surprise baby, now a first grader with wild red hair like her mom. The mischief in her eyes looked just like Janelle, too. Claire smiled. Nathan had always envied a big family like that, but Claire had been content with her one lovable child.

Janelle saw her examining the photo and winked. When she hung up, she eyed Claire and frowned. "Pardner, you look like you've been rode hard and put up wet."

Claire shrugged. "No such luck."

Janelle laughed, but compassion softened the green eyes. "I know it's a rough day. Do we need to get together and drink tonight?"

Claire hadn't mentioned the third anniversary of Nathan's death to anybody; in fact, she'd done everything she could to pretend it was just another day. But Janelle remembered.

"No, I won't project my gloom on you. But how about lunch?"

Janelle grimaced. "Can't. I've got clients any minute and we're doing three showings in a row. Sweat city. How about tomorrow?"

"Great. How'd Danny's game turn out?"

"Eagles win!" Janelle lifted a fist. Janelle's husband Les was a part-time PE teacher and full-time father, an arrangement that suited them both. "Danny had two tackles for a loss and an interception. We won't be able to live with him. As if we could before."

"Hey, he's in junior high. It's his job to be obnoxious."

The front door of the office opened with a gust of heat, setting off a wind chime that served as their doorbell.

"That's my client," Janelle said. "I'm showing the one in Olmas Park—again. Keep your fingers crossed." She gathered her clipboard and shoulder bag. "You have a phone message on your desk. From Winfield." She made a face.

Janelle had met Claire's ex-husband only once, the day of Nathan's funeral, but she knew their history and detested Win on principle. Claire had given up most of her bitterness toward Win, which seemed inconsequential compared to the loss of their son. Still, it irritated her that he called more often now than he had when Nathan was alive.

"Swell," Claire said. "Maybe I'll be out when he calls again."

Janelle lowered her voice. "You have that doctor's appointment, don't you?"

"Umm," Claire said.

Janelle gave her a stern look before walking away. "Do it, honey. It might help."

Claire wandered back to her own office. Another Slim-Fast-at-the-desk Monday.

For two hours she did paperwork, avoiding the pink message slip with Win's Dallas phone number. If he was suffering remorse for his neglect, that was his problem.

*Don't be so hard on him, Mom. He came around a lot when I was in high school, remember?*

Yes, but he virtually ignored you for your first twelve years, she thought.

She glanced toward the corner table in her office, where Nathan's photo in his football uniform sat next to a vase of daisies. She got up to change the water in the vase, her eyes lingering on another photo, this one of her and Nathan together. He was fifteen then, a sophomore. She was thirty-four, her face still smooth and full of hope. She felt much different now, only five years later.

Irv's voice called from up front. "Line one's for you, Claire."

Probably Win. Too late to pretend she wasn't in. "Do you know who it is?" she called back.

"A Mr. Johnson. And he sounds happy."

*A fish on the line,* Nathan said. *Reel him in!*

Enveloped in the overstuffed cushions of Dr. Reuben's leather recliner, Claire felt like a little girl, too small for the furniture. She wondered if this was intentional or whether, like so much else in the world, the chair was simply designed for the comfort of men. Large men like Dr. Reuben, who sat in a matching chair at a right angle to hers, taking notes.

She assessed the doctor with Nathan's eyes: six-two, two seventy-five, but too soft in the middle for a lineman.

"You mentioned conversations with Nathan," Dr. Reuben said. The tenor voice coming from that grizzly-bear body was startling. He sounded as if he'd never gone through puberty. "You called them *mirages.*"

Claire looked out the windows to the office courtyard. The oleander was in bloom, its glossy foliage unscathed by the heat, the pink blossoms fresh as a child's face. She envied the shrub's toughness, and its optimism.

She took a deep breath. "Yes. He appears sometimes, sort of shimmery and transparent, like a heat mirage. And we talk about things."

"What kinds of things?"

"How his high school's football team is doing. Whether I've sold any houses this week. Sometimes we talk about funny things from his childhood."

"Not about the accident? Or where he is now?"

"No. It's like when you're dreaming and know it's a dream, but it's absolutely real at the moment. My imagination has made him up, and since I have no concept of what happens to us when we die, he can't talk about that."

"Do you ever ask him?"

"God, no. It's hard enough as it is."

"So these mirages are painful for you."

"Afterward, yes. But when he's there and I have him back for a few moments, it's wonderful. The only time I ever feel happy."

"But afterward?"

"It's like being filleted alive." Claire watched the oleander blossoms blur into pink brush strokes against the glossy leaves.

"Is the pleasure worth the pain?"

She smiled without humor. "Apparently so. I keep having the mirages."

"When Nathan appears to you," Dr. Reuben said, "do you ever argue?"

"No."

"Ever talk about the times he got in trouble or disobeyed?"

Claire thought a moment. "He never got in trouble, really. Not as a teenager, anyway. He was a good kid."

"I understand that, from what you've told me about him. But even good kids break curfew, or go someplace without permission once in a while. Sneak off and drink a beer."

She shook her head. "Not Nathan."

"Really."

"You sound like you don't believe me. Nathan was always mature for his age. We sort of grew up together." Claire smiled. "We even had the same birthday, March 15. He called it the Ides of March. You know—from *Julius Caesar*. I was nineteen when I got pregnant and my husband left us. Abetted by his wealthy parents. They were against the marriage from the start."

"So the focus of your whole life was Nathan."

"For seventeen years. He was the reason I went to work, and the reason I came home."

"It's hard to fill a void like that."

"I fill it with work. I would work twenty-four hours a day if I could."

"But you're here," he pointed out. "So work must not be enough."

"I'm here because my friend Janelle badgered me until I agreed to see someone. But you're right. Work isn't enough. It's not as if my job is healing the sick or feeding the hungry."

"You help people find shelter."

"Yes. That's true. And I'm proud of my business."

Dr. Reuben shifted in his chair, like changing paragraphs. "When was the last time one of these mirages happened?"

Claire tried to shift positions, too, but the chair had sucked the strength from her limbs. "This morning, while I was showing a house. But we didn't talk, because I was working. I just saw him in the backyard."

"What was he doing?"

"Just sitting there. And then he was gone."

"Tell me about the last time Nathan did talk to you."

She paused, felt her chest closing up like a clamshell. "I don't sleep well, so I was up wandering the house after midnight. I went into his room—I call it his room, though he never lived in this house. I put all his things in one of the bedrooms when I moved. I couldn't just throw them away."

"So you went to Nathan's room when you couldn't sleep."

"Yes. Sometimes it helps."

"Are you able to sleep better there?"

"I don't sleep there. There's not even a bed. Just his beanbag chair, and his desk. Photos, his football stuff, things like that."

"You feel close to him in that room."

"I feel close to him everywhere. But more so among his things. Yes."

"Why didn't you put his bed in the room?"

"What?"

"You said there's no bed. I'm sure he had one in your previous house. What happened to it?"

"I gave it to Janelle when I moved."

"Why was that?"

She shrugged. "Because her youngest needed a bigger bed."

"And you were able to get rid of his bed when you couldn't part with his other things."

Claire turned her head to look at him. "There's nothing Freudian about it. Janelle's baby had outgrown her crib."

Dr. Reuben's face was impassive. He recrossed his legs. "Have you dated anyone since Nathan died?"

She turned her face away again. "No."

"How about when he was growing up?"

"Occasionally. Never anything serious."

"You're a young woman, quite attractive. Didn't you ever think about wanting to get married again?"

"Not really. Once burned, twice shy."

"What about Nathan's father? Did he come around much?"

"Not even once until Nathan was five. We saw him occasionally after that, but he never asked to take Nathan for weekends or summers. Not that I'd have let him. When Nathan started playing high school football, Win came pretty regularly. I guess football gave them something to talk about."

"So Nathan was the man of the house for his whole life."

"That's an odd way to put it. I earned the living and made the decisions, if that's your definition of 'man of the house.'"

"That's not my definition. I meant he was the only male presence."

"Pretty much."

"Did you ever have any kind of physical relationship with Nathan?"

Claire struggled up in the chair and turned to face him. "What the hell's that supposed to mean?"

"He was the only man in your life for seventeen years."

"He was my *son*. We did not have a sexual relationship!"

"It's not as rare as you might think, Claire."

"I *know* it happens. But it did not happen in my family. *Jesus.*"

"It's good to see you're capable of anger."

"There's a *second* load of crap. You think I wasn't angry about the obscene unfairness of my son's death? One night I broke an entire set of dishes." She looked at his placid face and wanted to break something now. Maybe his jaw.

*What the hell am I doing here?*

She stood up and looked for her purse. "You know what? We're finished here."

The doctor watched her flustered search. His high-pitched voice was matter-of-fact. "Your bag's on the floor on the other side of the recliner."

She grabbed the purse and hung it on her shoulder. "I came to you for help, and instead I get this…*sick* suggestion."

"Do you expect me to be able to help you after just one meeting?"

"For the money I'm paying, that would be swell."

"Do you want to sit back down?"

"I'll stand, thank you."

"Okay. Here's what I'm seeing." Unruffled by the fact that she was ready to bolt. "You haven't been able to give up your grief because you're afraid of the chasm that would be left without it."

"Very perceptive. I could have told you that myself."

"You've repressed the real, human things about Nathan, like times you argued or when he got in trouble. You've made him into something perfect."

She said nothing. *Maybe he was perfect. Did you ever think of that?*

"You've enshrined your son's memory like a saint. Nathan has become your fantasy lover."

"*Bullshit.* I ought to throw up on your carpet."

Dr. Reuben's expression never changed. "When you ask for an opinion, there's always the risk that you won't like what you hear."

She turned and jerked the door open. It flew out of her hand and banged against the wall. In the waiting room, a milk-faced man looked up from his magazine with shocked eyes.

"Save your money," she hissed, sweeping past him. She opened the outer door and plunged into the midday heat.

The closed car was an oven, and it felt good. She sat without opening the windows, shivering, while her heart slammed and skipped. When the heat finally soaked in, she started the car and turned on the air-conditioning. She laid her head on the steering wheel and aimed the metal-scented air into her face.

The son of a bitch. How dare he try to turn her love for Nathan into something unnatural and warped. So much for psycho-frigging-therapy.

*Who cares what he thinks,* Nathan said. *He sees too many perverts in his line of work.*

Maybe so, she thought. But it's the last damned time he'll see me.

# Chapter Two

The flowers were always white. The bouquet sat on the shaded patio outside the French doors—creamy calla lilies mixed with baby's breath and a multipetaled, snowy bloom that Claire couldn't name. Even the ribbon and vase were white as bleached bone, the awful purity broken only by a deep green background of foliage.

For three years the white flowers had arrived on the anniversary of Nathan's death. Every time, they were just as unexpected and devastating. She knew there would be no signature, not even a florist's card. Untraceable.

Her knees shifted like sand as she brought the bouquet inside. It hadn't been there long; the vase was still cool in her hands. She touched the waxy petals, her throat painfully tight, and looked for the card she knew she wouldn't find. The floral scent roiled her stomach.

The first year she'd assumed the flowers came from her ex-husband but didn't ask. The second year she did ask him, and Win denied sending them. She had asked Janelle, other co-workers, even her estranged father who lived in Seattle. They all denied. The anonymous remembrance felt eerie and bizarre, and she resented the sender. And yet, there was a cruel comfort in knowing that someone else remembered her son. She set the flowers on the breakfast room table and tried not to look at them, but she couldn't throw them away.

That night it took more wine than usual to put herself to sleep. She drank two glasses with her microwaved, frozen dinner and the rest of the bottle while she watched late-night news, her eyes seeing scenes more tragic than those on the screen. When she finally turned off the light, she was blessedly groggy and longing for mindless rest.

She would not go into his room tonight; she would leave the door locked.

Every night she made that promise. And most nights she failed.

The wine worked like a sedative until the dreams started. She awoke sweating, the sheet tangled around her legs. Her insomniac's clock projected the time on the ceiling in red letters—2:30 a.m. She'd been asleep less than three hours. Her head was pounding.

Sometimes the dreams were unspeakably sweet—Nathan as a little boy with a burr haircut, full of energy, his brown eyes rich as mink. Then she'd wake to the crashing knowledge of his violent death, and it was like losing him again. Other nights she fell into a dream loop of the night he died without dying, hooked up to a breathing machine though his brain waves were flat. Over and over, she had to make the gruesome decision to let the doctors harvest his blameless heart, his other organs too damaged to be useful.

Harvest, they said, like wheat or vegetables.

Tonight it was the recurring nightmare from her childhood: the murky, greenish pool; her parents' distended faces, blurred like runny watercolors; her father's accusing voice. *It was all her fault....*

Claire sat up and pulled on her robe.

Outside the floor-to-ceiling window of her second-story bedroom, the lights of San Antonio stretched from the base of the hill to the horizon, a glittering horde of fireflies in the muggy night. Somewhere in the spangled maze lay the River Walk, La Villita, the historic Alamo. Above the city, the stars paled like a reflection in water.

There weren't many hills in San Antonio, and she had bought the house for this view. At least that's what she'd said. The real reason was the day, less than a year ago, that she'd gone home to the modest frame house she'd inherited from her mother and couldn't make herself unlock the door. Nathan had lived there for most of his life, after her mom got sick and Claire moved home to take care of her. But that night, with her mother and Nathan both gone, she couldn't face those empty rooms. She'd sat on the front step with her arms wrapped around her knees until it got dark, then she'd driven to a motel. The next day she called a client who owned this house in Oak Cliffs and made him an offer he couldn't refuse.

It was too much house for one person, but she might as well be lonely in a big house as a small one. For the first time in her life she had plenty of money—more than one person deserved when so many families were teetering on the chapped lip of poverty. When Nathan was a baby, they'd once lived for a week on a dollar.

She turned away from the windows and her slippers whispered down the carpeted stairs, across polished hardwood to the kitchen. She filled a mug with water and set it in the microwave, shook two tablets from a pill bottle into her hand. Beneath the domed skylight, the white cabinets glowed like ghosts, showcasing modern appliances where she hadn't prepared more than half a dozen meals to eat alone at the kitchen bar. Her mother would have loved this kitchen. Marie Jameson had never owned a range top she didn't have to light with a match.

The microwave dinged. Claire dropped her tea bag into the steaming mug and inhaled the vapors. When she was small, before her father moved away, he used to drink until he would pass out for twelve hours or more. It had scared her then; she thought he might never wake up. Now she envied that oblivion. All she got was the headache.

She carried her tea to the living room and sat on the floor by a glass wall that faced her backyard. From here she could watch the first streaks of dawn marble the sky. Now the rationalization began, like an alcoholic talking herself into another drink. She shouldn't go to his room—that was morbid and destructive—but she couldn't go back to bed.

In the distance a siren wailed, and from the greenbelt below the house, a coyote howled in answer. She shivered, and the familiar dark grief rose around her like a poisonous fog.

Her legs pushed up from the floor; her feet climbed the stairs and padded down the silent hallway. The key in her robe pocket was cold in her hand, heavy beyond its weight. She twisted it in the lock and the door swung open.

No one but Dr. Reuben knew about this room, and she was sorry she'd told him. Janelle knew about her mirages, but not about this place.

A trace of Nathan's scent lingered here among his things. She stood in the doorway and breathed it in. Chilled air curled around her feet.

Nathan's football jersey, tacked up on the wall, loomed like a scarecrow in the dim room. On a shelf, his scarred helmet and spikes dwarfed the Little League trophies lined up like miniature soldiers. High school yearbooks lay mute on the secondhand desk where he used to study; one wall was a floor-to-ceiling photo gallery.

Dr. Reuben was right about one thing. The room was a shrine to Nathan. To her smart, considerate, responsible son. What was wrong with that? If she didn't keep his memory, his short life would disappear into the universe like a wisp of smoke. She couldn't let that happen.

Moonlight slanted through dormer windows that offered the same view of the city as her own bedroom. She sank onto the padded window seat with her knees pulled up, feet tucked under the hem of her robe. And waited.

Beside his desk, a butter-colored beanbag chair still held Nathan's shape. She found it hard to breathe.

There was a shimmering, transparent at first. It thickened like ice and took on color, until finally she could see his face.

*Get a grip, Mom. I know you miss me, but you need to get a life.*

"I know, Nathan. I'm trying. I'm just so damned tired."

His eyes were hollow as a skeleton's, his face blank of emotion. *So how's my team doing?*

"I don't think their season has started yet," she said.

*Two-a-days in the heat. You gotta love it. Every year one or two of the guys passed out.*

Familiar ground. She smiled and felt a sensation like floating. This was why she came, these few moments of bliss before the awful wrench of his leaving. She breathed carefully, gripping the window seat.

"Nathan? How was your day? Are you all right?"

*My days are all the same.*

Too soon his shape began to fade, his voice drifting. *You should go back to bed, Mom. Get some sleep.*

"Please don't go." But his outline was already shimmering.

He disappeared like a draft of air sucked out of the room.

When she could breathe again, Claire laid her head on her folded arms and cried until her insides were hollow, nothing left to spill.

She wiped her face and blew her nose. What kind of life was this? Hallucinations, no sleep. She was losing her mind. She wasn't even safe at work—and her business was all she had. She laid her head back and tried to breathe deeply.

Other people lost children and learned to move on. How did they manage?

A photo album lay on the window seat and she opened the book on her lap. Tilting it toward the moonlight, she turned the pages, touching each photo with her fingertips. A white paper slipped from the back of the album and fell to the floor. She picked it up—an envelope—and in the milky light she made out the return address for the Texas Organ Sharing Alliance. She didn't remember such a letter; it must have arrived in those first weeks after the accident when she could hardly remember her own name.

She unfolded the letter and held it close to the window. It was handwritten, the letters graceful and uniform.

Dear Stranger: You don't know me, but you are my hero. My husband, Mason, received your son's heart. You have given him a new life.

"Oh, God," Claire whispered, her chest closing up.

The letter had been forwarded to her by TOSA. At the time she hadn't been able to read past the second sentence. She had shoved it back in its envelope, stuck it away, put it out of her mind. Now she read the rest:

The Organ Sharing Alliance says I can tell you my husband's first name only. Mason is a musician, a violinist. He is only forty, but he's had a heart defect all his life. Then he had a major attack, and the doctors said he wouldn't live more than a few days.

Nothing I can say will ease your loss. Thank you for your courage and your generous spirit. We will never forget you or your son. If someday you'd like to contact us, you can do so through the Organ Sharing Alliance. Sincerely, Mason's wife.

Claire dropped the letter on her lap and sat for a long time with her eyes closed. When she could see again, she picked up the letter and reread it. The man would be forty-three now—if his body hadn't rejected Nathan's heart. If he was still alive, did he ever wonder about the young man whose heart he carried?

In the humid darkness outside the window, thunderclouds gathered. Lightning silvered the rooftops and trees tossed in a rising wind. Through the foggy glass, Claire saw a vision of a small lake, with sunshine and willows overhead. A man whose face she couldn't see stood beside the water. He was slender, slightly tall, and she felt that he was waiting. She walked toward him as if she were wading through water, and reached out her hand. She placed her palm on his chest and felt the beating of Nathan's heart.

At daylight, Claire awoke on the window seat in Nathan's room, still holding the letter. Welcome rain streaked the windows.

# Chapter Three

At the Brown Bag Deli, Claire and Janelle stood in line with the late-lunch crowd to order sandwiches. They picked up their drinks from a side bar and slid into one of the elevated booths by the front window. On the sidewalk outdoors, a few lunchtime shoppers straggled through the heat.

"Some people pay good money for a steam bath," Janelle said, "when all they need to do is visit San Antonio after a rain."

Claire squeezed lemon into her iced tea. Her legs perspired against the wooden bench, but the Brown Bag kept its thermostat set on sixty. Soon they'd be shivering. "How did your showings go yesterday?"

Janelle made a face. "Lookie-loos. I'm not sure they could qualify for a loan." She twisted the cap from a bottle of cream soda and poured it over ice. "Did Win ever call back?"

"Yeah, he's coming to town in a couple of weeks and wanted to have dinner."

"Like I'm always telling my kids, just say no."

Claire shrugged. "I did, but he's trying to be nice. You just hate him because he's rich and you're a Democrat."

"Hey, I don't have anything against money. Just the attitude that so often goes with it."

Claire couldn't explain her patience with Win, especially to Janelle. Even though he'd come late into Nathan's life, they'd begun to make a connection that was important to Nathan. Apparently it meant a lot to Win, too; he had taken his loss hard.

Claire rolled the cold tea glass across her forehead and Janelle frowned. "Got a headache again?"

"Umm."

"Did you see that shrink?"

"Yup."

"And?"

"He's an asshole. Accused me of having sex with my son."

Janelle's face crumpled. "Oh honey. I'm so sorry. What a jerk."

Claire blinked quickly, shaking her head. "He did make me ask myself some questions. Like why I've never dated anybody seriously—there were actually a couple of guys I really liked, but I pushed them away. It seems I was living my son's life instead of mine even before I lost him. It's a wonder he didn't turn out weird."

"You were a great mom. Try another doctor—it's like picking out a pair of jeans. Keep trying them on until you find one that fits."

"I have a different idea." She took the letter from her purse and laid it on the table. "Do you remember that night at the hospital when the doctor talked to me about donating Nathan's heart?"

Janelle frowned. "Yeah."

"Last night I found this. It's from the wife of the man who got his heart."

"What do you mean, you *found* it?"

"It came a few weeks afterward, and I couldn't even read it. I thought I'd thrown it away."

A waitress appeared with ham on rye for Janelle, a turkey wrap with avocado and sprouts for Claire, chips on the side. She set the baskets in front of them.

"Mustard?" Janelle asked.

"I'll get you some," the waitress said. They waited until she'd dropped the packets on the table and gone away.

Janelle bit off the corner of three packets and slathered the contents onto her ham. "So what about the letter?"

"The man's name is Mason, and he's a musician. A violinist. If he's still alive." Claire picked up her wrap, looked at it, put it down again. "Do you remember if the doctor said where the man was from?"

Janelle chewed. "I don't think he said. Probably in state, because I know there's a time limit for getting organs to the donors. Lindsey might remember. She was there that night, and I remember she was asking the doctor a lot of questions."

"I wish I'd asked more questions, but my mind was blown." Janelle had stayed with her for two days, afraid to leave her alone.

"And you're wondering about this why?" A spray of pickle juice caught the sunlight when Janelle bit into her spear.

"She said I could contact them through the Organ Sharing Network. But I wonder if there's a way to find out about him anonymously. I'd just like to know where he lives, what became of him. You're an Internet whiz. Any suggestions?"

Janelle's eyes narrowed, calculating. "Can't be too many job opportunities for a violin player. But are you sure it's a good idea?"

"Why not?"

"What if he turns out to be a jerk, or what if you find out his body rejected the heart and he's dead? Is that something you really want to know?"

"Wow. And you think *I'm* morbid."

"I'm just being realistic." Janelle leaned her arms on the table and lowered her voice. "I can't even imagine losing a child— my eyes tear up just saying it. But sugar, it's been *three years* and you're still bleeding. I'd hate to see you do anything that might make it worse."

Claire looked at her. "I'm not sure that's possible."

Janelle met her eyes, bobbed her head. "That's a point."

Claire pushed her sandwich away half-eaten. "Last night when I pictured meeting this man, I felt like there was something to live for. What if he has a nice family and he's contributing to the world with his music? Maybe if I knew that, Nathan's life wouldn't seem so wasted."

Janelle sniffed and wiped her nose on a paper napkin. She scanned the menu boards behind the counter. "I wish they had wine in this place. We could use a drink with this conversation."

"I do enough of that at night. If I'm not careful, I'll become an alcoholic like my father."

"Damn, honey. What are we going to do about you?"

Claire tossed her napkin on the table. "Sorry I screwed up lunch. Sometimes I need somebody to talk to, and you're it, you lucky duck. You must have built up some bad karma." She dropped a tip on the table. "You've got mustard on your chin. Are we ready? I've got clients in fifteen minutes."

"Just about." Janelle drained the last of her cream soda.

In Claire's car, with the air-conditioning blasting, Janelle said, "Come have dinner with me and the herd tonight. It won't be relaxing, but you definitely can't be lonely."

"Thanks, but I'm too tired to be decent company. I think I'll go home and crash."

"You ought to get a dog to keep you company in that big house."

"And leave him alone all the hours I work? That wouldn't be fair."

"A cat then. Cats sleep all day when they're alone, and they'll cuddle up on the bed at night."

"Cats make me sneeze."

Janelle shook her head. "I give up. You're too damned hard to please." Her family had two cats and The-Dog-That-Ate-Fort Worth.

In the agency parking lot, Claire cut the engine. Janelle's hand hesitated on the door. "Call me if you can't sleep again tonight, you hear?"

"Sure. Les would love it if I rang your phone at 3:00 a.m.

I'll be okay." She waved to a young couple just driving up. "Oops, my clients are early."

In the steaming heat, Claire showed the young couple and their fussy baby three houses in their price range. None of them pleased anybody, not even Claire. She dragged back to her desk at five-thirty, her scalp prickly and her blouse sweated through. The bottled water on her desk was tepid, but she drank it anyway. Janelle had already gone home, but a pink sticky-note in her loopy handwriting centered Claire's blotter.

*Oh, no, not another phone call fromWin.* But this one was something different entirely. The note read:

There's a Mason McKinnon listed among the violinists
on the Austin Symphony Web site.
Check www.austinsymphony.com.

Claire almost laughed. Could finding him be that easy?

Could be a coincidence, of course. Mason wasn't an uncommon name. Then again, maybe she was meant to find him. She wondered if she'd know it when she saw him, feel a kinship in her bones—but that was silly.

Confronted with the Web address, she hesitated, her stomach feeling queasy. What if it *was* the right man? She stuck the note in her purse and headed home.

That evening she went into Nathan's room before dark, hoping to stave off the late-night terrors. Once again she curled up on the window seat, watching out the window while shadows lengthened across the landscape. A blue jay screamed from the live oaks and triggered a memory. Instead of seeing Nathan at seventeen, she saw him years before, when he was four.

"Mommy, look! I think his wing is broken." Nathan's face shone up at her like a dandelion. He cradled a young blue jay in two hands. "I took him away from the neighbor's dog. Can we fix it? Can I keep him?"

The baby bird's feathers were wet clumps on pink skin. Tiny jet eyes glared at her, frightened but defiant. The wings drooped but didn't seem to be broken.

"Get a cardboard box from the garage and we'll make a place for him. But, honey——" she stopped his quick movement with her hand "——sometimes baby birds won't eat from people. He may be hurt too badly to live."

"He'll be all right, Mom. Don't worry."

Nathan yanked open the screen door and was back in the kitchen with a box before the door could slam. He settled the jay in the box and began a search through kitchen drawers for an eyedropper.

The front porch of the house in Dallas where they lived then was wide and cool, shaded from the sun by a deep overhang. Nathan hovered over the cardboard box all afternoon, bare legs folded under him. She watched through the kitchen window as he offered the jay a drink from the eyedropper, then combed the lawn for worms and tiny grasshoppers. He mashed these with a Popsicle stick and offered a bite to the clamped beak of the sad little bird, his own lips pursed as tightly as the jay's. Claire smiled, but not with a clear heart. Wounded wild things were hard to save.

That night, she followed padding feet and door squeaks to the front porch where the baby jay squatted in its box, caught in a shaft of moonlight.

"Why doesn't he sleep?" Nathan asked.

She knelt on the porch beside him. "Maybe the door opening woke him. Or maybe he wants his nest. Let's go back in."

Rewatered and rekissed, Nathan lay in bed, wide eyes glittering in the darkness. "Tomorrow I'll get him a different flavor of bugs."

"Try a mulberry from Mrs. Anderson's tree. Some birds like fruit."

"Yeah! I'll bet he'll like that."

The next morning, Nathan was on the porch in his pajamas when she got up. She made coffee and watched from the window. The jay was still sitting up, but its wings drooped even lower than before.

"Come and eat, honey. We need to get ready for church."

Before leaving the house, they checked on the jay again. Its feathers were dull, its face gray. Three untouched mulberries lay in purple stains on the floor of the box.

Nathan sat quietly on the drive to church and all through Mass. But he was much more cheerful on the way home.

"Mommy, when Father did the part about our own inventions, what did you pray for?"

"Our own *intentions,*" she corrected. She had prayed the same prayer she always prayed: Keep my son safe. Let me be a good mother. "I prayed we'd always be happy and healthy," she said.

"I prayed that Blueboy would get well," he said proudly. "I'll bet he's better by the time we get home."

A lump rose in her throat. Absolute faith was a dangerous thing.

Nathan pulled the door handle before the car completely stopped in the driveway, and she scolded him for it, as usual. But he was halfway to the porch and her words fell into the wind. She gathered her bag and the church bulletin and climbed out of the car.

He was crouched over the box, his head tilted in an attitude of disbelief. The young jay lay on its side in the box, eyes finally closed. Tiny black ants had already found the carcass. Nathan looked up with eyes that were as fierce and dry as the jay's had been when she'd first seen it. Without a word he ran into the house.

She followed slowly into his room. He was sitting in his little rocking chair, pretending to read a dinosaur book. The rocker rumbled furiously on the floor.

She sat down beside him. "Shall we bury Blueboy in the backyard?"

"You can do it. I don't want to look at him."

After a moment she got up, but paused by the door. "Honey, we don't always get what we pray for."

"Why not?" he demanded, eyes fixed on the book.

"I don't know. Maybe because we don't always know what's best."

He turned a page in the book, still rocking fast. She went to her own room to change clothes, feeling both betrayed and betrayer.

Sometime in the night Nathan's doorknob clicked and her eyes opened instantly. A bump against her bed told her he was there.

"Mommy?"

She lifted the sheet and he crawled in. "Have a bad dream?"

"Yes, but I don't remember it now." He snuggled next to her on the pillow, holding the limp brown rabbit he always slept with. He was quiet a moment.

"Mommy, what's it feel like when you die?"

"I'm not sure, honey. I think maybe it's like just going to sleep."

"Can I stay in your bed for a while?"

"Sure."

Like going to sleep. Was that what it felt like for her little brother, when he drowned? She'd learned about death too early in her life and wanted to spare Nathan that knowledge.

Moonlight cast thin shadows on the ceiling. Long after his warm breath fell evenly against her arm, she watched the ghostly branch of a tree toss up and down the wall.

The next Sunday Nathan dawdled at his breakfast. "I don't feel like going to church today."

She looked at him closely and knew he wasn't sick. "Me, either," she said.

They stayed home that morning and built a farm with clay, a tractor and a barn and little blue animals that would never die. The next day Nathan was back to his optimistic self, the baby bird forgotten. But Claire felt as if she'd lost something that she would never quite regain.

Darkness blanketed the world outside the dormer windows, and Claire watched the lights of the city wink on. She rose and left the room, locking the door behind her.

In her office downstairs, Claire booted up the computer and called up the home page for the Austin Symphony. Scanning the links, she pictured a somber violinist playing classical music while beneath his tuxedo shirt Nathan's heart pumped a country-and-western beat. The idea made her smile.

She clicked a link that said "Orchestra." The musicians names were listed beneath their sections: violin I, violin II, viola, cello, double bass, flute, oboe, clarinet, bassoon, French horn, trumpet, trombone, tuba, timpani—*good grief, so many*—percussion, harp and piano.

What in the world was a timpani? And what was the difference between violin I and violin II? A Texas schoolgirl whose clothes came from the thrift shop didn't have much chance for a musical education. But that was no excuse for not educating herself now. She loved all kinds of music.

Under violin I she found Mason McKinnon.

There were fourteen other names with his, seven women

and seven men. She scrolled again, hoping to find background on the individual musicians. No luck. Another link led to the symphony's season, outlined by dates.

Janelle was always telling her she should do something besides work. She clicked *Buy tickets now* and found two seats available in the center front of the lower balcony. That seemed like a good place to be—close enough to see the musicians but far enough away to feel anonymous. She ordered by credit card and clicked to confirm. If it wasn't a school-event night, she'd get Janelle to go with her.

Waiting for her confirmation to print out, Claire sat back in her chair and took a deep breath. Maybe it was far-fetched to think this McKinnon was the man with Nathan's heart, but she was willing to drive to Austin to find out.

# Chapter Four

Winfield O'Neal hung up the telephone and swung his desk chair toward a wall of glass that looked out over the Dallas metroplex. He laced his fingers together and thought about the phone conversation he'd just had, if you could call it that. Claire talked to him like a stranger, her voice guarded and impersonal. She didn't want to see him. When he got to San Antonio on business next week and called her again, he knew she would make some excuse, the same as last time. By now this shouldn't surprise him, but it did. He wasn't used to being avoided.

Win poured a bourbon and water at the wet bar in the corner of his office and carried his drink to the window. He rarely drank before five, but today he was bracing himself for a lunch meeting with his father and two company attorneys, where they would finalize plans for transferring leadership of O'Neal Enterprises from his father to him. He looked down on the matrix of streets and expressways crawling with traffic. From thirty-four floors up, the cars looked like toys. This view usually excited him, made him feel like an eagle surveying his territory. But today what he saw was a smog-stained sky and a dizzying distance between him and the ground. It felt damned lonely.

On a sidewalk below, a young woman was striding along with a baby strapped to her back, her long hair pulled back in a ponytail. She reminded him of Claire when they were first married and attending UT—the happiest months of his life, until Claire accidentally got pregnant. Then he'd left her to have their child and raise him alone.

He watched the young woman below disappear into the fitness club a block over, and he hoped the father of her baby had more guts. If Nathan had lived, he would have been about twenty now, in college somewhere, maybe wanting to get married. Win was married even younger, and though his parents counted it as a mistake, he never did. The mistake was running away from what he'd started. It was easy to see your mistakes in hindsight, but not so easy when you were an overindulged, self-centered kid.

The ice had melted in Win's drink and it tasted watery. He drank it anyway.

In two weeks he would become CEO of O'Neal Enterprises, the sprawling, diversified company that grew from a chain of retail furniture stores owned by his grandfather. Win ought to feel proud about his new position. Did feel proud of it, most days. His sister Maureen, who long ago had moved out from under their mother's domineering influence, would be a silent partner who reaped the benefits of his decisions. He would take care of Maureen's interests just as his father had looked out for his own sister, an alcoholic until her indecorous death.

A pattern was repeating itself. Win had become his father, and like Gerard O'Neal, he'd let his son grow up without him during those years when a boy really needs his dad.

Not that Claire hadn't done a good job with Nathan. By the time Nathan reached high school, Win's second marriage had dissolved and he finally began to spend some time with his son, more than the occasional visits when Nathan was younger. Nathan was unimpressed by the O'Neal money, but Win was definitely impressed with his son. Win had expected him to be smart, but Nathan was also levelheaded and polite, which seemed to Win a rare thing in a teenager. And he was one hell of an athlete. Overprotective of his mom, maybe, but that was understandable given the circumstances. Win was conscious of that only because his own mother had exerted such a controlling influence on her offspring.

In Nathan's last few years, Win had tried to build a relationship with his son, and he could see Nathan wanted that, too. Win did his best to see him once a month, and he attended most of Nathan's football games his junior year. He'd begun to fantasize about bringing Nathan into the business and someday handing down the leadership of O'Neal Enterprises. But that dream, along with all of Nathan's bright potential, had died with him on a diesel-reeking stretch of unremarkable highway. Three years ago today.

Nathan would have been a better man than the two generations of O'Neals who had come before him. With all the jackasses left to wander the world until old age, why in God's name did an accident like that happen to a kid like Nathan? Win and Claire held this tragedy in common, this unconscionable loss. It seemed to him they might help each other, *should* help each other, but clearly she didn't agree. He guessed he deserved that.

The intercom buzzed and he turned toward it. "Yes, Grace?"

His secretary's modulated voice floated from the box on his desk. "You're due at the Derrick Club in twenty minutes."

"Okay. Thanks."

He set his empty glass on the wet bar and returned to his desk. Quickly he scanned the contents of a folder about the transfer of the company leadership. He wanted the details fresh in his mind, though nobody at the table would be likely to ask him anything. Not with Gerard there. At lunch the attorneys would assure Win and his father that the paperwork was in order for turning over the reins, and they'd all pointedly ignore the elephant at the table. The fact that his father was dying.

Win took the fifth-floor breezeway that crossed from his building to the skyscraper next door and then rode the elevator to the forty-fifth floor. He exited onto port-colored carpet that muffled his footsteps. At the entrance to the club, an attractive hostess in a tight-fitting black dress recognized him. "This way, Mr. O'Neal."

The club room occupied the entire top floor of the Hightower Building and was encased on three sides by glass. Only the main dining room was open at lunch. Most days the prairie winds dissipated the smog and gave a spectacular view, but today a gray pall hung over the rooftops. He followed the graceful hips of the hostess as she swerved among white-shrouded tables mostly empty at this hour. This lunch crowd arrived closer to one o'clock, which was why Gerard had called the meeting for noon.

The lawyers, senior partners at Foley & Smith, were already at the table. "Win, good to see you," Fred Foley said. Both men stood to shake hands. Anderson Smith had been a friend of the family for years.

"Fred, Andy," Win said, and took a chair with his back to the windows. His father would arrive last. Even now, Gerard liked to make an entrance.

Gerard O'Neal's prostate cancer had gone undetected for too many years. At sixty-five, he was retiring only because he didn't want his associates and employees to see him suffer through chemotherapy. Chemo might slow the process, but it was too late for a cure. Win had talked to the doctors. In his father's place, Win thought he might end it himself rather than go through the long process of physical disintegration. Then again, retirement might kill Gerard O'Neal before the cancer. Spending that much time in close quarters with Win's mother could be deadly.

Win ordered a bourbon and water from the waitress and looked up to see his father coming across the room. The waitress saw him, too, and waited. "Vodka martini, Mr. O'Neal?"

"Make it a double," Gerard said, his voice gruff. He motioned for the men to stay seated, pulled out a chair and sat heavily. "Morning, everybody." Though it was past noon.

Win saw the dark lines of fatigue in his father's face that hadn't been there six months ago. Here was a man who'd thought he was invincible, and now he was facing death at a younger age than his own father had. Win had disagreed with his dad over many things for many years, but his breath came short whenever he confronted the fact of his father's mortality. *Life's a bitch, and then you die.*

But no, that wasn't true of Gerard O'Neal. He'd lived a good life. He had traveled, had a family; he'd known power and wealth. Nathan didn't get a chance at any of those things.

The year before the accident, Win had invited his father along to see Nathan play football. Gerard had declined, but Win saw something in his father's eyes. *He wants to go,* Win had thought, *but seeing his grandson isn't worth listening to my mother rail about it.* His parents had never acknowledged Win's son, as if Nathan were some bastard offspring of the king. And so he never talked about the accident with them, though they had to know. Win did his mourning alone, attended his son's funeral very much alone, standing awkwardly beside Claire at the graveside. Two days later Gerard had come into his office, fidgeted a moment with something on his desk, and finally said, "Sorry about your boy," before he turned and walked out.

Win's drink arrived and he drank half of it at once. They ordered more food than men who did no physical labor needed. Fred Foley launched the business discussion. Everything was proceeding smoothly, he said. Gerard gave him terse answers to a few questions. Anderson Smith outlined the succession of documents that would complete the transfer of Gerard's leadership.

"Everything will be ready on Monday," Andy said. "We'll circulate the papers by courier to collect both your signatures."

"Send them out to the house," Gerard said, his voice rougher than usual. "Today's my last day in the office."

Both attorneys looked shocked. "Sure, Gerard. I wasn't aware of that," Foley said.

Win hadn't known this, either, but he was no longer shocked by his father's sudden decisions. He cleared his throat. "Why don't I bring them out to the house, Dad, and we can sit down and sign them together."

His father wouldn't meet his eyes. "Naw. I've got to go to the damned hospital on Monday. No telling how long that will take. Just have the courier drop them off."

"Whatever you say." Win finished his drink and motioned the waitress for another.

There were some awkward silences after that, while they cut meat and chewed and drank. Fred and Andy tried to fill in with talk of sports or developments in the Mideast. Gerard kept his eyes on his plate, leaving it to Win to keep up the conversation.

When the check came, Gerard signed it to his account without finishing his steak and abruptly stood. "Andy, I need to update my will, too. Get the papers together and call me."

"Sure thing, G. Right away."

Gerard O'Neal's shoulders sagged as he weaved his way out of the dining room. The three other men watched him go in silence.

"Damn shame about your dad, Win. I'm really sorry," Andy said.

*It was a damn shame about my son, too, but nobody ever mentioned that.* "Yeah. Me, too."

Not all the jackasses of the world lived to old age after all. Nevertheless, Win felt the loss of his father keenly, as if it had already happened. In their own awkward way, he and his father loved each other, understood each other. When Gerard was gone, there would be no one in the world who loved Win except for Avis O'Neal, and his mother's self-interested affection was more of a curse than a comfort.

Win went back to his office, but he didn't get much done that afternoon. He kept seeing the date on his desk calendar and thinking about Nathan. He thought about Claire, too, and the rough day she must be having. Neither of them had mentioned what day it was during their brief phone call, but it loomed between them like a gallows. He wondered if he caught the three-ten flight to San Antonio and drove out to the cemetery, if he'd find her there today. Then he remembered; she'd once told him she couldn't stand to visit Nathan's grave; it hurt too much to think of him in that casket underground, and his heart missing.

It was after six when Win finished making changes on a franchise agreement and left it on Grace's desk for her to type up tomorrow. He retrieved his BMW from the basement garage and inched out into the stifling traffic.

The weekend stretched before him, and the thought of spending it in his Richardson condo seemed bleak and lame. He decided to pack a few things and drive out to the family's lake cabin east of the city. He had some good memories there, especially the weekend Nathan had gone out with him.

Nathan was a fisherman. He had all the gear and he loved being outdoors, on the water. Win had never done much fishing before, but that weekend had made him a fan. They'd rented a metal boat from the marina, Win running the motor from the backseat while Nathan sat up front and scouted for good water. He cast and retrieved with a smooth, practiced motion, and Win wondered who had taught him that skill.

It was early spring, the weather golden, the wind miraculously calm. Nathan had hooked into a six-pound black bass that fought like a badger. Win remembered how the kid whooped with glee, his rod arched nearly double as he fought the scrappy fish. Win had watched him, grinning. That day he'd sat in the back of the boat with the sun on his shoulders and felt uncommonly lucky, envisioning all kinds of good times ahead.

There were rods and reels stored at the lake house. Nobody had used them since. Tomorrow he'd take one down to the dock and try his luck, but it wouldn't be the same.

# Chapter Five

The first time Win met Claire Jameson, she was changing a flat on her old junker in the high school parking lot. She had the trunk open, the old-fashioned jack already wedged beneath the back bumper, and she was laboring to pump the thing up. Win watched her for half a minute before he stopped to help. He liked the determined curve of her neck, and the roundness of her butt in the faded jeans. Caramel-colored hair fell forward and obscured her face, but he was pretty sure he recognized her. He'd seen her in the hallways but didn't know her name.

"Want some help?" he said, throwing his letter jacket on the hood.

She glanced up at him. "That's okay. I've done it before."

He touched her shoulder, smiling, and jerked his head to one side. "No charge." She stood up and he stooped to the jack handle.

"This your car?" he said, not looking at her.

"Why else would I be changing the tire?"

Okay, it was a dumb question. He kept pumping the jack, though, and she relented. "Yeah, I paid for it myself. As you might guess by looking."

"It gets you around, right?"

"Most of the time." She rolled the spare over beside him. It was aired up, which was pretty amazing, but the tread was thin. He used the end of the jack handle to unscrew the bolts on the flat, took off the tire and heaved the spare into place.

She squatted beside him and handed him the bolts one at a time.

"What's your name?" he said.

"Claire Jameson."

"I'm Win O'Neal."

"I know. Thanks for the help."

He stood up, wiped his hands on a tissue she gave him. "Want to go get a Coke or something? That's my car, over there."

He drove a red Corvette his parents had paid for, his future pre-ordained by family and wealth. It was obvious they came from two different worlds. Maybe that was part of the attraction.

Claire's eyes assessed the expensive car, then him. "No, thanks. I have to get to work."

"Where do you work?"

The slightest hesitation. "Burger King." There was a challenge in her eyes.

He grinned. "No wonder their burgers are so good."

"Oh brother. Does that line actually work?"

"We'll see." He gave her the smile that did always work. "What time do you get off? Maybe we could see a movie."

It was a Friday night, early spring. A warm breeze blew soda straws and French fry wrappers across the high school parking lot. "I'd have to go home and change first," she said and wrinkled a lightly freckled nose. "They make us wear uniforms."

"Name the time and I'll pick you up. Here—write the address on my hand." He gave her a ballpoint.

Her printing was neat and small. "Can you find it?"

He glanced at the address in his palm. "Sure."

It turned out to be a tiny house in a run-down neighborhood. She said it was her father's house, which sounded odd but Win didn't question her. He didn't understand until years later that for kids who grew up poor, independence was survival. He just admired the fact that she could take care of herself. She had let him change the tire, but she didn't *need* him to.

They had dated most of the summer before she admitted that her father had moved west years ago and left the house for her and her mother. Her mother had relocated to San Antonio in hopes of a better job, and Claire was living on her own in the crumbling house so she could finish high school in Dallas.

He was miffed by her secrecy, but more impressed with her than ever. "Why didn't you tell me before?"

"Because I didn't want the school to find out and send a social worker out here. And I didn't want you dropping by uninvited or thinking you could spend the night."

Which was exactly what he would have done.

Claire teased him about being pampered, which of course was the truth. Except that pampered wasn't exactly the word for Avis O'Neal's exacting supervision of her son's life. When Win had been dating Claire for several months, Avis began to question. And somehow she checked Claire out, because by that fall she ordered him to stop dating her.

"The girl has no background, no family," Avis pointed out. A divorced father and a mother who worked as a salesclerk didn't count in Avis's view. "She's not in your league," his mother said, her penciled eyebrows arching upward.

So Win saw Claire on the sly and told his mother he was seeing the daughter of one of their country-club friends. It was a lie bound to self-destruct, but meanwhile, in spite of Avis's objections or maybe aided by them, Win thought he was falling in love.

The sexual attraction between them colored his days and dampened his nights. The week before graduation Claire finally agreed they could spend the evening at her house instead of going out to a movie. Their lovemaking was frenzied and innocent in her tiny bedroom, the sagging mattress cradling the wonder in their young bodies.

He convinced Claire to elope that summer and go off to college with him.

It was the first time he'd ever openly defied his mother. Avis was furious and threatened to get the marriage annulled. Win said if she tried, they would run away to another state. He was eighteen by then and didn't need her permission. His father, of course, wasn't home for this discussion.

So Avis retreated and bided her time.

The first semester at UT, they played house in a one-bedroom apartment. He was giddily happy, going off to class in the morning, plenty of sex in the afternoons. But by second semester he began to covet the frat parties his friends invited him to, the beer busts, the all-guy trips to Padre Island. Then Claire got pregnant, and a vision of himself as a father at twenty rose like a gargoyle in his mind. He couldn't possibly be a dad; he was still a kid. So he went home and told his mother.

He waited for her to say I-told-you-so, but she was too crafty for that. She simply paved the way for him to enroll in a school back East that fall, and she engineered the divorce. Even Win's dad said it was the best thing.

For years he'd blamed his cowardice on his parents, but the truth was that his parents had only enabled him to do what he'd wanted—to escape. Avis barely hid her delight in bailing him out. Win left the state before the baby was born and tried to forget he'd ever been married.

Claire never sued for child support. Avis had preempted that possibility by offering Claire a substantial sum—Win never knew how much—in exchange for her promise to relieve the O'Neal family of all responsibility for her child.

"You bought her off," Win said to Avis on a summer night, the first time in two years he'd been home from New Hampshire.

"And she was glad enough to take it." Avis sniffed. "You're well rid of that girl. Such a trashy mouth."

They were sitting on the flagstone patio with their drinks, brought to them by the maid, while they waited on Gerard to get home for dinner.

Win turned the highball glass in his hand without drinking, the taste of gin suddenly revolting on his tongue. "Why shouldn't she take the money? She needed it for medical expenses, and a house for her and…the baby." His knee jittered. "Do you know if it's a boy or a girl?"

Avis lifted her narrow chin, looking off across the lawn where fireflies had begun to rise from the grass. "I have no idea. And you're better off if you don't know, either."

He'd never loved his mother less than he did at that moment.

The next day he'd called an old high school buddy and met him for lunch. At Win's request, Drake made a few phone calls and found out Claire had a baby boy, and named him Nathan.

"Janie saw them at the mall," Drake said, his sympathetic expression undermined with what Win thought was a thin trace of satisfaction. "She said the baby has dark eyes and looks just like you."

"Thanks, asshole."

"You're welcome."

Claire's old phone number was disconnected when he tried it that weekend, and he found no listing for her in the book under either O'Neal or Jameson. He took that as a sign.

That fall he went back to Dartmouth and stayed until he earned his MBA and came home to take a vice president's position in his father's company, five years after Nathan was born. This time his inquiries about Claire turned up empty, and finally he asked one of the company attorneys to trace her. The lawyer reported that she'd moved to San Antonio to live with her mother, who was virtually housebound with severe emphysema. Claire was working as a real estate agent, supporting the three of them with the help of her mother's Social Security. It was just so typical of her that it pissed him off.

When he phoned, she was surprised and defensive. He'd expected that, of course. At first she didn't want to let him see Nathan, so he reminded her he had legal rights that he could use if he had to, and she relented. "Let me think about it. Call back in a few days."

He didn't ask to see the boy alone; he wouldn't have known what to do with him. They met in a park, where he could watch Nathan play. Claire wouldn't look at him, and gave one-word answers to his questions. Win had brought a baseball and glove, which was too large and too difficult to handle for a five-year-old. So Win pushed him in a swing for a while, then the boy gravitated to some kids his age on the jungle gym. After an hour, resentful and embarrassed by his own inadequacy, Win thought *screw it* and drove away, back to Dallas and his six-figure job and high-rise apartment.

Sherry, his second wife, was an attorney who worked in the same building. They kept running into one another in elevators and bars, and finally started dating. She was tall, big-boned and graceful, like a racehorse. Career-oriented and smart, she'd already decided she didn't want children. That was okay with him. They were married for seven years— three of them good—before carving one another up verbally became their only means of communication. Finally they agreed to split up. He moved out of the high-rise to a condo in the burbs, and began asking himself questions about what kind of man was divorced twice by age thirty-three and didn't know his own son's middle name.

The week Win's father entered the hospital to start a strenuous regimen of chemotherapy treatments, Win flew to San Antonio to meet with the manager of their franchise there, a man whom he suspected of living some kind of double life. Weird rumors kept floating back to the home office about that particular mega furniture store. The manager toured him through the store, the offices and the warehouse. He was odd, all right, but the store's profit margin was unassailable and his employees were loyal. The man swore ignorance about the rumors when Win confronted him directly. Win left his office feeling as if he'd just interviewed a Mafia lieutenant in the witness protection program.

From his room at the Hyatt Regency that evening, he phoned Claire, but she wasn't home or wasn't answering. All he could do was leave messages on both her home and office numbers. Undoubtedly she had a cell, but he didn't know the number. He left his own cell number and asked her please to call. He counted on the fact that she was chronically polite, and sure enough, at about ten o'clock his cell began to vibrate in his pocket.

He was in the hotel bar, having a nightcap before he turned in. He glanced at the incoming number before he answered.

"Win, it's Claire," she said. "You called?"

"I was hoping we could have dinner. I'm in town."

"So you said. Well, it's late now. I'm sure you've eaten."

"Eating wasn't exactly the point," he said. "I'd like to see you."

"Why?"

How could he answer that? *I want to know if we could ever mean something to each other again.* It was too far-fetched to say aloud. "Just to talk, I guess."

"Oh. Anything in particular?"

He smelled defeat. "Not really."

"Okay. I'm really tired. I'm going to sign off now and get to bed."

She did sound tired. "Thanks for calling back. I'm sorry I couldn't reach you earlier."

She offered no explanation. Didn't owe him one. He was about to ask for her cell number when she said good-night. "Claire?"

She was already gone.

Win hung up and saw he had a voice mail waiting, from his mother. He ordered another drink before he called up the message.

*Gerard isn't doing well,* Avis O'Neal's wintry voice said, as if reporting an inconvenience. *Please come to the hospital.*

# Chapter Six

Claire did her best to ignore the gradual decline of the white bouquet, but by the evening of the symphony performance, white petals littered the breakfast room table like tiny seashells, browned at the edges. The foliage had curled and dried. A faintly sour odor confirmed that the bouquet had to go.

Only a single calla lily whose pointed tip hadn't yet turned brown was worth saving. She placed it in a crystal bud vase on the table and washed the white urn, setting it in a cupboard beside two others, each different, each chalk white.

*Who? Why no name? How many years would the flowers appear?*

The anonymous source of the flowers was just one of the mysteries Claire wondered about on the hour's drive from San Antonio to the University of Texas campus in Austin. She parked close to the LBJ Library and walked past the towering fountain. In a previous life, she had met Win by that fountain after their classes. This evening the campus was quiet, only a few students strolling singly or in pairs toward the library. Had her face ever looked that fresh and young?

Bass Concert Hall, home of the Austin Symphony, sat kitty-corner from Darrell K. Royal-Texas Memorial Stadium, home of the Longhorns football team. It seemed like only months ago Claire had toured the campus with Nathan in anticipation of a scholarship offer from UT. He would have been a junior now, maybe not here but somewhere, and coming home on weekends with a rucksack full of laundry.

A steady trickle of patrons climbed the steps to Bass Hall, older couples in suits and cocktail dresses, college kids in casual clothes. No one was alone except Claire. One of Janelle's kids had a ball game and she couldn't come.

A volunteer at the door handed her a program and directed her to the elevators. Thanks to construction on the interstate north of San Antonio, she had missed the preconcert talk, but she had done some homework on the Internet. She'd learned that the violin ones played the melody, the twos played harmony. And that *timpani* meant kettledrums. She also knew that coming in late or talking during the program was *verboten*— and she was almost late.

An usher pointed out her seat in the center of a long row. Claire squeezed past the knees of half a dozen people, apologizing as she went. She sat next to a well-dressed woman in her sixties, leaving an empty seat on her left. The vacancy seemed pitiful: Here's a woman who couldn't rent a friend to attend a concert.

Some of the musicians were already on stage, warming up. The men wore dark suits or tail-less tuxedos; the women, black dresses or slacks. Claire examined each violinist but from her balcony seat she couldn't distinguish facial features, only hair and skin color. She should have brought her mini binoculars. She'd bought them for Nathan's football games, to watch him in the huddle or zoom in on heart-stopping moments when he lay still on the field, a knot of trainers hovering over him. Those nights she had wished he played in the band, instead. Now, perhaps he did.

The houselights dimmed and the woman next to Claire whispered, "This should be wonderful. The guest violinist is world renowned."

"It's my first time to attend," Claire said. "Can you point out the violin one section?"

"On the left side, closest to the audience."

The orchestra sat at attention for the entrance of the concertmaster, who cued the musicians for a final tuning of their instruments. Which one of the violinists was Mason McKinnon?

Everyone quieted, waiting, until the conductor strode onstage and applause swept through the hall. The maestro bowed and welcomed the audience, briefly previewing the two parts of the program: a Mendelssohn concerto and a symphony by Mahler. Then he introduced the featured artist, a violinist only twenty-one years old, and the program began.

The young violinist's technique was expressive and subdued, his long black coattails flashing glimpses of scarlet lining when he leaned into the movement of his bow. Claire was amazed by the emotion he was able to convey to her untrained ear. Why had she never attended these concerts when she was a student here? For a few minutes she lost herself in the music, then the movement changed and the spell was broken. Remembering her mission, she focused on the violin section.

Eliminating the women and three gray-haired men, there were still half a dozen musicians who might be McKinnon. She couldn't tell where the violin ones left off and the twos started. Maybe they were listed in some sort of order in the program. But until intermission when the lights came up, it was too dark to read.

The first half of the program ended with enthusiastic applause and Claire filed out to the lobby with the others. The line at the ladies' room was longer than the one at the bar, so she stood in the bar line, paging through her program until she found the list of musicians.

Mason McKinnon's name was not there.

She dropped out of line and found a quiet place to stand so she could check the list again. No McKinnon. Claire glanced around the lobby for the lady who'd been sitting next to her, and saw her standing with a man Claire guessed was her husband. They were sipping champagne. Claire threaded her way toward them.

"Excuse me," she said, smiling. "Are you regulars at the symphony?"

The woman had friendly eyes. "Yes, we're season ticket holders. I'm Marguerite Wilson and this is my husband, Charles."

"Claire O'Neal."

The husband switched his champagne glass to shake her hand. "Pleased to meet you."

"Are you acquainted with the musicians?" Claire asked. "I was looking for someone I used to know, a violinist who was listed on the symphony Web site. But I don't see his name in the program."

The couple looked at each other. "We know one of the percussionists, but none of the violinists, I'm afraid," he said.

"We could ask Bruce when we go back in," Marguerite volunteered. "That's the gentleman sitting by Charles. Bruce is on the symphony board and he knows *everything* about the orchestra."

"Thank you. I'd appreciate that."

By the time they were seated again, the lights dimmed and the man she took to be Bruce was just coming in from the opposite aisle. Claire squirmed. Now she would have to wait until the concert was over to talk to him.

The Mahler portion of the program began with an explosive arrangement that melted into a funeral dirge. Claire listened without hearing, wondering why Mason McKinnon's name was missing from the program. Janelle had warned her that some transplant recipients lived only a few years. If McKinnon had died, did she really want to know?

*Take a deep breath. You're not even sure he's the right man.*

Finally the concert ended and the audience stood. The applause was thunderous, and there were shouts of approval. Claire joined the ovation, applauding because it was over, anxious to buttonhole Bruce-who-knew-everything on the way out.

But the crowd kept clapping. The conductor returned for a second bow, and brought out the guest artist. The applause went on until Claire's arms ached, and she feared an encore.

After final bows by each section of the orchestra and then the entire group, however, the applause abated and people began to file out.

She followed the Wilsons to the side aisle. Charles Wilson was talking and laughing with his friend. She tapped Wilson's arm and smiled.

"Oh, yes. Bruce—I'd like to introduce…Ms. O'Neal, wasn't it?"

"Yes. Claire O'Neal." She extended her hand to the other man.

"Bruce Masterson." He shook her hand firmly. Masterson was tall, with a slim face and dark hair that ringed a bald pate he made no effort to disguise. Wire-rimmed glasses magnified his sharp eyes. "Charmed to meet you, Claire. Are you from Austin?"

"San Antonio."

"Ah. We're pleased to have you here. I hope you enjoyed the Mahler."

"Very much. But I was hoping to see someone I used to know, a man named Mason McKinnon. He's a violinist."

"Yes. Indeed he is. Or was." Bruce made a brief troubled face.

"*Was?* What do you mean?"

He must have read alarm on her face, because he touched her elbow as they moved up the aisle toward the exit. "Mr. McKinnon had…personal problems. He missed a few rehearsals and was forgiven. But then he actually missed a *performance*." Apparently this was inconceivable. "So of course the maestro had to let him go."

Claire frowned. "Really. Was it his health, do you think?"

"I couldn't say." His tone indicated that indeed he could say, but chose not to. "A shame, too. He was quite talented. If he'd stayed long enough and worked hard, I think he'd have made first chair."

They took the stairs down instead of the elevator. Bruce inclined his head toward Claire and lowered his voice. "His wife played for us, too, at one time. Did you know her? She was a cellist."

"No, I didn't." *Except from her letter.* "What became of him when he left?"

Bruce shrugged. "That I don't know. I heard several months ago that he'd left Austin."

He looked at her as if he wanted to ask how she knew McKinnon, but they were in the lobby now and he was greeted by people he knew. A woman with a face like a greyhound hooked bony hands onto his arm and beamed at him. Bruce ignored her.

"I hope to see you here again, Claire." He reached into his coat pocket and handed her his card. "If you'll let me know, I can arrange to sit with you down front. It's a totally different experience from there."

She did her best to look grateful. "Thank you. I'll keep that in mind."

He made a small bow and let the greyhound lead him away.

On the interstate traveling home from Austin, Claire set the cruise control at the speed limit, her headlights spearing ahead into the darkness. For three years she had avoided driving this stretch of southbound road where Nathan was killed. Her hands stiffened on the wheel as she approached the fatal mile marker, and she steeled herself for Nathan to appear. But the seat beside her remained empty, her solitude absolute. She passed the spot with a shudder and sweaty palms, then her breathing eased.

She unclenched her hands and turned on the radio. After the stately music of the symphony, the pop music sounded silly and she turned it off again. The Lexus was quiet inside, only a slight hiss of tires on pavement and the muffled rush of wind sliding past. She took a deep breath and blew it out like a sprinter.

Through the bug-spattered windshield, Claire saw her life unfold in a series of leavings. First her father, when she was a child. Then her husband. She saw her mother's lingering death, and Nathan's sudden, premature one.

She flashed on the dream of the murky pool, her mother sobbing, her father raving, and she shivered. *We can't help what we dream, but that doesn't mean we aren't responsible for our nightmares. I let my little brother drown. And I was talking with Nathan on his cell phone when he missed his turnoff and ended up on this road.*

Claire couldn't remember her little brother, Todd. He was only two when he died, and she only four. In her memory he had no face except the baby pictures she'd found years later in her mother's album. Her mother refused to talk about him and wouldn't let Claire ask questions. But she did have vague memories of the arguments before her father left, of hiding in a closet while their voices grew louder and angrier, her father's slurred from drinking. *Don't you dare blame her,* Marie's voice growled. *She's too little to watch out for a baby!* That's how she had known it was her fault when Buck Jameson left them, moving out of the little house in Dallas to an apartment on the other side of town. She'd seen him one weekend a month until she was thirteen. Then he moved half a continent away and didn't come back until her mother's funeral, when Nathan was six.

After the funeral, she and her father had argued. Buck flew back to Seattle and she hadn't seen him since. Somehow, though, he had learned about Nathan's accident and called her. She'd wept on the phone. The memorial service was over by then and she'd told him not to come, there was nothing he could do. Now he phoned periodically and sent a poinsettia plant each Christmas. Maybe he sent the white flowers, too, and had denied it because of the accusing tone in her voice when she asked him.

A semi rig roared past her in the left lane and the draft rocked Claire's car. Yellow lights outlined two boxy trailers behind the cab. She gripped the wheel and cursed the truck driver.

She might never find an answer to why Nathan died. But at least she could find out if Mason McKinnon carried her son's heart, and if so, what had become of him.

# Chapter Seven

The last calla lily yellowed overnight, its waxy petals veined with brown. Claire tossed it out before she left for work on Saturday morning.

She disliked hosting open houses; they were so often boring and unproductive. But her clients, a young couple who'd made a bid on a house in another city, needed to expedite this sale. So she'd advertised the event and posted flyers around the adjoining neighborhoods. She took along a folder of paperwork and her laptop in case nobody showed up.

The heat had relented slightly, and Claire was surprised by a steady trickle of lookers who passed through the house. By the time she locked up on Sunday evening, she had two solid prospects. She rewarded herself by taking Monday off to clean her own house.

In her shorts and tank top, hair tied up in a bandanna, she

scrubbed and swept and sweated until the house was spotless. The physical activity felt good; maybe she'd sleep tonight. At midaf-ternoon she pulled off the bandanna, made a tall glass of iced tea and went out to retrieve her mail.

Among the handful of bills and flyers was a letter from Lindsey Sanchez, Nathan's high school girlfriend. Lindsey was starting her junior year at the University of Missouri on a scholarship in journalism. She was a striking girl, with thick, dark hair and penetrating eyes, the most self-directed teenager Claire had ever met. Nathan was infatuated with her, and Claire had worried that he was setting up for his first broken heart. In hindsight that seemed like a silly concern.

Lindsey kept in touch with her on and off, phoning on holidays when she came home to see her parents, dropping by on summer break. Sometimes Claire caught herself resenting Lindsey for having college experiences that Nathan was denied. At the hospital after Nathan's wreck, when Claire wavered about giving consent for organ donation, Lindsey had been certain Nathan would want to donate any usable organ. Both had checked the donor boxes on their driver's licenses. In her grief, Claire had resented that, too. It was a low emotion that made Claire feel ashamed.

She tossed the other mail on the kitchen counter and slit open the envelope from Lindsey. It was postmarked on the anniversary of Nathan's death, and Claire took a deep breath before reading. But the letter contained only innocent news about Lindsey's course work and her job on the *Columbia Missourian* newspaper. At the end, there was a hesitant admission that she had started dating someone. Claire skimmed the letter again, an idea forming in her head.

Lindsey had added her e-mail address at the bottom of the letter. Claire carried it to the computer in her home office and wrote a brief answer. At the bottom of the note she typed a request. Do you have access to a database of old newspaper articles? I'd like to get copies of the news pages from the Austin paper for September 21, 22 and 23 of 2002. I'm looking for an article about a musician who might have received a heart transplant.

Claire reread the note and hit Send. Then she went upstairs to shower.

It didn't take long to get an answer. That evening there was an e-mail from Lindsey: Attached is the news article you're looking for. As if she'd already known the exact one.

Claire downloaded the file and brought it up on the screen— an article from the *Austin American-Statesman* on September 23, 2002. The headline read: Violinist Receives Gift of Life.

Mason McKinnon, a violinist with the Austin Symphony, received a heart transplant this week at an Austin hospital. Prior to the surgery, McKinnon had suffered from long-term heart disease and was declining rapidly, according to family sources.

"We can't believe our good fortune," said McKinnon's wife, Julia. "We're so thankful to the doctors and all the hospital staff who've been wonderful to us. And we're especially grateful to the family of the donor."

McKinnon was reported to be resting comfortably and adjusting well to antirejection drugs. He is expected to remain in the hospital several weeks for monitoring. Hospital sources say his prospects are good for a complete recovery.

McKinnon has played with the symphony for four years. Julia McKinnon played cello for the orchestra in the past but now gives private lessons from her home. The couple is expecting their first child.

Claire reread the story twice, her breath shallow.

They'd been expecting a child.

Irv Washington lived alone in an apartment on the west side, and he answered his phone on the third ring. Before becoming a Realtor, Irv had worked twenty years on the San Antonio police force, part of it as a detective. Claire didn't know much about his life as a cop, only that his wife had divorced him back then but he still kept a picture of her on his desk. He had a couple of grandkids in Colorado.

On the phone, Irv sounded older than he did in person, his Texas drawl magnified.

"Sorry to call you at home," she said, "but I need to ask you something that I didn't want to talk about at the office."

"No problem at all," he said. "This phone rings so seldom I'm glad to know it still works. What can I do for you?"

Claire got a mental picture of a bachelor apartment in dark colors, Irv watching TV alone in his sock feet. "I want to find someone who used to live in Austin but moved away. Where do I start?"

"How long ago did she move?"

"It's a he. I'm not sure, but I think it was within the last year."

"Would he have a police record?"

"I doubt it. He was a violinist for the Austin Symphony until recently. I have a newspaper clipping about him, but it's three years old."

She heard his voice change, the lawman coming out. "That's a start. Let me have a copy of it, and I'll make some inquiries. I still know a few guys on the force. One of them's a detective."

"I know I can trust you to keep this to yourself."

"You have my word. But if I knew why you were looking for him, that might give me something to go on."

"The man's name is Mason McKinnon. He got my son's heart."

There was a short silence on the other end. "I see. And does he not want you to find him?"

"I don't want him to know I'm looking. That's why I don't want to go through the organ donor network." Claire paused. "I just want to know where he is, and how he's doing. Maybe something about his family. I don't even want to meet him. Not yet, anyway."

"I understand." Irv cleared his gravelly throat. "Why don't you fax that article to me? I'll make a couple of calls. It might take a few days, but people usually aren't very hard to trace unless they're trying to hide."

"Thanks, Irv. I really appreciate this."

"Glad to help. Reminds me of my misspent youth on the force."

That week Win left a message on her voice mail at the office. He was in town and wanted to have dinner. Claire cringed, but people who didn't return phone calls were one of her pet peeves. She waited until ten o'clock, too late for dinner. Win's voice sounded so much like Nathan's—though older and sadder—that she gripped the receiver in both hands, her pulse throbbing. She got off the phone as quickly as she could.

Lying awake again that night, watching the red minutes click past on her ceiling, she thought about the letter from McKinnon's wife, and about the newspaper story Lindsey had sent. She wondered about their child, and what she would do if she did find McKinnon. For several nights she had avoided going into Nathan's room, but now she heard the echo of his voice in her head and missed him so much she could hardly breathe.

Her legs felt heavy when she rose and went downstairs to the kitchen. Instead of tea, she made a tall wine spritzer and drank it eagerly, closing her eyes. The cold cut a path through the tightness in her chest, a knifepoint of pain puckering her eyebrows. She finished the drink and made another.

In Nathan's room, she sat on the floor and leaned her back against the wall. It seemed like an hour before he appeared. She heard his voice before she could see him.

*Sounds like Lindsey's doing all right.*

His shimmering outline sprawled in the beanbag chair, long legs extended. Gradually he solidified, a vague smile on his face.

Claire squinted to see him. Already her head was aching. *Yes, she is. She's going to start dating again. I think she wanted me to say it was okay.*

Nathan had nothing to say about that. His face was less distinct than usual, especially his eyes. Instead of the addictive, floating feeling that usually accompanied his visits, a weight like an elephant squatted on Claire's chest.

*So you closed on the house in Terrell Hills?* he said.

*This morning. The Johnsons will be happy there, and it was my own listing.*

He grinned. *Money makes the world go 'round.*

*No,* she said slowly. Her tongue felt thick. *Money's just a substitute for what's missing.*

His legs had faded away; only his upper body remained.

*I miss you, Nathan.* She was fading, too. Her vision was a dark tunnel with Nathan at its center, in a vortex of piercing light.

*Buck didn't send the flowers,* Nathan said. And then he was gone.

Friday morning, in the thick of eight o'clock traffic, Claire felt the deflating clunk of a flat tire. She maneuvered off the busy street into a parking lot, got out and looked at the tire—as if staring at the ravaged rubber would change anything.

*Damn.* She was supposed to meet clients at her office in twenty minutes. Even with AAA on her speed dial, she'd never make it.

She pressed the cell phone to one ear and plugged the other ear with her fingers while traffic whistled past on Fredericksburg Road. The dispatcher said help would arrive within forty-five minutes.

"Forty-five minutes!" Claire said.

"Sorry. It's crazy out there today. All our subs are already out on calls."

*Swell.* She tried the office number but nobody was in yet. While she was leaving a disgruntled message on Janelle's cell number, a white pickup pulled into the lot and parked a few spaces away. Hope surged, then faded. It hadn't been five minutes since she called AAA, and there was no garage insignia on the truck's door. She stood up straighter and gripped the car key like a weapon.

The man who got out was stocky and hairy armed, with a face that looked vaguely familiar, like a dozen guys she'd seen at service stations or hardware stores. He touched the brim of his Peterbilt ball cap. "Need some help, ma'am?"

"You're not from AAA, are you?"

"No, ma'am, but I can change a flat in five minutes." When she frowned, he added, "Job I used to have, we had tire rodeos. See who could rope and tie 'em in the best time."

She glanced at her watch again. What could go wrong in full view of a street full of drivers? "Thanks. I'll be glad to pay you." She popped the lock on the back end where the spare was stored.

True to his word, the guy was fast at the job. He put everything away, even checked under the hood, for what she wasn't sure. She had a twenty-dollar bill ready for him when he finished.

He shook his head. "Not necessary. You have a good day now." He tipped his ball cap before driving away. Chivalry was alive and well, at least in Texas.

Luckily, the clients were running late, too. At her desk, she ran a comb through her hair and was stashing her purse in the desk when Irv stuck his head in the open door.

"Morning, boss."

"And a Friday morning, at that."

He stepped inside and laid a brown envelope on her desk. "Next time give me something hard."

She glanced at his face, then toward the front office. No one was within earshot. "You found him?"

He nodded. "It's all in there."

"Thanks, Irv. I owe you."

He waved it off and turned to go. It was easy to picture him as the detective he used to be. "I just hope you don't hurt yourself with it," he said. "There's such a thing as too much information."

Claire picked up the manila envelope, testing its slim weight, but the phone rang before she could look inside. She slipped the envelope into the drawer beneath her purse and picked up the receiver, hoping her clients weren't going to cancel.

It was Win.

*Don't you just love Fridays.*

Her first excursion with Brad and Melissa Rankin and fifteen-month-old Mandy had been an endurance test, and Claire braced herself for the second round. But today the baby wasn't fussy and the temperature was only muggy instead of stifling. The Rankins liked two of the three houses Claire showed them. In Claire's office that afternoon, the young couple held hands while Claire completed the paperwork for their offer on the nicer house. Their excitement was contagious.

"I'll call you just as soon as we get a response from the seller," Claire told them. "They'll probably make a counteroffer, but we can make this work."

It was past three when the Rankins left. Janelle came into Claire's office and plopped into the chair, kicking off her shoes. "Is it happy hour yet?"

"It is for me," Claire said. "I think I just put that cute family in a great house."

"Well, I sold the house in Olmas Park—*ta-da!*"

Claire gave her a thumbs-up. Janelle lowered her voice. "Any news about the violin player?"

"Close the door."

Claire pulled out the brown envelope and slid the contents onto her desk. On top was a publicity photo of a man in a tux, a violin and bow held casually in front of him. His expression was sober, but the square set of his jaw and a light in his eyes hinted at a smile.

Janelle leaned across the desk for a better view. "Is that him?"

"Apparently so."

"He looks like a sculpture," Janelle said. "Very arty."

In black and white it was hard to guess his coloring, but the eyes were light and his hair was either light brown or dark blond and wavy. Maybe a perm, maybe natural. It was long enough to brush his shirt collar. His face was angular, not exactly handsome, but interesting. And it looked younger than forty-three, which McKinnon would be now. She turned it over, but there was no date.

"Where'd you get this stuff?" Janelle asked.

"Irv dug it up for me. But that's confidential."

She handed over the photo and leafed through the other papers. One was a bio on symphony letterhead. It read like a news release and centered on McKinnon's background in music. He was the son of middle-class parents who recognized his gift for music early and gave him lessons at a young age…pursued music through high school and college, winning honors in competitions…graduated from the University of Texas, taught music in an elementary school, then at a community college. The bio might have described any number of musicians, Claire thought. It said nothing about the health defect that required an organ transplant.

There was a copy of his marriage certificate to Julia Elizabeth Rothschild, but no current information about her or their child. She handed over those papers for Janelle's inspection and picked up the last sheet, a plain piece of paper with four lines written in Irv's generous hand. Claire read aloud.

Mason McKinnon now resides at 427 La Malinda Avenue, apartment 213, in Santa Fe, New Mexico. Phone 505-555-5378. Employed as a piano player at Santero's Bar & Grille.

"He went from a symphony violinist to playing piano in a bar?" Janelle said. "That's quite a change. I wonder what happened."

Claire picked up the photo again and examined his face. She wondered if this shot was taken before or after he got Nathan's heart. Probably before, when he'd first started with the symphony. His face looked smooth and healthy, with the untroubled arrogance of youth.

"If I took some vacation time, could you look after the office?"

"Sure," Janelle said, meeting her eyes. "Unless you'd rather I go with you."

Claire shook her head. "I don't know how long I'll be gone, and you can't leave your family indefinitely. Besides, I need you to take care of things here."

"When will you go?"

"Next week, if I can. I'll gather up my files and summarize what I'm working on. You and Irv can either take my appointments or farm them out to Charlene and Greg."

"The new guys would be glad for some leads." Janelle frowned. "Are you sure you want to see him?"

"No. But I'm sure I have to."

"It's a hell of a way for you to take some time off, but Santa Fe's a neat place. I hope you'll relax and enjoy it."

"Maybe I will," Claire said absently. In her mind, she was seeing the vision of a man standing beside a pool of water, lacy trees overhead. Now she could also see his face, and imagine the beat of a familiar heart.

# Chapter Eight

In the fluorescent pallor of the *Columbia Missourian* newsroom, Lindsey Sanchez typed the last sentence of her report about the city planning commission meeting. The story would appear in tomorrow's edition and outline the commission's action on seventeen agenda items. Nobody in his right mind would read it all the way through.

Lindsey huffed a breath and pushed a strand of dark hair behind her ear. Her reporting skills were underused here, but it was part of paying her dues as an underclassman. Once she had her degree, she could apply at the *Dallas Morning News* or the *Kansas City Star,* work her way up the food chain until her byline meant something, like Molly Ivins or Maureen Dowd. She'd decided to specialize in Hispanic issues and immigration, maybe add a law degree to her credentials later on, when she could afford it.

The bluish glow of the computer screen reflected on her face as she reread the report, cutting words. At the same time, the other side of her brain spun out a fantasy about scientists someday discovering insidious, lethal electrons emanating from computers. If they did, she was toast. But so was everybody in the business world.

The strand of hair fell over her eyes again, and she impatiently gathered all of it into a long rope behind her head. She twisted the hair into a knot and skewered it on top of her head with a pencil, never taking her eyes from the computer screen. When she was satisfied the writing was tight and clear, she proofread a final time and filed the story electronically—no paper needed, no wasted trees. That was one of the good points about computers. For that, she would risk a few renegade rays.

While she was online, she checked her e-mail and was surprised to find a message from Claire O'Neal. She'd written Nathan's mom a letter last week, on the anniversary of Nathan's death. She hadn't mentioned that in the letter, but she knew Claire would be thinking about it all week. This was the first time Claire had ever answered one of her letters, and it pleased Lindsey that Claire was willing to share her e-mail address.

Lindsey had taken half a dozen psych classes at college, including one on the psychology of grief offered by the mortuary science department, but she'd never been able to break through the emotional wall Nathan's mom had built around herself after his accident. Lindsey knew Claire had walled off her grief as a survival mechanism, especially in those early months. But emotional isolation could be a dangerous thing.

Lindsey had seen her grandfather do that after her grandmother's death. Eventually he'd lost his will to live, and then his mind. She felt the need to stay in contact with Claire. They were the only two people in the world who understood how much they'd lost.

Lindsey scanned the impersonal lines of Claire's e-mail, everyday news about her job and the San Antonio weather, but she stopped cold at the last sentence and read it again. Claire was looking for information about the man who'd received Nathan's heart.

*I'll be damned. It sure took her long enough.*

If Lindsey had been Nathan's sister or mother, she could have contacted the man who got Nathan's heart through the Texas Organ Sharing Association three years ago. But as his seventeen-year-old girlfriend, she'd had no rights. She found that out the hard way when she'd contacted TOSA. The lady on the phone tried to be kind, but she said they forwarded letters only for family members. Lindsey did consider herself part of Nathan's family, and the rejection had cut her.

A few days later she'd found an article in the newspaper with the recipient's name. Chill-bumps had flashed over her when she scanned that headline and then read details about a musician who'd received a donated heart. Everything matched—the date, the proximity of the hospital. There was no doubt in her mind about the source of the heart. She'd carried the article around with her for days. But after the refusal from TOSA, she had felt unworthy to contact Nathan's recipient. She had no standing, no sanction. She wasn't family.

If it happened now, Lindsey wouldn't hesitate to take action on her own. But she was too young then, crushed by her loss and shy about her rights. She'd felt sure Nathan's mother would contact the musician, and then she'd get to meet him, too. But Claire never wanted to know, until now. And she was asking for Lindsey's help. In the milky fluorescent hum of the news office, Lindsey bit her lip and blinked back tears.

She closed the e-mail program and logged on to a database that could search the archives of every major newspaper in the U.S. While she waited for the site to recognize her password, Nathan's well-remembered image arose in her mind. She always pictured him in his jeans and football jersey, the number thirteen emblazoned on the front and back, his coffee-colored eyes smiling—the way he'd looked the night before he and Kent had gone to A&M on their recruiting trip.

After the accident, the newspapers were full of stories about Nathan's life and his death. Lindsey had clipped every one and kept them in a scrapbook. She pictured its burgundy cover on the shelf in her closet at home in San Antonio, in the too-small bedroom where she'd faced down boogeymen and teenage acne. The scrapbook lay under a stack of college texts she'd taken home to save, and she hadn't looked at it for a year now. But she remembered every article and could quote most of them from memory.

Claire O'Neal didn't need to review all the gruesome details of Nathan's accident or the recaps of his short life. There was only one article Claire needed, and Lindsey knew exactly which one it was.

Typing Nathan's name into a search box on the computer screen, Lindsey felt like a medium at a computer séance. She was calling him up from the dead, or at least from that cyber netherworld where people and old Web sites lived forever. She could feel his presence in the room.

When the search results had loaded, she scrolled through the familiar reports without stopping to read them. The bitter taste of Feta cheese stained her tongue....

On the September afternoon when her friend had phoned her about the TV news report, Lindsey was eating a salad with Greek cheese at the scarred kitchen table where she and her mother, her stepfather Carlos, and grown stepbrother Jimmy ate dinner together almost every night. Jimmy had his own place now, and he worked for the same construction company as Carlos. They were two peppers from the same vine, her mother always said. Neither had a peppery disposition, though, and Lindsey was grateful for that. She and her mother had fled one man, Lindsey's real father, because of his temper.

That Saturday afternoon, though, no one else was home. Lindsey was feeding tiny crumbs of the cheese from her salad to Eduardo, the Amazon Grey parrot who'd been her companion since before her mother married Carlos. Eduardo pursued the crumbs on the tabletop in his awkward, bobbing walk, and Lindsey was smiling at him when she answered the phone.

Marla didn't even say hello. "Do you have the TV on?" Her voice was urgent.

"No. I just got home from work."

"Oh, girl. I just saw the awfulest thing. There was a bad wreck on I-35, two teenagers severely injured. The TV report didn't give names, but—girl, they showed an old red Explorer just like Nathan's, and it was *wasted*." Marla knew Nathan and Kent had gone to A&M that weekend.

"*Madre de Dios*," Lindsey whispered. "I gotta go."

She hung up and switched on the small TV in the kitchen, flipping channels, but no local stations had news now. Marla must have seen a special bulletin.

She tried Nathan's cell number—no answer. Tried his house, too, though he probably wouldn't be home by now even if the wrecked car wasn't his. Frantic, not knowing what else to do, she called her mother at work.

Maria came straight home from the hotel downtown where she worked behind the front desk. She made phone calls. By the time someone had thought to phone Lindsey from the hospital, she was already racing toward Austin, frozen on the seat beside her mother, who wouldn't let her drive.

Even now, the remembered taste of Feta cheese nauseated Lindsey.

She kept scrolling through the information on the computer screen until she found the article from the *Austin American-Statesman*, September 23, 2002, page fifteen. She scanned it quickly, the words as familiar as the prayers she lip-synched in church. She saved the article to a file she could e-mail and logged off the site, asking herself a hard question: Did she still want to meet Mason McKinnon?

The idea felt like a step backward. Only this semester had she begun to feel like a normal college student instead of a twenty-year-old widow. She was even dating someone, sort of. Yet if Mason McKinnon's donated heart still beat, it was all that was left of Nathan O'Neal, her first true love. At unexpected moments, the feel of his body or the smell of his skin washed back to her so powerfully she had to stop what she was doing and remind herself to breathe. She wished they had made love; she could have carried that memory forever. Instead, she was a virgin at twenty, a rarity among her friends.

Lindsey sniffed and lifted her chin. No breakdowns allowed. She was the girl who had it all together—ask anybody. Marla still called her from UT to ask Lindsey's advice about her love life; her classmates sought her out to study with them before exams. Even her mom and stepdad had asked her opinion on whom they should vote for in the last election. Sometimes she felt like the mother of the world. At Christmas, her stepbrother had given her a sweatshirt that said I Am Invincible. "I couldn't find a cape," he said, only half joking.

What would they think if they had seen her last night, curled into a tight ball around Nathan's old T-shirt beneath her covers? She'd stopped wearing the faded gray shirt to sleep in when she gained a roommate in the college dorm. But she hid it under her pillow every morning and never washed it, saving Nathan's scent like sacred air. Even her mother, her best friend, didn't know about the shirt.

Lindsey straightened her spine in the chair, and her hands were steady as she typed a short reply to Claire O'Neal's e-mail. She attached the file and clicked Send. *The story's all yours now, Claire. For me it's old news.*

Time to go home. She straightened the desk she shared with two other student reporters, sliding her papers and notebook into a designated drawer. The computers stayed on; they never shut down here. She found that comforting, as if some great, gray intelligence was always awake, watching out for things.

Lindsey shouldered her backpack and crossed the campus in late-September light, the long shadows of buildings spilling over the sidewalks. The nights were cooler lately—football season. Soon the leaves of the huge trees on campus would turn red and gold, and then fall away. As Robert Frost said, "Nothing gold can stay."

It was midnight when Lindsey switched off her desk lamp and quietly got ready for bed. Her roommate was already asleep, her back turned to the light. The central heating unit droned white noise, a benign companion on the nights she stayed up late to study. Its breathy hum helped shut out distractions and lull her to sleep.

She stretched out on the stiff mattress and pulled Nathan's T-shirt from under the pillow. She laid it across her stomach beneath the sheet. In the dim glow through the window blinds she studied the familiar crack in the ceiling above her bed. It was shaped like the profile of a pregnant woman, or the outline of half a violin. And she thought again of the last time she'd seen Nathan, the night they'd harvested his heart.

She'd been lying awake as she was now, but in her bedroom at home, safe in her mother's house. She had sat all that day at the hospital, in the same waiting room as Claire and her friend Janelle, but slightly apart from them. Now her tears were dry, her senses numb. But she couldn't sleep.

She had watched Nathan's spirit gradually materialize beside her bed, his skin a pale glow in the darkness. She remembered the strange scent of apples in the room. At first she was terrified, her limbs rigid in the bed. But gradually she felt his calmness, that he was safe and whole, and relief flooded her chest.

She'd lain absolutely still, afraid that even her breath might dissolve the apparition. Finally she said, "Nathan? You're okay?"

*Yeah, I'm okay,* he said, as if that fact surprised him. *How about you?*

Tears slid onto her pillow. "I don't know what to do."

He was quiet a minute. *I miss you, too.*

She'd wanted to sit up and touch him, but she was afraid her hand would pass right through him like smoke.

She was not dreaming; she was certain of that. She sensed that he was not in pain, but he was troubled and restless, his spirit not yet free of the world he'd left too suddenly.

His voice was a whisper. *Lindsey?*

"Yes, Nathan."

*Am I real?*

Her chest constricted. "You are to me."

He had stayed with her that night until she fell asleep, but he never came back.

In her chilly dorm-room bed, Lindsey rolled onto her side and hugged her knees to her chest. She pressed his T-shirt to her middle and wished Nathan would come to her again.

# Chapter Nine

Lindsey had run across Kent Woolery in her second year on campus. She'd just come from her psychology class, where they were discussing body language. The professor said that an observant person could learn to decipher people's feelings, even their self-images, by the way they sat and stood and moved. Lindsey was still thinking about that when she saw a guy sitting by himself at a table in Brady Commons, one leg propped awkwardly on a chair. Her first assessment of him was *self-conscious*.

But there was something else, too, in the droop of his shoulders and the forward tilt of his head. He looked sad, she thought. Defeated. Only then did she realize his profile looked familiar.

Lindsey didn't have time for lunch between psychology and her journalism lab, halfway across campus; she'd just stopped at the student center to grab a soft drink. Filling a cup with ice and cola, she watched the profile of the guy at the table.

He looked a lot like Kent Woolery—Nathan's buddy who'd been in the wreck. But she hadn't seen Kent since high school, and why would he be here at Missouri? Besides, this guy was thin, and Kent had been a real bruiser in high school. Still, she was curious enough that she went out of her way to walk past his table.

*Oh my gosh. It is Kent.*

Or at least a shadow of him. A book lay open on the table beside his paper plate of pizza, but she could see he wasn't reading. His mind was somewhere else.

She walked closer. "Kent?"

He looked up. *Defensive,* she thought. As if he couldn't handle meeting one more stranger. She was almost sorry she'd spoken.

But then he recognized her and his face transformed into a smile. "Lindsey! I can't believe it."

His cheeks flushed and for a moment he looked healthy, but the color drained away again into a raw-chicken pallor. He was still smiling, though, and he took his leg off the chair so she could sit down. That's when she saw the metal contraption anchored over his sneaker. Vertical braces disappeared beneath the hem of his jeans.

*Madre de Dios. The wreck left him crippled.*

He saw her notice it, and the expression on his face nearly broke her heart. She put her drink on the table and sat down, dropping her loaded backpack on the floor.

She made herself smile. "I didn't know you'd started school here."

"It's my first semester. My brother and his wife moved to Columbia a couple years ago, and he talked me into it. I'm staying with them," Kent said.

"That's nice. Beats the dorms, I'm sure."

Kent nodded. "Sure is good to see somebody from home. You look great."

"You, too," she said, but both of them knew it wasn't true. He was fifty pounds thinner than he'd been in high school. Even the blue of his eyes looked faded.

She checked her watch. "I've got class in ten minutes. How are you doing?"

He shrugged. "Getting by. You're, what, a junior by now?"

"Yeah, plus some. I've been loading up, hoping to graduate early."

He raised his eyebrows. "Just like high school." But that was an era neither of them wanted to talk about. "I got a late start," he said. "Probably wouldn't have gone to college at all except for Tim's badgering. He drops me off in the morning and Carrie picks me up later, so I don't have to hoof it from the commuter lot."

She nodded, glanced at his leg. "That's from the wreck?"

"Yeah. The leg that was broken quit growing and the other one didn't. Two years of surgeries and physical therapy and still I walk like a carousel horse."

He laughed it off, but she saw in his eyes what it had cost him. Football had been Kent's whole focus in high school. Obviously, he would never play the sport again.

She poked at the textbook that lay open on the table. "Who'd you get for English comp?"

"Hastings."

"Ouch. *El chupacabra*."

"I'm glad to hear it. I thought he just hated me personally."

"He hates everybody. If there's a frat boy in your class, make friends with him. I hear there's a network that passes out copies of Hastings's old tests, free of charge." She picked up her book bag. "I gotta run. I usually eat lunch in here on Wednesdays. Maybe I'll see you tomorrow."

"I'm always right here," he said expansively, "pretending to study while I eat." And she could read in the way he opened his arms how much he hoped she would keep him company.

They had lunch together every Wednesday the rest of that semester, at ease among the crowd and clatter of the student center. Coming from the same high school gave them something in common, like matched logs in a lake of strangers. Lindsey edited his freshman compositions. But he never wrote about the accident. When his assignment was "an event that changed your life," he wrote about losing his dog when he was fourteen. Kent avoided the Tiger football games, even when she invited him to go with her and several friends.

Next semester their schedules changed, but they stayed in contact, meeting to study at the library or for lunch at the Commons. Kent took physical therapy on campus twice a week. Once she went with him. She watched his face go pale when the tech put him through the stretching exercises, sweat beading his forehead. Immediately after the sessions, his limp was always worse.

Sometimes when they walked across campus—Lindsey slowing her pace to allow for his gaited steps—or while they were stuffing on pizza after morning classes, she could feel Nathan's presence between them like a heavy curtain. Yet they never mentioned his name. She had the feeling Kent needed to talk about him, and about the accident. And he wanted to talk about it with *her*. She dreaded that conversation, but she would not back away. Maybe she needed it, too.

On a late-winter evening when a preview of spring scented the air, Kent borrowed his brother's car and they drove to a movie off campus. She hadn't dated anybody at MU, and this wasn't a date either, she'd told her roommate, just two old friends catching a flick together. Gaylene had rolled her eyes. "Whatever."

After the movie, they sat in the parking lot outside her dorm and talked. A fresh breeze through the open car windows smelled like ozone, and a thunderhead built in the distance. Lindsey inhaled deeply, slouching back in the seat. "Doesn't that smell remind you of high school? How everybody got crazy just before spring break?"

Kent laughed. "Yeah. Nathan said ozone made people horny and that somebody ought to bottle it for sale."

It was the first time he'd voluntarily brought up Nathan's name. Safe in the darkness, Lindsey smiled. "You guys used to do some crazy stuff."

"Like the day we climbed out the window of the biology lab to avoid going to assembly?"

"And Nathan sprained his ankle, because the lab was on the *second floor*," she said, pretending disapproval.

"You should talk. You conned him into dressing in costume for that Halloween dance and then showed up in your regular clothes."

Lindsey laughed. "That was a dirty trick, I admit. But he had it coming. He kept making faces at me in Hickson's class when I was trying to give the speech that counted as our nine-weeks' test."

It seemed Nathan was a part of everything they'd done. Crickets chirped from the hedge along the parking lot, and Kent slid his seat back and straightened his braced leg. One after another, they told Nathan stories, until finally there was only one memory left.

"I still miss him," Kent said. "There's never a day when I don't wonder why I lived and Nathan died."

Lindsey had wondered the same thing right after the accident, but she wouldn't say that to Kent. She hung her ponytail over the car seat and sighed.

Kent suddenly struck his palms against the steering wheel. "Ten inches. If that truck tire had come over ten inches farther, it would have been me. Nathan would be alive today."

Lindsey watched the silhouette of a coed against the curtained square of a dorm-room window. The girl was leaning forward, drying her long hair.

"Or five minutes," she said. "If you'd passed through that spot five minutes earlier—or later—it would have missed you. You'd have both gone on with the lives you had planned." She turned her head to look at him. "Doesn't the irony of that piss you off?"

He snorted. "I spent the whole second year of physical therapy being mad as hell. It helped get me through the leg lifts. When the pain started, I'd grit my teeth and think about how damned mad I was. But that wore off after a while, and then I used the pain to punish myself."

She frowned. "For what?"

"For being the one that's still alive."

"Jesus." She looked at his face in the shadows. "You've got to get over that."

He turned toward her without moving his damaged leg. The yellow glow from a streetlight angled through the windshield and touched the backs of his hands. He watched them flex and open as if they belonged to someone else, as if he didn't recognize his own hands.

"Can you forgive me, Lindsey?"

The crickets stopped chirping. Or maybe she couldn't hear them for the suffocating silence inside her chest.

She almost said *there's nothing to forgive. Nothing was your fault.* But he'd heard that before, from his family and half a dozen counselors, and it hadn't helped. He was asking her for absolution. Maybe because he couldn't ask God.

"I forgive you," she said. Like some phony deity. As if she had the ability to give him what he needed.

She put her hand on his arm and felt the hardness of bone. In high school, those arms could tackle anything on foot. His hand on top of hers was fever-warm. In the darkness, she saw the glitter of tears in his eyes.

Lindsey looked away, watching a blue moon rise over the parking lot, wishing she was somewhere else.

"Shit happens to everybody," she said finally, her voice husky and tired, like a mother with too many kids. "All we can do is keep moving, and drag the bad stuff with us. If we're lucky, someday it starts to fall away."

By the time they both went home to San Antonio that summer, Lindsey had accepted the fact that they were dating. But it was an odd kind of dating. They held hands, they sat close together with their knees touching, but they never kissed. Before they drove back to Columbia together, Kent took Lindsey to a country music club that had a live band. They sat out the fast numbers, watching couples two-step around the floor in a clockwise pattern, most of them from another generation. Then a slow dance came up, and Kent guided her onto the floor and held her close, his metal brace scraping softly against the wood floor in an odd rhythm of its own. When they didn't kiss good-night at the end of that evening, she realized they probably never would. No matter how much time they spent together, they'd always be a threesome.

In October, a week after Lindsey had sent Claire O'Neal the e-mail that would start her search for Nathan's heart, Lindsey awoke in her dorm-room bed from a sweaty nightmare. She and Kent had gone swimming in a remote lake—but he couldn't swim. She'd tried to pull him to shore, but Kent struggled and dragged them both underwater. The metal leg brace turned into concrete; they drifted down and down and she was running out of air. When they hit bottom, she jerked awake, gasping.

A few days later, when a guy in Lindsey's Broadcast News class asked her out, Lindsey said yes. Darren was a frat boy, with a handsome face and *GQ* clothes, and eyes that were almost as brown as Nathan's.

# Chapter Ten

Hob seldom drove the interstates anymore, not even the six-lane loop that circled San Antonio. Too many eighteen-wheelers, and he didn't like to look at them thundering down the road. When he'd sold his own rig, he was through with that life forever, even if his sweat still smelled like diesel. Now Hob stuck to the city streets on his way to work, sitting patiently in the traffic that clotted up behind the stoplights.

Waiting for the light to turn green, he looked at his hands resting on the steering wheel, the cuticles rimmed with black that wouldn't wash off even with gasoline. He'd started out as a mechanic, before he was a driver, and he'd come round in a circle. Same job, different garage. But that was okay. These days he had a purpose beyond repairing engines.

Hob switched on the radio and country music filled up the silence in the cab of his pickup. When there was too much silence, sitting at a stoplight or at night before he fell asleep, he heard that awful, wrenching sound again, like a machine-gun burst only quicker. Sometimes he even heard it in his sleep. He guessed that sound would be with him forever.

In that first instant when he'd heard the rapid-fire crack of bolts snapping, his mind had tried to deny it. But his hands had felt the jolt in the steering wheel and he'd known damned good and well what it was.

*Jesus, I've thrown a wheel.*

He'd been on the interstate, running north for Dallas at seventy miles an hour. He'd glanced quickly at his side mirror, and he had seen the big tire hit the concrete median and leap up like a missile. Nothing he could do to stop it.

*Holy shit. I sure hope it don't hit somebody.* He kept his foot to the pedal.

He knew which tire it was. The one he'd changed a hundred miles ago, that was due to have the lug nuts tightened again. But he hadn't taken time to do it on this haul, trying to beat his delivery deadline and get the bonus pay. Those bolts were put on with an impact wrench, eight of them. They ought to hold.

But they hadn't.

The light turned green and an impatient driver behind Hob tooted his horn. He slid his boot off the brake and goosed the accelerator of his geriatric pickup. It was a Friday, the traffic meaner than usual, everybody running late. But Hob was in no hurry. For him every day was just like the next. He drove three blocks before another red light caught him. Even with the radio on, the silence settled in his brain again.

*His foot to the metal, a September afternoon. He'd told himself he only imagined the screech of tires behind him on the opposite side of the highway. The rumble of his diesel engine hid the muffled clash of metal as his truck raced on toward Dallas. He hadn't dared to look back.* Even now, sweat broke out all over him when he remembered.

A few miles outside of Dallas that evening, he had pulled into a truck stop and put on a new tire. Told the attendant his had gone flat and ruined the rim and he'd left it in a ditch out by Abilene, which was nowhere near his real route.

That night he'd watched the TV news in his motel room. He saw the report about a freak accident on I-35, the vehicle so mangled you could hardly tell what it had been, a seventeen-year-old kid nearly decapitated and another one broken up. Hob went outside and threw up his hamburger and fries in the parking lot.

He hadn't waited out the night, just got back in his rig and hauled ass.

They couldn't prove anything, he'd told himself, even if they found him. And they never did.

For the next few weeks, he'd signed up for the longest hauls he could get. He expected every Texas State Trooper he saw to pull him over and ask where he was the afternoon of September 21. At first there had been articles in the papers about looking for the truck, and then nothing. A quote from one lawman said the guy in the truck probably never knew his tire was responsible. That made him feel a little better. Gradually Hob had stopped flinching at the sight of every patrol unit. But he'd lost his taste for the road, and he sold his rig.

He knew diesel engines inside out, and most any other kind of engine as well, so it wasn't hard to get a job in San Antonio. Hob had kept all the newspaper clippings, and those made it easy to find her. Maybe it was morbid, but he'd felt compelled to find out about the mother of the boy his loose truck tire had killed.

He knew from the clippings that her name was Claire, but when he thought of her, he called her The Mother. If he called her by name it seemed too personal, as if he were stalking her. Stalkers had bad motives, just the opposite of his.

The Mother was a pretty thing, slim with shiny brown hair, and when he finally got close enough to see her face he could tell how sad she was. It was her only child, the papers said. There was no mention of a husband. She had her own real estate agency and seemed to be doing all right. Just the same, he'd decided he should keep an eye on her. It was the least he could do.

But Hob didn't want to do the least. Not this time. He'd lived for fifty years doing the least that he could about everything. School, his job, his marriage. All half-assed. For once he wanted to do something right, to do the right thing. And so he'd appointed himself as Claire O'Neal's guardian. Not a guardian angel; he wouldn't pretend to qualify for that. But he could watch out for her without her knowing, be around when she needed some job done that required a man. Make sure nobody took advantage of her. God knew she'd been hurt enough already.

One night a few months back, when he'd driven by her house, she was sitting on the front step, her arms wrapped around her knees. It worried him to see her out there alone in the dark. He'd stopped to see if she was all right, staying back so she couldn't see enough of his face to remember it. She said thanks and waved him away. The next weekend he saw the moving van and followed it to her new house. Everything in the old house probably reminded her of the boy. He felt really bad about that.

Hob never had a son, or even a daughter. Wendy had bailed out of their short marriage without getting pregnant, a couple thousand years ago. He thought about Wendy now, on his way to work, and wondered what she was doing, whether she'd married again.

If they'd had a son, Hob could have been a good dad, he told himself. He'd have been highly proud of his son's accomplishments, especially if he played sports. Unlike his own dad, who criticized his kids all the time. Hob's dad, Ezra, had been a driver, too, for a while. He'd also been a roughneck, a mechanic and a gas passer in the days when people didn't pump their own. Ezra kept on moving from one thing to the next, never happy with any of them. Life hadn't treated old Ezra well, and it was as if he was determined to pass that on to his kids. Hob wouldn't have done a boy of his own that way.

If Hob had a daughter, though, he wouldn't have had a clue. He didn't understand women at all, not his mom, nor his half sister, Margaret. And for damned sure he hadn't understood Wendy. She'd made that quite plain.

Even so, Hob thought he could imagine how much pain Claire O'Neal must have gone through when she lost her only child for no logical reason, something out of the blue that she couldn't foresee or protect him from. The unfairness of it rankled in

Hob's chest. The damned tire might have just spun off the road without hitting anything. But no, it took out an innocent kid's life and left Hob with this huge, oily stain on his conscience.

Hob took a piece of nicotine gum from his shirt pocket and popped it into his mouth. He had quit smoking after his dad died of lung cancer at sixty-five. But now he was addicted to the damned gum.

At the next intersection, Hob spotted a familiar bronze Lexus in a parking lot alongside the buzzing traffic. He straightened up in the seat. A woman was standing beside the car, looking at a flat tire.

He maneuvered into the right lane, turned off and circled the block. It was The Mother, all right, out there on the pavement that already simmered with heat though it was still early. She had a cell phone pressed to her ear.

It wasn't unusual to see her on his way to work. He'd bought his small, frame house because it sat on the edge of the addition where she used to live. The upscale neighborhood she'd moved to was only a mile or so away, on the opposite side of this main thoroughfare. And he'd memorized all her routines.

Hob pulled into the lot where the Lexus sat and parked a short distance away, giving her some space. Usually he kept his distance but today would have to be an exception. He killed the engine and climbed out.

He could see when he approached that she was wary of him. That was all right. A woman alone ought to be wary.

He touched the brim of his ball cap. "Need some help?"

She wanted to know if he was from AAA. He made some joke about tire rodeos, where he could change a tire in five minutes. He didn't push, and in a minute she seemed to decide he wasn't dangerous. She let him change the tire.

It was a darned nice vehicle she drove. Had a fancy jack, and the tire was in good shape except for a nail she'd picked up somewhere. He finished up and wiped his hands on a rag he kept in his pickup.

She stepped toward him, holding out a folded bill that he could see was a twenty. "Thanks for your trouble. I really appreciate it."

He didn't take the money, of course, but it was nice of her. "I work at a repair place," he told her. "If you want, I'll take the tire with me and get it fixed."

"Thanks, but you've done enough. There's a garage close to my office, and I'll leave it there."

He reached in the glove box and found a card from the garage where he worked. His thumb left a little smudge in the white margin when he handed it to her. "If you ever need repairs, I'd do a good job for you, at a fair price."

His heart jackhammered a few seconds while she glanced at the card. But his name wasn't on it, and she had no idea. She put it in her purse, then smiled and handed him *her* card. Said if he ever needed to buy or sell a house, to let her know.

Hob got back in his pickup and tucked her card above the visor, like a souvenir. It was the first time he'd actually talked to The Mother. She seemed like a real nice lady. He'd probably never have the guts to tell her who he was. What good would it do, anyway? He couldn't undo what was done.

He was twenty minutes late getting to work, but if the boss noticed, he didn't say anything. Good mechanics were always in demand, like nurses. As long as he got his work done, the garage owner left him alone. So did the other mechanics. Everybody knew Hob didn't like to talk much. When they sat around together at lunch eating their burgers and fries, he listened to their stories, adventures in the service or on long hauls, the single guys boasting about their sexual exploits, the married guys bitching about their wives and mothers-in-law. He knew it was all good-natured bullshit, but he had nothing to add. *Once a tire came off my rig and killed a kid, nearly cut his head off. Messed up his buddy, too.* What would they say if he told them that?

It was hot in the big tin building where they worked on the cars, even with the doors open on both ends and two turbo-size fans blowing air through. In a back room, Hob stripped down and tossed his jeans and T-shirt on a chair before sliding on his striped coveralls. They were tighter to zip up than they used to be. He was getting a paunch from too much fast food and beer.

On his coveralls, a little red-and-white patch above the breast pocket said *Hobby.* His real name was Hobson, which had been his mother's maiden name. So of course the kids at school right away called him Hobby Horse, and he'd used that for his trucker's handle. Nowadays he wished they had just put Hob on the patch.

Two diesel tractors waited for him out on the floor, the kind he used to drive. Their hood-and-fender assemblies were pulled up to expose the big engines, like a gal with her skirt thrown over her head.

There wasn't much in the way of automotive engines that he didn't understand. It was one of the few things, maybe the only thing, he'd ever been good at in his whole life. The intricacies of an engine were like a puzzle, and he enjoyed getting all the pieces to fit perfectly and make a lubricated sound.

Hob started up the first tractor and let it idle while he walked around it and listened to its deep-throated rattle. It was popping out through the air breather. Probably a stuck exhaust valve, or a burned one. He set to work running a compression check on the faulty cylinder. Fixing engines was kind of like housework. You did the same things over and over. Some of the younger mechanics got bored with it—he could see it in their eyes. And then they got sloppy. But Hob took a simple pleasure in each repair job.

And no matter the reason that a vehicle came into the shop, on every one, large or small, he tightened all the lug nuts on the wheels.

# Chapter Eleven

The tip jar was filling up.

On a Friday night, late-season tourists and business types shouldered together in the bar, most of them waiting for tables in the restaurant next door. Mason watched them with a sardonic eye, his fingers automatic on the piano keyboard. He'd eaten in the restaurant one time, when he first got this job. The food was good but pricey, and he didn't like sitting alone at a table with linen cloths and too many forks. Julia would have loved the place, though; she'd grown up with crystal and silver even at breakfast. Mason had adjusted to all that when they got married, but he didn't have the patience for it anymore.

One of the regulars came in and gave Mason a wave. He dipped his head without missing any notes. Most of the regulars stayed away on weekends, but some of them liked the atmosphere of the place when it was crowded. On a night like this, sooner or later somebody would yell, "Play 'The Piano Man,'" and Mason would honor the request with a silent apology to Billy Joel. He felt like a phony singing that number, but it was Mason's job to make the customers happy, and the song never failed to galvanize the house and fill up the tip jar.

He finished up a jazz set and launched straight into Gershwin. Variety was the spice of employment. Once in a while he mixed in a classical piece to remind himself of the world he'd left behind, and to amuse himself by making big Tommy squirm. Tommy was a good guy, but he took his job as bar manager way too seriously.

The piano was a Steinway grand, a privilege to play, its black lacquered surface mirror-bright. An instrument like that was an anomaly in the bar. Its presence hinted of a classier past, before the area around the bar had gone to seed. But that was Santa Fe for you—art and squalor and money and kitsch all squashed together like an overpriced sandwich. That's what made the place interesting. And a good place to get lost.

A tourist stuck a five in the jar on his way to dinner and Mason showed his teeth. *Can you spare it, buddy?* The guy had on a seven-hundred-dollar suit and would probably tip his waiter at least twenty.

The Steinway was the reason Mason was here. The piano and a huge stone fireplace were the signatures of Santero's Bar & Grille. On the lighted sign out front, some anonymous artist had rendered the two symbols with a few Picasso-like strokes. Now the sign was cracked and the *e* had fallen off *grille,* subtracting ten bucks from the price of dinner. But folks could still get a sandwich with fries or some faux Mexican cuisine in the bar, if they didn't want to spend the bucks to go next door. It all came out of the same kitchen.

His gig at the bar was from seven to twelve, five nights a week, and it wasn't a bad deal. While his butt was anchored to the bench, his mind could travel anywhere. Even if he didn't want to go there.

He traveled now to the day he'd drifted into Santa Fe with his money running out. He'd sold his car to pay the deposit on a cheap apartment and a few months rent in advance. The bar was within walking distance, and he had gone inside because of the sketch of the piano on the neon sign. He hadn't touched his violin in months, and he was starved for music. But that afternoon the Steinway sat closed and silent. He'd watched it with a melancholy feeling while he drank his beer, running his eyes over the piano's curved top, imagining the feel of the cool ivory keys. After one more beer he went up to the piano and cranked out a dozen tunes in a row, just for the hell of it.

The piano had needed tuning, but it still sounded pretty good. Hardly anybody was in the place that day, but the few patrons gave him a round of applause and hooted their approval. Tommy had hired him on the spot. The pay was lousy, but the tips were good and the drinks were free.

He finished the Gershwin set with *Rhapsody in Blue*. A woman with fake-red hair sidled up to the platform and asked if he could play "Malagueña." She'd probably played the piece back when she took lessons, same as he had. He launched into it, giving it plenty of drama, and she looked thrilled. Sometimes he felt like Liberace, without the rhinestones.

Inside the piano bench, Mason had found stacks of old sheet music, but he never used the scores when he was on the clock. Ever since he was a kid and started taking piano lessons, his fingers could find the notes automatically. It was a skill that impressed the customers. Tommy, too. Once, the big barkeep had asked how Mason could memorize that many songs. Mason told him he could read the sheet music in the bench with his ass.

The redhead pushed a few ones into the tip jar, beaming a smile at him. "Excellent," she said. As if she'd know.

Mason signaled Renee to bring him a beer, then he settled into a semiclassical piece. It wasn't like playing the violin, but at least it was music. And that sent him traveling again, thinking of Julia. He wondered what she was doing today, this minute, in her expensive Swiss sanctuary.

If they hadn't both been musicians, he'd never have met Julia. Her family was rich, and he was the son of an insurance salesman and a schoolteacher. Looking down at the keyboard, he pictured Julia's hands, her slender, gifted fingers. Julia was an angel on the harp, but the cello was her real love. The first time he'd seen her holding that big cello between her knees, bringing out those pure, resonant sounds, he'd known immediately he was in love. He wanted to be that cello.

He was twenty-eight then, she even younger. What a pair they made, him with his defective heart and Julia with her fragile psyche, broken before they met. Even passion couldn't cure them. But they'd had a few amazing years before their private demons played the finale, *Stürmisch bewegt,* and she'd escaped to her parents' chalet in Europe. He hoped her parents could protect her from the world, and from herself. He hadn't been man enough for the job.

Time for his break. He finished the Debussy piece and stepped down from the raised platform where the piano sat. Several pa-trons spoke up with compliments as he passed among the tables. He acknowledged them with a half smile. One of them offered to buy him a drink but he kept moving, pretending he didn't hear.

At the far end of the long, oak bar he leaned against the area kept clear for the servers and lit a cigarette while Tommy drew him a beer. With his meds, Mason didn't have any business with either the cigarettes or the alcohol. That's exactly why he had them.

Tommy set a foaming mug in front of him. The bartender was handsome in the way a natural monolith is handsome, with some kind of Indian heritage that made him look ageless. He wore tiny hoop earrings in both ears and a turquoise ring the size of a tuba.

"Was a lady in here asking about you earlier," Tommy said, his brown hands sliding a white rag over the bar, polishing, always polishing.

"Yeah, the tourists love me." Mason took a long drag on the cigarette.

"She didn't look like a tourist. Looked more like a banker ready to repossess your car." Tommy grinned. "If you *had* a car."

Mason acknowledged the jibe with a nod, exhaled smoke, washed the taste down with a sip of beer. Julia couldn't look like a banker if she tried, but just to be sure, he said, "What'd she look like?"

"Late thirties, maybe. Slim, brown hair, nice eyes."

Julia had black hair and an olive complexion. Mason blew it off with a puff of smoke. "Doesn't sound like my landlord, so everything's cool."

He saluted Tommy with his beer and made his way through the smoke and the noise toward a hallway that ran past the restrooms. He hit the metal crash bar on the back door and went out into the alley for some fresh air.

The door swung shut behind him, cutting off the noise of the bar. A low adobe wall separated the alley from an arroyo behind the building. The ditch had grown up in mesquite and brittlebush, and sometimes he saw jackrabbits or coyotes out there. Mason propped his back against the building and lit another cigarette. The damn things didn't even taste good, but it gave his hands something to do when he wasn't playing.

He inhaled and listened to the silence. Tonight there were no coyotes, only an owl calling to its mate with a mournful sound. There was no water in the arroyo except after a big rain in the mountains, and even that didn't stay long. Like good health and true love.

Evenings in Santa Fe were always cool and dry, except in winter when they were cold and dry. A zillion stars speckled the cobalt sky and he took a minute to look at them. Living in humid Texas all his life, he'd never seen this many stars.

A person could get addicted to this climate, like Phillips and Blumenschein, those two early artists who stopped at Taos when their wagon wheel broke and never left, enchanted by the special quality of the light. He understood that. Often, looking at the muted desert colors, the acute shadows, he thought about how he would paint them. He'd taken quite a few art classes in college. He wasn't good enough to pursue it professionally but the classes had taught him how to see light. And once you learned how to really *see,* you sometimes saw things that were painfully beautiful.

Before he sold his car, he'd driven up in the Santa Fe Mountains northeast of town and watched the sun set spectacularly on the opposite side of the valley. He wasn't sure he could stand that again. But if he still had wheels, he would drive up to Taos, seventy miles to the north, and have a look around. His gaze raked the skyline in that direction as if he might see it from here.

Time to get back inside. Mason ground out his smoke and poked the combination on a keypad to open the back door. Inside, the stone fireplace painted the room with flickering light and the scent of piñon smoke. The tables were full and people stood around the long curve of the bar, talking too loud and laughing, intent on having a good time. Tommy was jawing with the customers, setting them up as fast as Renee and Joanne could carry them away. The room felt hot after the cool evening air.

Mason went back to the piano and launched into a Scott Joplin medley. He felt weary, but that was nothing unusual. Most of the time he felt better than he had any right to. One of these days a rejection episode would catch up with him. If he was lucky, it might be fatal.

Renee approached the platform and smiled. "Need anything?"

"Sure, bring me another beer." The stuff was watered down; he could drink them all night and still play. "But don't set it on the piano," he said, then softened the warning with a smile when the girl looked offended.

During the week, Renee was the only server in the bar, but on weekends Joanne came in to help out. They were nice kids, both in their early twenties, Joanne a college student some-where. They respected him because he was a musician, and he smirked at the irony of that.

He concentrated on the syncopated rhythm of "Maple Leaf Rag" and when he finished, applause swept through the bar. He acknowledged it with a public-relations smile and swung into the intro for "The Entertainer." Joplin was always a crowd pleaser.

And the tip jar runneth over.

On Saturday night, Mason had played halfway through his weekend repertoire before he noticed a woman sitting alone in the corner by the fireplace, across the room from the piano. She was watching him play, and not idly like most of the cus-tomers. A music buff, maybe. Or just an attractive woman alone who liked musicians.

He wondered if this was the woman Tommy had mentioned last night. Tommy had said "lady" instead of "woman," an un-conscious choice. But it fit. This woman looked different from most females who came alone to the bar. Mason was usually conscious of all the customers in the room, the way you're aware of things in your peripheral vision without really seeing them. He couldn't be certain, with the bar so crowded tonight, but now that he'd noticed her, he was pretty sure she'd been there all evening.

To entertain himself, he picked out a song and played it for her. He often did this to help pass the time, choosing one customer without the person's knowing, like a game. He'd try to match a song to his impression of the stranger, what Julia would have called their *psychic auras.* If the customer came up and put money in the jar when the song was through, he'd scored. If they got up and left, he lost the game.

For the Lone Lady at the Corner Table, he picked "The Shadow of Your Smile." It was the theme from an old Elizabeth Taylor movie, something sappy and romantic, but it had a haunting melody he'd always liked. The Lone Lady didn't leave, but she didn't come up to the piano, either. No points awarded.

He switched to something contemporary, a Norah Jones song, and on the second chorus he sang the words, glancing back at the corner table so he could give her his Liberace smile if she looked directly at him. His voice wasn't wonderful, but he had perfect pitch—like Willie Nelson without the twang.

Most of the dinner customers had moved through by now and the room was quieter, except for a raucous fellow at the bar who was entertaining his friends with stories nobody wanted to hear. Mason saw Joanne go over to the Lone Lady to see if she wanted another drink. You had to keep ordering if you were going to take up table space on a weekend. It was an unwritten rule.

When Joanne walked away, the woman glanced up and saw him watching her. He didn't have time to flash a grin before she looked away, studying the flames that licked around the piñon logs in the fireplace. *Maybe she has a crush on me.* He smiled at the joke. If that was it, she would change her tune fast in daylight. He was a stick man these days, hollow as a wood flute. Nothing of substance about him.

That thought reminded him of an old blues song he hadn't played in a long time, so he launched into it. When he looked up again, the woman was gone.

The Lone Lady came back Sunday night, but by then he'd grown bored with trying to guess her story. If she wanted to sit there and drink alone every night, that was her business. A table full of tourists right by the piano kept him busy all evening with requests.

At midnight Mason cleaned out the tip jar, straightening the bills into a bank bag that Tommy kept in the safe for him. He'd be inviting trouble if he carried it home through the dark streets. He might be tired of living, but getting mugged wasn't his first choice for a finale. On Monday or Tuesday, his days off, he would pick up the tip money and walk it down to the bank in daylight, along with his weekly check. After that, he'd probably end up back at the bar to work on new arrangements for the next week. He had nothing else to do, and if he stayed away too long, he got lonesome for the touch of that big piano.

# Chapter Twelve

Claire circled the parking lot of Santero's Bar and Grille twice before she found a spot. That afternoon, when she'd first found the place, the bar was nearly empty. Apparently business was good on Friday nights.

She squeezed her SUV into a space between the Dumpster and a low-slung black compact car with fire-breathing lizards painted on the fenders. The lizards were beautiful and scary, like the gang art on bridge abutments in San Antonio. She locked the Lexus and walked toward the bar entrance, passing new Cadillac sedans, ten-year-old Honda compacts and dusty SUVs. Gravel crunched under her shoes.

She opened the carved wood door and stepped into the dim interior of the bar. Silver-haired couples occupied many of the tables, and young arty types in wrinkled clothes stood around the long oak bar. There were tourists, too, obvious in their bright cotton clothes and sneakers.

Oversize paintings hung on a rock wall, and a large stone fireplace spattered warm light on the drinkers. The place must have been classy once, but now the dark corners hid layers of dust and regret, like an old movie queen getting by on cosmetics and past glories. Maybe it was fashionably seedy, but definitely seedy. Any way you sliced it, playing piano here was quite a decline from the cachet of the Austin Symphony.

She stopped near the entrance and watched the crowd, listening to their brittle laughter. The only other time she'd gone into a bar by herself she was thirteen and looking for her father. Standing here in her business clothes, she felt very much an outsider.

Piano music floated through the noise. She edged around a knot of people and looked toward the grand piano on its low platform across the room. A slender man in a baggy jacket leaned over the keyboard.

Was that McKinnon? He looked smaller than she'd imagined. Through the film of smoke, she couldn't tell if his profile matched the photo in her purse.

Claire scanned the room for an empty table. A couple was abandoning a spot near the fireplace and Claire moved quickly toward it. She took a chair facing the piano and hung her jacket on the back of the other chair as if she were expecting someone. Maybe that would discourage prowlers. From here she could watch the piano player at a safe distance.

Most of the customers were talking, ignoring his music. If their inattentiveness bothered him, he didn't show it. He rippled through a familiar melody as if he were just passing time, watching the hubbub with a vague half smile, talking briefly with someone who approached the piano. He didn't try to compete with the noise by pounding the keys.

A pretty young waitress appeared at Claire's table. "Good evening. What can I get you?"

"Cabernet, please. House brand is fine."

"Coming right up."

"The piano player is quite good," Claire said. "What's his name?"

The girl smiled and flashed a look of admiration in his direction. "That's Mason McKinnon. Isn't he wonderful?"

Claire nodded, her smile frozen. The girl went away.

So this was the man with Nathan's heart.

She scooted her chair to get a better view of him. McKinnon leaned into his music, smiling at a customer who stopped to put folded money into a glass vase on the piano's shiny top. He made some wisecrack and the customer laughed. If Claire didn't know better, she'd have said he was born to play piano in a bar. She thought about the guest violinist she'd seen perform with the Austin symphony, his passion for the music and the instrument, and wondered if McKinnon had felt that way once. Why had he given it up?

Nathan's heart was beating inside that man's chest, keeping him and his music alive. Claire shivered.

The waitress returned with her wine and a tiny bowl of pretzel goldfish. The Cabernet tasted thin and cheap.

She'd been there an hour when McKinnon finished a set and

took a break, acknowledging the light applause with a half wave. She watched him step off the platform and walk over to the long bar. His jacket looked too big for him, like a child wearing his father's clothes. She imagined striking up a conversation with him, knew she would not.

McKinnon spoke to the bartender, then hooked an elbow over the rim of the bar and waited. In the shadowy light, he looked older than the photo she carried in her purse, the jawline more angular. But it was the same face, no question.

And he had an attitude. He lit a cigarette and lounged against the bar, surveying the crowd like a character out of *Casablanca*. Someone spoke to him and he responded with a lopsided smirk.

*He shouldn't be smoking. Especially not with a borrowed heart.*

His gaze drifted in her direction and she looked away. In the big fireplace, flames fluttered and jigged like the pulse in her neck.

She glanced back to see the bartender slide McKinnon a mug of beer. He scooped it up and carried it down a dark hallway at the back of the bar. She squinted after him, her face hot.

*Unbelievable.* The man was drinking and smoking. And he obviously wasn't eating right—he looked bony as a scarecrow.

What the hell was he thinking?

Her teeth twinged as if she'd bitten tinfoil. She saw herself march down the hall after him, grab him by the lapels and shake him until his eyeballs rolled. The fantasy felt great, but it wasn't practical. She flagged down the waitress.

"Another Cab?" the girl said.

"Yes, and ice water, please. A tall glass." Claire opened the collar of her blouse, her breath short.

She stayed at the bar until McKinnon stopped playing around midnight, then drove back to the upscale hotel where she'd checked in the day before. She plugged her laptop into the dataport and searched for information about follow-up care for heart transplant patients. For damned sure, it didn't involve smoking and drinking.

She took notes from the computer screen on the hotel stationery. McKinnon had to know what he should do to take care of himself. Why wasn't he doing it?

It was almost daylight when she fell onto the king-size bed and slept.

That night and the next, Claire sat by the fireplace at Santero's, sipped bad wine and watched McKinnon wasting his health and a providential talent. The idea was incomprehensible; the SOB was thumbing his nose at his second chance at life. Nathan had given him that gift—and so had she, by God, the night she'd agonized over the decision to let the surgeons take Nathan's heart.

McKinnon's behavior was *unacceptable.*

She bit the head off a pretzel goldfish. Only twice had she ever been this angry, both times on Nathan's account. Once was after the accident, when she'd raged against God for taking Nathan's young life. And twenty years ago, when Avis O'Neal had offered her twenty-five thousand dollars to divorce her pampered son and relieve him of any responsibility for their unborn child. Claire was nineteen then, alone and scared, with no income. For her baby's sake she took the money, then told Avis O'Neal to kiss off, promising to make her life a litigious hell if Avis ever contacted her again or tried to see her grandchild. And the woman never had.

Now it was Mason McKinnon who was shortchanging her son. Obviously the man had no scruples, no sense of wonder for the miracle of a healthy heart. What about his own child, who would be almost three years old now? Didn't he want to see his child grow up? Why didn't his wife stop his destructive behavior?

*Unacceptable.*

Driving from San Antonio, Claire had told herself that she would not interfere in Mason McKinnon's life. It wasn't fair, she reasoned, to inflict on a stranger her own inability to cope with her son's loss. But seeing McKinnon in this shape changed everything. He had forfeited his right to privacy.

Claire paid her tab and left the bar.

At ten minutes after midnight, when McKinnon walked out the front door, Claire watched from a corner of the parking lot where the streetlight didn't reach. She had backed her car into the space so she could face the bar entrance. Now she waited, her hand on the ignition. But instead of getting into a car, McKinnon crossed through the parking lot and set off walking down the darkened sidewalk.

She debated whether to get out and follow him on foot. But there was no telling where he might be headed, and the area around the bar looked too risky to be walking at night. She let him get a block ahead, then started the car and rolled slowly behind.

She could barely see his dark clothes moving in the shadows. At the corner she waited to see which way he went, then she circled the block and picked up his trail again. The streets were quiet, only a few cars about in the small hours of a Monday morning. She'd have to be careful so he didn't notice her. She also kept an eye out for cruising policemen, who might get suspicious of her behavior.

Three blocks from the bar, McKinnon turned left onto a four-lane thoroughfare. She sped up to catch him. The traffic here gave her camouflage but made it harder to keep track of him. She couldn't poke along at ten miles an hour without attracting attention. She turned off and circled a block.

She came back onto Cerrillos Road, a main thoroughfare lined with motels and retail business. She was going the other direction now, facing McKinnon as he approached. He walked purposefully, but without hurry. She passed him and got in the left lane to make a U-turn, thinking again of a night when she was thirteen, tracking her dad to a redneck bar on a weekend she was supposed to spend with him. That night she'd trailed her quarry on a bicycle.

She made the turn and glimpsed McKinnon cutting into the parking lot of a convenience store. She lost sight of him, but he hadn't gone inside; he'd gone past the store toward the back. She turned at the next block and glimpsed a figure passing through a gap in a dilapidated wooden fence. He came out in a parking lot that faced the side street she'd taken. The lot fronted a two-story apartment building that sat directly behind the quick-stop.

Claire pulled into the parking lot and doused her lights. Checked to make sure her doors were locked. In a moment she saw movement on a second floor walkway and McKinnon appeared, oblivious to anything but his own destination. She watched him unlock a door and go inside. Behind the drawn curtains a light came on.

Claire circled the parking area and pulled into a space so that her headlights aimed toward his door. Squinting, she made out a metallic reflection: number 213. Just as Irv's report had said.

She cut her lights again and waited. Stains streaked the stucco exterior of the apartment complex, and the shrubs along the front sidewalk looked anemic and thirsty. Spray-painted graffiti emblazoned the fence between the apartments and the convenience store.

The place gave her the creeps. According to Irv's research, McKinnon's wife had come from a wealthy family. Claire could not imagine Julia McKinnon living here. If Julia had left him, that could be the cause of his current habits. Or the result of them.

She waited for a long time, to convince herself he was living there instead of just visiting or buying drugs. At two o'clock his light went out.

Claire sat in the car with her arms wrapped around her, shivering. She watched his darkened window for another half hour, wondering what had brought him to this low place in his life. And how to save a man's life who didn't want saving.

# Chapter Thirteen

After midnight, the streets around Santero's lay quiet. Mason set out down the broken sidewalks on his way home. Low-riders and rusted-out pickups slept in dirt front yards where the occasional streetlights didn't reach. Nested between small adobe houses, an all-night laundromat sat empty except for an old woman dozing in a plastic chair. The windows cast rectangles of light across the sidewalk and into the street, like an Edward Hopper painting. The artists of Santa Fe wouldn't live here, though, where laundromats and bars intermingled with the houses. The successful artists owned expensive homes in the hills outside of town.

Mason stayed alert for the sound of other footsteps. At this hour the working stiffs were asleep, and anybody else could be bad news. After a few blocks he turned southwest on Cerrillos Road, away from the center of town. Traffic sizzled past in four lanes and streetlights erased the darkness.

His shadow bobbed along on the pavement beneath his feet. It was a six-block walk, so he wore sneakers to work with his jeans and sport coat. Tommy never mentioned a dress code, and Mason didn't give a shit what he looked like.

In two more blocks he cut through behind a convenience store and emerged in the parking lot of the City Suites apartments, an H-shaped structure that squatted in the halogen glare of two sentry lights. The marquee out front advertised cheap rent and two color TVs in each flat. It didn't mention there was no cable and the picture was always fuzzy.

His shoes on the metal staircase rang D-sharp into the quiet night. He found the key in his pocket and let himself in to number 213. Yellow lamplight flooded the cheap Southwestern furniture that came with the digs, not quite reaching into the ell of the kitchen. He walked through to the single bedroom and turned on another lamp beside the bed. His reflection caught in the glass of a Native American print that hung behind the bed, giving the illusion of other movement, and it startled him. He'd lived here nearly a year, but the furnished rooms still felt like a motel instead of home.

He emptied his pockets onto the faux-wood dresser and turned on the TV for company. The fridge held a quart of milk, a carton of orange juice and one shriveled apple. He was hungry but too tired to cook. Hell, he didn't cook even when he wasn't tired. He sniffed the milk and drank a few swallows left in the carton, then moved on to the shower. At least there was plenty of hot water in the middle of the night.

Afterward, damp and depleted, he slumped on the bed and piled both pillows behind his head. At 1:00 a.m. his TV choices were slim. He settled on an old movie channel but fell asleep before he could recognize the flick. Sometime in the night, he rolled over on the remote and woke up enough to hit the off button.

It was past noon when Mason awoke to the noise of somebody bumping and door-slamming in the apartment below, moving in or moving out. He tried to remember what day it was. Monday, the first of his two days off. The longest days of the week.

He lay there listening to the noise downstairs, feeling the vibrations of movement through the common walls. It reminded him of the old joke about a little boy who asked his mom if it was true what the Bible said, that we come from dust and return to dust when we die. She said, yes, what the Bible said was true. And the kid said, "Then somebody's either coming or going underneath my bed."

Somebody was coming or going underneath Mason's bed. He turned his head on the pillow and watched bluish light sift through the drawn curtains, the darker blues bunched at the top, spreading out to cerulean at the bottom. The gradations of light were beautiful, if you didn't know how much dust had amassed in the fabric. He couldn't think of one reason to get up. He was like those dust bunnies under the bed, weightless and transparent, a soul on its way out.

Finally he got up and went to the bathroom.

In the kitchen he dumped out an army of pills on the counter—two blue ones, a yellow horse pill, tiny white ones insidious with hidden power, a red that was bitter as a persimmon if it touched your tongue. He swallowed them with orange juice. What a waste. Thousands of dollars worth of medications every month to keep his worthless body from rejecting the lion heart he'd inherited from a healthy kid.

He didn't pay for the drugs himself—couldn't have. That was taken care of by an insurance policy his mother had taken out after his father died. She must have suspected he would inherit his dad's cardiomyopathy. Mason was in high school then and still healthy, so it was easy to get maximum coverage. Jessica McKinnon still paid the premiums and wouldn't hear of anything else.

Now *hers* was a heart worth saving. He ought to write his mom a note today, tell her how great he was doing, so she wouldn't worry. Every week or so he sent her one of those tourist postcards they sold at every cash register in town. If it weren't for his mother, he'd have stopped taking the antirejection drugs months ago, quit dragging things out. But if she didn't get the monthly statements from the insurance company, she would be on the next plane to Santa Fe, and he couldn't let her see him like this. Thank goodness his sister still lived in Austin, and the grandkids helped keep Jessica's mind off him.

The horse pill hung in his throat and he finished off the orange juice and tossed the empty carton in the sink. There was more bumping downstairs, and he walked to the front window and pushed aside the curtain. The sky was clear and sunny, but the TV weatherman had predicted thundershowers tomorrow. At this time of year, rain in town usually translated to snow at the higher elevations, and the winter economy here depended on the ski ranges getting good snow. The locals had been grousing about the need for precipitation; maybe they'd get it.

His second-floor window looked down on the parking lot, where a woman was carrying bags from her car to the apartment below. The top of her head disappeared beneath the balcony walkway and he heard her moving around in the apartment directly below his. He hoped she didn't have kids that played the TV loud in the mornings.

The pills burned in his empty stomach. He found a can of ravioli in the kitchen cabinet, dumped the contents into a bowl and set it in the microwave. While his breakfast heated, he lit a cigarette and turned on the TV news. Had to get some groceries today. Bananas and milk, and some kind of meat that was already cooked. And tortilla chips, his main snack. He also needed to bank the tip money from the bar.

Chores were a good thing, something to take up the time. But he was still dog tired, and there was no hurry. If he did all his chores today, he'd have nothing to do tomorrow. He watched the weather and the football scores while he ate the ravioli, then went back to bed for the day.

Midmorning sun angled through an arched window above the bar entrance and spotlighted Mason's scuffed sneakers beneath the Steinway. Mason saw it as a painting—the cracked shoes on the piano pedals, the skewed triangle of light. Some kind of metaphor for his life, probably, but he chose not to analyze that.

He opened the piano bench and lifted out a stack of sheet music, the pages yellowed, corners dog-eared by other musicians' fingers. He laid the stack of music on top of the piano and stood on the perimeter of the carpeted dais to sort through it. The platform echoed the grand piano's shape, with room enough to walk around it, if you didn't drink too much.

Some of the scores were older than he was. He handled the sheets gently, in honor of all the musicians who'd played the music before him. In his mind he saw a parade of faces, some of them long dead, others still playing bars in some other city. Maybe some had moved on to bands or orchestras, chasing their dreams.

Maybe one of them played violin with a symphony.

But that's not the way it worked. You didn't move up from playing bars; you moved down to it—unless you were born to play the clubs, like Satchmo.

He picked out six songs and set them on the latticed music rack above the keyboard, stacking the rest back into the bench. He got bored playing the same stuff every night, and every so often he had to add some new tunes. One afternoon, with nothing to do in his claustrophobic apartment, he'd tried to write a song of his own, sitting at the kitchen table with a score sheet improvised from notebook paper. But a gray light had fallen across the lined page and suddenly he'd seen himself as if from a distance—the failed musician, pathetic and sad. He quit before he got the song right.

One line of the melody kept playing through his head, though, when he was walking to work or taking a shower. It had a distinct country flavor, and that struck him as odd. He'd never much cared for country music until the last few years. Maybe it was his Texas roots cropping up.

Mason ran a few scales on the Steinway's keyboard to warm up his fingers. Then he opened the first sheet of music, sight-reading it first, humming the notes in his head. He played through the piece easily and repeated it several times with more expression. After five rehearsals, he closed the music and tried it from memory. Soon his fingers took over and added notes of their own.

By now the angle of sunlight had changed and showed a thin layer of dust on the black surface of the piano. He could feel it on the keys, too—smoke from the bar patrons, and from the fireplace that burned every night. He stepped down from the platform and went behind the bar. From the bin where Tommy kept his clean bar rags, Mason fished out two soft cloths and dampened one, wringing it almost dry. With the damp cloth he cleaned each piano key individually, then polished it with the dry cloth. After he'd finished the keyboard, he wiped down the lacquered wood, starting with the winged top and working his way down to the legs, taking his time. When he started playing here, the guy who cleaned the bar was using a cheap cleaning spray on the keys and wood alike, if he cleaned it at all. It made Mason's teeth ache to think about it. Right away he'd set a rule that nobody touched the piano except him.

Tommy came in at noon. His black hair was slicked back into a ponytail at the base of his neck, and his T-shirt was so white it glowed in the dim light. So did his grin when he saw Mason at work.

"Morning, maestro. When you get finished there, start on the tables, will you?"

Mason nodded. "I'll check my contract."

He liked being here early when no one was around but Tommy and the chef next door in the restaurant's kitchen, a Mexican man with a weathered face who always got there before them. Manolo either didn't speak English or pretended not to. Mason seldom saw him, but the smells of sautéed onions and bell peppers and other fine aromas wafted through the brick archway between the bar and the dining room. Sometimes he could hear Manolo singing while he cooked. Once in a while he sent his helper out with a sausage soufflé for Mason and Tommy, or thin pancakes laced with brandy syrup.

With Manolo to run the kitchen and Tommy to manage the bar, the guy that owned both places seldom came around, which suited everybody fine. Tommy said the boss owned property in several Southwestern cities and traveled a lot.

When the piano was spotless, Mason tossed the cloths onto the bar. "It's time to get the piano tuned again," he told Tommy.

"Unh." Tommy nodded, stocking bottles of booze in the racks behind the bar.

Mason went back to his sheet music, working on an old Cole Porter tune next. He practiced the new pieces until he felt ready to add several of them to his nightly repertoire. Then, reluctant to go, he just fiddled around, picking out a song he'd listened to on CD on the long drive out here from Austin.

"I like that one," Tommy called when Mason stopped playing. "What's it called?"

"'One Flight Down.' Written by Jesse Harris and sung by Norah Jones on that CD that won a Grammy in 2002."

Tommy shook his head. "You're too smart for this place. I'll tell Gordon you need a raise."

"You do that."

The next time through, to entertain Tommy, Mason sang the words. The song was about finally hearing the music that was in your head all along. The first time he heard it he'd nearly cried. He was a mess back then, before all the scars healed over. But he was a tough guy now, all right.

It was nearly time for the bar to open, so Mason put away the sheet music and asked Tommy to get his tip bag from the safe. He stuck the bag up under his shirt and set out walking.

Outdoors, a pristine sunlight cast crisp shadows across his path and fractured the desert colors into a dozen subtle shades. Yellow chamisa bloomed along the dry gullies and sprouted up from the cracks in the sidewalk. The air smelled so good it hurt his chest. Moments like this kept him putting one foot in front of the other, day after day, when it made a whole lot more sense to flush his meds and call it quits. He shook his head, disgusted by his own weakness.

At the drive-through bank window on Alameda, the girl behind the bulletproof glass remembered him, not startled anymore as she'd been the first few times he arrived on foot. She smiled and spoke into her microphone, her voice sounding faraway and hollow through the speaker.

"Good morning, Mr. McKinnon. I heard you play the other night. Really enjoyed it." She counted the cash twice and filled out the deposit slip for him. He kept a couple hundred for his pocket.

From the bank he walked to a local market, bought milk and cereal, bread and bologna. He touched the smooth grapefruits, imagining their pungent taste and smell, but those were forbidden fruits with his medications. He bought apples, instead, one mango and two bananas, limited by what he could carry in two bags.

Lugging the sacks up the stairs to his apartment, he was conscious of the fatigue in his legs, even though he'd had plenty of sleep. The fatigue was getting worse every week, and he was long overdue for his heart checkup. What the hell.

He put the groceries away and made himself a pimento cheese sandwich. He turned on the TV with the sound muted and sat down at the vinyl-topped table to eat, using a paper towel for a plate.

Silence ticked around him. His eyes traced the outlines of the generic furniture, the cheap prints on the walls. When his gaze came to rest on the black case of his violin inside the open door of the closet, he got up and closed the closet door. Poor, abandoned Serena. The Antonazzi violin was worth at least two hundred thousand dollars. If he sold her, he wouldn't have to worry about money for a long time. But he could come nearer to cutting off his leg.

He turned on the TV sound and flipped channels, pausing a minute on *Animal Planet* to watch a show dog trot around a ring, its long hair flowing like water. On another channel, a talk show host was interviewing some author. "Why do you think so many writers are alcoholic and suicidal?" the host asked.

"I don't know," the writer said. "Maybe it's because of the long afternoons."

*No shit.* Mason snorted and switched off the TV. He lit a cigarette and threw away his paper-towel plate.

And then there was nothing left to do.

Nothing.

On his days off, the hours expanded like a noxious gas. If he had a small keyboard, he could pass the time. He had Serena, of course, but he hadn't played the violin since Julia left. Couldn't make himself pick it up.

He stopped pacing and faced the hollow room. The wall clock ticked. He changed clothes and went out to walk the streets.

At 3:00 a.m. Mason awoke, alert as a cat. His job had turned him into a night person, and when he went to bed at a normal time, it threw his body clock off. He lay still for a while hoping drowsiness would overtake him again, but it was no use.

He dressed in jeans and a long-sleeved T-shirt, pocketed his room key and cigarettes and stepped outside. A thundershower had moved through and the night air felt cool. He thought about going back for his sweatshirt but didn't.

The second-floor walkway circled the building and led to a sundeck around back, which overlooked a flowered *placita*. To him it was the best feature of the City Suites. He often went out to the deck at night when it was abandoned and sat in a wooden chair beneath the stars. From there he could see the mountains in the distance, their snow-dusted tops incandescent with moonlight.

Tonight he lit a cigarette and leaned his forearms on the deck railing, watching the lightning that flashed in the hills.

"You shouldn't be smoking."

The voice startled him. He turned toward it and saw the woman's legs protruding from the shadow of an umbrella table, her face and torso hidden.

A reformed smoker, no doubt. They were the worst.

"Sorry," he said, in a tone that let her know he wasn't. "I thought I was alone."

He turned back toward the mountains, pissed because she'd violated his privacy. And spoiled his requiem for the near dead. He'd just as well go back to his flat, but he'd be damned if he'd let her run him off before he finished his smoke.

"It's beautiful, isn't it?" she said. "The storm over the mountains." Her voice was low and slow, a Texas accent.

"Umm." He kept his back to her, not wanting conversation.

"I'm your new neighbor. Number 113," she said.

He stubbed out his cigarette in a flowerpot and when the butt was cool, he put it in his shirt pocket. "Welcome to Shangri-la. I sleep days, so I hope you're quiet."

She waited a beat before answering, but when she did, she mimicked his sardonic tone, giving back what she got. "I barely sleep nights, let alone days, but I'm *always* quiet."

He almost smiled. He turned to face the shadow beneath the umbrella. "So you don't have kids? I thought I heard kids this morning."

"Not mine," she said slowly. "You?"

"Me what?"

"Do you have kids?"

"No." *Just a baby named Michael, who never took a living breath.*

She recrossed her legs and ice clinked in a glass. She was wearing sweatpants and sneakers. A nightwalker, like him.

"My name's Claire," she said.

He nodded but didn't tell her his name. He was getting a funny vibe, as if he'd seen her before maybe, or she wanted something. Not a midnight bump-and-go; there was none of that in her voice. Whatever it was, he didn't want the involvement.

"Guess I'll turn in," he said. "Good night."

Leaving the deck, he glanced back as a gust of wind caught the umbrella flap and lifted the shadow from her face. She was looking away from him, toward the lightning, but her profile seemed familiar.

He was halfway to his apartment before he figured it out. She looked a lot like the Lone Lady from the bar.

# Chapter Fourteen

At midday when Mason opened his apartment door to pick up his newspaper, he almost stepped on a foil-wrapped package. He stopped, frowning.

Something another resident had dropped, unnoticed? More likely something gross left as a joke by kids in the complex.

But it didn't smell gross. In fact, a delicious aroma curled up from whatever was inside. His folded newspaper lay beside the package like wrapped silverware.

He picked up the bundle and discovered it was a casserole dish, still warm. He lifted one edge of the foil. The smell made his mouth water. It looked like chicken, he decided, with rice in a creamy sauce. Who would have left him this? Then he saw the note that was under the dish.

The handwriting was neat and businesslike, and clearly feminine. "I made too much dinner and thought I'd share. Don't worry, no strings attached. Claire."

He shook his head. What was the deal with this woman? It stretched the boundaries of coincidence that she'd shown up at the bar for several nights, and then moved in here. Surely she wasn't the same person. He'd seen both women in semi-darkness; the resemblance was probably his imagination.

Either that, or she was stalking him.

He picked up his newspaper and took the covered dish inside. The aroma made his stomach growl. There were vegetables, too, broccoli and tiny carrots and mushrooms in the rice. He poked at it with a fork, then took a bite. Healthy-looking stuff, but damn, it tasted good. If the neighbor was some kind of weirdo and had put poison in it, what did he care, anyway?

He sat down and ate half of his meal straight from the bowl, saving the rest for later. But after his shower, the aroma lingered in the apartment and he wasn't dead yet. So he took the casserole back out of the refrigerator and ate the rest.

When the last grain of rice was gone, he set the dish in the sink on top of the others and ran it full of water. He supposed she expected him to wash and return the dish, with a thank-you note. But he didn't want to encourage the woman or she might become a pest.

He carried a basket of laundry downstairs to the coin-operated machines, came back upstairs, and turned on *Animal Planet* while he wrote checks for his bills. While the clothes were in the dryer, he switched to CNN and caught the headlines.

It had rained a little that morning. Returning with his basket of clean clothes, he kicked off his damp flip-flops at the door. The apartment floor felt lumpy under his bare feet. He hated that. It had been a couple of months since he'd swept the place.

He rolled out the used Hoover upright and vacuumed the traffic patterns, too tired to move the furniture. Then he re-wrapped the cord and rolled the sweeper back into the closet beside Serena's black case, ignoring her like a maiden aunt. He shut the door feeling stupid about his guilt toward an inani-mate object.

But Serena wasn't inanimate when he played. When he *used* to play. Then, she was vital and elegant and his pulse raced when he held her.

Those days were over. He found his cigarettes and hunted for matches.

The apartment needed dusting, and the bathroom bor-dered on disgusting. It was hard to care. But he did need clean clothes to wear to work. He plugged in the iron and whacked it once to get it going. The beat-up ironing board was a permanent fixture in his bedroom. In the narrow space between the bed and the wall, he barely had room to stand and press the pants he'd taken from the dryer. Thank God for knit shirts.

He slipped on the pants while they were still warm and checked the clock. He'd succeeded in dragging out his chores so they ate up most of the afternoon. Soon he could go to work and warm up on the piano before the dinner crowd gathered.

He didn't like to show up at work much more than an hour early. That was just too lame.

He'd already shaved and pulled on a lightweight turtleneck when he remembered the casserole dish in the sink. He couldn't wash dishes now without splashing on his clean shirt, so he blew it off.

The dish would still be there tomorrow. And with his luck, so would he.

The midweek crowd at Santero's consisted of a few middle-aged couples and half a dozen after-work singles who camped out on the bar stools, hoping to get lucky or to tell Tommy what a crappy day they'd had. Most of them seemed to prefer the latter. Mason didn't know how Tommy stood it.

He didn't mind the small audience. Even when they had a good crowd, most of them only half listened to him play. He told himself he didn't perform for the audience anyway, not even for himself. Only for the music.

He scattered the new numbers from the old sheet music among his regular lineup. They sounded good, and he managed to anesthetize himself for three hours. By then his neck was stiff and his butt numb on the bench. He took a break, carrying his beer and cigarette out back to the alley.

The evening felt cool and dry. Big surprise. At least tonight his stomach wasn't growling, thanks to all that chicken and rice. The Lone Lady hadn't appeared in the bar, and he dismissed the idea that she and his food donor were one and the same. The idea was just too weird.

Nothing was moving in the arroyo tonight, no coyotes afoot or owls on the wing. And he was getting chilly. He ground out his smoke and went back to work.

The rest of the evening, Mason kept glancing back at the table where the Lone Lady had sat. A lot of the weekend bar patrons were tourists or businesspeople on short visits to the city. Undoubtedly she had been one of those, just a transient customer. He was transient, too, and not just in Santa Fe. The days of transplant recipients were numbered, and he was counting down.

The tip jar was less than half full at midnight when he stashed the money in the bank bag, bid Tommy good-night and walked home. The scent of chicken and rice still lingered in his apartment. He wished he had saved some for breakfast.

There was no foil-covered dish on his mat at noon the next day when he opened his front door. But beneath the rubber band on his newspaper he found a folded slip of paper that advertised a housecleaning service. It was photocopied on pink paper, probably by some housewife needing extra money. Budget rates, it said. Satisfaction guaranteed. The phone number had the same prefix as his.

It wasn't a bad idea. He hated cleaning his apartment, and it seemed obvious by now he was never going to do it. The tip money was counting up, and his paycheck covered cigarettes and bologna sandwiches and most of the rent. Maybe he would call and see what "budget rates" meant. Maybe tomorrow.

He tossed the flyer on the kitchen table and spent a couple of hours reading the local newspaper, even the ads. He worked the crossword puzzle, watched a veterinary show on *Animal Planet,* then switched over to ESPN to check the Big 12 scores. He never used to follow football, but now that he had time on his hands, he liked to see how the Texas teams were doing.

It was still too early to go to work. Shamed by the pink flyer, he soaked a week's dirty dishes in soapy water. When he finally got them clean and draining in the rack, he dried the one that belonged to the woman downstairs and set it on the table.

On his way to work, he left the dish outside her door along with a scrap of paper that said only "Thanks." He didn't sign the note or brag on the food. He rang the bell at 113 and hurried away before she answered.

At ten-thirty that night, when he came back to the piano from his cigarette-and-beer break, the Lone Lady was sitting at the same table in the darkest corner of the bar. Huh. Maybe she wasn't transient after all. Without getting closer, he couldn't tell if she looked like the new neighbor whose profile he'd only glimpsed in the dark. And by the time he shut down the Steinway at midnight, she was gone.

It was the same dish he'd washed and returned. This time the covered bowl held beef stew and came with a square of buttered corn bread. She had wrapped the warm corn bread separately, along with a small dish of peach cobbler. He couldn't help it; his mouth watered.

This really had to stop, he told himself while he wolfed down the food. But man, this was home-style cooking like his mom used to do, not the bird food Julia cooked and ate. When they were first married, he used to take Julia out to dinner twice a week so he could get a steak or a pork chop, something substantial.

But he couldn't keep taking food from the neighbor downstairs. Sooner or later she was bound to expect something in return. She'd want a leaky showerhead fixed, or the TV adjusted, and he had no skills in either area. He especially had no interest in chatty conversations or neighborly visits. Being polite to people he didn't know was too much of a strain. He was required to do it on the job, and that was all he could manage.

Still, he wasn't sure how to order somebody to stop being nice to him. If he rang the bell and waited for her to answer, there was no avoiding an awkward conversation. Passive ungratefulness seemed the best method, and it was definitely easiest. He would return the bowl without even a note.

The housecleaning ad was under the rubber band on his newspaper again the next day. This time he dialed the number. His shower was caked with hard-water scum and the rusty stain in the commode was getting scary. His sink was full of dirty dishes again.

A woman's voice answered.

"Are you the one who advertised for housecleaning?"

"Oh!" She sounded surprised. "Yes, I am."

"What would you charge for a small apartment, basically two rooms with a kitchen at one end? And a bathroom."

"Umm. Is thirty dollars too much?"

A sucker born every minute. She must be new in Santa Fe and didn't know what the market would bear. Obviously she didn't have much experience, but for thirty dollars it was worth a try.

"That's quite reasonable," he said evenly. "The problem is I sleep days, and work nights. Are you willing to come after six? I could leave a key under the mat." He didn't want to be here while she cleaned, and there was nothing worth stealing except for Serena. He could carry the violin to work, or maybe leave it with the apartment manager. As if it would be any safer with Bald Bingham than with the house cleaner.

"I'd prefer days," she said primly, "but you're my first customer and I need the work. Did you want cleaning every week?"

"Let's just start with one time. I probably can't afford every week."

"That's okay. I can come this evening, if you like."

"Sure. I'll pick up some of the junk. My name's Mason McKinnon, City Suites apartments, number 213. Do you know where that is?"

"Yes. I live quite close." He could hear her smile. Happy for the work, he guessed.

"I'll stop by late tomorrow afternoon to see if everything is okay," she said. "And to collect my fee."

"Fair enough."

After he hung up he realized he didn't get her name. But what did it matter?

When he got home after midnight, the apartment was spotless. She'd even rearranged a few pieces of furniture in a way that made the living room seem larger, and she'd put fresh flowers in a water tumbler on the kitchen table. He'd forgotten to take Serena with him and was relieved to see the black violin case, sans dust, still in the closet.

The ashtrays, though, were missing. At first he thought she'd stolen them, but then he found them washed and put away in the back of a cupboard, a small mistake.

Mason resolved to hire her once a month. He laid out thirty-five dollars on the table and took the key from under the mat.

At 5:00 p.m., when he'd returned from buying cigarettes and orange juice at the quick-stop, the doorbell rang. He picked up the money from the table and answered the door in his baggy jeans and T-shirt.

"Hi," she said, smiling. "I'm your house cleaner."

Mason stared. "Wait a minute. Aren't you...?"

"What's the matter? Wasn't my work satisfactory?"

"Everything looks great. You're the woman in 113, aren't you?"

Now that he saw her in daylight, he knew damned good and well she was also the woman from the bar.

"Yes. I'm Claire," she said brightly, as if she were pleased he remembered. She was close to his age, a little younger maybe, with a painfully open face and wide eyes. She didn't look like a kook, but neither did Dr. Jekyll.

She glanced inside the apartment, which he took as a hint to invite her in.

He ignored it. "And you left food outside my door."

She smiled again. "Yes. I took my dish back yesterday when I cleaned. Did you like the stew?"

"Very tasty. But you've got to stop doing that."

"Why?" That innocent expression again. She ought to quit that; it made her look like an easy mark.

"Look, I don't know what you're up to, but I'm not interested in any kind of relationship—"

"Believe me, neither am I," she cut in, more emphatically than he thought necessary. "Is that for me?" She took the money out of his hand. "Oh, thanks! A tip! See you around."

She walked away while he stood there with his mouth open, his empty hand still extended. Her steps rang down the metal staircase—a perfect G. He felt the reverberation of her apartment door closing beneath his feet.

What the hell.

Mason began to get used to the idea of food appearing outside his apartment door. He was careful not to depend on it, or to thank the ditzy neighbor with too much zeal. Still, his pants rode on his waist again instead of hanging from his hip bones, and he was using a wider notch on his belt. She might be crazy, but she sure could cook. In a sort of passive gratitude, he agreed to let her clean his apartment every two weeks.

He was surprised that she didn't stop by to chat or suggest they go someplace together. It was as if she had her own agenda, maybe working off some kind of bad karma. As long as she didn't demand anything of him, that was okay with him.

But the next time she came to clean, there was a problem. Not only were the ashtrays missing, his cigarettes were gone. Three packs!

That was just plain stealing, and he was irritated as hell when he rang her doorbell.

Her face registered an odd look when she opened the door—more resolved than surprised, as if she'd expected him.

"You took my cigarettes," he said.

She didn't even deny it. "You shouldn't smoke. It's bad for you."

"You *stole* my cigarettes!"

"Not exactly."

"What do you mean, *not exactly?*"

"I didn't take them, I hid them. If you don't see them lying around all the time, maybe you won't smoke so much." Her voice was calm.

"What the hell do you care? It's not your business. You may be a great cook and a good house cleaner but you're not my keeper. Where did you put the damned cigarettes?"

A normal person would have furred up when he raised his voice, but instead, she smiled. "I'll make you a deal. If you can go one whole day without them, I'll tell you where they are."

He couldn't believe it. The woman was nuts.

Anger wasn't getting him anywhere. He ran a hand over his uncombed hair and looked out across the parking lot while he counted to ten. Sunshine sparkled off windshields and bumpers.

"It's a beautiful day, isn't it?" she said, as if they weren't in the middle of an argument. "I love this dry air in New Mexico."

He tried a different tack, enforcing a patient tone. "Claire. Please. Just tell me where you put them. Are they still in the apartment?"

"Sure."

She came out on the sidewalk and scanned the sky. "The temperature's perfect. I'm going to make a picnic supper and eat around back on the sundeck. Want to join me?"

"Some other time," he snapped. "I'll be in my room hunting for my own damned possessions. Don't expect me to recommend your cleaning service to anybody else if you're going to hide my stuff."

It actually surprised him when her benign smile disappeared. The expression that replaced it sent him backward a step. Her eyes turned flat and hard.

"Just go one day without smoking. You can give them up one step at a time. You know damned well they're bad for your heart."

She stepped back inside her apartment and slammed the door.

*Bad for his heart?* He stood there a full minute listening to its steady percussion.

## Chapter Fifteen

The door of the white limousine sent by the funeral home snapped shut with the solid sound of money. Win offered Avis O'Neal his arm and helped his mother cross the grassy apron of the cemetery to the open grave where Gerard O'Neal would be interred. Win's father had chosen his weapon in the duel with cancer, electing the toughest and most damaging course of chemotherapy. "It'll cure me or kill me," he'd said, in the same voice he had used to annihilate a competing business. Gerard was hospitalized for the three weeks it took to kill him.

Win's sister, Maureen, walked behind them, one hand locked with Joe, her rotund husband, and the other with Joe Junior, their frail-looking son. Maureen and Joe had forgone the limousine in favor of their own Buick. They were an odd little group, but whatever their family dynamic was, it seemed to work for Maureen. Win was glad for her, as long as he didn't have to spend much time with any of them.

His mother's spike heels punctured the sod and she clung to his arm for balance. Even discounting the shoes, which seemed to him offensively inappropriate for a funeral, Win was surprised by the tentativeness of her steps. Avis North O'Neal had always been sharp edged, even more so than his father. Gerard made tough business decisions, but family matters were Avis's realm, and compassion never clouded her vision of appropriate behavior for the O'Neal family. She had made all of Win's decisions for his first thirty years, with the one notable exception of his elopement with Claire Jameson when he was eighteen. And Avis had managed to expunge that decision within two years' time.

So it had shocked Win, the day after Gerard's self-engineered death, when Avis handed him the sheet of instructions his father had left and withdrew to her bedroom suite, leaving Win in charge. If the phone rang, Win dealt with it. When the funeral director had questions about the service, Win had answered them without disturbing her.

This morning, while they waited in his parents' mansion for the family car that would drive them to Gerard's memorial service, his mother had sat quietly in a wingback chair in the formal living room, a chair Win had supposed was intended only for torturing business clients. He began to wonder whether his mother would bounce back from her husband's illness and death, or whether he'd have to look after her from now on, along with the O'Neal conglomerate of companies. A sick feeling began to grow in his stomach.

Win stood with his mother while six men in tuxedos rolled the elaborate coffin on a wheeled cart closer to the grave site. In concert, they lifted it onto the pulley contraption that would lower his father into the earth. Foley and Smith, the two attorneys, were among the pallbearers. The men looked ridiculous in formal attire, but that detail was part of the instructions Win had inherited. Undoubtedly Avis's idea. All six men were business associates; Gerard had no friends who were social contacts only.

When the casket was in place and cloaked with flowers, the family took their seats beneath the flapping green awning, their knees only inches from a steel railing around the earthy-smelling hole. The sun pressed down on the tent and Win perspired in his black suit. The sweet fragrance of flowers was stupefying. He glanced sideways at his mother, but Avis looked completely cool, a plaster of makeup absorbing any dampness on her face. She wore no sunglasses against the morning glare. Her expression was blank.

A minister Win didn't know delivered a brief scripture and a prayer. The eulogy and testimonials had been recited at the church service previously. Win sat like stone, the words deflecting from his surface without soaking in.

A welcome wind swept through the tent and cooled his face. *Before I die,* Win promised himself, *I'll leave instructions to be cremated and skip the folderol.* By then his mother would be gone, and his son was gone already. Nobody would be left who gave a damn.

But a mere scattering of ashes would not have been due recognition for Gerard O'Neal's life. In Win's eyes his father stood like a giant, despite his lack of attention to Win and his sister when they were young. Gerard was intelligent and shrewd, ruthless when he needed to be but never dishonest. Nobody had ever worked harder to build a business. Win admired those qualities, ones he wasn't sure he possessed in great enough measure for the challenge that lay ahead. He was smart enough, maybe even shrewd. But since the death of the son he'd abandoned and the disintegration of his second marriage, he lacked the single-minded devotion to business that had made Gerard an icon in the Dallas business world.

*Goodbye, old man. I'll give it my best shot. And in my own way, I'll miss you.*

When the prayer ended, a long line of sympathizers passed along the narrow space between his mother's knees and his father's grave, shaking hands, expressing regrets. Finally the stream of people withdrew to give the widow and children a moment alone. Maureen's son was threatening to faint, which gave her an excuse to escape the tent and seek the air-conditioned Buick. Maybe Joe Senior had bribed the kid.

Avis sat a moment longer, regarding the flower-mounded bier with sober eyes. "I never thought he'd leave me alone," she said. Then she stood and walked away.

Win followed, catching her elbow lest one of her sharp heels sink into a gopher hole and send her sprawling on the cemetery lawn.

On the drive back to the O'Neal estate, Win sat alone in the backseat and regarded his future. He could see himself spending more and more hours in the office tower where O'Neal Enterprises occupied the top five floors. He could see his mother making more and more demands on his time and his patience. From here, his life looked more joyless than it was already, dominated by profit margins and stock holdings he didn't care much about.

How would his life have been different if he had a family of his own? What if he'd had the guts to stick it out with Claire and their baby? Nathan might be alive today. Might even have had a sister or a brother. No one could predict a fickle accident, but the slightest change in a person's history could put him in an entirely different place in time. Nathan might not have been on that highway, on that day, at that hour.

The long car pulled up in front of the O'Neal mansion, chauffeuring Win back to reality. He was being foolish, thinking like a naive kid. He could almost hear his father's voice telling him to suck it up. He couldn't dream away the past; what was he going to do about the future?

If Win didn't like what he saw coming, it was up to him to change it. That's what Gerard O'Neal would have done.

All afternoon, the mansion bulged with people and food and more people and more food. Avis retired to her room after a decent interval, leaving Win and Maureen to host. Win couldn't get away without insulting his parents' friends. Everyone wanted to talk to him, to express condolences, to press the hand of the new head of the O'Neal empire. Several divorcées in tight black dresses prowled the queue.

Even Maureen's husband was receiving an unaccustomed amount of attention. Win could see Joe was enjoying it. He was standing up straight, trying to hold his gut in. Maureen, truly bereft today, sat in her father's favorite chair in the living room, looking pale and lost. Win was past that stage; he'd gone through it weeks ago while he watched his father recede and die. Maureen came home for the death but not for the dying. That was just as well. By now Win's grief had subsided into relief for the end of his father's suffering. For Gerard, at least, the ordeal was over.

Around four o'clock, the last of the guests straggled home. Fred Foley and Anderson Smith were among the last to go. Andy pulled Win aside, into Gerard's wood-paneled study, for a private word.

"Gerard made a change in the will last week that I'm not sure you know about," Andy said, his hand on Win's sleeve. "He had set up a portfolio in trust for your son, with you as trustee. He hadn't changed that after your son died."

Win met the attorney's kind, watery eyes. "He left a trust for Nathan?" His chest felt hollow.

Andy nodded. "Last week he called me in to make a change." Win saw him hesitate. "He put the trust in Claire Jameson O'Neal's name, with you still the trustee."

"You're shitting me. I can't believe he even remembered her name."

"It seemed strange to me, too, but you know your dad." Andy shrugged. "He ordered me not to tell you until he was gone."

Win nodded. Gerard always did have his own code of justice.

"Mom doesn't know about it, either, that's for damned sure. She hated Claire." Win fixed Andy with a look he'd learned from Gerard. "And there's no need to tell her."

Andy nodded. "I understand. If you need Fred's or my assistance for anything, anything at all, please let me know, Win."

"Thanks, Andy. I'm sure I will." He knew the offer was sincere. For a fee.

When everyone else had gone, Dorothy, the longtime housekeeper of the O'Neal home, quietly circled about picking up glasses and snack dishes that sat abandoned in every corner like leftovers from a party. Rich people were pigs in somebody else's house. Without comment, Win began to help Dorothy clean up.

"You don't need to do that, Mr. O'Neal," she insisted, and he saw the liquid in her eyes.

Dorothy had served on the fringes of this family for a generation, but nobody acknowledged her loss. He put down a brace of glasses and wrapped her plump body in a hug. "For God's sake, Dorothy, I'm just Win. We buried Mr. O'Neal."

At that she broke and cried. A lot of good he was at comforting anybody. He patted her back awkwardly and turned her loose to do her job. Dorothy was most happy when she was helping someone else.

He mixed a highball at his father's bar in the library and walked out the French doors onto the flagstone terrace. The view was all greens. Mostly golf greens. A flawless lawn sloped slightly toward a landscaped water hazard, far enough away from the house that errant white missiles from the other side wouldn't break the windows. Willows and sycamores bordered the pond, and an arched bridge wide enough for a golf cart spanned one narrow end. From the gazebo at the edge of the lawn, Win's father could watch golfers on the other side of the lake putting for par.

Win refilled his drink and carried it down to the gazebo. He sat there while the gathering darkness drove the last golfers from the course and the tree frogs raised a chorus that echoed across the water. Automatic tiki torches popped to life around the gazebo and spread their thick, citronella scent to the waning breeze. Fireflies by the dozens arose from the grass.

Win lifted his glass to the end of an era. The king is dead; long live the king.

Dorothy came halfway down the lawn and called to him. "Win? Would you like me to stay over tonight? I'll be glad to, if you need me."

He waved to her. "We'll be fine, Dorothy. Go on home, and thanks for everything."

She turned and labored back up the incline. A few minutes later he heard her car start and drive away.

After a while, the light came on in Maureen's third-floor bedroom and the one next to it where Joe Junior slept. No light showed in his mother's room, and he thought perhaps he should check on her. But he couldn't face the prospect of those blank eyes again. For tonight, at least, he'd leave her alone. She'd probably taken something to make her sleep, like a double bourbon.

Lights from a distant fairway shimmered on the still surface of the lake. He'd never felt so alone in his life.

*If you don't like the way the future looks, what are you going to do to change it?*

Maybe Anderson Smith had given him a lead. Win took out his cell phone and pushed the program button where he'd stored Claire's home number.

# Chapter Sixteen

On Lindsey's first date with the too-handsome guy from her Broadcast News class, Darren Dillingham told her about summers on his dad's yacht, cruising the blue Caribbean. Darren planned to become an anchorman on a major network, but he had no intention of spending years in the trenches first. Nor did he want to serve as a foreign correspondent where he might get shot at or kidnapped. He had a habit of cracking his jaw after he made a point. But worst of all, he never read a newspaper.

Darren kissed her good-night with lips as dry as old money, and Lindsey was already bored. Why was it that the guys her age seemed shallow or immature or needy? Nathan had never seemed that way to her. Maybe she wasn't ready to start dating, after all.

She still saw Kent Woolery, but less often than before, mostly for lunch in the crowded Commons. Not wanting to hurt him, she had told him up front that she was going out with Darren.

Kent's eyes had looked everywhere except directly at her. "Sure. I never expected you not to date other guys."

"Kent, you and I weren't really *dating*," she said, and realized she had used past tense, as if whatever connection they'd had was already gone. "I mean, you never kissed me, we never talked about the future. Just the past."

Kent's face flushed. He watched his thumb circling the rim of his soda cup. "It's hard for me to picture much of a future. I just get through one day at a time."

"I know. And that's not a bad philosophy if you could enjoy the day you're in."

He gave a dry laugh. "Yeah, right."

She could see that he *was* hurt, no matter her careful intentions.

"So can we still get together sometimes?" he said. "If it doesn't bring you down too much?" Finally he looked at her. "I'd hate to lose the one friend I have on campus."

*Don't beg, Kent. Don't be pitiful.* "Sure," Lindsey had said, but she had a feeling he wouldn't be back next semester. He'd already started missing classes.

Darren called her twice more, but she made excuses and he got the hint. Unfortunately, she still had to see him twice a week in the broadcasting class. She sat on the opposite side of the room, but when they met in the hallway and were forced to speak, he was catty and defensive, reinforcing her opinion of guys her age.

By contrast, she found nothing shallow or immature about Dr. Cordell Thayer, an associate professor in the J-school. Dr. Thayer was younger than the other instructors, fresh from a real job on the *Washington Post,* and he'd taken a special interest in Lindsey's future. In Cordell Thayer, she'd found a mentor.

She first met him as a freshman in his Principles of American Journalism class, where he'd entertained the budding journalists with his firsthand experience at the epicenter of American government and world affairs. It was a large class, and he took no special notice of Lindsey even though she got A's on her papers. Lindsey always made A's.

The next semester, Lindsey had signed up for his section of news reporting. That's when she began to get the feeling he was singling her out. He made her work hard for her grade— sometimes, she thought, harder than the others. In class he often challenged her responses, playing devil's advocate even when she knew he agreed with her. But the day he returned one of her papers with a C scrawled at the top—and no explanation—she was furious.

She'd never made a C in her life. She scheduled an appointment to see Dr. Thayer during his office hours and tossed the offending paper on his desk.

"If Sami or Jason had written this," she huffed, naming two suck-ups in the class, "you'd have given it an A."

Cord Thayer's eyes were gunmetal gray. He watched her with an amused expression she found insulting. He pushed back in the chair behind his desk, legs crossed casually, and didn't invite her to sit. She stood before him like a supplicant, getting more and more steamed.

"You're right," he said eventually. "I expect more of you than I do of them. You have more potential."

Was he mocking her? His expression was interested, but the corner of his mouth still played with a smile.

"That's bullshit," she said finally, but without much heat. "You didn't even say what you found wrong with my story."

"Figure it out on your own. Then you won't make that mistake again."

The weight of his gaze made perspiration break out under her sweater. She left his office flustered, and without the grade adjustment she'd hoped for.

That night Lindsey took apart her story sentence by sentence and saw that she had supported an important fact with her opinion instead of a solid source. It was subtle, but it was there. *"Damn,"* she said.

Dr. Thayer had warned them: "In a straight news story, don't tell me what you think—tell me what you know. A journalist has to make that distinction, in his own work and in the news he reads every day."

She'd redoubled her efforts in the class and earned her A. The next semester she didn't have a class with him, but when he ran across her in the hallway outside the *Columbia Missourian* office, his angular face opened in a smile.

"Lindsey," he said, "it's good to see you." As if he didn't remember how she'd made an ass of herself in his office.

"How's your semester going?" he said, pulling her aside from the flow of students in the hallway. He asked what classes she was taking, what her plans were for next semester. "Do you have time to grab a cup of coffee?"

"Um, sure," she said. "Okay."

There was no amusement now in the penetrating way he watched her face. Maybe he'd really meant it when he said she had potential. She tried not to be flattered by his interest, but of course she was. And she had the uneasy feeling he could read those thoughts.

Twice that month they had coffee together, spontaneous encounters that sprouted from accidental meetings. He talked to her like a colleague instead of a student; he respected her point of view. He told her his friends called him Cord.

Cord was intellectual and much more worldly than anyone Lindsey had ever met. He encouraged her ambition to become editor of the *Latina,* a bilingual publication that was produced on campus. "You ought to apply for the Washington program, too," he said. "You could spend a semester in the capital working with the best news professionals in the country. Most of the interns are grad students, but they take a few seniors. With your column in the *Missourian* next year, you'll be a known quantity in the J-school. I think you'd have a good chance."

Unfortunately, the students had to pay their own expenses in D.C., and most of the intern positions paid little or nothing. Lindsey couldn't afford it. Nevertheless, she was hugely flattered that he had offered to write her a recommendation.

They began to meet intentionally, mostly at an off-campus coffee shop. She loved listening to his stories about working on the *Post.* He'd actually met Bob Woodward in person, and sat in press conferences with Helen Thomas. Like Lindsey, he had an active interest in the environment. She went home from these conversations with her mind zinging, her head full of aspirations. He was the most professional journalist she'd ever met, and he believed in her.

The night that changed everything, they had both attended a guest lecture in the liberal arts auditorium to hear a former editor from the *L.A. Times*. Unfortunately, the speaker turned out to be a self-important cynic who snorted at his own attempts at humor.

Sitting beside Lindsey in the lecture hall, Cord muttered comments under his breath. Ten minutes into the speech, he was pulling at threads on his socks and casting glances toward the ceiling.

"Shh," Lindsey warned him, half smiling.

He leaned close to her ear, his breath warm and minty. A shiver ran down her back. "This guy blows," he whispered, none too softly. "Let's get out of here."

With guilty pleasure, she followed him out the side door.

They walked a long way through the chilly evening, their coat collars pulled up, the scent of wood smoke in the air, to a family-run Italian restaurant off campus. It was a dark, hole-in-the-wall place, and Lindsey saw no one who might be from the university. Cord chose a corner booth lit only by a stubby candle stuck in the neck of a Chianti bottle.

When she slid onto the seat opposite him, every hair on her body felt polarized, as if lightning were about to strike. Was it possible to be more than friends with someone like Cord Thayer?

He ordered wine for them both. She had recently turned twenty-one, but she rarely drank. She didn't trust the lack of control that came with alcohol. The musky red wine left a bitter aftertaste, like seaweed.

Cord recommended a pasta dish she couldn't pronounce and ordered for her. The sauce flooded her mouth with a flavor so exquisite she could hardly keep from humming. Cord watched her eat, smiling. "I like to see someone enjoy her food. It indicates an appetite for living."

Halfway through dinner, he pushed his plate away and leaned his arms on the table. In the dim light, his dilated eyes looked dark as coal, the candle flame flickering in his pupils. Lindsey shivered.

"School policy forbids instructors at MU from dating their students," Cord said. "If we're caught together, the consequences would be worse for me than for you. I'd lose tenure for sure, possibly be fired. All you'd have at stake is your reputation."

Lindsey heard the distinct growl of the dump truck—not at all what she'd expected. How could he dump her when they weren't even dating? Blindsided, she looked down at her plate.

"Sure," she mumbled. "I understand."

"Do you? Because I want you to be clear about the risks. For both of us."

"I get it," she said impatiently, not looking at him.

"Good." He got up and slid onto the bench seat beside her. *What the hell...?*

"We'll have to be careful," he said, his wine-scented breath warm against her face.

No one had ever kissed her like that. Not even Nathan. Nathan's kisses were honest and warm and wonderfully sweet.

But this was a kiss that knew things, and it melted her legs like candle wax.

Then Dr. Cord Thayer paid the check and walked her back to the dorm without so much as touching her hand.

# Chapter Seventeen

At dawn Hob was dozing in his old white pickup when the flashing lights woke him. The police cruiser had parked right behind him, the headlights illuminating the back of his head like a targeted animal. "Shit," Hob said.

It was still half dark on the shady residential street where he'd parked in the night, half a block from The Mother's house. The cop took his time getting out of the patrol car and Hob figured he was calling in the license plate, checking for wants and warrants, as they said on TV. He wouldn't find any. Not even a parking ticket. Hob had kept his record clean as a factory engine. Still, ever since that accident on I-35, it made him nervous as hell to have any contact with a police officer.

In his rearview mirror, Hob saw the cop get out of the cruiser and amble toward the driver's side of the pickup, one hand on his sidearm, coming up to the window cautious and slow. Hob wiped the sleep from his face with a rough palm and rolled down his window.

This was going to take some explaining. He wished he could tell the cop that The Mother was missing. He hadn't seen her in three days, and so he'd watched the house all night. He knew he would doze off, but he'd parked so that if anybody turned into her driveway, the headlights would shine right in his eyes and wake him up. She hadn't come home. Something was wrong, but he couldn't say that to the cop. The cop would want to know why he was watching her.

Hob had to think fast, and that wasn't his specialty. He was no good at lying.

A flashlight beam ricocheted inside the cab. "Hobson Jeeter?" the cop said.

*Christ.* It was a lady cop. That made him even more nervous.

"Yes, ma'am." Since when did they send female cops out on night patrol, alone? That wasn't fair, was it?

"May I see your license and registration, please?"

"Yes, ma'am." He reached for the glove box and from the corner of his eye saw the lady cop step just behind the cab, arm cocked on the gun butt. "Don't worry, Officer. I don't have no gun."

He moved slowly, holding up the paper so she could see what it was. She took it and Hob went to his hip for his wallet. The cop kept her flashlight trained on his lap, the hot center right over his pecker. He'd been sitting there all night without re-lieving himself and he nearly did it now. He fumbled with the wallet until he got hold of his license and handed it over.

The cop checked both items with her flashlight. "Is the address on your license current?"

"Yes'm."

"So you don't live on this street."

"No."

"Want to tell me what you're doing out here all night?"

Hob took a deep breath. "Lady paid me to watch her house while she's out of town." He tried to think ahead, check each thought for believability before he said it out loud.

"Which house?"

He hesitated only a second. "That 'un." He pointed to The Mother's house.

He risked a glance at the officer's face while she was looking up. It was getting light outside now, and he could see that her hair was pulled up under the cap. She wasn't bad looking even without any makeup, but she was a big gal. As tall as he was, with better developed shoulders, as if she worked out with weights. Maybe that was required for women cops.

The officer shone her light around until she found the house number and he knew she was making a metal note of it. "What's the lady's name?"

"Mrs. O'Neal," Hob said, as confidently as he could. "I'm her mechanic. But she asked me to keep an eye on things, so that's what I was doing." He couldn't tell if she was buying his story or not. He looked away before she glanced back at him, so he wouldn't have to meet her eyes.

"You'd better go on home, Mr. Jeeter. You're making the neighbors nervous." She handed him back his license and registration. "You realize we'll check this with Mrs. O'Neal. Anything bad happens in this neighborhood we'll naturally come looking for you."

Hob bobbed his head. "I can see that, yeah. But you won't get hold of Mrs. O'Neal, 'cause she's out of town."

"When's she supposed to be back?"

"I don't know." That seemed unlikely, so he amended. "She just said she'd let me know when she got home, and pay me then." *Jesus. A minute ago he'd said she already paid him.*

"All right, Mr. Jeeter. You go on home now, you hear? And I'd advise you not to sit out here again."

"Sure thing. Thank you, Officer."

He started up the engine quick as a cat and drove off with the lady cop still standing in the street watching him, her shape growing smaller in the rearview mirror until the road curved off and she disappeared.

"Shit," Hob said again. He spit his stale nicotine gum out the window and pulled a fresh piece from his pocket. He could use some strong coffee, too.

Maybe the cop would just go on with her shift and forget about him. But he'd better check with that real estate place, just in case. See if he could find out if The Mother really was out of town and get his story ready in case the cop checked and it turned out The Mother was sick or just staying somewhere else for some reason. Hob reached above the visor and pulled down the business card she'd given him when he changed her tire out on Fredericksburg Road.

He crossed the main thoroughfare and drove slowly through

the sleepy neighborhood that bordered the one where he lived. He parked in the driveway of his small, frame house and calculated he had a couple of hours before he needed to get to work. The clock in the pickup hadn't worked for years. Should have brought his watch along on his vigil, but he was out of the habit of wearing one.

Mealy had heard him drive up and was waiting just inside the door when he opened it. The cat zipped between his feet and escaped outdoors, yowling as he went.

"Be careful, cat," Hob said, and went on inside.

Last time Mealy got out, he hadn't come back for two days. But Mealy had been feral once and he still had his claws, so Hob figured the big tom could hold his own with any critter in the neighborhood. Hob had picked him up as a stray kitten on one of his long hauls, back when he was driving. The cat had liked riding with him, stretched out on the dashboard of the big truck cab, and they'd logged a lot of miles together. Hob named him Mealy because he was the color of oatmeal, and because he was always looking for a free meal.

At the rust-stained kitchen sink, Hob drew water for coffee and started it brewing, then turned on the TV to fill up the quiet. He showered and put on clean clothes and sat down at the kitchen table with a Sara Lee cupcake and his coffee. The TV was playing the morning news but he didn't listen. He laid the business card for O'Neal Realty on the Formica tabletop and looked at it while he ate.

The Mother's office was a twenty-minute drive from here. He'd driven by it yesterday, looking for her car. He had enough time to go by again this morning before he went to work, but it would be too early for the real estate office to open. Phoning wouldn't do any good; he'd already tried that, from the pay phone at the garage. The woman that answered said Mrs. O'Neal wasn't in the office, but somebody else could help him. Then she put him on hold, and he hung up.

He'd have to go there in person on his lunch break. It would be tricky trying to find out where The Mother was without drawing too much attention. He didn't want anybody in the office remembering his face. But he needed a plausible explanation in case that policewoman decided to follow up.

Besides, he was beginning to worry about The Mother. He knew she hadn't moved; her stuff was still in the house. But she had no family to check on her, and it was his duty to make sure nothing else bad happened to her. He knew what came from being sloppy, not checking on things he was supposed to check. He wouldn't make that mistake again.

# Chapter Eighteen

Claire had expected McKinnon would be angry about his cigarettes. When she'd hidden them in his apartment, she knew he probably wouldn't let her inside again, not even to clean. So she'd made sure she learned everything she could.

In a drawer beside his bed she had found his handbook for heart recipients and a list of his medications. She sat on his bed and read the handbook from start to finish. Other than rejection, the most serious danger to a transplant patient was some kind of infection. The immunosuppressant drugs that stopped his body from rejecting a foreign organ also stopped its natural defenses. A cut finger, a cold, a virus—any of them could spell serious trouble for McKinnon. The book advised patients to stay away from crowds, and there he was working in a bar, for heaven's sake.

In the quiet of his apartment, her skin crawling like a thief's, she had copied down the names and amounts of his medications—nearly a dozen pills each day, dispensed from breakfast to bedtime. On his bathroom shelf she found a blood pressure cuff and the log where he was supposed to record the reading twice a day, along with his pulse rate. Too many spaces in the chart were blank. He'd managed to log the BP rate once a day—usually—but there was no pulse rate recorded for at least two months.

At her own apartment that evening, she had logged onto an Internet site that was listed in the handbook. She read about the possible side effects of the drugs, like the danger of chemical dependent diabetes, loss of bone mass and skin integrity, increased growth of body hair and gum tissue. None certain, all possible.

She searched out the closest transplant care center and found there was only one in New Mexico—the Presbyterian Heart Center in Albuquerque, an hour away. The next day she had phoned the heart center and talked to a nurse.

She told the nurse she was a family member of a recipient—not completely untrue; she was related to McKinnon's heart. She said she wanted to help him. "I'm afraid he's not doing his follow-up visits. What should his schedule be?"

"How long ago was his transplant surgery?"

"About three years."

"At three years out, he should be seeing a cardiologist two or three times a year."

"Can you check to see if he's been doing that?"

The nurse was sympathetic but she wasn't allowed to give out patient information to someone on the phone. "It's a privacy issue," she said. She told Claire he should also have a blood test every six weeks, a biopsy once a year, a coronary catheter every two years.

"My God, if he did everything by the book, he'd hardly have time for a normal life," Claire said.

"The protocol pretty much *becomes* the normal life for organ recipients," the nurse conceded. "In the aftermath of the surgery and all these lifestyle adjustments, depression is common. That's another reason they need the follow-up visits."

Claire thought about McKinnon's cynical attitude, his twelve-hour sleep marathons, his disregard for his health. All could be symptoms of depression.

"A lot of people have to follow such a strict routine," the nurse pointed out. "They adapt. We have support groups here at the center that are a big help to some patients."

Right; she could just see McKinnon in a support group. They'd throw him out on the first visit. But the nurse had a point. Other people adapted to the requirements, and so could he. She would see to that.

After her confrontation with McKinnon at her apartment door, Claire had to regroup. She had hoped to establish a neighborly friendship with him, on her mother's theory that you could catch more flies with honey than with vinegar. Now he was pissed about the cigarettes, and though she wouldn't back down, it wasn't in her best interest to alienate him.

So far he hadn't turned down anything she'd cooked; maybe another good meal would take the edge off his anger. She chose a recipe from her newly purchased Italian cookbook, made a list of ingredients and went shopping at the market.

That evening she stayed away from the bar, intending to give McKinnon time to cool down. Alone in the grim little apartment that reminded her too much of the houses where she'd grown up, she yearned to hear a friendly voice. But Janelle didn't answer at home or on her cell. Claire left voice messages on both phones, then watched an old movie on the grainy TV until she heard McKinnon come home after midnight.

Janelle called back the next morning, her voice sounding tense. "Hey, girl. What's up in Santa Fe?" Claire pictured Janelle in the San Antonio office, her desk cluttered with contracts and loan applications and photos of her kids.

Claire was mixing tomato sauce and spices in a pot on the stove, her hair pinned back like a fast-food worker. "You sound kind of stressed," she said.

"Don't mind me. I'm just having a nervous breakdown. When are you coming back? We miss you around here."

"What's wrong? Is nobody selling anything?"

"Business is fine. But I'm drowning in this paperwork."

"I know," Claire sympathized. "You'd think we worked for the federal government. I'll tell the accountant that the agency percentage this month goes to you."

"No way. I wouldn't do this for money. Only for love."

Claire grinned. "Well, you'll get the money anyway."

She heard the squeak of a spring-back chair and the sound of file folders falling off a desk. Janelle said something obscene and the chair squeaked again. "Really, though—what's keeping you? You're not opening a Santa Fe office, are you?"

"Hardly. You told me to take some vacation time."

"Since when do you do what I tell you?" Janelle's voice got quieter. "Did you meet McKinnon? Does he know who you are?"

"Yes and no. I'll tell you about it sometime." She switched the cell phone to her other hand and stirred the sauce. "Listen, I know it's asking a lot, but I need you to manage things a while longer. Send me some of the stuff I could do online, and I'll work on it here on my laptop. I used to do that at home a lot."

Janelle snorted. "If I took paperwork home, it would come back stuck together with peanut butter and jelly." She heaved a sigh. "Ignore my whining. I'll survive. I just hope you're okay."

"I'm fine. Enjoying the climate. And I've taken on a project."

"What's that noise? It sounds like you're *cooking*. That can't be right."

"Yes, Miss Smart Ass. I'm cooking. I'll let you go, but call me if you have any questions. Or just to visit."

"Here's a question. Win phoned me the other day. He said he needed to talk to you and wanted to know where you were. I said I wasn't authorized to give out that information."

Claire smiled. "Sorry about that. If he calls again, you can give him my cell number. At least then he'll bug me instead of you."

They said goodbye and Claire laid veal cutlets in a skillet to sauté. She missed Janelle. She missed the camaraderie of the office and the daily satisfaction of running her business. But Janelle was right about the paperwork—she didn't miss that part at all.

She added the sauce, sprinkled grated Parmesan on the cutlets and put a lid on the skillet. Cooking was actually fun when you had lots of time. McKinnon never commented on the meals she left him, but the dishes came back empty and his face didn't look quite so skeletal as it had before. That was what counted. In a way, she was cooking for Nathan again.

She shelved the cookbook alongside the other new one she'd bought at a neat little bookstore close to the plaza. The books were her badge of honor—they'd saved her from a purse snatcher as she was walking home. A neighbor in the laundry room had warned her it was dangerous to explore the city on foot, but she'd thought the woman was exaggerating. Claire liked the exercise, and the October days here were magnificent. She felt perfectly safe wandering down Canyon Road, a narrow street lined with art galleries and quaint shops. It was her favorite haunt. She'd taken a side street off Canyon when the thief surprised her.

She was thinking about the presents she'd just bought Janelle and Lindsey when she heard footsteps approaching fast from behind. He was already on her when she wheeled around—a tattooed stranger who grabbed for the purse on her shoulder.

She'd reacted without thinking, swinging the plastic bag of books like a ball on a chain. She didn't even scream. But the mugger did, when the heavy books connected with his ear and knocked him off his feet. Then she'd started yelling, all her junior-high street language coming back in a rush. She called him names in Spanish, threatened him with nonexistent mace in English. She swung the bag at him again as he scrambled to his feet and ran.

After he'd disappeared, she stood in the quiet street with her head pounding and knees trembling. The encounter had lasted all of ten seconds. It had been many years, thank God, since she'd needed to defend herself physically. But apparently she hadn't forgotten the lessons learned in a rough school. She shivered, partly at the thought of what might have happened on that deserted street, and partly at the violence of her own reaction. It reminded her too much of her father's temper.

Claire glanced at the clock and turned on the oven. McKinnon would have veal parmigiana for lunch, if he wasn't too mad to eat. With a green salad and fresh-baked bread. Sliding the loaf of dough in the oven, she felt like the witch who fattened up Hansel and Gretel.

While the aroma of baking bread leavened the apartment, she emptied a clutch of shopping bags onto the kitchen table and reviewed the loot she'd bought last week—a turquoise-and-silver pendant with matching earrings for Janelle, a bolo tie for Irv. He'd get a kick out of that. She had come across an anthology of women journalists and bought it in advance for Lindsey's graduation from college. At the same bookstore, she'd picked up two copies of a flyer about the Santa Fe Symphony and Chorus.

Claire resacked the gifts, listening for McKinnon's footsteps overhead. His schedule was sadly predictable. He slept until noon, and after that she would hear the water running, the toilet flushing, the muffled drone of his TV until he left for work about six. But she never heard the sound of his violin. She had wiped a layer of dust from the black case stored in his closet. From all reports, he was quite a virtuoso on violin—a gift that ascended to the level of art. A musician with such a talent, she thought, surely couldn't give it up without suffering. Another possible contributor to depression.

At noon she dished up the veal, wrapped two slices of warm garlic bread in foil, and shook Italian dressing over the salad. Using a cookie sheet for a tray, she carried everything up the metal stairs and down the balcony walkway. She had bent down to put the dishes on the mat when McKinnon's door jerked opened.

Her heart lurched. "Oh. Hi." Caught in the act of feeding the hungry. "I was leaving a peace offering." She stood up.

He grabbed her elbow and pulled her into his apartment. Her adrenaline surged.

"Show me where you hid my cigarettes," he demanded. "Those things are three bucks a pack."

She scowled back, gripping the empty cookie sheet in both hands. "Smoking is a major cause of heart problems." She struggled for calm, but her voice sounded angry. "I'm sure you know that. Why do you persist?"

His grip on her arm tightened for an instant before he let go. He puffed an exaggerated breath and ran a hand through his hair. He cast a glance toward the ceiling as if beseeching a higher power. "What the hell's wrong with you, lady? Skulking around the bar, bringing me food? It's none of your business whether I smoke. I happen to have the heart of a teenage athlete!"

The light around her turned blue, like a flashbulb going off. She reacted on impulse. The snap of her palm against his face hung in the air like an obscenity.

McKinnon's eyes widened and his mouth gaped open, speechless.

She couldn't believe what she'd done. Her face burned as if she were the one who'd been struck, but she didn't apologize. *"You son of a bitch,"* she hissed. "I know that heart better than you do. It belonged to *my son*."

His hand moved slowly to touch his cheek. "What? I just meant my heart is strong...."

She set her jaw, her eyes filling. *Figure it out, piano man.*

Knowledge dawned in his eyes. "Holy Mozart...you're his mother?"

"He has a name. Nathan O'Neal."

McKinnon's face paled. The wiry eyebrows pinched together and for once he had no snappy comeback.

"He was seventeen," Claire said, pounding each word. "Yes, he *was* an athlete, and smart and considerate. He loved country music and football and a girl named Lindsey." Her voice cracked. "He loved *me*."

McKinnon shook his head. Said nothing.

She straightened her spine. "You owe my son your life. So when you smoke and don't eat right and stop playing the music you're meant to play, it is *very much* my business."

He shook his head again. "I had no idea...."

"Of course you didn't. You never bothered to find out anything about him." She stepped closer, holding the cookie sheet to her chest like a shield. "Let me tell you something, mister. You are *not allowed* to waste my son's gift. You are *not allowed* to kill yourself by neglect and abuse."

"Ye gods. I'm the victim of a crusade."

"Victim! You're not a *victim*. You're the *survivor,* piano man. Get that straight."

The cookie sheet clanged on the doorjamb as she plunged out of his apartment. She strode down the walkway, calling back over her shoulder.

"Take out your violin, McKinnon. It's lonesome in there in the dark."

Her feet pounded down the staircase. She slammed the door to her apartment and leaned against it, breathing hard.

*What a childish, idiotic thing to do. He'll probably call the police, get an injunction to stop me from harassing him.*

She dropped the cookie sheet and held her head. A sharp pain bloomed behind her eyes. She hadn't meant to tell him like that. Didn't intend to tell him at all except as a last resort, to guilt him into shaping up.

She paced the apartment from front to back. What was he doing now? Calling the manager? Dialing the cops? Maybe he would disappear, and she'd lose track of Nathan's heart forever. She listened for sounds through the ceiling. Her heartbeat stuttered.

*I think you blew it, Mom.*

"Jesus!"

Nathan was sitting at the kitchen table, one leg crooked over the other knee. He was wearing his high school football jersey, the same one he had on every time he appeared. His face was as white as the number thirteen on his chest.

*Nathan. You're back.*

The room tilted. She dropped onto the threadbare carpet and hugged her knees, breathing like a guppy. He hadn't materialized since she'd arrived in Santa Fe and she'd begun to believe that the visions were gone.

*Smells good in here,* he said. *What have you been cooking?*

She couldn't answer. Couldn't remember.

*You used to make great chili. Remember? Texas chili.*

He never talked about the hard stuff. Just like Win, when they were young. She stayed on the floor, arms folded tightly, rocking herself like a child.

*I'll see that he takes care of your heart, Nathan. I promise.*

Already he'd begun to fade. Claire braced herself for the departure, like wind through a tunnel. Only his face and shoulders remained, his voice turning sad.

*What about your heart, Mom? Who's going to take care of that?*

That night she lay awake in the bed, a wet washcloth folded over eyes that felt like bruises. She heard McKinnon come home after midnight, his footsteps crossing the floor above her. The plumbing zinged to life and water trickled through the pipes in the walls. She heard drawers opening and slamming, something dropping on the floor, a muffled epithet.

Looking for his stupid cigarettes.

Her head pounded. She waited for the squeaks and cracks of his weight in the bed, but that sound didn't come. His footsteps ranged through the rooms, pacing. And then he stopped.

She uncovered her eyes and watched the red minutes click past on her ceiling.

Just when she thought he must be asleep, she heard another sound, something she hadn't memorized. A soft plucking, then a hum. A few thin wails, like the cry of a cat.

She held her breath.

The silvery strain of a violin slid through the dark, the music breathing, full of grace. Her mouth opened, airless.

She pictured him laying open the black case. Finding the three packs of cigarettes she had tucked around the curved edges of the violin. Frowning at the symphony brochure she'd slipped beneath the strings.

She saw him lifting the violin with two hands, like a baby. Tuning it. The polished wood gleaming gold in the lamplight. She felt its coolness beneath his chin, so familiar and right. The tautness of the strings beneath his fingers.

Listening wide-eyed in the dark, her hair full of tears, she felt the pull of the bow across her hollow bones.

## Chapter Nineteen

Sometimes Mason dreamed about the young man who'd given him a heart—the boy he had wished to die. In his dreams, he could never see the young man's face, just a nebulous, blue-jeaned presence that Mason couldn't look at directly, like the face of God.

Now that presence had a name. *Nathan O'Neal*. And his mother lived right downstairs.

The days before his transplant, when he lay in an Austin hospital dying by slow degrees, were a fog in Mason's memory. Through the drugs and the haze, he'd been aware of only two things. One was a sense that Julia was growing more and more distant; and the other was that in order for him to live, someone young and strong had to die.

He'd tried not to wish for it, and he'd failed.

When it comes down to smelling death's awful breath, most people recoil and want desperately to live. And so had he. He was in love with Julia, with his life, with the music they shared. They were the magic couple, both accepted into the symphony, living their dream life. Her chronic depression had been effectively controlled with drugs, and until his doctor discovered the harsh extent of his cardiomyopathy, they'd been planning a family. Then he became ill, deteriorated quickly and was hospitalized.

A parade of nameless doctors had faded in and out of his hospital room during those weeks, but it was the surgeon himself who came in one day when Mason was more lucid than usual and told him they had the perfect donor. It was a teenage athlete who didn't drink or use drugs, killed in a traffic accident.

That's all Mason knew. The doctor didn't tell him the young man's name, and Mason had been so riddled with sorrow he couldn't ask. *The perfect donor.* Which meant an innocent young person was brain-dead, his organs kept functioning with a respirator. What had Mason ever done to earn the right to that boy's heart?

Later he learned that he wasn't even first in line for the transplant. Another man had been waiting longer but that day he had diarrhea, which disqualified him for the surgery. Mason never asked, was afraid to know, if the man lived or died.

Julia had stayed with him every day, but he could feel her drifting away. She didn't tell him until after the surgery that she was pregnant and facing the idea that she might have to raise their child alone. Or that she feared the effect of drugs on her pregnancy and had stopped taking her medication.

When the doctor told them about the donor, they wept together. Julia became hysterical, and he'd thought it was relief, because she loved him so much.

In the months he spent recuperating after the surgery, returning to the hospital over and over for tests, they inhabited their house like two ghosts. She was withdrawn, unreachable. He felt abandoned. He turned to his violin for comfort and its music spilled through the rooms, a liquid grief that nearly drowned them both.

After she was gone, he had put the violin in its case and left it—until tonight, when he'd finally realized where Claire O'Neal must have hidden his cigarettes.

He had opened the violin case, and Serena lay waiting. His hands shook when he reached for her, tossing aside the packs of cigarettes, discarding a paper threaded under the strings. He cradled the instrument under his chin and felt her familiar weight, the flawless balance. His fingers tightened and tested the strings until each note sang true. Then he drew the bow across, and let her weep.

His beloved Serena.

*I'm sorry, Serena. And Julia, and Claire. I'm a sorry, sorry man.*

His eyes were blind when he replaced the violin and snapped the latches on the case. A brochure about the Santa Fe Symphony lay on the floor. He tossed it on a table, unread. Did she have any idea how cruel that was?

Probably not. When she'd told him about her son—about *Nathan*—the pain on her face was like looking in a mirror. He'd understood her purpose instantly. His heart was all she had left of her child and she was trying to save him. What wouldn't Mason have done to rescue his own tiny, breathless son?

Her face had told him something else, too, something even she didn't know. Claire O'Neal was fighting not only to save her son's heart, but to save herself. There was something admirable in that. He'd forfeited his battle months ago.

But did Claire O'Neal's bravery give her the right to drag him back through his grief? He couldn't take that, not even with his young-man's heart.

Somehow he had to make her go away.

She wasn't at her usual table when he started his first set the next evening. He knew she would come, though; she had to come, looking for her son. He played a number in her honor: "I Know You by Heart."

Claire arrived after nine. There was a decent crowd for a weeknight, and a middle-aged couple had taken the table where she usually sat. Mason half expected her to ask them to move. But she settled at a table closer to the bar and waved to Renee, who waved back and brought her a glass of red wine.

Mason played a medley of old standbys, letting his fingers do the work while the music soothed his brain. He thought of Serena, and of the steady beating of his heart. It was hard to lose himself in the music tonight, when he knew what he had to do.

At ten o'clock he took his break. He went to the men's room and washed up, splashing water on a face that looked older than deceit. Then he collected a beer from Tommy and carried it to Claire's table.

He pulled out a chair without asking. In the dull light he saw her eyes widen, like a fox ready to jump. She said nothing when he set his glass on the table and straddled the chair, facing her. Tommy had started the jukebox, some modern cut with a whiny female vocalist that seemed like an anachronism in this place.

Claire eyed him, frowning.

"Look," he said, spreading his hands amiably, "no smoke." He smiled, turning on the rusty remains of what used to pass for charm.

She nodded. One corner of her mouth twitched, more a sign of relief than a smile. "That's a start." She glanced pointedly at the beer.

"You can't expect me to quit my smokes *and* beer," he said reasonably. "Besides, beer has been clinically proven to be good for the heart."

"I think that was red wine."

"Oh. Well, I've got to have something to do on my break. I don't think one beer will do much damage."

She exhaled as if she'd been holding her breath. "I don't, either. Not just one."

Her shoulders relaxed, but only a little. He squinted, reading her. This was a woman who hated confrontation, but reacted fiercely. That scene the other day must have tortured her. He counted this as a mark in his advantage.

"I notice you don't keep beer at home," she said. "Or hard liquor. That's good."

He shook his head, self-deprecating. "I can't believe I actually let you into my apartment, and now you know all my dirty secrets. What you're doing is stalking, you know. I could call the police."

She shrugged. "You answered my ad. All the rest is just co-incidence." She tucked a curve of brown hair behind her ear. "At least that's what I'd tell them. Which one of us do you think they'd believe?"

Her laugh was honest and low pitched. Thank God she didn't giggle; he hated it when grown women giggled. In an-other life he probably would have liked Claire O'Neal, and in honor of that he decided to play it straight.

He took a pull on his beer, set it back in the same wet circle on the table. "What will it take for you to go back where you came from and leave me to live my pedestrian life the way I choose?"

She didn't look away. "San Antonio."

"What?"

"I came from San Antonio."

"Okay. But that's not the question."

"I've already told you. Take care of my son's heart. That means taking care of yourself. I know the protocol you're sup-posed to be following."

"What if I don't want to? What if I'm content doing just what I'm doing? Do I have no rights?"

"Nope. No rights at all." This time she didn't smile.

He looked at her, assessing what she needed and whether he could stand to give her enough of it to make her go away.

"Tell me about Nathan."

"As much as you want," she said. "But right now the bar-tender is giving you the look."

"Tommy can't help it. He was born that way." He didn't even glance at the bar.

"Why don't we talk about it at home. I could make an early dinner tomorrow, before you go to work."

"Let's talk now."

She took a deep breath. "Or we could talk now." She sipped the wine as if bracing herself.

"Nathan was seventeen when he died, a senior in high school. On his way home from a recruiting trip to Texas A&M, where he'd have probably played football four or five years while he got his degree. He was six-two, dark hair, brown eyes, which he got from his father. National Merit finalist. I was extremely proud of him." The slightest tremor in her voice on this last phrase.

Mason nodded, wiping condensation from his beer glass with his thumbs. He held the glass tightly so his hands didn't shake. "I can see why. What else?" He could hear his heart thumping.

"He didn't drink or smoke, mostly because of athletics, I imagine. And he had a strong sense of ethics."

"You said he was in love."

"If you can be in love at that age." Her eyes flickered. "Which you can, whether it lasts or not. The girl is a college student now. Still comes to see me sometimes."

"No wonder you can't give him up. He sounds like the perfect son." He glanced up and caught a defensive look passing across her face.

"Nobody's perfect," she said, but it was a rote response, as if she didn't believe it. "But I wouldn't have changed a thing about him."

"Tell me."

She drank the last of her wine and held on to the glass like a life raft. "When Nathan was fourteen, he got suspended from school for three days for fighting. I came down on him hard, because I'd raised him never to hit. A week or so later, a woman I didn't know stopped me in the grocery store. She was the mother of a chubby kid who wore glasses and didn't make friends, and she thanked me because Nathan had taken up for him when he was being humiliated by a bully. The bully was a guy on Nathan's football team, somebody he used to run around with. But when the guy wouldn't quit picking on Sammy, and had him backed into his locker trying to cram him inside, Nathan decked him." She looked up at Mason. "He hadn't made any excuses or explained to me what he'd done. Just served out his grounding."

In school, Mason had been a lot like Sammy. Only skinny instead of fat. He drained his beer. "Why did you decide to find me, after three years?"

She waited a beat. "Because I found a letter from Julia. One she'd written shortly after the transplant."

At the unexpected mention of Julia's name, Mason flinched. He looked away.

"It's a beautiful letter," she said. "She sounds gracious and compassionate."

Something gave way in his chest, melting outward to a weakness in his limbs. This was off-limits. He hadn't meant to talk about his wife. In self-defense, his voice turned hard.

"Julia suffers from clinical depression. She's living in Switzerland now, under the care of her parents and a good doctor there." He felt the weight of her eyes.

"What happened to your child?"

He moved the empty beer mug on the table, obliterating the wet ring. "He was born dead. Most likely a heart defect inherited from me." He looked at her, keeping his face expressionless, wielding the words like a blunt instrument. "His name was Michael. So I understand something about losing a child. Julia tried to kill herself."

He saw her face crumple and for a moment regretted his acid tone. Below the noise of the jukebox, he read her lips: "I'm sorry."

*Screw it.* It was her fault for tracking him down like some damned bounty hunter. Mason stood abruptly and snagged his glass from the table. "I've got to get back to work."

There was no food outside his door the next day, and she didn't show up at the bar that night. Mason's relief was tempered with an odd disappointment. He thought she was tougher than that. He wondered if she would go back to San Antonio and turn into a hollow shell, like him.

On his break, he couldn't tolerate the silence of the arroyo out back, so he sat at the far end of the bar and talked to one of the regulars, a guy named Vince, while Tommy's jukebox twanged.

Vince drove a delivery truck up to Taos twice a week. Mason bought him a beer.

"I've never been up that way," Mason said. "I hear it's pretty country."

"Hitch a ride with me sometime," Vince said. "I'd be glad for the company."

Mason finished his beer and signaled Tommy for another round. He'd always wanted to see Taos. Maybe it was time to move on.

# Chapter Twenty

A cold front rolled down the mountain slopes and covered the city with a low, white ceiling that smelled of snow. By nightfall, when Claire walked across the parking lot at Santero's, lazy flakes floated from the blue-black sky and caught in her hair. A muffled silence lay over the streets, as if the city were holding its breath.

Claire pulled open the big carved door and stepped from the frosty silence into the noisy, overheated world of the bar. Logs blazed in the stone fireplace, and the room buzzed with loud talk and laughter, the crowd energized by the prospect of the first snow. Tommy had gone all out for Halloween: jack-o'-lanterns grinned from the alcoves and crepe-paper spiders dangled from the vigas in the ceiling.

Music from the jukebox meshed with the noise. Claire edged around a group of standing drinkers and glanced toward the piano. The Steinway sat sleek and quiet as a black cat, the piano bench vacant.

It was only nine o'clock, too early for his break.

Someone bumped into her back and beer foam flecked her sleeve. "Sorry," the guy yelled, grinning like a pumpkin before he turned away.

She found a single empty stool at the bar and brandished a ten-dollar bill, waiting for Tommy to notice it and come over to take her order. He was setting up drinks with both hands, his black hair slicked back into a ponytail that glistened beneath the track lights. But he didn't look happy. The dark eyes clouded when he saw her.

"What'll it be?" He slapped down a coaster in front of her.

"Cabernet, please." Her voice rose above the noise. "Where's Mason tonight?"

Tommy scowled. "Damned if I know. Didn't show up."

He turned away, poured her wine and two beers, slid the beers down the polished bar. He set the wine on the coaster in front of her. "You don't know where he is?"

"Why would I know?"

He shrugged. "Until you came in, I figured maybe he was with you."

"Not likely," she said. "Maybe he's just late."

Tommy shook his head. "He's done this before. But never on a weekend. Boss threatened to fire him over it last time." He cleared half a dozen glasses from the bar and dunked them in a vat of sudsy water. "I don't know what he's thinking."

He moved away, summoned to the other end of the bar by

the server named Renee. Someone called out, "Hey, where's your piano player?" Claire saw the worried look on Renee's face when she glanced at Tommy.

"Who knows?" Tommy shot back. "Musicians!"

Surely McKinnon hadn't skipped out because of her. He'd seemed upset by their conversation, but she couldn't believe he was affected enough not to show up at work.

Claire set her untouched wine on the ten-spot and left the bar.

It was snowing in earnest now, the air thick with huge flakes that wet the concrete as they melted. She drove slowly down the route Mason had walked to his apartment, her windshield wipers slapping an urgent rhythm.

On the darkened sidewalk, a gaggle of hobgoblins bobbed along the sidewalk, flashlight beams jerking ahead of them. They were flanked by two adult figures wrapped in mufflers, and she thought of Nathan's first trick-or-treat night, when he'd gone as a peanut-butter-and-jelly sandwich, in a home-made costume she fashioned from two sheets of foam rubber painted brown at the edges. Nathan's body was the grape jelly, in a purple sweat suit. She heard the children's chatter through her closed window as she passed. No sign of McKinnon.

When she parked at the City Suites, his apartment was dark. She jogged up the stairs and pounded on the door. No answer. She tried the knob and it was locked.

"Mason? Are you in there?"

Nothing but silence.

She turned and looked across the parking lot. Snow sifted

through cones of light beneath the streetlamps. Nothing else moved in the lot or on the street.

If she called the police, what could she say? That a guy she barely knew hadn't shown up for work in a bar?

She pulled her jacket closer, her breath coming out in steamy puffs. Without a car, where could he have gone? What if he was ill, unable to answer the door? She'd read about rejection episodes after a transplant, but none of the literature said how severe the episodes might get.

More likely he was hung over and sleeping it off. There was nothing she could do. Surely he would turn up by tomorrow.

She clumped down the stairs to her own apartment, changed into pajamas and fell onto the lumpy couch with the remote control. For three hours she shifted from one sitcom to another, muting the sound at every commercial, listening for movement in the apartment above. At 1:00 a.m., with the national anthem playing, she roused from dozing and peered out the window into the parking lot.

The snow had stopped falling. The cars looked like lightly frosted cupcakes. No slouched figure in sneakers materialized from the night. She turned off the TV and went to bed.

The next morning, she dressed in warm clothes and two pairs of socks for her daily walk and climbed the stairs to knock on McKinnon's door again. The sun dazzled in a severe-clear sky. The only evidence of last night's snow lay in wispy strings along the shaded walkway next to the building. She rapped on the door to 213 and called his name, but the apartment was quiet, the windows dark.

The apartment manager's office was attached to his quarters in number 101. It sat in an ell between two wings of the building, where a ground-floor breezeway passed through to the courtyard in back. Two green plastic chairs in the breezeway held a thin rim of snow.

The office door was locked, a note taped to the outside. "Doctor's appointment. Back at noon." Claire swore under her breath and started off for her walk.

She was waiting in one of the green chairs when a car finally parked in the manager's space. Mr. Bingham extracted his considerable paunch from an ancient white tank that had once been a luxury car. He came toward her with a rolling gait, his arms full of shopping bags. *Doctor's appointment, my ass.*

The landlord puffed and wheezed under his load. Sunshine reflected from his bald head. "Good morning!" he called, though it was well past noon. "Are you waiting for me?"

"Yes." Claire stood up. "I'm concerned about Mr. McKinnon in 213. He didn't show up at work yesterday, and he's not answering his door."

Bingham smiled, juggling his bags while he unlocked the office. "Well, that's not too unusual around here. No cause for alarm."

His sunny tone irritated her, but she nodded. "You're probably right. But Mason takes a lot of medication, and I'm worried he could be unconscious and need a doctor. Could you please open his door and check on him?"

Bingham pushed the door open and she followed him into the small, gloomy room where she'd first come to rent her flat.

Dusty curtains clustered in the windows and unidentifiable black marks scuffed the off-white walls. It was the kind of room where nobody spent much time.

Mr. Bingham dumped his bags into an orange vinyl chair beside the cluttered desk. "I hate to violate people's privacy, Miss…"

"O'Neal. Claire O'Neal. I'm in 113."

"You're a friend of Mr. McKinnon?"

"Yes," she lied. "It's not like him to be gone and not tell me."

He gave her a sideways glance, his face full of fake compassion. "The two of you have a quarrel, did you?"

Like lightning, she saw her fist shoot out and plant her turquoise ring into his smug, pudgy jaw—but only in her imagination. She kept her voice level.

"Not at all. That's why I'm so worried." She sighed. "If you won't check on him, I guess I'll have to get the police out here."

"Now, now. I didn't say I wouldn't check on him. I just don't like to meddle in other people's affairs."

"Yes, you've made that clear," she said, louder. "But if he's lying up there sick or injured, and he dies while you're trying to make up your mind, I can see all kinds of legal problems in your future." *If you're going to lie, lie big.* "Did I mention that I'm an attorney, back in Texas?"

"Sure you are." He gave her a patronizing look, but he pulled out a drawer and began fumbling through it. "Keep your shirt on, I'm trying to find the right key."

She followed his baggy trousers up the stairs to Mason's door. Bingham knocked and called out loudly, twice, then tried several keys on a four-inch ring before finding one that turned the lock. He leaned his torso inside. "Mr. McKinnon? You here?"

Claire pushed past him. No one in the living room or bathroom. The bed was made. The violin was still in the closet, and so were his clothes. At least he wasn't lying on the floor dead. She let out a breath like escaping steam.

Bingham stood in the doorway, rattling his key ring. "Looks like he'll be back. We'd better lock up now."

Behind him, Claire saw a white panel truck pull into the apartment parking lot. "Yeah, thanks," she said.

The battered passenger door of the truck opened and a man's legs stepped out onto the pavement. The man slammed the truck door and glanced up at the open doorway of number 213 where Bingham stood.

The manager turned to see what Claire was watching. It was clear he didn't recognize Mason McKinnon. But McKinnon recognized him. Even from this distance she could see his clothes were more rumpled than usual, his face unshaven.

He couldn't have seen her standing in the shadows of his apartment, but he glanced toward her car in its parking space. Instead of coming upstairs, he turned and walked away from the building.

Claire brushed past Mr. Bingham. "Sorry I bothered you." She set off at a trot down the second-floor walkway.

McKinnon was nearly a block ahead of her by the time she pounded down the stairs and rounded the corner of the building. She caught a glimpse of him as he turned into the residential area adjacent to the apartments. He was walking fast, heading toward a neighborhood park that she'd discovered on her walks.

She picked up her pace, but when she reached the edge of the park, she'd lost him. The park was a block square, with a small pond where children came to feed the ducks. Her eyes scanned the playground and picnic tables. Through the thinly leafed trees beside the pond, she saw his navy-blue jacket.

She jogged toward the row of trees, rounded them at a walk, and stopped. McKinnon was standing at the water's edge, throwing tiny pebbles. No, not pebbles. He had bought a handful of corn from a dispenser shaped like a clown's head, and he was tossing them a few kernels at a time into the center of the pond. Swirls below the surface revealed the movement of fish. A noisy group of mottled ducks sailed fast from the other side, leading a vee of silver ripples.

"Are you okay?" she called.

His face registered no surprise. He tossed another missile into the water. "That's too tough a question."

She walked closer. "Tommy's worried about you."

His smile twisted to one side. "No. Tommy's mad." Corn sailed over the water and sank with tiny plops that sent the ducks scrambling.

"Okay. *I* was worried about you."

He turned to face her, frowning, and leaned one elbow on the clown's white scalp. "I thought you'd given up and left town."

"I don't give up easily."

He shook the grains of corn in his palm, thinking it over. "That's a good quality. I used to admire that."

Sunlight spangled the pond, and to his left, a few lacy willow leaves still clung to their branches. Backlit against the water, the scene looked like an old photo with its colors faded, a picture of someone lost.

She'd seen that picture before. Her neck shivered. She knew what would happen next.

Mason glanced at her, then looked away. "I'm sorry about dumping my baggage on you the other night. It was a crappy thing to do."

She saw the knot slide up and down in his throat, saw his eyes blink in slow motion. In the distance a dog barked, and she heard the echoed shout of children, the close commotion of hungry ducks.

The light turned an eerie color she'd never seen before. *Nathan's heart is beating in his chest.*

She moved forward as if she were walking through water. When she came close, he tossed away the grains of corn and squared his shoulders. His hands hung loose at his sides.

She stopped.

"It's all right." His voice sounded hoarse, barely more than a whisper.

His shirt felt cool to her fingertips. She watched her hand, not his face, as she lay her palm flat against his chest. She closed her eyes and felt the beating of her son's heart.

It was almost enough.

Her throat tight, she pressed her ear against his chest. There…a rapid, steady pulse. The heartbeat she'd once felt beneath her own, before Nathan was born.

His arms wrapped slowly around her. He stood still, his breath regular and patient. But his voice was tight when he spoke. "If I could give him back to you, I would."

"I didn't come here to make you feel guilty."

"You didn't have to. I've been guilty since the day I realized that the only way I would live was if somebody else died."

She raised her head and stepped away, dried her face on her sleeve. His eyes, too, were wet, and the angular cheekbones made shadows on his face.

"It's not your fault that my son died. No one blames you for that."

He nodded. Shrugged. "Shall we walk?"

They waded through the sea of jabbering ducks along the sandy perimeter of the pond, watching their own feet. A crisp breeze pulled at their jackets and Mason zipped his up.

"Every time the weather gets cool like this," he said, "I get a craving for chili. And I never did before." He glanced at her and smiled. "Did Nathan like chili?"

She smiled, too. "He loved it. Especially my homemade Texas chili. Do you also have cravings for George Jones?"

She was teasing, but he seemed to consider the question. "Not specifically, but I do like country music more than I used to. Sometimes I hear it in my head."

He stooped to pick up a pair of small rocks, examined them, flung one into the pond. The ducks stormed in and swam toward the ripples.

"Some people believe there's such a thing as cellular memory," he said. "Science hasn't proven it, but they can't disprove it, either. How else can you account for animal instinct, when even the young who've been abandoned know things about where to hunt or what to eat?"

Claire looked up at the sky, where a jet contrail cut through the blue. "Geese and hummingbirds find migration paths they've never traveled before." They came to a park bench that faced the pond and sat.

"My parents have no particular musical abilities," he said. "But when I was five, I sat down at a neighbor's piano and played a melody that was in my head. Turns out I had a great-grandmother who had a beautiful voice and sometimes made up her own songs. Maybe you can attribute musical ability to DNA, but where did that *melody* come from?"

Claire said nothing, pulling her jacket close around her. A tiny bird dipped above the pond to drink on the wing.

Mason's gaze followed the bird into the distance. "I think we carry in our brains—or our cells—certain mannerisms and preferences, maybe even stories, that belonged to generations of ancestors we never knew."

"I'd like to believe that," she said. "It would be comforting. Like we're less alone."

The sun had moved overhead now, silvering the pond. Ducks swam leisurely through the fractured light, preening and oiling themselves.

"I'd like to hear about Julia," she said. "If it's not too hard."

He took a breath. "Julia had problems with depression since high school. Her parents had taken her to the best doctors money could buy, and by the time we met they'd figured out a combination of drugs that controlled it. She seemed as happy as anyone I knew. Moody sometimes, but most musicians are. We fell in love the first time we met."

"What does she look like?"

"About your height, and slim. Too slim, really. She always ate like a rabbit. Dark hair, almost black, and dark eyes. There's something Oriental about the cheekbones, though she had no Oriental heritage she knew anything about." He smiled. "But she did really like Chinese food."

On the pond, two drakes squabbled and nipped at each other, then swam apart.

"She played cello?"

"Like an angel." He was quiet a moment, drifting. "Julia learned she was pregnant while I was in the hospital waiting for the transplant, but she didn't tell me. They had told us I wouldn't live more than a week if I didn't get a heart."

Claire shook her head. "How awful. For both of you."

"It's a hell of a thing, to be told you're about to die. And worse, that the only way you'll live is if somebody else dies accidentally. You try like hell not to hope for it, but of course you do hope. You hope for the heart, not the death, but you can't have one without the other and you feel like a ghoul. I think it was even harder for Julia. They kept me sedated, and I was getting so little oxygen I slept eighteen hours a day."

Claire thought of another room at a different hospital, where Nathan lay hooked to a respirator. In those same hours, Julia was watching her husband die, unable to help him, and expecting a child.

"Then the news came that a heart was available," he said. "The doctors warned us that I might not make it, or my body might reject the heart. I went into surgery not knowing if I'd ever see Julia again." Mason cleared his throat, pulled apart a seedpod he'd found on the sand. "But I came through the surgery fine. Then it was a matter of adjusting to the antirejection drugs, finding ones I could tolerate. All of them have side effects, and they're unimaginably expensive."

"Will you have to take the drugs from now on?"

"As long as I live." His jaw flexed. "After I came home from the hospital, Julia finally told me she was pregnant, and that she'd stopped her depression meds because she was afraid of their effect on the baby. Probably due to stress, she nearly miscarried and was confined to bed for a while. Eventually the baby's heart sounds stopped, and Julia went into labor two months early."

Claire's breath felt impossibly heavy. *Stop, I can't hear any more.* But she swallowed hard and kept quiet.

"Julia insisted on seeing the baby. After that she withdrew so far even the drugs couldn't help. One day I came home and found her unconscious on the bed, an empty pill bottle on the floor."

"It's a wonder you didn't lose your mind."

"They pumped her stomach and saved her life, but she stopped talking and she wouldn't open her eyes. When I came into the room, she'd become agitated, her blood pressure spiking, and the nurse would ask me to leave. I think Julia hated me because I didn't let her die."

Claire shook her head. "If she's ever okay again, she won't hate you."

"I doubt I'll see her again. Her parents took her to a clinic in Switzerland that they thought was the best in the world, and I didn't fight them. She's still in the institution but comes home to their place in Berne on the weekends sometimes, and for holidays. She rarely talks, and never about me or the baby. Her mother thinks she doesn't remember. I hope she's right."

Claire huffed a breath, stretching her legs out in front of the bench. "Sometimes life just sucks, and there's no explanation."

He glanced at her face. "You're not religious?"

"I believe in God, I guess. Or I used to. But it's the old question of why the innocent suffer. I have a cousin who's a priest, and we talked quite a lot after Nathan died. He said he has doubts, too, sometimes, but his faith is strong enough to withstand the doubts. Mine wasn't."

Across the lake, a young mother pushed a stroller along the sidewalk, a small boy ricocheting around her from the water's edge to the corn dispenser.

"What about you?" Claire said. "What do you believe?"

He shrugged. "I think anything is possible. But believing is the hard part."

The young mother passed behind them on the sidewalk and the boy ranged close, collecting stones. "Here's a good one," Mason said, and held out his hand. "I picked it up on the other side."

The little boy glanced at his mother, who smiled and nodded. He ran forward and plucked the rock from Mason's palm. "It has sparkles! Thanks."

Mason watched them go. "Michael would be about that size now if he'd lived. I don't think I could have kept up with him."

"Sure you could, because you'd have to. And you'd probably still be playing with the symphony."

"I don't know. Julia and I used to go to rehearsals and performances together. I just didn't have the heart for it anymore." He stopped. "Sorry. Poor choice of words."

Claire smiled. "Don't apologize. I'm not that fragile."

"No. You're very strong."

"Huh. My friends and onetime shrink would disagree. They think I'm copeless. Obsessed with my son's memory."

"Are they right?"

She looked out across the pond, debating. "I see Nathan sometimes," she said quietly. "He appears to me, and we talk to each other." A stray breeze stirred ripples on the pond and a shower of leaves fell around them. "That sounds quite insane when I say it aloud."

"Everybody who's been through trauma is probably a little insane. Whatever gets you through the afternoons, I say." He paused. "Did it ever occur to you that he might not be a hallucination?"

A shivery feeling brushed over her, like spider steps on her skin. "I'm afraid to consider that. Somehow it's scarier than thinking I'm crazy."

"What's left to be afraid of? You've already been through the worst that could happen."

A puff of breeze rained yellow leaves onto her open palms. "When I saw you standing by the pond," she said, "I had this feeling that I'd known you for a long time."

He smiled. "Maybe you have. Our ancestors might have met around a campfire a few thousand years ago. Yours was cooking caveman chili. And mine was playing a flute carved from a thigh bone."

Claire laughed, the image flickering in her mind. She looked at him until he met her eyes. "I'm glad you have my son's heart."

He put his hand over hers and glanced away, squinting into the light.

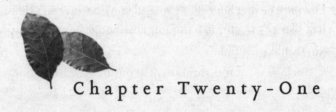

# Chapter Twenty-One

Tommy the bartender set a glass of wine on Claire's table. "It's on the house," he said. "You left a full one last time."

Claire smiled up at him. "Thanks." She was used to seeing only the top half of Tommy behind the bar, and he looked even taller standing beside her table.

Renee was busy with a group of tourists on the far side of the room, the only other patrons in the bar. Claire motioned toward an empty chair and Tommy sat, swiping the table with his omnipresent bar rag. They both glanced toward the piano, where Mason was breezing through a medley of state songs, entertaining the tourists.

"Why didn't you fire him?" she asked.

Tommy looked disgusted with himself. "I didn't tell the boss he skipped. But if one of the customers rats him out, my ass is grass. It's the last time I'm covering for him."

Claire smiled. Big Tommy was just a teddy bear in a pony-tail. He fidgeted a few seconds, seeming uncomfortable at the table, then rose and ambled back to his usual place.

With the tourists satisfied for the moment, Renee brought over a bowl of pretzels. "Hi, Claire. Can I get you anything else?"

*Where everybody knows your name.* She'd become a regular at a bar, like a character in a sitcom. The thought gave her pause. "No, thanks. I'm fine."

"You look great tonight. Love that outfit." And Renee moved on.

Claire thought about the first night she'd come here, when she'd felt like such an outsider in her pantsuit and heels. To-night she was wearing a denim skirt and a cotton blouse painted with Southwest icons, her hair longer and looser. Her real life in San Antonio seemed far away. Sometimes she missed it.

Mason changed tempo and she recognized "The Shadow of Your Smile," a haunting melody he played almost every night. It must be one of his favorites.

For an hour she nursed her wine and listened to him play, watching the customers come and go. She speculated on their private tragedies and lost dreams, the parts of their lives they came here to forget. But she couldn't guess their stories from the outside; Mason McKinnon was proof of that. Sometimes when she looked at him, she forgot to think about Nathan's heart. She had started to see him as a person instead of a proj-ect, and that made her uncomfortable. She wasn't sure why.

Mason took a request for a show tune, and the tourist table sang along. He'd apparently stopped smoking, at least when she was around, and his face looked fuller and healthier. What worried her most now was his outlook. He didn't seem to care about anything.

On break, Mason picked up a beer from Tommy and came over to her table. He sat down and looked at her. There was no bulge of a cigarette pack in his breast pocket.

"Hi," she said. "Heard any good country songs lately?"

A faint smile played across his face. "Want to get something to eat when I get off?" he said. "I know an IHOP that's open after midnight."

They ordered blueberry pancakes and talked about music. She asked when he'd started playing the violin.

"I was about ten," he said. "My school had a junior orchestra and I wanted to be in that. I'd been taking piano lessons since first grade. My dad wasn't into music at all. I always felt like I disappointed him because instead of playing football or basketball, I was a skinny kid who played in the band."

"I guess all kids worry about disappointing their dads. Even girls." But she didn't want to talk about fathers—or even sons. She steered back toward her purpose. "It must be amazing to play with an orchestra. To be on the inside of something like that."

The waitress stopped to refill their coffee.

"It's unbelievable," Mason said. "With all those first-rate musicians working together, the music becomes larger than all of us. It's like—" he spread his hands "—your body *expands*. And you play better than you know you can."

The only such magic Claire knew was the way her heart expanded when she'd watched her baby son sleeping, or watched his school programs with tears in her eyes. "How could you possibly give that up?"

"Without Julia, it wasn't the same." He leaned back in the booth, his face quiet. "One day I woke up alone again, and I could feel the days falling around me, silent as snow. I was suffocating."

Claire thought of the night she'd huddled on the front step of her old house, unable to go inside. "How did you end up in Santa Fe?"

He sipped his coffee, his voice changing. "I had good memories here. My parents and I came here once on vacation, before my dad died. Oddly enough, I like playing piano at the bar. I'm right there with the audience. A lot of them are talking instead of listening—that's just part of the gig—but some do listen. Maybe they'll request a song that's meant a lot to them. And for a few minutes, I can make them happy." Then he shrugged it off and went back to his pancakes.

Claire watched her hands line up her knife and fork on the table. "In the arts section of the newspaper I saw an article inviting musicians to audition for the Santa Fe Symphony. Apparently they're open to new members."

His smile twisted. "I am way too out of practice."

"You could fix that."

He gave her the cynical-piano-player look and didn't answer.

"Have you seen them perform?" she asked.

"No."

"Me, either. I went to the symphony in Austin—looking for you, actually—and I loved it."

But his faced had closed. *Baby steps,* she thought. The waitress refilled their coffee for the third time and left the check. Claire reached for it but he got there first.

"My treat," he said. "Tips have been good lately."

She narrowed her eyes. "Are you trying to run me off with kindness now?"

"Nah." He pulled bills from a tattered wallet without looking at her. "I kind of hope you'll hang around."

The spicy aroma of Texas chili saturated Claire's small apartment. She dipped a wooden spoon into the stew pot and blew on a test bite while she held the cell phone to her ear. *Garlic. That's what it needed.*

"Just tell me straight," Janelle said. "Are you ever coming back?"

"Of course I am," Claire said. "What's wrong?"

"Charlene is quitting to go back to teaching. She'd rather have time than money."

"The idea is to have both," Claire said.

"I wouldn't know. Do you want me to advertise for another agent?"

"Umm. How were the sales numbers for October?"

"I'll e-mail them to you. Down a little, but nothing abnormal for right after school starts. Irv's been hot lately—three closings this week."

"Go, Irv. Let's not worry about a new agent right now. I'll deal with that when I get back." She laid a clove of garlic on the cutting board and rummaged in a drawer for a paring knife. "How are Les and the kids?"

"They're fine. Les grumbles about my long hours, but the kids don't care as long as there's food in the house and I show up at their events." Janelle heaved a sigh and Claire heard her desk chair squeak. "I miss talking to you. What are you doing out there, besides cooking?"

Claire considered how to answer. *I'm taking over a man's life, uninvited.*

*Guarding a vital organ I used to know.*

*Learning to get through the day without hallucinating my dead son.*

"Getting perspective," she said. "Exercising. Shopping. I'll bring presents when I come home."

"Presents are good. What about McKinnon? What's going on with him?"

Claire switched the phone to the other ear. "I like him. But his life is a train wreck. He needs some work."

"He's not working?"

Claire laughed. "He's not working where he *should* be."

"My clients are coming in the door," Janelle said. "I'll have to go. Oh—do you know a mechanic named Hobby? I'm not sure whether that's his last name or a nickname."

"I don't think so. Why?"

"A guy came in here last week saying he wanted to look at houses. Somebody had recommended you as an agent, and he wouldn't be satisfied with me or even Irv. Wanted to know where you were and when you'd be back."

"My reputation among mechanics is impeccable."

"I told him to check back in a week or two. But he kind of gave me the creeps."

"Uh-oh. Then don't give him my cell number, please. Maybe he'll go away."

"Take care of yourself, cowgirl. We miss you around here."

Claire hung up and stirred garlic into the chili. Despite a tight stitch of homesickness, she always felt better after talking to Ja-nelle. She'd have to find a way to repay Janelle for managing the agency while she was gone. The cell phone warbled again and she picked it up, grinning. "What did you forget?"

"Pardon me? Is this Claire?"

"Oh. Win." Her shoulders sagged. "I thought Janelle was calling me back."

"So you're still in Santa Fe?"

"Yes." She kept her voice light. "Everybody thought I should take a vacation. Now they want me back home."

"I guess they didn't expect you to stay a month," he said.

"I guess not. So. Janelle said you'd been calling. What do you need?"

She heard him pull in a deep breath and exhale. "My dad died last week."

"Oh." Her lighthearted mood hissed away. She knew Win idolized his father. "I'm sorry to hear that. Had he been ill?"

"He had cancer," Win said. "Things went faster than we expected. Which was probably for the best."

She couldn't think what to say. "How's your mom doing?" Though it was hard to care.

"She's putting up a good front. You know Mom."

*Indeed.* "So you're in charge of the whole family business now."

"I'm CEO, yeah."

"Congratulations—I guess."

"Right." He moved on. "I know this will surprise you, but Dad had set up a portfolio of stocks in a trust for Nathan. Mostly in O'Neal Enterprises, of course, but some other issues, too."

"You're kidding. Gerard did that?"

"I didn't know about it, either. Just before he died, he put the account in your name, with me as trustee. Odd, isn't it?"

Odd was hardly the word. Win's father had never acknowledged his own grandson, let alone Claire.

"We need to discuss what to do with it," Win said.

"That's pretty simple. It should have been put in your name. I'll sign the stocks over to you."

"It isn't mine," he insisted. "It's Nathan's." She was surprised at the heat in his voice. "Since neither of us really needs money, I thought we might do something with it that Nathan would have liked."

She paused, taken aback. "That's a lovely idea, Win. Let me think about it until I get back to San Antonio."

"When do you think that will be?"

"I don't know. I'll call you."

"No you won't."

She huffed a breath. "I said I would. Don't try to guilt me, Win. This came out of left field, and I need time to think about it. I'll call you when I get home."

"Okay. I'm sorry." He waited a beat. "Meanwhile, I'd like to send a copy of the portfolio contents and values by FedEx, so you can look it over."

"All right." She gave him the address and apartment number. "And Win, I am sorry about your father." She flipped the phone shut and sat down, suddenly short of breath.

Incredible. Gerard O'Neal had included his disowned grandson in his will. Once again proving she didn't know anything about anything.

An eerie feeling crept up her spine, and she waited for Nathan to appear, even hoped that he would. But Nathan didn't come. She was quite alone, and hollow as a timpani.

At noon she left the foil-covered bowl of chili on the mat beside Mason's newspaper, along with a packet of carrot sticks and green onions. On top she placed an envelope containing two tickets to the Sunday afternoon performance of the Santa Fe Symphony. She did not knock.

Nor did she go to Santero's that night, giving Mason time to think it over. She was still awake when she heard his footsteps cross the floor overhead, then the sounds of running water. He didn't come downstairs, though he must have seen her light when he came home.

By noon the next day she still hadn't heard him moving around upstairs. Nor did she hear his TV. But that afternoon she found the clean bowl in front of her door, empty except for the envelope containing both symphony tickets. She picked them up with a sinking feeling.

Damn. She'd gone too far.

# Chapter Twenty-Two

On Sunday afternoon Claire went to the symphony alone. The Lensic Performing Arts Center occupied a beautifully restored, historic building on San Francisco Street. Smaller than the Bass Concert Hall in Austin, the Lensic felt more intimate, even from Claire's seat in the balcony. An ornate proscenium arched high above the stage, painted with the colors of Santa Fe—turquoise, terra-cotta, silver. The stage was draped in black.

Claire's mood was black, as well. She'd been so sure she could persuade Mason to attend with her—arrogantly sure. She was wrong, and now she'd risked the fragile rapport they'd started to build, a personal bond that might protect her son's heart.

Sitting in the darkened concert hall, Claire probed another layer of worry, too, an anxiety that lay beneath her concern for his heart. She cared too much about Mason McKinnon. She wasn't surprised that she felt a connection to him, because of

Nathan. But did that account for her watching his hands while he ate, for knowing there were three small crescents on the right side of his mouth when he smiled, but only two on the left?

It was getting too weird, too complicated. Maybe she should pack up tomorrow and go back to San Antonio. If Mason really wanted to self-destruct, he would do it with or without her interference.

The maestro lifted his baton and a tsunami of music surged through the hall, catching her in its rising wave. For a few moments, her distress washed away in the harmony of strings. *Mason ought to be here, inside that wonderful sound.* Maybe it was presumptuous, but she knew in her gut that this music was the one thing that could make him value his life again. She wanted that for him, and not only because of Nathan's heart.

When the concert was over, Claire dreaded going back to the bleak apartment, so she wandered down San Francisco Street among the late-afternoon tourists. The crowd was thinning as evening approached, and the scent of tortillas and salsa wafted from the doorways of family-run cafés. On a narrow sidewalk south of the Plaza, a beautiful Gothic building caught the sunlight, and she crossed the street to have a look. A sign out front identified The Chapel of Loretto, built between 1873-1878. The Sisters of Loretto had established an academy on this site even earlier. She had read about a famous staircase in the chapel, so she paid admission and strolled inside.

Only a few other visitors milled silently through the small chapel. An ornate ceiling arched high overhead, its multicolored dome glowing with light. A bank of dwarf candles flickered at one side of the altar railing; sculptured saints looked down from the walls. Claire paused before the intricately carved altar, all white and veined with gold. As a girl, she had spurned the pomp and ritual of the Catholic mass. But the baroque details of Loretto Chapel seemed beautiful to her, and somehow spiritual.

The famous staircase stood at the back of the chapel, a magnificent spiral of burnished wood. Her gaze followed the stairs through two complete turns from the floor to the choir loft, where a stained-glass window caught the afternoon light.

Near the staircase, a video played softly, and Clare drew close to hear the story. The builders of the chapel, two architects from Paris, had designed the choir loft without a staircase. Women were not allowed to sing in European choirs, and men used ladders to ascend to the loft. But the Loretto Chapel would be used by the Sisters and their female students. Climbing a twenty-foot ladder in long dresses and habits would be terrifying. The architects had left no room for a traditional staircase, and the sisters faced a dilemma. So they began a novena, a nine-day period of prayer, to St. Joseph, patron saint of carpenters.

On the ninth day of prayer, a grizzled carpenter leading a donkey came to the school and offered to build the needed staircase. Using only a few basic tools, he fashioned a perfectly balanced spiral staircase of a wood that is now extinct. Each step was secured with square wooden pegs—no nails, no glue and no center support. According to the video, architects and engineers still marveled at its construction. When the staircase was finished, the carpenter disappeared, never asking for his pay. The nuns believed that the old carpenter was St. Joseph, the father of Christ.

The recording fell silent. Claire was alone in the chapel. She imagined the nuns in their long, black habits ascending the circular stairs. They never doubted the mystical appearance of their carpenter. What would they have believed about Nathan's mirage?

That night Claire lay on the sagging sofa in her apartment, staring at the TV without seeing its flickering images. The rooms upstairs were silent. She pictured Mason at work, breathing secondhand smoke and hoping she would disappear and leave him alone. Near midnight, she carried a book to bed and read herself to sleep.

She was sitting in a darkened concert hall, adrift in an ocean of empty seats. A young violinist played alone on the stage, his coattails flashing scarlet, the music drenching her like wine.

*Lento, espressivo.* With exquisite longing.

Claire came awake, her heartbeat ragged in her throat. The red numbers on her ceiling read 2:13 a.m. Violin music melted down through the ceiling.

She sat up, holding her breath.

Mason was playing his violin. *Lento, espressivo.*

The vibration sent a thrill down her spine. She could see him leaning into the music, feel the curve of his fingers on the strings.

She slipped out of bed and pulled a long coat over her gown. Forgot her shoes.

The concrete walkway was cold beneath her feet, the stairs silent as she ascended. Outside his apartment she stopped and tapped gently, laying her forehead against the door. Only the sound of the violin seeped through.

The knob turned silently in her hand.

Mason sat on a kitchen chair, his eyes closed. His face in profile looked transfixed. His body moved like an extension of the violin, swaying with each stroke of the bow, inseparable from its sound.

A draft of cold air snaked around her legs. She stepped inside and closed the door.

When the latch clicked, his eyes opened, and she saw that they were rimmed with tears. The bow faltered for only an instant, then the silver rope curled out again, its emotion so raw it hurt her chest.

When he finished and lowered the violin, the air still rang. "Mason?"

He glanced at a letter that lay open on the table beside him, blue handwriting on a single page of ivory paper. She stepped closer and saw a Zurich postmark on the envelope. *Julia.*

His voice was dry as reeds. "It's from her mother. Julia suffered a relapse when the doctors tried to recall her memory."

Claire's eyes filled. She shook her head.

"She won't take food unless they feed her," he said, "and she never speaks. She just sits looking out a barred window. Someone gave her a rosary and she worries the beads until her fingers bleed, and weeps if they try to take it away. The doctor doesn't think she'll ever come back."

Claire put her hand on his shoulder. Wished for something she could say. "I'm so sorry."

He laid the violin and bow on the table. It seemed a great effort for him to stand. He put his arms around her and rocked back and forth, as if comforting a child.

She held him, barely breathing. The muscles in his back were bunched wire, his face unreasonably hot. For long moments, they circled together like slow moons.

His breath rasped in her hair. "Stay with me tonight. Please."

She lay with him beneath the sheet, still in her gown, her body cool against his burning skin. She listened to the rush of her own blood and tried not to think.

Gradually his breath came easier and his spine softened.

"I can't make love," he said, his voice drowsy in the darkness. "A side effect of the drugs."

Her breath caught. She laid her arm across him, moved her face from his shoulder so he wouldn't feel her tears. "Neither can I."

For a long time after he fell asleep, she listened to the strangeness of a man's breath beside her. How long had it been? The sounds of distant traffic drifted through the walls, and the call of a night bird whose name she didn't know. A quiet percussion of sorrows.

Predawn light diffused through the blue curtains when she rolled carefully away. She stood beside the bed and looked at his face, troubled even in sleep. His hair was a fracas of curls on the pillow, his fingers relaxed on the sheet. Something shifted in her chest.

*What am I doing? He has my son's heart!*

She found her coat on the floor, pulled it over her gown and slipped out the front door.

# Chapter Twenty-Three

Mason awoke shivering, his face hot as fire. His damp T-shirt clung to his chest. He knew immediately what was wrong; he'd expected it for a long time.

Rolling over, he caught the scent of Claire's shampoo on the pillow. She'd been next to him, but now she was gone. Or maybe that was another of his feverish dreams.

He stumbled to the bathroom and drank water. His face in the mirror looked bloated, his fingers stiff as cigars. When he looked into his red-rimmed eyes, he saw Julia, sitting beside a window, worrying her rosary beads. He had dreamed she was fleeing through snow-covered mountains in a tattered dress, pursued by white-coated keepers. And Mason had stood apart, playing the violin like Nero with Rome burning.

Maybe she was better off with her mind completely gone

than drifting back and forth, knowing what she'd lost. He hoped that wherever she'd gone, it was peaceful there.

Unexpectedly he thought of Jessica McKinnon, his decent, long-suffering mother. He was grateful she couldn't see him now.

And he thought of Claire. The heart she wanted so much to save was failing. His body was attacking it, set off by some virus or infection. He could feel the battle waging in his chest and in his brain.

If he skipped his meds this morning, the process would go faster.

Somebody once said *not to decide is to decide*. He turned away from the mirror and switched on the hot water in the shower.

He sat on the commode to shed the clothes he'd slept in. When steam billowed out and obscured the mirror, he stepped into the spray and leaned against the cracked tile, limp as a phony excuse.

The water washed over him until his legs wouldn't hold him up anymore, then he toweled off and slipped on a pair of sweatpants. He was sitting on the rumpled bed, struggling with a clean T-shirt, when he heard the knock on his apartment door. He glanced at the clock. It had to be Claire, coming to check on him. Probably bearing food.

He was too tired to answer. But the door wasn't locked; if he didn't respond, she would come in anyway. He almost smiled, thinking about the ways she had tried to save him. Now he was about to disappoint her. The knock came again, and this time her voice, calling his name. He shuffled to the door barefoot and pulled it open.

Even with the fever addling his brain, he could read her emotions—or thought he could. He watched her take in his puffy cheeks and bleary eyes. Alarm lit her face like a billboard—she was trying to relate his condition to last night, to what happened, or didn't happen, in his bed. Then he saw her eyes soften and knew she'd remembered Julia. She thought he was mourning his lost wife.

"It's a rejection episode," he told her, his voice flat. "Anything can set them off. Even a cold." He turned away.

She stepped inside and shut the door, all business now. Her hand was cool and dry when she felt his forehead. Her eyes widened. "Get dressed. I'll drive you to the heart center in Albuquerque."

Of course she would already know about the closest transplant care facility. He felt a surge of sympathy for her dedication to a lost cause. He shook his head. "I don't want to go—"

She held up a hand, cutting him off. "We're going. Right now. We need to take your blood pressure log with us. And the list of medications." She went straight to the place where he kept these and started rummaging.

"Get dressed," she repeated.

He felt woozy, exhausted. Resistance took too much effort. While he slowly worked his leaden legs into a pair of pants, he heard her in the living room on the tiny cell phone she always carried. She was calling ahead for an appointment. She had made his decision for him. Maybe that's what he wanted.

He was zipping up when she appeared in the bedroom doorway, phone still in her hand. "They want to know if you've been to this facility before."

He tried to think. "Eight or nine months ago."

"Good. Then they'll have your records."

They were on the road within half an hour, heading toward Albuquerque on I-25. It was an hour's drive in normal traffic, but Claire was speeding, keeping an eye in the rearview for flashing lights.

He laid his head back and melted into the soft leather seat. His body ached. His mind felt drifty and surreal. "Is this Monday?"

"What? Um—yes." She was scanning the highway ahead for cops.

"That's good. I won't miss work."

"You don't wash your hands often enough at the bar. That's probably where you picked up some kind of bug."

She reached across and laid her cool palm on his forehead again. He wished she would put it over his eyes; they felt like hot stones.

"Do you have symptoms other than fever?"

"Some fluid retention. More tired than usual."

"For how long?"

He shrugged.

She made an exasperated face. "Why didn't you say something? Or do something about it?"

He rolled his head toward her. She wouldn't like the real answer. "Because I'm a useless slug?" He gave her a weak smile.

"From your lips to God's ears." She blew out a breath. "Okay, I'll lay off. But this is scary, Mason."

"I'll be okay. It's happened before."

She glanced over at him. "What if the rejection gets too severe? What happens then?"

He didn't answer.

He dozed in and out, his head lolling with the motion of the car. When they hit the outskirts of Albuquerque, he pointed to the Central Avenue exit and directed her toward the Presbyterian Heart Center in the hospital complex.

She took his arm while they walked toward the glass doors. "I hope some big, burly nurse chews your ass out good," she said.

The nurses, however, were sweet tempered and efficient. Within minutes Mason was summoned to the inner sanctum to be checked out, leaving Claire to cool her heels in a waiting room. He waved to her stupidly as they whisked him away. This was going to take a while. Maybe she'd call someone on her cell phone, or finish a crossword puzzle somebody else had started in a ragged magazine.

In a windowless exam room, he was disrobed, swathed in a hospital gown, and ensconced on a rolling table. A nurse wrapped his legs in soft sheets and spread a warmed blanket on top. Then it began—first the vital signs, and an elephantine injection of steroids. With the steroids would come an emotional roller coaster, extra hair, maybe other side effects, as well. Next the echocardiogram, to get his heart's ejection fraction. The technician frowned at what he saw.

He was wheeled through a succession of rooms, the ceilings all the same, the equipment and personnel different. He decided that med techs everywhere were uniformly polite and informative, if you cared to ask questions. They did their best to treat him like a person, but in reality he was a challenge, a lab specimen. A scientific problem to be solved. In between tests, he dozed.

They extracted vials of blood, hooked an IV to his arm. He closed his eyes and let them do what they would. He'd been through it so many times, the needles, the tests, the endless drugs. All the necessary struggles to keep him alive. Why did they think he was worth it?

A distinguished-looking cardiologist examined him. Asked more questions, wrote notes. Mason was too tired to remember his name. The doctor ordered him admitted to the hospital. Finally they were through with him and he was wheeled back to the room where he started—or he thought it was the same room. He rested in foggy submission.

"I'll go tell Mrs. McKinnon she can come in now," a nurse said, and he thought *How did my mother get here?*

But in a few minutes Claire came into the room. The nurse had assumed they were married. That was funny, and he roused himself enough to smile. Claire smiled back and held his hand.

"You're a beautiful person," he mumbled. "Did I forget to tell you that?"

"We're going to admit Mr. McKinnon to the hospital," the nurse said to Claire, "and do a heart biopsy tomorrow morning. The doctor will adjust his medications and keep an eye on him for a day or so. Then he'll need another biopsy in a few days, or maybe next week."

"He'll be here a week?"

"Probably not. If he responds to the steroids and the changes in his meds, he can probably go home. If so, it's important that we set an appointment for another heart biopsy next week."

Claire nodded. "Just let me know when. How do they do that, exactly? The biopsy."

"We'll numb an area in his neck, over the jugular vein." The nurse touched the base of her throat on the right side. "Or sometimes they go through the groin. The doctor inserts a small needle into the vein and introduces a catheter that's threaded through the vein to the heart."

Mason could have given the speech himself, if he'd been alert enough. He watched Claire take it in, her face intense.

"We'll measure the output of the heart—the ejection fraction—and compare the readings with his last visit," the nurse was saying. "A bioptome is inserted through the catheter. It's like a tiny forceps, and the doctor uses it to clip some tissue samples."

Claire's face pinched. "Is he awake for this?"

"Yes, but usually they don't feel much."

"What do they do with the biopsy?"

"The samples are examined for the kind of cells that might invade heart muscle and try to destroy it."

Claire looked at the plastic tubes snaking from his arm and his nose. He could see she was feeling sorry for him, and he appreciated that.

The nurse checked the IV tube briefly and patted the thermal blanket over Mason's knees. "They'll be here to transfer you in just a few minutes." She gave him a smile that was way out of proportion to his situation, and left the room.

Claire's face was pale. She sank onto a straight chair and leaned her head against the wall.

"Are you okay?" he asked.

"Better than you." She looked at him bleakly. "I haven't been inside a hospital since Nathan died. I'm feeling a bit ragged."

"You don't need to stay. Really."

"Right." Her smile looked tired. "You can take the bus home." She slipped off her shoes and fanned herself with one of them.

"I'd appreciate it very much if you could come get me when I'm dismissed," he said, making an effort to speak clearly. "But tonight I'll be zoned out in a room where they pipe in electronic music. It's no fun to watch."

"It's what you deserve for neglecting yourself."

"I guess so. Of course if you do go, you'll miss a chance to bully me while I'm defenseless."

"And that's my mission in life," she said. "So I guess I'll hang around."

They settled him in a hospital room with a tray of overcooked food. He convinced Claire to go find the cafeteria and while she was gone, he sank toward sleep. Whatever they'd given him in those injections really kicked butt.

When he awoke, stripes of orange sunset angled through the blinds. Claire lay pushed back in the vinyl recliner next to the window. Her eyes were closed, her breathing even.

He watched her sleep. With her face relaxed and her profile outlined in rosy light, she looked like a painting, a post-

Renaissance Madonna. She had a firm chin and a nice, unapologetic nose. He could picture her as a young mother, so serious and conscientious. Overprotective, without a doubt.

If he'd had the chance to know his own son for seventeen years, he suspected the loss would have been seventeen times worse. No wonder she was hanging on so fiercely.

*Nathan, old buddy, they gave your heart to a self-pitying asshole. But I'll do what I can to repay your mom.*

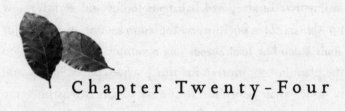

# Chapter Twenty-Four

In her high-heeled boots, Lindsey Sanchez carefully navigated the glazed sidewalk around Francis Quadrangle on the MU campus. A preview of winter had arrived that week in Columbia, with three days of biting north wind. Icy pellets drove students across campus, their coat collars turned up, faces obscured like bank robbers in black-and-gold mufflers. But tonight, on her way to a preholiday party sponsored by the Ad Club for the whole J-school, the wind was still, the stars cold and bright.

After Thanksgiving came finals, when no campus events were allowed, and after that students scattered quickly, going home for the holiday break or off on ski trips. Lindsey would load Christmas presents for her family into her road-weary Hyundai and start the fourteen-hour drive to San Antonio. She hadn't been home since summer and she was lonesome to see her mom. The little house in San Antonio would be strung with lights, and she and her mother would cook for days—homemade tamales, empanadas drizzled with chocolate, chili rellenos made with peppers her mother had bought in season and frozen for the Christmas feast.

But first Lindsey had five tests to ace and an interview for the editor's position of the *Latina*—one of her major goals since her first semester on campus. She was also on the planning committee for this J-school party. She would be more than ready for the break at Christmastime; the only thing she regretted was that she wouldn't see Cord Thayer for nearly a month, until she came back to campus in January.

Lindsey piled her coat and muffler on a table outside the double classroom that was already decorated for the party. She'd spent the afternoon setting up refreshment tables and helping the band string amp cables beneath a black tarp on the floor. Now the food committee was cheerfully at work, covering the red tablecloths with platters of cookies and cheese balls, bowls of chips and dips. Flying in the face of political correctness, they'd decided to go with a traditional Christmas theme.

Carly glanced up at her and waved. "Hey, Lindsey." Her arm was ringed with tiny bells.

"Hey, Carly. It's looking good."

Two of the three band members had arrived, wearing stereotypical busted-out jeans and longish hair. All three were music majors on campus. She'd heard the band before and liked their sound. Felix was tuning up his electric guitar and testing the mics. Lindsey waved to him and set to work help-ing Carly pile cheese cubes on a red plastic tray.

Most of the J-school faculty would put in an appearance at the party. She and Cord would say hello without too much eye contact, and she'd make a point not to show more interest in him than in the others. They would leave separately. Afterward, she would drive the four blocks to his apartment.

Students began to sift in, singly and in groups. The band tuned up a rock version of "Winter Wonderland." The song re-minded her of her last Christmas with Nathan; the whole hol-iday season had glittered with magic. But she wouldn't think about that tonight.

The first hour of any party was slow, this one even slower because they couldn't serve alcohol at a campus event. No lu-brication for the social interaction. But as the room grew more crowded and the band changed to contemporary hits, voices grew louder. Some of the students started to dance.

Laughter surrounded a bulletin board of inept headlines from real newspapers. *Many Antiques at DAR Meeting. Iraqi Head Seeks Arms.* Lindsey had got a couple of art students to draw a cartoon illustration for each one. The favorites were *Panda Mat-ing Fails; Veterinarian Takes Over* and *Clinton's Firmness Got Results.*

Two faculty sponsors came in and gave Lindsey a thumbs-up from across the room. She watched students chat up the profs in hopes of a better grade. In the postgraduate world, they would call it networking.

The band switched to "Blue Christmas," the drummer doing a darned good Elvis impression. Lindsey saw Darren Dillingham approaching, a crooked leer on his movie-perfect face. She braced herself.

"Hey, Linds. Whatzup?"

His breath smelled of beer. "Hi, Darren. I see this isn't your first party of the evening."

She tried to move away before he asked her to dance, but Darren moved with her.

"Goin' home for the holidays?" he said.

"Yeah. Right after finals."

"Thought maybe you were stayin' in town." He smirked. "You and Dr. Thayer."

Lindsey turned toward him and made her face completely blank. She affected a bored tone. "Is that some kind of innuendo, Darren?"

He shrugged. "If the foo shits, wear it."

"As usual, you don't know what the hell you're talking about."

She turned her back on him and headed toward a group who worked on the *Maneater* staff, where she knew Darren wouldn't follow. But her pulse was pounding. *Did Darren know? If he did, others did, too.*

Sara Lorquia touched her elbow. "I need to talk to you a minute," she said, her voice low. "It's about your interview."

Lindsey looked at Sara's dark eyes and saw something urgent there. "Sure. Let's head toward the ladies' room."

They didn't go in. Sara steered her to an empty conference room at the end of the hall and shut the door.

Twenty minutes later Lindsey stepped back into the noisy party room, but her mind was somewhere else. Her eyes scanned the room blindly until she saw Cord standing in a corner farthest from the band with several other faculty members. He glanced up and met her eyes. She smiled, her pulse lurching, then moved away in the opposite direction. She made sure the snack tables were replenished, the punch bowls and soda bin full. Finally she arrived at the knot of faculty members where Cord stood with a plastic cup of pink punch in his hand.

"Hi, everybody. Thanks for coming out tonight." Doing her hostess duties.

"Great job on the party, Lindsey," Ms. Masterson said. "That's a good band. Unlike last year." She rolled her eyes and the others laughed.

"I hear you're up for the editor's job at the *Latina,*" Dr. Savoy said. He was chairman of the J-school, teetering on the verge of retirement. "Good luck."

"Thanks." Lindsey smiled and showed crossed fingers. But she thought of Sara Lorquia, who was vacating the editor's job, and her stomach jittered. "See you later," she said, and moved away.

Around ten she saw Cord in her peripheral vision as he separated from the group and found his coat. At the doorway he glanced in her direction, inclined his head imperceptibly toward the exit. Her answer was a slow blink of her eyes.

The party broke up early, most of the students moving on to off-campus venues. Alcohol-free campus parties were just a prelude on a Friday night. It took Lindsey and her committee only twenty minutes to clean up and vacate the building.

When Cord didn't answer her tap on his apartment door, she turned her key in the lock and stepped inside. She started to call his name but the silence stopped her. She'd been here several times and the room looked just the same, except that the living room was dark, lit only by a trio of candles on the coffee table.

She hung up her coat and went into the kitchen, where a small light shone above the stovetop. He wasn't there. She walked down the hall to his bedroom.

Cord sat in a chair beside a low window that looked out on leafless trees silvered with ice. But he wasn't looking out; he was looking at her. He'd been waiting.

Something Latin was playing on the sound system. She stopped in the doorway, a silhouette against the faint light, and waited for her eyes to adjust so she could see his face.

"I miss you already," he said, and she wondered if he was talking about the holiday break, or something that would last much longer.

She leaned down and unzipped her boots, tossed them aside one at a time, and stood barefoot on plush carpet. She pulled the tail of her silk blouse loose from her skirt and waited for him to come to her.

His hands were warm in her cold hair, his mouth hungry. Sometimes, in her rigid dorm-room bed, the memory of his masculine scent roused her from a sound sleep. She felt his breathing accelerate, and she smiled. "Merry Christmas."

He held her head in both hands and looked into her flushed face. "You're going to ruin me. And I won't even care."

Afterward, as she lay beside him on his loopy waterbed listening to his soft dozing, she thought he could be right.

If her interview tomorrow went the way she thought it would, she might well be his ruin.

Mr. Villaverde's office was on the second floor of the administration building. Lindsey arrived five minutes early. He'd set the interview for Saturday morning, he said, so it wouldn't interfere with her classes or her work schedule at the *Missourian*.

The front door to the ad building was unlocked, but all the first-floor offices were dark. She climbed the stairs to the second floor.

Villaverde wasn't a professor; he didn't have the qualifications. His official position was Assistant to the Dean of Student Affairs, and he taught two sections of business communications. His father had been a vice president, his grandfather a dean. Villaverde family money had underwritten the *Latina* for three generations, and that entitled him to a spot on the review committee for the new editor.

A trapezoid of light angled from the partially open door of his office. Lindsey took off her coat and folded it carefully over her arm. Perspiration collected under the turtleneck of her sweater. She cleared her throat and rapped on the door.

"Mr. Villaverde?"

"Come in, come in, Lindsey!" His voice sounded jovial. She stepped inside, leaving the door ajar.

"You're right on time," he said. "I like that."

His smile revealed too much space between his teeth, as if they'd shrunk. That was the one thing she remembered about him from the only other time they'd met. Shark teeth.

"Have a seat, have a seat," he said.

She guessed him at late forties. He was beginning to bald, and he had the soft look of a man who seldom exercised. She sat on one end of the leather sofa that faced his desk and laid her coat on the seat beside her. Even across his desk she could smell his expensive cologne.

"You look lovely in that sweater," he said, beaming at her. "Do you like this cold weather?"

"I'm from San Antonio. I prefer the heat."

"Like the old movie, huh? Some like it hot!" He boomed a laugh.

She had no idea what he was talking about. She crossed her legs, smiled politely without answering.

He leaned his arms on the desk. "So. Tell me why you want to be editor of the *Latina*."

She took a breath, put on her interview smile. "I've admired the publication ever since I've been on campus. Sara's done a great job with it, and I'd like to continue the community focus she's developed."

"Ah, yes, Sara. That she has." His eyes traveled away for a moment, then returned. "I've looked at your résumé and it's excellent. You have high recommendations from the faculty. Especially Dr. Thayer."

"Thank you."

"But there are two other applicants. Did you know that?"

She blinked. "No. I didn't."

"They are also qualified. So the committee has a hard choice, you see."

"I understand."

"And it's my vote that will make the difference."

"Really."

He smiled, leaned back in the spring-loaded chair. "Quite so. Quite so." The chair squeaked. "Unfortunately, it's come to my attention that you have an...inappropriate involvement with a faculty member." Now the smile was gone.

Lindsey's face flashed hot. "What do you mean?"

The shark smile again, his eyes hard. "Let's don't play games, Lindsey. You're having an affair with Cordell Thayer."

She met his gaze directly, managed not to flinch. "My private life has nothing to do with my qualifications for this job."

He shrugged, but a slight smile showed he was pleased by her indirect admission. "Maybe not. But it does compromise your integrity. And as for Dr. Thayer, if this gets out, it threatens not only his tenure, but his continued employment with the university. Surely you know that."

"No," she lied. "I didn't realize."

"Yes, yes. It puts you both in a precarious, em, *position*. But I suppose you've been there before." He leered, to be sure she got the implication.

Lindsey's hands clenched and unclenched on her lap. "So you're going to veto me for the editor's job."

"I didn't say that. I happen to be on your side. I think you're *absolutely* the best qualified to lead the *Latina* in the direction we want it to go. You're very bright, and you've shown excellent leadership. A wonderful example for our Hispanic underclasswomen." He cleared his throat. "Except for this one thing.

Thank goodness, I'm the only one on the review board who knows about that."

She waited. "Okay," she said slowly. "What do you recommend?"

"Well, it seems to me we're in a position to do each other a favor here. You're an attractive young woman, Lindsey. And one of my hobbies is photographing beautiful young women."

"Is that right. Clothed or unclothed?" She let him hear the sarcasm.

He smiled. "Let's just say that choice is up to me. The photos are quite artistic, and of course, for my own enjoyment only." He opened a desk drawer and removed what looked like a photo album. "Now I know you're a close friend of Sara's, and that you wouldn't do anything to hurt her. Would you like to see the photo she posed for?"

"No."

"Are you sure? It's quite beautiful. And of course I gave all the negatives to Sara. It's a onetime favor, no strings. No harm, no foul."

He placed the album on the edge of the desk in front of her and flipped open the cover. And there was Sara Lorquia, her eyes full of shame.

Lindsey tried to remove her gaze but could not. She imagined what lay on the pages behind Sara's photo in the book.

"It turns out this wasn't the first photo of this kind Sara had made," he said, "and she didn't want anyone to know that. Luckily, her secret is safe with me." His voice became low, confidential. "I'm very good at keeping secrets, Lindsey. I certainly can't tell anyone about my photos, or I'd lose my job. And next year, you'll graduate and go on with your life and never see me again."

She reached out and flipped the album shut. "How many years have you been blackmailing students like me?"

"Blackmail? Did I ask you for money? This is a favor, strictly voluntary. And in return, you'll have that editor's job you want so much. And Dr. Thayer will still have his...position."

She fixed him with a level gaze. "You slimy germ. I'll bet you kept a set of negatives for everything in your little photo album."

He laughed. "Not very trusting, are you, Lindsey? Smart girl. Of course I gave up all the negatives. But if you're worried about that, I could give you one other choice."

"Which is?"

He came around the desk and stood behind the sofa. Placed his hands on her shoulders where her muscles were tense as guy wires. His coffee-stained breath hissed warm against her cheek.

"I'll lock the door. It'll be over in twenty minutes and never mentioned again. You and Cord Thayer will be home free."

The door banged open behind them. The ebony face of Newt Bradley, the campus cop, scowled in disgust. "That's more than I can say for you, Villaverde."

"What the hell are you doing in my office?" he shrieked. "I'll have your job for this!"

"You okay, Lindsey?" Newt said.

She stood and picked up her coat with shaking hands. "Yeah. I'm okay." From her coat pocket she removed the mini cassette recorder and extracted the tape, handed it to Newt. "I hope the mic picked up everything."

"I heard most of it, anyway."

She took the photo album from the desk and tucked it under her arm. "I need to destroy these. I don't want them used as evidence."

Newt frowned, thinking it over. "Go ahead. With the tape and what I heard, we don't need those to charge him."

"Charge me? With what?" Villaverde demanded. "Those photographs were voluntary. I haven't done anything illegal."

"We'll see," Newt said. "The dean may feel otherwise."

Villaverde lifted his chin and Lindsey saw the flicker of victory in his eyes. "Go ahead and tell him. See who he believes."

"*Madre de Dios,*" Lindsey said. "The dean already knows. Are you blackmailing him, too? Or does he get copies of the pictures?"

She told Cord everything—right after she posted the story. They were sitting in the late-afternoon sunshine at a coffee shop inside a chain bookstore.

"I didn't use your name," she told him, "but somebody will. If Darren knew and Villaverde knew, there's no way to keep it secret."

Cord's face looked stung, defeated. *This is the end of it,* she thought. *I've lost him.*

"I'm sorry," she said. "But the lousy SOB had to be stopped. And somebody will write up the story—it might just as well be me."

In this light, his eyes looked more blue than gray. He looked out the smeared glass toward the parking lot without speaking. Red and green tinsel dangled from the lampposts, swaying in the wind. Early Christmas shoppers flocked toward the store.

"Cord? Just say it. Tell me what you're thinking."

"I'm thinking—" he stopped for a sip of cappuccino, not looking at her "—that maybe I'll resign before they fire me." He shrugged. "I could go back to newspaper work. Pay's lousy either way."

The story broke two days later in the *Maneater* and the *Columbia Missourian,* and was picked up by the wire services. Lindsey's byline hit forty university newspapers and twelve of the majors, including the *Kansas City Star.* The *Star*'s city editor phoned her at the *Missourian* office and complimented her investigative reporting.

"Come see me when you graduate," the woman said.

Lindsey took down the editor's name and number. "I have one more year," Lindsey said. "But do you have any openings now? I have a friend with experience on the *Washington Post,* and he might need a job."

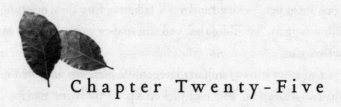

# Chapter Twenty-Five

Claire stayed at the hospital the first night, dozing in the unforgiving recliner beside Mason's bed. The doctor checked him the next morning before she'd even had coffee, and later a tech in green scrubs came with a cart and ushered him downstairs for his heart biopsy. Claire followed them through the busy hallways, sat in another waiting room until they brought him out again. The doctor wanted to keep an eye on him another night, maybe two.

That afternoon Claire drove home. She stood in the shower for twenty minutes, dried her hair, then called Tommy to let him know Mason was ill and wouldn't be at work the next day. Tommy was sympathetic, and said Wednesday nights at the bar were slow anyway.

Claire slept like a monolith in the sagging comfort of her apartment bed and drove back to Albuquerque Wednesday morning. Mason's face was still puffy, but his eyes looked clear and he seemed in good spirits.

"How are *you* feeling this morning?" he asked. "Get some sleep?"

The doctor dismissed him to go home that afternoon. In the car, Mason was relaxed and more talkative than she'd ever seen him, with little trace of the cynicism she'd come to expect. He remarked on the intense color of the sky and told a story about jackrabbits on his grandfather's ranch outside of Dallas. "Mom had to sell the ranch, finally, and we both regretted that."

Claire smiled. "Somehow I can't see you living on a Texas ranch miles from civilization."

"I didn't say I wanted to *live* out there—just keep it in the family." Then he laughed, and she realized she'd rarely heard him laugh before.

His refrigerator was empty, so she brought up a healthy lunch from her own kitchen and then left him alone to rest. That evening, sitting at her kitchen table to go over the agency reports Janelle had e-mailed her, she heard his violin. Not the heavy dirges of before, but *allegretto* passages that rippled down through the ceiling like a waterfall. She listened, both puzzled and pleased. Perhaps the letter from Julia's mother had released him from the burden of false hope.

Mason began to play his violin every day. Most of the apartment residents were at work in the afternoons, but Claire wondered if the ones who were home would complain about the music. Instead, he became a novelty and a mystery to his neighbors. In the laundry room, Claire overheard two women talking about the violin player upstairs; rumors floated around him. The sound of strings became as indigenous to the complex as piñon smoke on a desert evening.

He logged his blood pressure and pulse rate every day, even when she didn't remind him. His energy level increased. The next week when she drove him to the heart center for his biopsy, she was antsy and worried, but Mason seemed relaxed.

"After you've been through it a dozen times, it sort of gets to be routine. Besides, they have me on antidepressants," he said, and grinned.

Claire shuddered. "I'm sorry, but the idea of taking little chunks out of your heart gives me the willies." She realized she'd said *your heart* and not *Nathan's heart*.

The procedure went smoothly and they sent him home the same day.

Frown lines melted from Mason's forehead. At Santero's, the cynical twist disappeared from his smile, and classical pieces showed up more often in his piano repertoire. This perplexed Tommy, but Mason had become a sort of folk hero to the bartender, and he held his peace. Until Claire told him, Tommy hadn't known about Mason's transplanted heart.

On evenings he didn't work, Mason sometimes played his violin on the sundeck behind the apartments, facing the mountains. Oval notes echoed like bells above the crisp brown ghosts of asters in the deserted courtyard. With her fleece jacket wrapped around her, Claire would lie back in a deck chair and listen, drifting like the hawk that etched spirals on the evening sky.

They carried a picnic lunch to the park one warm afternoon. Near the pond where she'd first felt his heartbeat, they ate hero sandwiches and laughed about their childhoods in Texas. They talked about their parents, about Nathan and a little about Julia. But they never mentioned the night Claire had stayed in his bed.

For Claire, the memory vibrated like a note that couldn't be unplayed. When she was cooking or walking or shopping, she tried to name what had happened that night. But she couldn't pigeonhole the amalgam of unsettling emotions. *What if he had wanted sex? What would I have done?*

Gradually her uneasiness faded—except for the night she dreamed that Mason and her son were one and the same. That night she awoke sweating, a sick feeling in her stomach.

On the calendar on her kitchen wall, she marked off fifteen days since her last visit from Nathan. Each day he didn't appear she felt stronger. Each day he didn't appear she regretted the loss. Sometimes a wave of melancholy left her holding her breath, waiting for him to materialize. Were his visits nothing more than hallucination?

On her weekly pilgrimages to Canyon Road, Claire had come to love the watercolor paintings of high-desert land-scapes. Now the galleries were hosting shows for their premier artists, and she promised herself an original when she found the right one. The day she found it, she stowed the wrapped parcel behind the car seat with a giddy feeling of self-indulgence. She couldn't wait to show Mason. With his artist's eye, he would love the painting, too. That day on her way home she stopped by the office of the Santa Fe Symphony.

Half a dozen tenants stood in the parking lot of the City Suites when she returned, their faces turned up toward the second floor. She hit her brakes. *My God, is the building on fire?* She parked hurriedly on the row nearest the street and switched off the motor. Then she heard it—violin music ringing through the crisp, autumn air.

Claire stepped out of her car and looked up toward the sound. Mason stood by the railing, barefoot, his curly hair uncombed, sawing away like a fiddler on the roof.

A childlike grin lit his face. He finished the song with a flourish and his small audience cheered. Mason responded with a formal bow and waved to her.

Claire jogged up the stairs to his flat carrying an audition application for the Santa Fe Symphony. It was time.

Candidates for the symphony were provided an audition list, material they would be expected to play to demonstrate "technical expertise and prowess," the director had told her. At the appointed time, all candidates must show up and draw a number. Auditions took place behind a screen, so that the committee couldn't see or recognize the candidates.

"No danger of that in my case," Mason said. "But it's supposed to keep politics out of the process."

She was in his apartment, watching him put new strings on his violin. He had picked up the orchestral scores yesterday. "Who's on the committee?" she asked.

"The conductor, and five musicians who remain anonymous. After the preliminary round, two or three final candidates play again. Only one is invited to play with the symphony, for two performances. That's part of the process, too. To determine how the new musician fits into the 'corporate and musical culture' of the group."

Claire raised her eyebrows. "Sounds kind of political to me."

"Social politics, I guess." He shrugged. "There's always a social element among the musicians. They have to be able to work together."

Claire thought about the crushed hopes of the musicians not chosen at the audition, all of them rejected but one. She hadn't fully realized the risk he was taking. Second thoughts roiled her stomach.

"It's a fairly standard process, except for the two performances before a contract is offered." Mason tightened a string with the wooden peg, plucked it several times and moved on to the next. "The Santa Fe group is a cooperative, so the musicians have more say in who plays. If the two performances are successful, the new guy will be offered a probationary contract. And that might or might not result in an offer of a tenured contract at the end of the season."

"Wow. That's intense."

"This is the formal process. I've never gone through it quite like this before."

"Not in Austin?"

He turned another peg until the string was right. "Sometimes you're lucky enough to fill in for a member who's on leave of absence. If you fit in well, the orchestra committee can vote to invite you on a permanent basis. With the consent of the conductor." He looked up at her, his forehead creased. "That's how I came aboard in Austin."

"Do you know how many others are auditioning?"

"Not a clue."

With the last string in place, he bowed and tuned the instrument. She watched the sure, swift movement of his hands.

He looked at her expression and stopped the bow. "Quit worrying. If I don't make it, I won't jump off the roof of the Lensic Center. I can always try again."

She smiled. "I know you'll do well." But she worried anyway.

The day of his audition, she offered to go along but he shook his head. "If I'm terrible, I don't want you to hear it."

So she lent him her car and wished him luck. Her stomach was a beehive as she watched him load Serena onto the backseat and drive away. She stood in the parking lot, waving him off like a mother sending her child to the first day of school.

Chores. That was the ticket—just the thing to keep her from fidgeting.

She washed the windows in her apartment inside and out, which she was pretty sure had never been done in the history of the building. Finished with that task, she washed the windows in Mason's apartment. She did a load of laundry, baked a lasagna, answered her e-mail. After three hours she'd run out of chores and spent the next hour pacing by the front window.

How could it take so long? He was out of the habit of driving; could he have had an accident in the short distance to the concert hall? Maybe he'd chickened out and was sitting right now with the street people in the grassy Plaza, afraid to come home.

Perhaps the audition had gone badly and he'd driven off to Taos again—this time in her car.

Finally she saw the Lexus turn into the parking lot. She ran outdoors, slowing to a walk before she reached the car. Her fingernails dug into her palms.

He climbed out with Serena's curved case under one arm and a bouquet of flowers in the other. His face looked like a sunrise.

She sucked in her breath. "Tell me everything."

He plopped the flowers into her hands and gave her a quick, loud kiss. His voice shook. "I got the chair."

"Wahoo!"

"Still on probation, of course."

The violin case poked her ribs when she hugged him. A neighbor carrying laundry looked down at them from the upstairs walkway and Claire gave her a thumbs-up. The woman smiled.

She led him toward her apartment, her feet as giddy as if she'd crossed a high bridge without disaster.

"Lucky for me, there were only three other violinists," he said.

"Phooey. Luck has nothing to do with it. When do you start rehearsals?"

"Next week. The chair is in the violin two section, which I haven't played before, so that'll be a challenge. I brought home the scores to practice."

He sat on the edge of her kitchen table while she filled a tumbler with water for the flowers. "My first concert is a week from Sunday." He was still smiling as if he couldn't quite believe it.

"Wow. That's fast."

"That's the way it is with symphonies. Musicians at this level are expected to know the scores when they show up. We'll rehearse together only four or five sessions the week before the performance. They rehearse in the afternoon, so I can keep the gig at Santero's, just find somebody to cover Sunday night once a month."

She made a face.

"Nobody can live on symphony pay alone," he reminded.

She set the flowers on the table and faced him. "We should celebrate."

They drove a long, winding road up the Santa Fe Mountains. The slopes rippled with aspen gold and the peaks beyond were laced with white. At a snow line turnout that overlooked a high valley, they set out a tailgate picnic of champagne and lasagna and French bread. Claire shivered in her puffy coat.

The champagne cork sailed over the railing and disappeared down the mountainside. They toasted with plastic cups held in gloved hands.

"Here's to the healing powers of music," Claire said.

He met her eyes. "Here's to *you*."

# Chapter Twenty-Six

Claire was probably overdressed for the symphony, and she didn't care. She'd bought a classic black dress, a feather-soft shawl woven with turquoise and silver accents, and a pair of impractical, strappy heels. The mission she had staked out on her first week in Santa Fe was about to be accomplished. She felt like a CEO who'd saved a corporation from bankruptcy, a Coast Guard seaman who'd pulled a drowning man from the sea.

*Aren't you full of yourself.* She made a face at her gloating reflection while she fastened on silver earrings, brushed her hair and misted it in place. Was it her imagination, or did that face look a lot healthier than it had a month ago? The longer hair felt good against her neck. When she went back to work, though, it would have to go. Long hair was too high maintenance.

The phone rang and she scooped it up, smiling. "Can't get the bow tie right, can you?"

"Good guess," Mason said. "Can you help?"

She'd gone with him to rent the tailless tux that was a requirement for symphony players. The bow tie was mandatory, too, and the sales associate had shown them how to tie it. But it was easier from the outside than in.

"Come on down," she said. "I'm almost ready."

The concert was to start at four, but the musicians assembled an hour early. They entered the Lensic Center through the artists' entrance off the alley. Mason led her through the dark backstage area, where technicians buzzed with activity and power cords snaked across the black-painted floor. When Mason held her elbow so she didn't catch a heel, his hand felt clammy.

At a draped archway that led into the grand hall, he turned her loose. "I'll meet you in the lobby afterward."

She could tell that his mind was already on his music. "Break a leg, or whatever musicians say."

He gave her a distracted smile and disappeared backstage.

The empty concert hall lay suspended in a cathedral-like hush. Claire walked up the aisle toward the lobby, her steps silent on padded carpet. Ushers weren't on duty yet, but a lady at the ticket window gave her a program. Claire returned to the hall and found her seat in the fifth row center. From here she would see the expression on every face, the color of the maestro's socks.

A few other patrons drifted in, probably family of the musicians. They found seats among the empty rows. A small group gathered at one side of the hall for the preconcert talk. Claire thought of joining them, but she was too fidgety. Instead she opened her program and read about the afternoon's performance—"From Russia with Love," featuring selections by Gluck, Tchaikovsky, Ravel and Stravinsky.

The hall gradually filled and musicians came onto the stage a few at a time, Mason among them. She shifted in her seat to see his face. He looked serious, focused on his warm-up. If he was as nervous as she was, it didn't show.

The string players tuned their instruments and played a few passages, each doing his own thing, a pleasant cacophony. Then the concertmaster entered and the musicians came to attention. Their anticipation stilled the audience. The magic Mason had described to her was about to happen—she almost could feel it herself. The conductor entered, took his bows and briefly welcomed the audience. Then he turned to the musicians and raised his baton.

The first dramatic notes struck her breathless. Her eyes blurred, just the way they used to when she watched Nathan in his school programs. *Okay, Mason, show them how terrific you are.*

The music swelled and ebbed, pulling her in, casting her up on waves of sound. She strained to hear one particular violin, which of course was impossible.

At intermission she stayed in her seat, too expended to move. She fanned her face with the program. *God, that was almost like sex. As best I remember.*

The program ended with Stravinsky's *Firebird Suite,* and the audience stood to applaud. Claire clapped until her hands hurt and her face ached from smiling. Afterward, she filed out and stood among the milling crowd in the lobby, expectantly watching the faces that passed by as if someone might stop to congratulate her. *Good grief. I'm acting like a stage mother.*

At last Mason appeared, looking wasted and happy, and carrying Serena in her black case. She hugged him and whispered, "You were fantastic."

He grinned. "I bet you say that to all the guys."

A distinguished-looking man approached them and Claire recognized the concertmaster. "Well done," he said to Mason, pumping his hand. His smile was genuine.

Mason straightened his shoulders and introduced her to Jacob Jordan. Jordan had silver hair and friendly lines around his eyes, like somebody's grandfather. He gave a small bow when he took Claire's hand.

"Some of us are going for drinks and dinner at Geronimo's," he said. "We'd love to have you both join us."

"Thank you," Mason said. "I appreciate that very much, but we've already made plans." Claire glanced at him, careful to keep her face neutral.

"Perhaps next time," the master said.

"We'll count on it. And Jacob, thanks for your help and encouragement."

When he'd walked away, Claire raised her eyebrows. "What about fitting into the 'corporate and musical culture'?"

"I'm not ready to be social at that level tonight," he said, and she could read the tension around his eyes. "I'd rather get out of the monkey suit and have a quiet dinner. In fact, I made us a reservation."

The Hideaway sat in the vee of a narrow canyon a few miles out of town. It was a place of white tablecloths and fresh flowers, with original art displayed on mottled, adobe walls. A charming *placita,* lighted by flickering *chimeneas,* offered outdoor seating in warmer weather, but tonight they sat indoors in an alcove to themselves. Mason had changed into slacks and a jacket, but she still wore her black dress.

Claire gave him a look as they took their seats. "This place seems awfully romantic."

"So what's wrong with that?"

The waiter—"my name's Raoul"—lit candles and recommended the roast duck with a special Merlot. Who were they to disagree? Claire felt fuzzy even before the wine arrived.

Mason sat back and took a deep breath. "Red wine is good for the heart," he quoted, and lifted his glass.

"Seeing you in your monkey suit in the middle of that wonderful orchestra is good for *my* heart."

"If it weren't for you, I never would have played violin again."

She wrinkled her nose. "Sure you would, eventually."

"No." He shook his head. "I was working on dying, the slow and gutless way." His eyes deepened. "Whatever time I have left, you've given it back to me."

Claire swallowed hard. She had a vision of placing her palm against his cheek and feeling the vibration of violins in his jawbone. She put both hands in her lap. "This conversation is getting way too serious. Let's talk about the concert." She leaned forward conspiratorially. "Did you see that bassoonist's hair? I mean, what was she *thinking?*"

He smiled, but his eyes didn't change. "I *want* to talk seriously."

"Bummer. Then you'd better pour me some more wine."

He obliged, but she noticed he was nursing his first glass. *Taking care of himself. He's going to be all right.*

"The night you stayed with me—not at the hospital, at my place—I told you I couldn't make love. I talked to the doctor about that, and he adjusted my drugs. And gave me another one, for special occasions." He looked at her hopefully.

"Mason—"

"I'm not propositioning you," he said quickly. "I just wanted you to know. In case… In case it might make a difference."

Did it? She didn't know.

"Claire, I know you've been trying to refuse what's happening with us, but I think we could fall in love."

Fall in love, she thought. Did people still say things like that?

She met his earnest eyes and felt a different kind of falling. "God, have I tried to refuse it. I don't think I could handle that."

"Why not? Isn't love a good thing?"

"Not for us. Not the kind of love that comes with sex. You know why."

He took his time answering. "Because I'd never know if you loved me, or just my heart. And you wouldn't know, either."

She swallowed a mass in her throat. "I can't separate them. How could I make love to you knowing it's my son's heart I felt against me? That just seems *wrong.*"

"It isn't wrong." He paused, softening his words. "It's my heart now, Claire. It used to be Nathan's, but now it's mine. It's an organ, not a person."

"I know. I know that *in my head*. But what we know doesn't always govern what we feel."

He nodded. "I agree. And I feel that I've found a soul mate, somebody who's made me human again. I don't want to lose that."

"Why do we have to? There are lots of ways to love somebody."

"Like brotherly love?" He huffed a sigh.

She scowled. "My ex-husband and I used to argue about this back when guys still tried to hit on me. He insisted it was not possible for a woman and man to be close friends. That for a man, sex always entered into it. If he really liked the woman, he was bound to want sex. Do you agree with that?"

"Is this a trick question?"

"Just answer it."

"I don't agree with the *always*."

"Thank you."

"Of course it's possible for people to love each other without sex," he conceded, and shrugged. "Lots of married couples do it."

Claire laughed. "Like everybody's parents, we all hope."

"But I know what your ex meant. Sex can be an incredible experience, not to mention a lot of fun. We're not old. Is non-physical love enough?"

With dubious timing, the waiter appeared bearing duck. Claire was saved, at least temporarily, from a question she couldn't answer.

My-name's-Raoul fired the glaze at tableside and served the portions with grand flourish. When he'd gone, they looked at their plates and then each other. Claire's eyes felt as glazed as the duck.

"All that sex talk made me hungry," Mason said. "Let's eat."

The duck was juicy and fragrant and only a tiny bit gamy. They ate like Romans.

"You're driving," she told him, and finished the Merlot. Mason ordered coffee.

On the ride home, Claire's head felt misty, only partly from wine. Mason didn't repeat his question, and for a long while they didn't talk at all. The motion of the car soothed her, and she was almost asleep when a new question came at her out of the dark.

"You told me you were estranged from your father but at the time you wouldn't say why. So now I'm asking."

She rolled her head toward him on the seat back and said something she'd never said aloud to anyone. "Because I let my little brother drown."

Mason pulled the car off on the shoulder and stopped, letting the engine idle. He put the gearshift in park and turned toward her. "Tell me."

"I don't remember it, really. Just my parents' shock afterward. I was four, and Todd was two. I think I was supposed to be watching him."

"And your father blamed you for it?"

She shrugged. "He left us about a year later. What else would a child think?"

"Claire." He touched her face. "Nathan's death was not your fault. And neither was your little brother's. You need to talk to your father."

He put the Lexus in gear and drove home.

In the apartment parking lot, Mason waited until she'd found her house key in the tiny purse. She assured him she was sober enough to use it, and he ascended the stairs while she walked to her door alone. A full moon floated overhead, casting amorphous shadows across her path.

Another dark shadow clotted in the green plastic chair that sat on the sidewalk close to her door. When she approached, the shadow gathered itself and stood up.

She lurched backward in her unstable shoes, the key poised in her hand like a weapon.

A familiar figure stood just beyond the reach of the sentinel light. "Don't be afraid. It's just me," Nathan said.

# Chapter Twenty-Seven

Claire's heartbeat stuttered. "I thought you'd gone away forever." Her voice sounded hoarse in the darkness.

The tall figure stepped out of the shadows. Moonlight angled across his face. "What do you mean? I've been trying to see you for a long time," Win said.

"Oh my God. It's *you*." Her knees wilted. She dropped into the chair her ex-husband had just vacated. In the milky light, the resemblance between father and son was incredible.

"Claire? Are you okay?"

"I thought you were Nathan."

He winced. "*Jesus.* I'm sorry. I did try to call first—I left two messages on your cell."

"I didn't take it with me tonight." She held her head in both hands, her temples pounding. "What are you doing here?"

Win crouched beside her chair and touched her arm. She

could smell his cologne, something subtle and expensive. Even in high school he'd always smelled rich. "Let's go in off the sidewalk, can we?" he said.

He offered a hand to help her up. He took her key and unlocked, returned the key and opened the door.

She stepped in ahead of him. "I'll be back in a minute."

She headed to the bedroom and closed the door. Her insides felt like negative space. She tossed the shawl on her bed and slipped off the high-heeled shoes. In the bathroom, she pressed a cold washcloth to her temples.

When she came back to the living room, Win was still standing, a worried look in the too-familiar eyes. Once again she was surprised by the resemblance. She hadn't seen Win in a long time. He looked as if he'd lost some weight; maybe that made him look younger.

She cleared her throat. "Why don't you sit. And tell me what you're doing in Santa Fe."

He folded himself onto the low sofa, sinking almost to the floor. She took the lone chair. He propped his hands on his knees and looked at her.

"I came to see you."

She frowned. "I told you I'd need some time to think about the funds your dad set up for Nathan."

He didn't seem to hear her. He was looking at her hair, the slim black dress. "You look—" he searched for a word "—terrific. You must have gone someplace special tonight."

"Yes. I did." He waited but she didn't volunteer more.

"Are you seeing someone?" he asked.

"Not exactly."

"Not exactly," he repeated. "I don't know what that means."

"It means that it isn't your business. And I don't appreciate your showing up here unannounced and scaring me like that."

"I'm sorry I startled you." He sighed, spread his hands. "But I said that already."

She looked at his anxious face, his knees poking up from the sofa like grasshopper legs. Except for the slacks and sport coat, he looked more like an awkward teenager than a business tycoon. Or an ex-husband.

She huffed a breath. "Well, since you're here, shall I make us some decaf?"

"That sounds good." He smiled, his face relieved. "I guess we are hitting the decaf age, aren't we?"

Her insomnia had nothing to do with age, but the point wasn't worth disputing. She trudged to the kitchen alcove and rummaged in the cabinets for coffee and filters. When she turned to draw water in the glass carafe, Win had appeared by the refrigerator and she nearly bumped into him.

"Damn! I'm going to tie a bell on your neck."

"Sorry again." His smile melted away. "About what happened before. Do you…sometimes think you see Nathan?"

She poured water into the top of the coffeemaker and switched it on before turning to face him. The drawer handles poked into the small of her back, a hard comfort.

"I don't *think* I see him. I *do* see him."

Win's face contracted as if the idea hurt him. Either that or he thought she was insane. Something mean rose up in her; she wanted to appall him with the truth. "He's quite real," she said. "We talk sometimes." She waited for Win to ask if she'd gotten professional help. She tried to imagine his face if she told him Dr. Reuben's perverted suspicion.

But Win surprised her again. "What do you talk about?

Looking at him, she realized something that had never occurred to her. Win was lonely. The urge to shock him drained away.

"Mostly we talk about trivial things," she said. "He won't talk about anything important, even when I ask. Just like you used to do."

"This has been happening ever since he died?"

"Yes. But not lately."

He searched her face. "Why didn't you tell me?"

She stared at him, incredulous. "Why in the world would I tell you? We rarely spoke to each other for seventeen years. It's not as if we were friends."

"We were married once. That's a lot more than friends."

"I disagree. We are divorced, and that's a lot *less* than friends." The coffeepot gurgled in the silence.

Win looked down at the polished toes of his shoes. "It doesn't have to be. If you had told me, I would have understood."

A thought sent her pulse lurching. She waited it out. "Have you seen him, too?"

He hesitated. "No. I wish I could say I had."

In that moment she realized she didn't know this older Win at all. She was certainly a different person from when they'd been newlyweds; had she thought he would stay the same?

Her voice lost its edge. "You haven't coped very well, either, have you?" And he had no one to talk to about his son. That's why he kept calling her.

"I was just getting to know him," Win said, "realizing what a great kid he was. And what I'd missed by being such a bastard when I was young."

He looked at her with Nathan's coffee-brown eyes. "Claire, I'm sorry I left you when you got pregnant. And for abandoning my son. I've regretted it a hundred times."

Claire frowned. Old resentments died hard. "Is this part of a twelve-step program?"

"No," he said, unoffended. "It's just something I've thought for a long time that I should tell you."

She believed he meant it. At least today.

"Okay," she said. "For what it's worth, I accept the apology. But that won't change the years you didn't see your son grow up."

She turned away feeling rotten and set two mugs down from a cupboard. She poured them full. "Still take it black?"

"Yes. I can't believe you remember that."

She handed him the mug. "I remember a lot of things."

They sat down with the kitchen table between them. She leaned on her elbows and looked at him. "Now what?"

"I brought the portfolio for you to look over. I would value your opinion."

"Okay, but you could have sent those by FedEx. What else?"

He looked at his coffee cup, and finally at her, then pulled a deep breath. "When Dad died I took a close look at my life—actually I've been doing that for some time now. It seems pretty hollow. Since my second marriage broke up, I've done nothing but work."

*The same thing I did after Nathan died.* The coffee tasted like metal; she hated decaf.

"Now I have control of the whole company," he said, "and I find it's a poor substitute for a family. For having someone who cares whether I come home at night."

*What about your controlling mother?* She washed down the thought with more bad coffee.

"I don't blame you for being skeptical," he said. "Look, young love's a onetime thing—that would have worn off even if I'd hung around. But I still care about you, and I'm not the same guy who ran out on you twenty years ago. I'd like to be part of your life again, if you'll let me."

She shifted in her chair without meeting his eyes.

"Your turn," he said.

"What do you want me to say? That I think we have a future together? I really can't see that."

"Can you see us spending time together? Just seeing what happens?"

"I don't know." She shook her head. "You think that would work because we have history. But for me, that history has more bad memories than good."

He turned his coffee cup in both hands. "Except for Nathan. And that time in our lives when we created him."

"Yes. I haven't forgotten that part."

Nor had she forgotten the man one floor above them. She heard Mason's footsteps crossing from his bedroom to the bath, water running through the pipes as he got ready for bed. What if she told Win the man with Nathan's heart lived right upstairs, a man with a poet's soul and magical hands? Would Win insist on meeting him? The idea disturbed her; she couldn't even picture them in the same frame.

A realization bloomed in her mind: *I am shutting them both out. What am I afraid of?*

Her eyes focused on the kitchen clock. It was midnight, and she needed to be alone. "I'm too tired to think, Win. If you'll leave the papers you want me to see, I'll call you to talk it over. I promise."

He nodded and pushed his chair back from the table. "All right." He took a brown envelope from his jacket pocket and handed it to her. "That's a summary of the stocks and their current values."

They said good-night at the door. Win disappeared into the shadows of the parking lot and she stood for a moment watching him go. He must have wondered why in the world she was living in this place. But to his credit, he hadn't asked. She locked the door and headed for bed, leaving their two cups of cold coffee on the table.

Despite a fatigue that was mental as well as physical, Claire couldn't sleep. She changed positions, pounded the limp pillows. The sheet crawled under her skin like ants and her calf muscles twitched. Finally she gave it up. She rose and slipped into her gray sweats, her comfort suit. Above her head, Mason's apartment was quiet. She hoped he was sleeping well.

She rinsed the coffee cups, filled hers with hot tea and honey, then slipped on a jacket and sneakers and pocketed her apartment key.

The night air was sharp edged. She zipped her coat and pulled up the hood. She climbed the stairs and followed the walkway around the building to the deck.

No one was about at this hour. The moon hung small and bright above the mountains. She sat at a table closest to the building, out of the wind—the exact spot where she was sitting when she'd met Mason for the first time. Tonight the canvas umbrella was battened down for the winter, and there was no lightning in the hills. Everything was different from when she'd first come here.

Everything.

She cradled the warm cup in her hands and closed her eyes. A passage of music from Mason's concert played in her memory, and she pictured him among the musicians, rapt in his special world. It was a place she could not go. She was wildly proud for him, and a little sad. He didn't need her now that he had his music.

Maybe that was selfish, but she wasn't ashamed. In the beginning, she hadn't cared about him, only about Nathan's heart. Somewhere along the line, that had changed. Now Mason was reclaiming his life, and if she'd helped make that happen, it was the second-best thing she'd ever done.

She thought of the moment she'd seen Win in the dark, looking so much like Nathan it melted her bones. Could she ever look at Win without that reaction? She'd spent years hating him for deserting her, for not loving her enough. She'd hated him for the sacrifices she had to make, hated him most of all because her son grew up without a dad. But that was a long time ago. Maybe time absolved everyone of young mistakes, and all that remained was for us to forgive each other, and ourselves.

Claire opened her eyes and looked up at the bright, cold stars. She listened to the night sounds of Santa Fe and inhaled the scented air. She loved the haunting beauty of the mountains, the excitement of that first snow. She was going to miss this place.

One man had her son's face; another had his heart. If she was ever to let go of her lost son, she had to let go of all three.

# Chapter Twenty-Eight

The day the pastor came by Hob's little house on Banderos Street, Hob was watching an old John Wayne flick he'd seen half a dozen times before. The house was just big enough for Hob and his cat, Mealy. It had two bedrooms, one where he slept and one where he kept his collection of Louis L'Amour audiotapes. Mealy slept anywhere he wanted to.

Hob had bought the Louis L'Amour cassettes when he was on the road, pushing the big rig five and six hundred miles a day. The westerns helped keep him awake. There wasn't a L'Amour tape made that he didn't have. Now, with no tape player in his pickup truck, he didn't have any way to listen to them. They just sat there collecting dust. Sometimes he went in and looked them over, reading the titles and trying to remember what each one was about. He wished the tapes were books instead, so he could reread the stories in the evenings when there was nothing worth watching on TV. Even the pro wrestling he used to like had gone all show business and phony.

But occasionally he found an old western, like the one he had on TV that Saturday. The chase scene had just started, John Wayne riding hard to escape a band of desperados, when Mealy yowled. Mealy always knew when someone was at the door, even before the knock rattled the screen. A watch cat, that's what he was.

"Well, who is it, if you're so smart?" Hob said. But Mealy didn't answer.

From his chair Hob could see a man's head in the wagon-wheel window at the top of the wooden front door. The buzzard was tall, whoever he was. Hob guessed it was some kind of salesman, because he wasn't expecting a delivery and certainly not company. He muted the TV and cast a regretful look at it before he got up. The chase scene was always followed by the shoot-out. He hated to miss it, and he didn't have one of those video recorder machines. He got up thinking he would get rid of the stranger fast and get back to his movie.

The man at the door was dressed all in black, like the bad guy in the western except that he wasn't wearing a hat. The black getup seemed odd right off, but then Hob had a look at the fellow's eyes and he couldn't look away. Like magnets, they were, and shiny as marbles.

The man looked a hole right through Hob, and then he closed his eyes and tipped his head back as if he was facing heaven. "Brother," the man said, "I can tell you're troubled. You've wronged someone, or someone has wronged you, and you need redemption. The Lord has sent me here to forgive you, and to help you forgive yourself."

"Horseshit," Hob said.

The man smiled. "Of course you doubt me. Who wouldn't? You don't know me, and you think I don't know you. But I know you need the Lord, Hobson Jeeter. We all need the Lord. I can help you find Him, but only God can give you peace."

He stuck out his skinny white hand and passed a piece of paper through a hole where the screen had come untacked from its frame. "I'm Reverend Willard Sampson. Come to my church, Brother. Sunday morning at ten. I'll be watching for you, and so will the Lord."

Then the fellow stepped down off Hob's porch and walked away. Mealy yowled.

Hob watched to see if the reverend went to every house on the block, but he didn't. Apparently he'd only come to see Hob. He kept walking until Hob couldn't see where he'd gone. Hob took a piece of nicotine gum out of his shirt pocket and popped it into his mouth.

How did that preacher know his name? Was his guilt written in some almighty book that only a man of God could see?

Hob slammed the door and went back to John Wayne, but the shoot-out was over and he couldn't concentrate on the rest. He kept seeing the minister's wild eyes that seemed to know exactly what Hob had done, and how he was still guilty about it.

On Sunday morning, Hob put on his cleanest pants and a shirt that Wendy had bought him twenty years ago and he'd only worn once. Clutching the piece of paper the reverend had given him, he walked down the street three blocks, turned left, and walked two more. The little church building had always been there, but Hob had never paid much attention. Once he'd seen it was for sale, but now the sign was gone and the parking lot was half-full of cars, maybe a dozen in all.

Hob climbed two steps to the metal door. The building was one of those prefabs, with nary a window, but somebody had given it a fresh coat of white paint. Hob guessed the reverend had started up a new church of his own.

The inside was so dark he had to stop a minute to let his eyes adjust. Then he walked through a lobby the size of a coat closet and sat down at the back of a small sanctuary. Instead of benches, the church had rows of metal folding chairs, most of them empty. The rows that weren't empty were all at the front.

Hob hadn't darkened the door of a church since he was nine years old. His mom used to go, and she'd dragged the kids along until they got big enough to fight her on it. Hob's dad never went, so of course he'd tried to imitate his dad. Stupid mistake, but what do kids know.

Hob wondered what kind of church this one was. His mother was a Freewill Baptist, but this church didn't look like any Baptist church he'd ever seen. There wasn't a baptismal well at the front, for one thing. And for another, the cross up behind the altar had a statue of the crucified Christ on it. Baptist crosses were always empty, and Hob was more comfortable with that. The church didn't look Catholic, though, because there weren't any statues of saints nor any kneeling rails. It looked to him like this preacher fellow made up the rules as he went along.

Before Hob could get up and leave, the Reverend Sampson swept in through a side door and stepped onto the pulpit. He lifted his loose black sleeves above the congregation. "Blessed is he who comes in the name of the Lord. All those who seek Him shall be saved!"

"Amen!" the crowd chanted, and Hob was too entranced to leave.

The minister had a way about him, as if he truly understood the problems people floundered through their whole lives. The sermon was about guilt, and the awful things it could do to the soul, and how even when people deserved to feel guilty—and they always did—they could be relieved of their sins by confessing and asking God to forgive them. It wasn't too late for anybody, the reverend declared, no matter what they'd done. If they were truly sorry and did penance for their bad acts, God would absolve them and take them up to heaven.

It had never occurred to Hob that his soul might go to everlasting hell because of what he'd done—or hadn't done—that caused that boy's death. Listening to the reverend, he began to think on that. It made him more and more agitated. He put a ten-dollar bill in the collection plate when it came around, and after the service was over he hung around in the sanctuary until the others filed out. Some of them gave him a peculiar look, others a knowing smile as if they already forgave him. When he thought they'd all gone, he went outside and there was the reverend standing on the step.

"Ah, Hobson Jeeter," the reverend said, and smiled. "The Lord has moved you to come to my church. Welcome."

"Thank you, Reverend. I wonder if I could talk to you a few minutes."

"Of course you can, Brother. Let's go inside."

They sat in two folding chairs facing each other, their legs crossed in opposite directions.

"How did you know my name and where I lived?" Hob asked.

Reverend Sampson nodded, as if this question was expected. "I found your name in the neighborhood directory. But the minute I laid eyes on you, I saw you were troubled and needed to find the Lord. I have that gift, Brother. I can't explain it. Maybe it's because I was once like you, in need of salvation."

Hob thought about that for a minute, while he popped two pieces of nicotine gum into his mouth. Then he explained to the reverend that he'd done something wrong a long time ago and had been suffering for it ever since. The reverend threw his head back the way Hob had seen him do on his front porch the day before, only this time the reverend's face was filled with bliss, as if he'd just won the lottery.

After their talk, Hob walked home feeling uneasy. He went back the next Sunday to make sure he wasn't being suckered in, and that the reverend really did have a pipeline to God. This time Hob watched the other folks who attended the service, and he saw the same enraptured look on their faces that Reverend Sampson had. These folks had come onto something, he decided, and maybe he ought to pay attention. His mother had always said he was a heathen just like his daddy, and someday he'd repent. Maybe Momma was right. Hob could see that just like Peter in the Bible story the reverend told, he'd been denying the Lord.

That night Hob tried to pray. He'd never done it before, at least not making up his own words. He told God about the accident three years ago, that he hadn't meant to kill that boy but he'd run away like a yellow dog instead of owning up to what he'd done. Then he took a dose of baking soda in warm water for his upset stomach and went to bed. He tossed and turned and belched most of the night.

When God's voice came to him, it sounded just like the Reverend Sampson's inside Hob's head. The voice said that before he could ask forgiveness of God, he had to apologize to whomever he'd wronged.

# Chapter Twenty-Nine

In the laundry room at the apartment complex, Claire found two cardboard boxes left over from somebody else's move. Mason was still asleep when she packed the boxes with the things she'd acquired in Santa Fe: cookbooks and kitchen utensils, the prized painting, gifts for Irv and Janelle, a candle from the Chapel at Lo-retto. But she couldn't pack up so neatly her reluctance to leave Mason. Her nose kept running as she carried suitcases and boxes and slid them into the back of her car.

By noon she had loaded everything and swept the apartment. She turned in her keys to Mr. Bingham and climbed the metal stairway for the last time. Outside Mason's door, she could hear his TV playing. Her hand hesitated before knocking.

How many goodbyes were required of a person in one lifetime? She'd had more than her share. Maybe that's why, when she had to say goodbye to Nathan, she'd simply refused.

Taking a deep breath, she made a fist and rapped on the door.

He opened it, smiling. He had on the baggy jeans he always wore at home. "Look," he said, motioning her inside. "They sent flowers to welcome me to the orchestra."

A lavish autumn bouquet dwarfed the kitchen table. In contrast with the elegant flower arrangement, the table looked cheap and temporary. It reminded her of the table in her mother's kitchen when she was a little girl. Somehow that made her even sadder.

"They're beautiful," she said. Mason's hair was damp from the shower and she smelled the familiar scent of his aftershave.

"I felt silly when the guy delivered them," Mason said sheepishly. "Who sends flowers to a man?"

She smiled. "Lots of people. I wish I'd thought of it." And that made her think of the all-white bouquet that arrived unsigned on each anniversary of Nathan's accident. She'd never asked Mason—but he couldn't have sent them. When she'd shown up in Santa Fe, he didn't even recognize her name, let alone know where she lived.

He noticed her cotton slacks and comfortable shoes, the handbag on her shoulder. "Where are you going?"

She paused a few seconds while something inside her began to sink like snow into a canyon, slow and bottomless. "I'm going home."

"Home?" He looked confused, as if she were already home. She saw his eyes change the moment he understood. "You mean San Antonio?"

She nodded. "I've neglected my business, and imposed on my friends too long."

Lines etched his face. "I've scared you away."

"No. It's more complicated than that."

If she could have found words to explain her realization under the cold light of the stars, he might have understood. But her throat was too tight and she'd promised herself she wouldn't get maudlin. "I just have to go. Please don't make it harder."

He touched her cheek. "Poor Claire. You whipped me into shape but you forgot to save yourself."

"That's what I'm trying to do."

"I know. I don't agree with the way you're doing it, but I'm a lousy one to give advice."

He hugged her, and she hugged back. "Promise you'll take care of yourself," she said, hanging on.

"If I don't, will you come back and straighten me out again?"

"Absolutely."

"Then I'd rather be bad."

He turned her loose and wiped her tears with his fingers. "But I'll stay straight so you don't have to worry. And I will see you again."

"I hope so." She kissed both his palms, and was gone.

Speeding south toward Las Cruces, the cargo in the back of the Lexus rattling with the rhythm of the road, she thought of their discussion over dinner, and Mason's unanswered question. Is nonphysical love enough?

*Lots of married couples do it.* His voice in her head made her smile.

She loved him like a friend, but he was more than a friend. Like the brother she'd lost, but more than a brother. How would she describe the way she felt about him if he didn't have Nathan's heart? The desert horizon gave back no answer.

At Las Cruces she caught I-10 to El Paso, then hummed across West Texas for hours on end, no navigation required. Jackrabbits and diesel fumes, and her mind ranging out like the stunted mesquite from the roadside to the sky. At Fort Stockton she got a room for the night at a roadside Super-8. By 7:00 a.m. she was behind the wheel again, coffee in a paper cup, two doughnuts in a napkin. She was gathering momentum, drawn homeward by magnetic force. She was homesick for her house, for Janelle, for the business that had saved her life after Nathan was gone.

At midafternoon she pulled into her driveway. Her backside was travel weary, her shoulders stiff and tired. She pushed the garage door opener half expecting it not to work, as if she'd been gone for years instead of weeks.

In San Antonio, November still brought Indian summer days that reached into the eighties. Sunshine angled through the car windows as she waited to drive beneath the garage door. Unaccountably, she thought about her father, up there in Seattle where the weather was cloudy and cool. *You need to talk to your father,* Mason had said.

Maybe someday. She parked the Lexus and killed the engine, leaving the overhead door open. First she would stretch her legs and air out the house, then begin to unload.

At the kitchen entrance with her hand on the doorknob, she pictured the vacant rooms, heavy with the memory of Nathan's ghost. She saw herself wandering the house in the sleepless nights, drinking too much, living in her memories instead of her life. Would it be any different now?

The door pushed open with a rush of stuffy air, as if the house had been holding its breath. She walked through briskly, turning on lights and opening windows. The place felt huge after the little apartment in Santa Fe, and deadly quiet. *Janelle's right. I should get a dog.* She adjusted the thermostat to blow out the stale smell.

She dragged the largest suitcase upstairs first, past the locked bedroom that held Nathan's things, and down the hall to her own. She flopped the case on the bed and went back for another.

A forgotten pot of English ivy sat on the kitchen windowsill, its leaves shriveled and brown. She'd meant to take it to the office, or at least set it outdoors in the shade so it could fend for itself. She carried the leafy corpse to the backyard and dumped the evidence in a flower bed. To atone for her crime, she scooped a coffee can of seeds from a plastic bin in the garage and carried it to the patio to feed the birds and squirrels.

Stepping onto the wooden deck, she stopped. Golden lantana spilled from the clay planters, glowing like phosphorous in the autumn light. Cockscomb sprouted from the center of the pots in spiky red shoots, looking better than it had when she left.

Those flowers should have been dead from heat and neglect. But they looked as if someone had watered them and trimmed off the spent blooms. Claire stuck her fingers in the potting soil; it felt damp.

She hadn't asked anyone to take care of her flowers. She had hired a lawn service to mow the grass while she was gone, but that was all. And Janelle was far too busy with her kids' schedules and supervising the agency.

She turned to fill the feeders and stopped again. The feeder with the broken lid had been fixed. Shiny nail heads dotted the frame. She could think of no one who would come here and renail the wooden feeder that a marauding raccoon had sprung. Certainly not the lawn service; it wasn't in their contract. In the seven months she'd lived here, she'd met only one neighbor, elderly Mr. Levitz who walked his white poodle down her street. He was sweet but far too arthritic to undertake this task.

She had an eerie vision of Nathan hammering nails into the bird feeder, standing over the flowerpots with a garden hose in his ethereal hand.

*Stop it. You just got here and you're creeping out again.*

She filled both feeders and scattered some seed on the ground, then went indoors and called Janelle's cell phone.

"Yes?"

"Hi, stranger. I'm back in town."

Janelle squealed. "You're *here?* Who is this really?"

Claire smiled. "Your boss, smarty-pants."

"Ah, I remember you now. Vaguely. Listen, I'm with a client but I'll call you back shortly. Are you at home?"

"Yes. Unpacking. You didn't happen to come over and water my plants, did you?"

"Uh-oh. Was I supposed to?"

"Not at all. Talk to you in a while."

Forty-five minutes later Janelle knocked on the back door and popped her head inside. "Claire? It's me!"

"Come in!" Claire dropped the laundry she was carrying to the utility room and they hugged like children, laughing.

"God, it's good to see you." Janelle stepped back and looked her over. "You look fantastic. *Fan and tit,* as Les would say."

"It's amazing what a little exercise and sunshine will do."

"And some food. You don't look like an anorexic orphan anymore."

"Screw you very much. How about some iced tea? My lemons went bad, but the tea's fresh."

They carried their glasses outdoors and sat on the patio. Long shadows had begun to reach across the lawn, and a pair of chickadees already had found the seeds. Janelle wanted to know everything about Santa Fe and Mason McKinnon, and she filled Claire in on what was going on at the office. Irv had sold one of the historic houses in the King William district for a million dollars.

"It belonged to a widow he happened to meet at some civic event," Janelle said. "I think they've been keeping company, too."

"Hurray for Irv."

Janelle checked her watch. "Oops. I have a kid to pick up." She hauled herself up from the chaise lounge and leaned down to give Claire a half hug. "You coming in tomorrow?"

"Bright and early. I'm ready to get back to work."

"Pardner, I sure am glad you're home."

In honor of his big sale, Irv took a well-deserved fishing trip, and Claire insisted Janelle take some time off, too. Their absence left Claire swamped, but it felt good to be up and running. She showed multilist properties in Olmas Park and her own Oak Cliffs addition, but she'd handed off her own listings when she left town and she needed new ones. On two blustery afternoons, she trudged door-to-door in upscale neighborhoods sticking colored flyers in the doors: *Thinking of selling your house? Let me help!*

She phoned former clients and asked them for leads and recommendations, a tactic that paid off with two immediate listings. Evenings, she worked in her home office on the computer, completing the storms of paperwork. She hung the painting from Santa Fe there, and thought of Mason whenever she looked at it.

Gradually her days returned to the same pattern as before her trip, except that Nathan's visits didn't recur. The day after she got home, she had unlocked the door to his room and left it open. It began to seem like a normal bedroom, not mystical nor haunted. She told herself that life was good, that she was content, and tried to ignore a current of restlessness that ran just below the surface of her days. Sometimes she caught herself thinking, *Is this all there is?*

She phoned Win, as promised, and suggested they donate the proceeds of Nathan's inheritance to a fund that helped the families of children who needed organ transplants. She had researched the fund through the Texas Organ Sharing Association and the Austin transplant center. Both TOSA and the nurse at the transplant center knew about the group and praised its work.

"That's a great idea," Win said. "I'll have our attorneys draw up the papers." He sounded surprised and disconcertingly happy to hear from her.

"I'm going to donate Nathan's college fund, too," she said. "The money your mother gave us when you left."

Win paused a beat. "I think Nathan would approve." He cleared his throat. "Come to Dallas for the weekend. You can stay in the company's VIP apartment. We could have dinner, see a show or something. Anything that sounds fun to you."

She declined, using the easy excuse that weekends were prime time for Realtors, and hung up feeling guilty for disappointing him. *What is it with me? There's not a reason in the world I should feel guilty aboutWin O'Neal, even if he is having a hard time.* Once again her emotions were overriding her brain.

In Santa Fe she'd established a habit of daily walking, and she continued that pattern, hiking through her neighborhood in the early mornings while only the birds and a few joggers were out and about. In those quiet times she thought of Mason. She wondered if he was eating properly and keeping his blood pressure and pulse log, and whether he felt lonely when he passed her apartment door.

Sitting at her desk one day, she picked up the phone on an impulse and called him. There was no answer, and he didn't have a message machine. It was early afternoon; he'd probably gone out for groceries or a symphony rehearsal. She called the next day about noon, when he usually got up. The unanswered ringing sounded so hollow that she didn't try again for a week. Why hadn't he tried to phone her? Maybe he'd made friends among the symphony members and his life was busy and full.

By late November, she was working twelve-hour days at the office. Irv had come back from his fishing trip looking sunburned and happy. She got the impression that he hadn't gone alone, but he rarely mentioned his personal life so she didn't ask. The Monday before Thanksgiving, as she sat at her desk tapping the computer keys, Irv warned her in his fatherly way, "Slow down. You'll burn out."

She glanced up from the screen and smiled, still typing. "Hard work won't hurt me. Never has."

He frowned at her over the top of his glasses. "For someone so young," he said, "you have a short memory."

Janelle invited Claire to have Thanksgiving dinner with her brood and a host of relatives. "I know darned good and well you'll have a Swanson turkey dinner from the freezer if you don't come over," she said.

"Busted. I bought the thing yesterday."

"Unacceptable," Janelle said. "I'll expect you at my table. Wear combat gear."

"What can I bring? Pies? Cranberry salad? Texas chili?"

"Not a thing. The Pie Palace is baking for me, and my mother-in-law has the cranberries covered."

"Not a pretty image."

"Sorry. Just bring your hungry self about eleven. If I don't serve this brood by noon, they'll start eating the wallpaper."

"Maybe I should bring wine for the cook."

"Now you're talking."

On Tuesday Win called again. He'd promised to take his mother to the country club for Thanksgiving dinner but wanted to make sure Claire wouldn't be alone. "I don't suppose you'd consider joining us. I could drive down tomorrow and pick you up."

The thought of seeing Avis O'Neal across the table sent a shudder over her. "No, thanks. I've got a date with about twenty-five members of the Landry-Jackson clan. Janelle's family."

"That's good. Lots of kids and commotion."

"And best of all, I can go home whenever I like. But I appreciate the invitation, Win."

"While you're feeling kindly toward me, how about dinner next weekend? I'll fly down there. Friday or Saturday, your choice."

This time she had no handy excuse, so she told him the truth. "I can't, Win. You still remind me too much of Nathan."

She heard him blow out a deep breath. "I would hope someday that will be a good thing, instead of something you dread."

"I hope so, too," she said.

"Call me when that happens. I'll be here."

Autumn was Nathan's favorite time of year, when shorter days and cooler nights turned certain trees to gold and the leaves shimmered down like yellow rain. The heart of football season. Claire missed him more at Thanksgiving than any other holiday.

The night before, she went to his room. The scent of him had faded since she'd been leaving the door open, but she still caught a faint trace, or imagined she did. She touched the helmet he'd worn in his last high school game. It was covered with stars he'd earned for completed passes, and their rough texture felt a little like the burr haircut he had when he was six. She picked up his junior class photo and looked at the hope in his face. No tears tonight, just a loneliness she suspected would be with her always.

She carried the photo to the window seat and curled up in the corner like so many nights before.

And waited.

*One last time, Nathan? Let me see you one last time.*

Silence ticked in the empty house. A neighbor's dog howled, and the clock downstairs chimed two solitary bongs.

A gust of wind blew yellow leaves against the window. Claire looked out across the tree-covered hills to the lights beyond. She pulled her feet underneath her robe and wrapped her arms around her knees. Nathan appeared not in a mirage, but in a parade of happy memories. A fourth-grade pilgrim in his Thanksgiving program. The eighth-grade essay that earned him a savings bond and a flag. Even the trip to the emergency room when he was five and stuck a BB in his ear.

The downstairs clock chimed the half hour and she drifted back even further, to a troubled little girl with scuffed sneakers, hiding while her parents argued, blaming herself. She laid her head back and closed her eyes.

When the chime struck three, she rose and stretched her kinked legs. She set the photograph on its shelf and went to bed. Maybe her mirages had truly gone away. She wondered if the sadness ever would.

# Chapter Thirty

Janelle and Les Landry's spacious, older home was as stuffed as the turkey. Including the addition they'd built during Janelle's unexpected last pregnancy, the house had five bedrooms, four baths, two living areas and a game room. On Thanksgiving Day, they needed every inch. The house was noisy and welcoming, rich with the aromas of turkey and pumpkin and Les's father's fat cigar.

Claire lost track of relatives' names after a dozen. Children of all sizes ran through the kitchen at intervals to steal bites of food. Janelle was serving buffet-style; it would have required a Viking's hall to seat everyone at one table. At noon the kids filled their plates and migrated to the game room, where Les had fashioned a table from a plywood slab laid over two sawhorses. Tablecloths the color of autumn leaves covered the slab. When the kids were seated, the adults descended on the feast.

Claire made her way through the line, piling carbs on her plate. She'd slept four hours the night before and propped herself up that morning with plenty of caffeine.

Janelle maneuvered Les's unmarried brother next to Claire at the long table in the dining room. A ceramic turkey squatted regally in the center of the table, and little Callie had decorated the linen cloth with crayoned cutouts of her Thanksgiving art. Claire looked at the table and thought how much Nathan would have loved this. He'd always envied his friends who had lots of cousins.

Les's brother Dale was a professional baseball player for a triple-A team. If he'd been a football player, Claire could have carried on an adequate conversation. As it was, she mostly listened to family anecdotes while stowing away mashed potatoes and giblet gravy.

Claire had brought four bottles of a Beaujolais that the man at the wine shop recommended with turkey. The bottles passed joyfully up and down the table, bypassing Janelle's oldest sister whose religion apparently forbade drinking, laughing, or anything else that might be fun. That probably explained why she was childless, Claire thought, a lucky break for the nonexistent kids. How Sarah and Janelle could have come from the same gene pool was a mystery.

Despite Claire's protests, Les set a slice of pumpkin pie with whipped cream in front of her after the main course. She ate a few bites to be polite, but her rib cage was getting uncomfortably tight. The house suddenly felt too warm and crowded; she needed fresh air.

Her legs wavered as she took her tea glass and slipped out to the patio. She leaned against a support post to catch her breath, perspiration coating her forehead. She felt weird. She wasn't used to eating this much; maybe her body was rebelling.

What was wrong with the gazebo in the backyard? The beams were all wavy....

The tea glass slipped from her hand and shattered. She slumped into a patio chair, mouth-breathing.

Dale stepped out the sliding-glass door. "Are you okay?"

"How embarrassing," she said. "I swear I had only one glass of the wine." She tried to pick up the jagged pieces of glass but was too dizzy to lean over.

"Don't worry about it." He knelt and picked up the glass. "You look kind of pale."

"I think all my blood went to my stomach. I hope these aren't Janelle's best glasses." She was still struggling to catch her breath.

"I'll throw this away and bring a broom for the fine pieces," Dale said. "Would you like to lie down somewhere?"

"Thank you, no. But I think I'll go on home. If I tell Janelle, she'll have a fit. Would you please give her my thanks, and I'll apologize to her tomorrow?"

"Sure. Are you okay to drive? I could take you home." Dale really was a nice guy.

"I'm fine. I just didn't get much sleep last night."

She retrieved her purse and walked around the outside of the house to the street. Luckily she'd parked where she wouldn't get blocked in. Her knees felt jittery. She took deep breaths to oxygenate her brain. What the hell was wrong with her?

The afternoon had turned muggy, gulf air flowing up from the south in cloud layers that covered the sun. Claire longed for the cool front that was predicted later in the day. She started the engine and sat for a minute with the air-conditioning aimed at her face. Then she drove through quiet streets toward the main thoroughfare.

Black spots floated in her vision. What if she passed out and ran into someone? She'd better get home fast.

Her pulse speeded up, and so did the Lexus. She turned onto Fredricksburg Road, thankful there wasn't much traffic because of the holiday. Only one vehicle sat at the stoplight across from her, a white pickup that she saw in a hazy oval. The traffic light turned green and she rolled forward, but dark edges were closing in.

She couldn't get her foot onto the brake. She steered toward the edge of the road, felt the bump of tires against a curb—and that was all.

Claire awoke stretched out on the concrete beside her car, panting like a beached fish. The silhouette of a man's face hung against the overcast sky.

"Claire? Can you hear me?"

How did he know her name?

Behind him, she heard the metallic sounds of equipment being deployed and saw the boxy white profile of an ambulance. When she could focus on the man kneeling beside her, she saw he was very young. His eyes and hair were black as jet.

"My name's Jeremy. I'm an EMT."

Her arms and legs were too heavy to move. "I'm fine, really. I just overate."

"We're going to check you over. People don't usually pass out from overeating. But then, I didn't see how much turkey and dressing you put on your plate." He smiled, showing unnaturally white teeth.

How did people get teeth like that, she thought. Mouthwash with Clorox? She closed her eyes.

Jeremy took her vital signs while his helper positioned a stretcher beside her. Another man loomed in the background, wearing a ball cap and workman's clothes. He didn't look like one of the EMTs. Maybe just a witness to her folly.

"I'm so sleepy. Turkey does that, doesn't it?"

The white teeth flashed again. "That's the rumor. But your pulse is irregular and your breathing's a little labored. I don't think we can blame the bird for that—unless you're allergic to it. Has this ever happened before?"

"No."

"I'm going to put an oxygen tube in your nose to help you breathe easier."

She nodded, accepting the prongs in her nostrils. She wanted to go to sleep and wake up at home. Surely this was a bad dream.

They transported her to University Hospital, which wasn't far from her house. Jeremy sat beside her in the ambulance, monitoring her pulse.

"What about my car?"

"Don't worry. Your friend was going to take care of it."

*What friend?* She was too tired to ask. If she had to, she thought groggily, she could walk home from the hospital.

The ambulance rocked to a stop and two attendants wheeled her through the emergency room entrance. Somewhere behind her, a woman asked, "Are you her husband?"

"No, ma'am," a man's voice said.

"We need someone to help us fill out the paperwork. Can you do that?"

"No, but I brought her purse out of her car. Maybe that'll help." Claire didn't recognize his voice.

They wheeled her into a room with a curtain for a door. It looked a lot like the emergency room where they'd taken Nathan. She tried to think of something else while the nurse took her blood pressure and shined a penlight in her eyes.

"My name's Judy," the nurse said, ripping loose the Velcro cuff. "Does your blood pressure usually run high?"

Claire licked her dry lips. "It usually runs low. I just don't like hospitals."

Using a bulky cell phone, Judy reported Claire's vitals and symptoms, presumably to the doctor on call. Medicine in the electronic age.

"The doctor wants you to have an electrocardiogram, okay?" Judy told her. Her voice was nasal and she dragged out *okay* as if talking to a child. Another nurse helped strip off Claire's clothes and replace them with a hospital gown.

"A technician will roll the machine in here and hook you up in a few minutes, okay?" Judy said. "Have you ever had an electrocardiogram before?"

Claire shook her head. "Is something wrong with my heart?"

"Probably not. Your heartbeat's a little irregular, but that's not unusual by itself. We're trying to figure out why you passed out. Okaaay?"

The other nurse, apparently a trainee, spread a warm blanket over her legs. Her name was Brenda and she looked about twelve months pregnant.

"Thank you," Claire said. "I'm really thirsty."

"I'll get you some ice water." Brenda had a voice meant for lul-labies. "Is there someone you'd like me to call?"

Claire thought of Janelle with her houseful of family. "No. No one, thanks."

Brenda moved out on quiet feet.

With water and another warm blanket, Claire was left alone in the sanitized bed that crinkled whenever she moved, a ceiling light assaulting her eyes. She felt like a specimen on a microscope slide. She thought of all the procedures Mason had been through, and would continue to go through on a regular basis the rest of his life.

*I'm such a wimp. And I'll never eat turkey again....*

She succumbed to a dogged drowsiness until the EKG tech came in. He wore tiny square glasses and a ponytail, and he didn't talk much. The tech dabbed cold jelly on her chest and wired her to the machine. The test took only a few minutes. He packed up his machine without offering any clues about the test results. As he was leaving, Brenda brought in Claire's purse and stashed it in a closet. She dimmed the light and assured Claire the doctor would be in soon.

In a hospital, *soon* has a different meaning to the staff than to the patients. Claire watched the second hand click around an institutional clock oddly mounted a foot below the ceiling. Finally she fell asleep.

When she awoke, a man was sitting in the straight chair against the wall. He definitely wasn't the doctor. His T-shirt and jeans were faded and he needed a shave. Rampant dark hair sprouted from his forearms, as if to make up for the bald spot on his head, which hung forward as if he were dozing, or praying.

"Excuse me." Her voice was hoarse and she tried to speak up. "Excuse me. I think you're in the wrong room."

The man's head lifted and she looked into pale, watery eyes. He uncrossed his legs and sat up straighter. "No, ma'am. I'm in the right room." His hands crushed a gimme ball cap that said Peterbilt above the brim.

Beneath the sheet, Claire searched for the call button the nurse had pinned to the bedding. "Who are you?"

"I'm the one called the ambulance when you passed out on the road. You really gave me a scare." Spidery eyebrows collided when he frowned. "You gonna be okay?"

Claire's hand relaxed on the call button, but she didn't let go. "I'm fine. They're just checking me out. Thanks for stopping to help."

"Your car's in the parking lot there at the Wal-Mart." His speech was a thick Texas drawl. "I locked it up and put the keys in your purse. Did you get your purse back?"

"Yes, I did. I appreciate all your trouble." She studied his face. "Have I met you someplace before? I'm Claire O'Neal."

He bobbed his head. "Name's Hobson Jeeter, Hob for short. I changed a tire for you one time. Out on that same street."

"Yes, I remember now. What a coincidence."

The jagged lump in the front of his throat worked up and down. "No, ma'am. It wasn't no coincidence." He looked down at the cap in his hands, fingering the warped brim. "I been sorta looking out for you for a long time now."

Claire frowned. "What do you mean?"

The colorless eyes met hers, pleading. Alarm began to buzz in her brain.

"You don't know me," he said, "but I know you." He spoke deliberately, as if he'd rehearsed. "You're the mother of that boy that got killed out on I-35. Three years ago September."

Claire's skin went cold. *Jesus. He's a psycho.* Her thumb jammed the red call button. Jammed it again.

"Why do you know about that?" she said.

"I'm sorry, missus. I don't mean to upset you. Here lately I started going to church, and the pastor said I should ask forgiveness from anybody I'd wronged. That maybe then I could forgive myself."

Claire jammed the button again. *Why didn't somebody answer?* "You've never wronged me. I don't even know you."

He inhaled, straightened his spine. "Yes, ma'am, I have. I've carried it around for three years, but I never got over it." The stubbly face creased with distress. "I'm a mechanic now, but I used to drive a semi rig. Long hauls."

Her hands lost the call button and went stiff at her sides. "Oh my God…"

He nodded, confirming. "It was my truck that threw that tire."

Claire's heart began jigging again, banging against her ribs. A pain spiked behind her eyes.

Nurse Judy pushed the curtain aside and stuck her head into the room. "Did you need something?"

But Claire couldn't speak. The nurse glanced from Claire's face to the man in the chair. "Is everything all right here?"

"Yes, ma'am," Hobson said. "I was just leavin'."

He stood up, wringing the hat in his hands. Someone in the hallway called the nurse's name. She cast a frown at both Claire and her visitor and then disappeared.

But Hobson Jeeter didn't go yet. He moved to the foot of her bed. "It was an accident," he said. "A horrible accident. But if I'd have retightened those lug nuts like I should have, it might not've happened." His eyes were red rimmed. "I didn't even look back. I was too big a coward."

Claire rolled her head on the pillow, closed her eyes tightly. "Please go away. Don't tell me any more."

"I'm apologizing, Mrs. O'Neal. I don't expect you can forgive me, but I'm asking anyway, like the pastor said. I want you to know how sorry I am about your boy."

Then he ducked through the curtain and was gone.

Claire felt the slight draft of his passing, the fabric partition falling shut. She lay in the cold room, her ragged pulse throbbing under her skin. From beyond the curtain came the murmured noises of a world that never slept. On her side of the curtain, only the fluorescent hum of the lights and the ticking of the white-faced clock.

Nathan's death was not a capricious act of God, after all.

Not some karmic punishment for her sins.

Nathan had died because someone forgot to tighten lug bolts on a truck that happened to be traveling the same highway at the same time. Just human error, and wretched luck.

# Chapter Thirty-One

It was after six when the doctor appeared. Claire hadn't slept at all since Hobson Jeeter left her room.

The doctor glanced at Claire's untouched supper tray and rolled the tray table out of the way. "Mrs. O'Neal? I'm Doctor Radison."

"Happy Thanksgiving."

He smiled. "Same to you."

He was about her age, with curly brown hair, close-cropped. His white jacket hung open over a casual shirt that had a spot on the stomach. Claire guessed turkey gravy.

"I'm sorry to take you away from your family today," she said.

He shrugged. "You didn't. I had to make rounds, anyway." He scanned the chart in his hands, then met her eyes. "You had kind of a scary day. How are you feeling now?"

"Just tired. And a little silly."

"There's nothing silly about passing out while you're driving." His forehead wrinkled above sharp, hazel eyes. "Let's listen to your chest."

He leaned over her, smelling of the outdoors. The stethoscope felt like ice, and she flinched.

"Sorry," he said. "I should have warmed that up. It's turned chilly outside this evening." He moved the disk on her chest and listened, then had her sit up and listened to her back. Luckily, his hands weren't cold; they were confident and relaxed, like a good dance partner. She wondered if Mason liked to dance.

Dr. Radison straightened the blanket and tucked her in. He stepped back a polite distance and fixed her with inquisitive eyes. "Your EKG showed some cardioarrhythmia. I suspect that's the cause of your fainting spell today."

"That sounds ominous."

"Not necessarily. It just means your heartbeat is irregular. Lots of people have arrhythmia in varying degrees and never even know it. Usually it doesn't require treatment. But when it starts giving you problems, it could be a symptom of something more serious. Have you noticed being short of breath lately?"

"Yes. For a year or so, actually. I thought I was just out of shape."

He noted something on the chart. "Any light-headedness before today?"

"Not that I recall."

*Except when Nathan appeared,* she thought suddenly. She'd been short of breath then, too.

"Your heartbeat sounds fine now," he was saying, "but I want to keep you overnight and have Dr. Tomay see you tomorrow. He's a cardiologist. If you're doing okay then, he'll probably send you home."

"I have to work tomorrow. I have two appointments with clients."

"The Friday after Thanksgiving?"

She gave him a look. "Are you working tomorrow?"

"Touché." His smile showed perfect orthodontia. She liked him anyway.

"I'm a Realtor. My clients need to look at houses when *they're* off work."

"Can you get someone to cover for you?"

She sighed. "Probably, if I want to mess up somebody else's holiday."

Dr. Radison frowned. He laid the chart on the bed and pulled up a tall stool, sitting with his fingers laced over a bent knee. "You work holidays so your colleagues can have the time off?"

"Well…sometimes, yes. Most of them have families, and I don't."

"I'll bet you own your own business."

"Good guess."

"How many hours do you put in each week?"

She hedged. "That's hard to say. It varies."

"Okay. How many hours have you put in this week so far? And no fudging."

Claire calculated. "If you count the paperwork I do at night—"

"It counts."

"Thirty-six, maybe forty hours."

"You've worked forty hours in three days?"

"Four days. I work Sunday afternoons. Usually I take Mondays off, but this week was really busy." She shrugged, feeling defensive. "I like my job."

"So do I. But I notice that when I start putting in too many hours, I get stressed out and overfatigued. And when that happens, I might make mistakes—or have health problems."

"Okay. I get it. "

"What did you have for breakfast this morning?"

She looked at him stupidly. "Breakfast?"

"Yes. You do eat breakfast, don't you?"

"Sure. I had…a blueberry muffin and coffee."

"How much coffee?"

"Um…three cups."

"Leaded or unleaded?"

"What's the point of unleaded?"

"Right. And at lunch, did you have some more caffeine?"

"Just one cup, with dessert. Oh, and iced tea."

"What about alcohol?"

"One glass of wine with lunch." She smiled weakly. "All things in moderation."

"Caffeine and alcohol exacerbate the arrhythmia. So do fatigue and stress. And so your body sends you a message by passing out."

"Bummer."

"I'm not a cardiologist. We'll let Dr. Tomay check you out. But I can tell you already that you're doing just about everything you can to make a mild arrhythmia worse." His hazel eyes lasered in, his face serious. "From preliminary indications, your heart seems to be healthy. But like any other part of the body, it can suffer from overwork and bad habits. The heart is just a muscle, after all."

After he left, pregnant Brenda rolled her through hallways and elevators to a room on the third floor of the hospital. On the bumpy ride, the doctor's parting irony echoed in her head.

*The heart is just a muscle, after all.*

The hospital room was pleasant enough except for the inevitable antiseptic smell. A flowered border crowned the textured walls, and a Monet print in an ornate frame hung on the wall facing the bed. Two different nurses settled her into the bed and asked the same questions she'd answered downstairs. When they'd gone, she retrieved her cell phone from the bedside table and found two missed calls from Janelle. She pushed the call-back button and looked out the window while she waited. The sky behind the half-closed blinds was dark, the pane smeared with a cold rain.

In a house with teenagers, no adult ever answers the phone. "Hi, Danny, it's Claire. Is your mom still in the kitchen?"

"Uh, nope. She's around here somewhere. Hang on."

Claire hung. Rock music played in the background, one of those girl singers that all sounded alike. *God, I must be old already.*

"About time you called me back," Janelle said, and the rock music disappeared. "Where are you? Dale said you were going home but I called there four times."

"I didn't quite make it. I'm at University Hospital."

"You're in the *hospital?* What happened?"

"An irregular heartbeat, apparently. That and stupidity. I'll be fine, but they're keeping me overnight."

"I'll be right there. What room are you in?"

"Don't you dare. It's cold and rainy out and I know you still have company. I'm settled in a room with a lovely view of the parking lot, getting ready to sleep like Snow White. Tomorrow I'm supposed to see a cardiologist, and then I'll go home."

"What can I do to help?"

"I'm going to see if Irv can take my appointments for tomorrow. I would cancel, but I don't have the clients' phone numbers here."

"Irv might be at his new lady friend's house. If you can't reach him, call me back."

"Thanks. I will."

But Irv Washington was at home watching football on TV. "Are you okay?" he asked.

"Just a little under the weather." She didn't mention the hospital.

"Rest up and don't worry. I'll take care of your people."

"I appreciate it, Irv."

She turned off the phone and climbed out of bed, holding her drafty gown closed. At the window, she pulled the heavy blind all the way up. Rain splattered on the parking lot and blurred the headlights that slid along the street beyond. Night sounds of the hospital floated in from the hallway, muffled voices of nurses and aides, the electronic ping of someone's call button. If it wasn't the loneliest sound in the world, it had to be second.

All over the city, families were gathering around turkey banquets, or else foraging for leftovers from an early dinner. Kid cousins were playing Clue and Monopoly, their parents and grandparents watching football or telling stories. She and Nathan had never had that kind of holiday, but they'd had good times, and thinking about that made her smile.

The floor was drafty and her feet were getting cold. She crawled back into the tall bed and covered up, running the head end up so she could look outside.

She thought of the truck driver—Hobson Jeeter. She'd never forget the name.

He must have carried a huge load of guilt if he'd been keeping track of her all this time, like some kind of misguided penance. It was creepy to think he'd been lurking just outside her awareness, watching her come and go. He was probably the one who watered her plants and fixed the feeder. *My God—he sent the white flowers.* That's why they were unsigned.

She could report him to the law and maybe he'd be arrested for negligence in Nathan's death, or for leaving the scene of an accident. But what purpose would that serve? He didn't seem dangerous; if he'd meant her any harm, he'd had plenty of opportunities. She didn't feel vindictive toward him, just uneasy, and bone tired.

She felt a flicker in her chest and laid her hand on her heart. This had been happening for a long time, but she hadn't paid attention to her own body. What if the cardiologist found a serious heart problem? Wouldn't it be the world's greatest irony if she needed a transplant from someone else, some unlucky young victim of an accident?

The heart is just a muscle, after all.

The view from a hospital window gave Claire a whole different perspective of the world. She saw quite clearly the things in her life that were worth hanging on to. And other things she ought to let go.

On her cell phone, she dialed information and then rang the number for Buck Jameson in Seattle.

# Chapter Thirty-Two

Claire's flight into Seattle-Tacoma Airport descended in a driz-zling rain. She'd requested a window seat, hoping to see the blue Pacific as the plane came in, or Mt. Rainier covered with snow. But a gray mist blanked out everything beyond the boxy win-dow until the last few seconds of their descent. The wheels struck tarmac and bounced, sending her stomach into a loop. She waited to feel her heart skitter, but it behaved just fine.

After her stint in the hospital and a complete physical and stress test, the cardiologist had found no evidence of heart dis-ease. But he confirmed Dr. Radison's warnings to cut back on caffeine, alcohol and stress, which meant working fewer hours.

"Often a lifestyle change works better than medication," Dr. Tomay had told her in his friendly Ukrainian accent. "If that doesn't do it, we try a prescription." She was to check back with him in six weeks.

Claire shouldered her tote bag and waded down the aisle behind a mother with two small children, going to Grandma's for the holidays.

"Nobody buys real estate the week before Christmas," she had told her father on the phone. "I was thinking I'd come out for a visit."

"That's the best present I could think of," Buck said, but he sounded nervous.

She hadn't tried to explain her sudden decision to visit. Partly she wanted to resolve old resentments, perhaps seek absolution for Todd's drowning. Partly she was seeking family again. Buck probably understood her reasons as well as she did, but he had to wonder *why now,* after she'd kept her distance for so many years.

The terminal was jammed with holiday travelers. Swags of tinsel festooned the concourse, and a motorized Santa waved from a shop window as she passed. Claire retrieved her suitcase from the baggage carousel and trailed it through sliding-glass doors into a shivery mist. She'd insisted on taking the airport shuttle to her father's house. Flight delays were common these days, especially in winter, and it was a long drive from the airport to the northwest suburbs of Seattle.

The shuttle had four passengers, and she was the last delivery on its long, circuitous route. The shuttle driver turned out to be a native Texan and he talked nonstop once he found out where she was from. It was dark by the time the airport van pulled into the driveway at her father's address.

The house was white with stone facing halfway up, just as

Buck had described it. Yellow light glowed behind the curtains, and a Christmas tree blinked in the front window. Another van sat in the driveway, a red one with a handicap insignia on the back. Was that her father's car?

The driver retrieved Claire's bag and wished her a merry Christmas. She tipped him extra and rolled her bag up the driveway in the misting rain. Then she saw the ramp.

A painted, plywood incline led from the driveway to a covered porch that sheltered the front door. She was still digesting what that meant when the door opened and Buck Jameson rolled out onto the porch.

Her second shock, after realizing Buck needed a wheelchair, was that if she'd met her father on a street somewhere, she wouldn't have known him. Undoubtedly he was thinking the same thing about her. They hadn't seen each other since Nathan was six. Nearly fifteen years.

Buck's hair was still thick and wiry but fully gray now, his face lined with the wounds and wisdom of sixty-five years. His eyes watched her take in the chair, the useless legs. Then he said, "You better come in, Sissy. Your hair's getting wet." The gruff voice was one thing that hadn't changed.

She took the ramp, rolling the suitcase behind her. When she stood beneath the porch overhang, she stopped again. "How long have you been…?" Her question trailed off.

"Crippled up? Ten years last August. An accident on the job."

"Why didn't you tell me?"

He shrugged. "I didn't want you feeling sorry for me. You had your hands full already."

When she could think of nothing to say, he filled in details. The company had paid all his medical bills, vested his retirement, and promised him a good-paying desk job for as long as he wanted it. She could hear how weary he was of that speech.

"In return, I agreed not to sue their asses off." He smiled. "It wasn't their fault, anyway. My own damned carelessness."

Still speechless, she merely looked at him.

"If I'd warned you, you might not have come," he said.

"Of course I would. Why would that matter?"

He shrugged. "It makes some people uncomfortable."

He held the door open for her, then maneuvered over the threshold with a practiced motion. The door hissed shut behind him.

Inside, the house looked larger than it did from the outside. The floors were hardwood—easier for rolling the chair—with spacious paths connecting one room to the next. In the living room, a maroon-and-navy plaid sofa and recliner anchored a handsome area rug. There was no coffee table to obstruct passage, but magazines and books spilled from the end tables. In a brick fireplace, yellow flames warmed the room with a pleasant scent.

"This is lovely," Claire said. "Did you decorate it yourself?"

He humphed. "Just the furniture. All these doodads are Annie's idea." Shelves on both sides of the fireplace held china collectibles and small woodcarvings whose details she couldn't see in the soft light.

"Who's Annie?"

"My physical therapist. You'll meet her later."

Claire stood in the middle of the room holding the extended handle on her bag. Buck seemed at a loss, too. For an awkward moment she wondered what in the world she was doing here—and realized that was exactly what her father meant about the wheelchair making people uncomfortable.

Finally she took off her damp jacket and hung it on a hall tree by the front door.

"I'll show you your room," he said, "and you can put away your things."

"Great. I think I'll put on warmer clothes. My feet are freezing."

She followed him past a heavy dining room table and down a hall with wide doorways. She had tried to picture what her father's house might look like, a longtime bachelor's habitat. Her imaginings couldn't have been further off.

"I had the house remodeled to accommodate my new mode of transportation," he said over his shoulder. "That's my room." He nodded toward an open door as he passed. "They built me a special shower and lowered the bed."

Lift bars hung from the ceiling above the bed. A long, narrow table with a padded top sat against one wall. A therapy table, Claire guessed.

The next bedroom, in striking contrast to Buck's, displayed a colorful quilted spread over a white eyelet bed skirt. Layers of fabric ruffled the windows. She assumed this was the guest room, but he moved past it and down the hall. The third room looked more like a bedroom-in-a-bag, obviously unused. But the colors were restful and pleasant, and a Tiffany-style lamp glowed beside the bed. In one corner, a wooden rocking chair with an ornately carved back held a flowered seat cushion.

A funny twinge etched through her stomach. "I recognize that rocking chair."

Buck smiled. "Do you?" He turned slightly to look at her. "That's the only piece of furniture I took with me when Maggie and I got divorced. My grandfather made it."

How odd to think of him with a grandfather. It was a relationship she envied; both of her grandfathers were gone before she could remember.

The curved arms of the chair, polished smooth by generations of skin oils, recalled a vague memory of being rocked on her father's lap. "The carving on the back is beautiful," she said.

"Yeah, I guess that's where I got my interest in wood. From Papaw. The chair will go to you when I die." He made a noise like a small cough and adjusted the angle of his wheelchair again. She'd already pegged this motion as a nervous gesture.

"Annie freshened everything up for you and put out clean towels in the bathroom across the hall," he said.

"It looks very comfortable." She lifted her bag onto a luggage rack at the foot of the bed.

"If there's anything you need or can't find, just give a holler. I'll be in the kitchen." He executed a three-point turn and wheeled away, calling back over his shoulder. "Dinner's ready whenever you are."

In jeans and sneakers, her face and hands washed, she retraced her steps down the hall. On the way past, she paused to look into the middle bedroom. A hand mirror and several bottles sat beside a hairbrush on the bureau. Somebody obviously stayed in that frilly room. Perhaps Annie was more than his physical therapist.

She followed an enticing aroma and the clattering of dishes to the kitchen. In the doorway, she stopped before he was aware of her presence. Her father's chair wasn't electric, and as a result his arms and upper body looked muscular and strong. She wondered how he managed his bath, his bodily functions, getting to and from work. The red van must be equipped so he could drive.

He had set two places at a small table in the kitchen. The fiddleback chairs looked like serviceable antiques. In fact, quite a few items in the house looked antique—good quality but comfortable and worn. Even his wheelchair seemed a natural part of the furnishings. She thought how easy it would be for him to isolate himself here and never go out of his comfort zone. The outside world had to be a challenge, regardless of accessibility requirements. Maybe that's why Buck had kept working, to avoid becoming a recluse.

She shuffled her feet so he'd know she was there. "That smells heavenly. You must be a good cook."

He made a growling noise that was not quite a laugh. "No, Annie's the cook. Left to my own devices, I usually eat frozen dinners."

"I eat a lot of those myself."

She watched him remove a hot casserole from the oven, his hands encased in Holstein-patterned mitts. He placed the hot dish on top of the stove with deliberate movements, closed the oven door, adjusted the position of his chair and transferred the dish to a countertop that had been lowered to chair height.

How difficult it must have been to learn that kind of patience, to adjust to a life where every simple task took time. The father she'd once known was not a patient man.

She picked up two tumblers he'd set on the table. "Shall I fill these with water?"

"Sure. There's ice and water in the door of the fridge. No ice for me."

On the refrigerator, fish-shaped magnets anchored the corners of three curling snapshots. She leaned close to see them and felt the telltale flip of her finicky pulse. One photo was of Nathan on his first birthday, another when he was about seven and dressed up for Halloween. The third showed him in his football uniform as a freshman in high school.

"You sent those in your Christmas cards, remember?" he said, his voice low.

"Yes. I do now."

Nathan would have been ten years old when Buck became disabled. Was that why he hadn't come to visit his grandson again? Or was it because she'd never invited him? If she had known about his accident, would she have brought Nathan to see him?

Standing by the refrigerator in Buck's modified kitchen, she saw again the view from her hospital window. *People create so much of their own sorrow. And for what?*

She filled the glasses and set the casserole on a trivet in the center of the table. Buck brought a salad from the fridge and pulled up his chair to one side of the table, locking the brakes. She sat opposite him.

"There's huckleberry cobbler for dessert," he said.

"Annie must be a gem."

"That she is. I wanted her to join us but she said we should have some time alone to get acquainted." He put his napkin in his lap and leaned back in the chair.

The blue eyes she'd inherited regarded her across the table. She recalled a younger version of that face fixing her with a stern look across the breakfast table when she was small. She couldn't remember what she'd done, only that she was in trouble.

The silence stretched. "I told Annie we might need her here tonight most of all," Buck said.

"I'm sorry. I just had a flashback from childhood."

"Uh-oh. Let's start with something easier." His eyebrows bunched together. "On the phone you said you'd spent some time in Santa Fe."

"Right." She smiled. "Hand me your plate and I'll dish up this great-smelling casserole."

She made it sound like an adventure—tracing down the man with Nathan's heart and reorganizing his life. When she told him about hiding Mason's cigarettes, Buck actually smiled.

"Transplant patients have so many rules to follow, so much to be careful of," she said. "Probably kind of like living in a wheelchair."

"I imagine so."

She told him about Mason's lost family, but not about the fine line between friendship and desire. Buck listened, asked questions, made grunting noises. And eventually, he began to ask careful questions about his grandson. Touched by his interest, she managed to talk about Nathan with only a few moments of wet eyes.

Halfway through dinner, he looked at her earnestly. "This is going pretty good, isn't it?"

Claire smiled. "Darned good, I'd say."

Buck offered her a second helping of casserole but Claire declined. He helped himself. "I gotta admit I was worried. I thought you were still mad, and finally coming out here to tell me off." He put the dish down, avoiding her eyes. "And I couldn't blame you. Seems like I was never around when you needed me."

Claire pushed her plate to one side. "Dad, I need to talk about that. I wonder if we can just get it over with tonight."

He set down his water glass and folded his hands.

"Why did you leave Mom and me? I always thought it was my fault. Maybe all kids do, when their parents split up."

He took his time answering. "It wasn't you, Sissy. It was because of Todd. Surely Maggie talked with you about it."

"No. Whenever I asked about him, she clammed up."

"Yeah," her father said. "I guess she would have. Maggie wouldn't talk about him, and she wouldn't let me. We were both devastated. But I needed to remember him, and she needed to forget."

"That's when you started drinking?"

"Naw. I was already doing too much of that." He shrugged. "But that's when it got out of control. Our grief was an awful, ugly thing. We blamed each other, and you were having night-mares. I thought the best thing I could do for everybody was get completely away."

Claire thought these were the most words she'd ever heard from her father at one time. "Every time you looked at me, you saw the son you'd lost," she said. "I overheard you say that to Mom during one of your fights."

He frowned, but he didn't deny it.

"You also said I let him drown."

Buck's leathery face winced. "I was stupid with booze back then, day and night. I know that's no excuse. I'm sorry, Sissy. Maybe I was a coward to move away, but I thought I was doing the best thing. I knew Maggie would take care of you."

"Mom saw Todd when she looked at Nathan," Claire said, her eyes moving away from Buck's face to a memory of the kitchen in her mother's house. "Sometimes she even called him by Todd's name, until he got old enough to correct her." Her mother had doted on Nathan, spent every moment with him that she could. Maybe she believed he was her son, returned to her in a slightly different body.

Claire cleared her throat. "I have this dream of standing by dirty water when I'm very small. You and mom are there, sob-bing. But it isn't just a dream, is it? I can't remember anything else about the day he died."

Buck growled. "Why do you want to go through all this?"

She felt the irregular bumping in her chest, and willed her-self to relax, breathe deeply. There was no light-headedness, though; her thoughts felt icy sharp.

"When you and Mom lost Todd, you went through the same agony I did when Nathan died. Somehow it's taken me all this time to realize that. And to forgive you for blaming me."

The lines on his face grew deeper. "I didn't really blame you. I blamed me, but I didn't have the guts to put a gun to my head."

"How did you get past it?"

"Time. Nothing helped but time."

"I was supposed to be watching Todd, wasn't I?" she said.

"You were four years old. It was not your responsibility. If Maggie and I hadn't been busy sniping at each other over some stupid thing, we'd have realized you and Todd had gone outside."

"Tell me what happened."

Buck's voice dropped to a low mumble. "He drowned in the apartment swimming pool. Those crappy apartments where we lived then. The pool was closed for repairs, but somehow you two managed to get the gate open. When you came screaming to get me, I knew he was already gone."

"I think," she said, her chest hollow, "that's part of the reason I couldn't cope with losing Nathan. If I let my brother drown, I must have let my son die, too."

His blue eyes flamed. "That's pure bullshit. You did not let your brother drown. It just happened. Same as Nathan's accident. If anybody was at fault for Todd, it was Maggie and me."

In the silence that followed, they heard boots on the front porch, the doorbell and the door bursting open in quick succession.

"Yoo-hoo!" a female voice called. "I brought ice cream for the cobbler!"

Buck's eyes looked relieved. "That woman has impeccable timing."

Annie Love—her real name, not a nickname—swooped into the kitchen. She was ten years younger than Buck, round as a teddy bear and mortally huggy.

"You're Claire! I'm Annie Love!" she declared, and surprised Claire with a vociferous embrace. She smelled like something fresh baked. "Buck's been nervous as a cat waiting for you to get here."

Buck's scowl turned slightly red.

Annie found lots to talk about while they ate their cobbler, and she laughed at everything. She stayed past eleven and said goodnight with more hugs. When she closed the front door behind her, it was as if a light went out in the house. Claire saw the way Buck looked at the door and decided that Annie might well be the glue that could keep her and her father from drifting apart again.

Over the next few days, Claire learned to accept Annie's affections without flinching. Buck grumbled every time Annie leaned over him and pressed her pink face against his, but Claire could see he thrived on it. When Annie was there, he was relaxed, even jovial in his guarded way. He depended on her for much more than his physical needs.

Buck seemed pleased that Claire and Annie liked each other. "Annie could get along with an IRS auditor," he said, which was apparently high praise.

"Well," Claire said, and sniffed. "That doesn't say much for me, does it?"

On Christmas Day, Annie laid out a smorgasbord of delectables that would have fed half the Boeing plant. They could coast for days on the leftovers. After dinner, while Buck pushed back in his recliner and rested, Claire and Annie did dishes together.

"Have you seen your father's carvings?"

Annie was drying the platter on which she'd brought a dozen deviled eggs. *He loves them,* she'd said with a wink. *That's how I used to bribe him into doing his exercises.*

"The ones on the living room shelves?" Claire said. "They're amazing. He gave me a little Santa and a Texas longhorn."

"Oh, he has lots more in his bedroom. You've got to see those."

When the dishes were finished and Buck was dozing or pretending to be, Annie led Claire into his inner sanctum. One wall was filled with glass-fronted shelves. Annie opened the doors and took down one carving after another, handing them to Claire. Moose and bears and wolves, no more than four inches tall, hand carved with primitive details that perfectly captured the essence of each animal. Some figures were painted, like the Santa, the others oiled to a warm, wood finish.

Claire smoothed her fingers over the curved lines. "These are really good," she said. "In Santa Fe they'd sell for hundreds apiece."

"Oh, he wouldn't sell them," Annie scoffed. "He says they aren't worth anything. He gives them away, especially to the neighborhood kids. He started doing them when he was first confined to the chair and needed something to do with his hands."

On an afternoon while Buck watched ESPN sports, Claire and Annie had raspberry tea on a closed-in porch that faced the tiny backyard. Languid snowflakes had just begun to collect on the bony branches of a twisted tree. In front of a two-seater swing, a ring of stones marked off a small, winter-browned garden, centered by a shallow pool. Claire wondered if her father had placed the stones before his accident. Beside the pool stood a plump gnome that resembled a standing Buddha, or Annie.

"I guess you know by now that I often stay overnight with Buck," Annie confided while they watched the snow sift down. "We ought to get married, but he thinks that because he's older than I am and needs the chair, that would be like taking advantage." She huffed, lifting a spring of gray-brown hair from her forehead. "He's such a stubborn old fart."

Claire smiled. "You could just move in, like the young folks do."

"I might," Annie said. The light sky reflected in her copper-rimmed glasses. "But for now I'm keeping my little house. My daughter's a minister's wife, and I'm not sure I could tell her I was living in sin." Annie's laughter bubbled, rising and falling like a fountain. Every time Claire heard it, she laughed, too.

"Of course, with Buck's paralysis," Annie added dryly, "there's no sin to it."

A whistling emanated from the kitchen and Annie popped from her chair. "There's the teakettle. I'll bring us some more hot water."

In her absence Claire watched the lazy snowflakes and thought about what Mason had said. Lots of married couples love each other without sex.

The day before Claire was to go home, the sky turned partly sunny. Annie volunteered to show her the sights of Seattle. "You haven't been two miles from this house since you got here. What would you like to see?"

Tight little lines around Buck's eyes had clued Annie that he was having some pain that day, so she'd ordered him onto the massage table and worked him over. Afterward he looked limp. He'd seen Seattle before, he said, and opted to stay home from sightseeing. When Claire and Annie left the house, he was ensconced in his recliner with a pan of popcorn and a football game on TV.

"He'll be asleep in ten minutes," Annie said, backing her Honda out of the driveway at an alarming clip. "I'll show you Pike Place Market down by the harbor. If we get too cold, we'll hit the after-Christmas sales at a mall. I know a great little antique place, too."

The next day, Buck seemed to feel better. He insisted on driving her to the airport in his specially equipped van, as if he wanted to prove his self-sufficiency. She rode beside him and Annie sat on the backseat, narrating the sights along the way. Clouds mounded in the sky, and more snow showers were predicted.

"I wish you'd got to see Mt. Rainier in the sun," Annie said. "It's good luck, you know."

Buck pointed out the Boeing plant from which he would retire in the spring. Claire sensed that he was uneasy about giving it up, but she could also see how getting to and from work everyday would tire him.

At the airport, Buck pulled up to the curb and Annie hopped out of the backseat. "I'll get your bag. You two can say goodbye."

Claire squeezed her father's rough hand. "I'll come again soon."

"I wish you would." His eyes were liquid. "We're all the family we've got left."

Claire leaned across the console and kissed his stubbly cheek. "Marry that woman," she said, pointing her thumb toward the back of the van where Annie was dragging her suitcase to the sidewalk. "Then we'll have somebody else in the family. Annie's a real treasure."

Buck bobbed his head. "Maybe I'll do that one of these days."

Annie smothered her with a final hug before Claire dragged her suitcase through the sliding-glass doors. Without Annie there, it would have been hard to go back to Texas and leave her father alone.

The winding line at the security checkpoint moved efficiently and her flight departed on time. Claire settled back in her window seat as the jet banked into a turn and rose steeply, breaking through the cloud ceiling. Brilliant sunlight glinted off the wing.

Claire squinted into the sudden brightness. And there in the distance stood the regal, blue-white peak of Mt. Rainier, thrusting up through the clouds like a promise.

# Chapter Thirty-Three

On New Year's Day, Claire telephoned Mason. It was early afternoon Santa Fe time. The phone rang and rang. She was about to give up when he answered.

"'Lo?"

"Mason? It's Claire. Happy New Year."

"Oh—Claire. Hi." He sounded distant, as if he didn't quite remember who she was. "I was rehearsing my scores and almost didn't hear the phone."

She tried to accept his preoccupation with the music as a reason for the detachment in his voice. She asked how he'd been, what he'd done for Christmas, other inane questions. The conversation was filled with little silences that pulled at her breath.

"I went to Seattle to see my father," she told him.

"Ah. That's good. I'll bet it was cold up there." No indication that he remembered telling her she should go.

*How's Nathan's heart?* she almost blurted. Instead she said, "I forgot to give you my phone numbers," as if he couldn't have easily found her through directory assistance if he'd chosen to call. She reeled off her home and office numbers and said good-bye with a hollow feeling in her chest. She wondered if she'd ever hear from him again.

Twice that month she spotted the white pickup—once, following her in traffic, another time parked outside the grocery store where she'd gone after dark. She had no doubt whose it was. That night she looked up Hobson Jeeter in the phone book.

When he answered, she used her business voice, polite but firm. "Mr. Jeeter, this is Claire O'Neal."

It took him a moment to respond; clearly she'd caught him off guard. "Yes, ma'am. What can I do for you?"

"I've seen your truck following me, and I want you to stop. Stop following me, and stop sending flowers every September. Do you understand?"

Another long pause. "Mr. Jeeter? Are you there?"

"Yes, ma'am. But——"

"You've made your apology, now you must leave me alone. I don't want to call the police about this, but if I see you again, I will."

"I didn't mean you any harm," he said.

"I believe you. But it's time to stop. Please give me your word you won't do this anymore."

Again he hesitated.

"All right," he said finally. "You have my word."

When she hung up, her hands were shaking. All her life she'd hated confrontation. But now it was done; she'd given him warning.

February brought signs of spring in suburban San Antonio—yellow forsythia and pink flowering peach. She and Janelle had made a pact for the new year: Janelle would take Sundays off to be with her family, and Claire would not work more than forty hours a week. She'd added two new Realtors to the agency and they were starting to take hold and produce sales.

At her follow-up appointment with Dr. Tomay, Claire got a good report and no prescription medication. Before she left his office, the doctor asked if she had any questions.

"Yes, I do." She'd been thinking for weeks about how to ask. "Could a lack of oxygen to the brain, as one might experience during a severe episode of arrhythmia, cause a person to hallucinate? Might I have seen something or someone who wasn't really there?"

The doctor had looked at her thoughtfully, tenting his fingers beneath his chin. He took several moments before answering.

"I have not observed that particular symptom among my patients," he said slowly, "but I would not discount the possibility. Many phenomena remain unexplained by medical science. The human body astounds us all the time. And so does the human spirit."

On her morning walks she had no shortness of breath, no heart palpitations, and was grateful for her health in a way she'd never been before. Still, at introspective moments, she looked ahead and saw herself doing the same things, day after day, until she was retirement age like her dad. The insight gnawed at her ribs as she approached her fortieth birthday, and she admitted as much to Janelle.

"I wouldn't know about that," Janelle said evilly. "*I'm* only thirty-eight."

The Saturday before Easter, on the birthday she and Nathan shared, Claire found her office filled with helium balloons and an obscenely large cake with *four-zero* emblazoned on the top in black frosting. All twelve agents crowded in to share the cake and to shower her with insulting cards. It was fun and messy and over in half an hour—the perfect birthday party, in Claire's view. Then they all got back to work.

She brought three of the balloons with her to the open house she had scheduled in Terrell Hills. She attached the balloons to the sign she hammered into the front lawn, where they bobbed in the breeze like bright Easter eggs. Bluebonnets spilled from the rock garden beside the front porch of the house. She stood a moment inhaling the perfumed air and felt again the sensation of something left undone.

Only three couples toured the house in the afternoon, and at five o'clock Claire took down the balloon-decked sign and locked up. On the drive home, she watched the cross streets and the rearview mirror out of habit, but she hadn't seen anything of the white pickup since her phone call to Hobson Jeeter. Someday she would stop looking over her shoulder.

The answering machine on her kitchen counter gave two red winks as she piled her purse and clipboard on the marble countertop. She kicked off her shoes and poured a caffeine-free cola over ice while the tape rewound.

The first message was Annie, calling from Seattle, her voice round and warm. "We just wanted to wish you Happy Birthday. Hope you got our card. We can't wait to see you in May for the big day," Annie bubbled. "Don't I sound silly, planning a wedding at my age? It won't be a big deal, just us and my son-in-law the minister. And of course, my daughter and her kids. Buck sends his love and says to call him when you have time."

Claire smiled, knowing that when she called back, Buck would talk a few minutes and pass the phone to Annie. That's the way it would be from now on; her father never was much of a talker.

The next voice that came on the machine stopped her cola halfway to her mouth.

"Hi, Claire. It's Mason."

She pounced on the machine and turned up the volume. "I'm in Austin visiting my mom this weekend," he said. "I'd like to drive down and see you before I go back...." He sounded like himself, not the distant stranger she'd phoned in Santa Fe. He gave the phone number at his mother's house.

Smiling like a banana, Claire pushed the rewind button and listened again, laying her hand on the machine to feel the vibration of his voice. Then she dialed the number.

The phone seemed to ring forever before Jessica McKinnon's voice explained in a gentle drawl that no one was home. Mason must have left already. Deflated, Claire left a message that included directions to her house, just in case, plus her home number and cell phone number. She hung up, but her hand lingered on the receiver.

The doorbell rang. She padded to the door in stocking feet and peeped through the spy hole. A man wearing a sport coat and baggy jeans stood on the porch. His hair was longish and wavy, and he was holding a stuffed rabbit.

She yanked open the door.

Mason grinned. "Trick or treat."

When Nathan was small, Claire sometimes looked at him and had the sensation that she was looking at herself, she knew him so well. She had that sense now, of looking at herself in a different body, with eyes the color of cool light.

She wrapped him in a hug that would have made Annie proud. They clung together, laughing. "Don't let go," she warned. "I'm not through hugging you yet." His scent, the sound of his voice, felt like home.

Finally she pulled away and looked him in the eyes. "What took you so damned long?"

"I was giving you time," he said, "so you'd see how much you missed me. Trouble is, it worked the other way." He smiled and handed her the flop-eared bunny. "Hoppy Easter."

She hugged the rabbit. "Come in this house."

She led him through the entryway and living room into the kitchen.

"What a great house."

"I'll give you a tour later. What would you like to drink? Coffee, tea, soda?"

"Whatever you're having."

She poured him a cola and handed him the glass. She couldn't stop smiling. "You look great—and healthy."

"I got the Good Housekeeping Seal of Approval from my original transplant unit in Austin yesterday."

"Terrific."

They sat at the breakfast room table, talking fast, catching up. Mason had started working days at a music store and playing with a couple of chamber groups. He'd given up the job at Santero's and moved into a nicer apartment.

She asked about his mom, and told him about Christmas at her father's. "Oh! I have something for you," she said. "It's in my bedroom."

His eyebrows went up. "That sounds promising."

She smiled. "It isn't. It's a wood carving. Come on."

From her bureau drawer, she lifted the tissue-wrapped bundle she'd brought home from Seattle. "My dad made this."

The carving depicted a rotund grizzly bear playing a violin, his eyes closed in an expression of bear bliss. Mason laughed out loud. "This is wonderful. He carved it himself?"

She nodded. "He has dozens of little figures he's made since he was confined to a wheelchair."

"I didn't know your dad was in a wheelchair."

"I didn't, either. He's getting married in May. Proving your theory."

"My theory?"

"That lots of married couples live without sex."

"Yeah, but it's overrated," he said, and they laughed again.

She took him on a tour of the house, ending in Nathan's room. "Here's my shrine," she said wistfully. "I don't know whether I'll ever be able to change it."

Mason fell quiet when he stepped into the room. He examined each photo on the gallery wall. She could read his face when he touched Nathan's jersey that hung on the wall: *I have this boy's heart.*

Finally he turned to her, his eyes shiny. "Do you still see him?"

"No. Not for months now."

"Are you okay with that?"

She nodded. "It's better this way. I'll always miss him. But it's not as hard as it used to be."

He put his arm around her shoulders and they stood together looking at the room. Outside the windows, dusk had fallen.

She cleared her throat. "I'll bet you haven't had any dinner, and I haven't, either. Let's see what we can find."

They worked side by side in the kitchen, Mason following orders, and in half an hour sat down to fettuccine Alfredo and English peas. They talked music and real estate. She told him about her visit to the emergency room, and the truck driver named Hob. They rinsed the dishes and loaded the dishwasher as if they'd done it together a hundred times.

Eventually, he glanced at his watch. "My God, it's midnight. You should have thrown me out."

"Why? I'm having a great time. And there's absolutely no reason for you to drive back to Austin at this hour, when I have a guest bedroom that's never even been used. Should you phone your mom?"

"Actually I'm not going back to Austin. I'm heading back to Santa Fe tomorrow."

"Tomorrow?" Her face fell.

He nodded. "I have rehearsals."

"What about your mom's car?"

He grinned. "That's *my* car, even though it's used. I'll have to take care of myself now, to outlive my car payments."

He brought in his suitcase and she made sure he had everything he needed to be comfortable, then said good-night. Down the hall in her king-sized bed, she fell asleep easily, relaxed and happy.

The next morning, standing by his dusty-purple convertible in the driveway, she hugged him goodbye. "You'd better call me," she threatened.

"I will. And I don't want to go four months without seeing you again."

"Me, either."

"Then it's your turn to come to Santa Fe."

"Right after my dad's wedding. I promise."

He opened the door, but she put a hand on his arm. "Mason...I had no right to insinuate myself into your life the way I did. I know I should apologize for that. But it wouldn't be sincere because the way things turned out, I'm not sorry."

He met her eyes before answering. "I'm not, either."

"Something of Nathan still exists on this earth thanks to you. I am so grateful."

"I'll do my best to keep it safe. Always."

He hugged her again and got into his car. She watched him

drive away, part of her riding with him. And part of him was still with her. Whatever happened in the months ahead, for now, this was enough.

# Epilogue

On spring break, Lindsey Sanchez was going to fly home to San Antonio. She hadn't been home since Christmas and her mother had surprised her with a plane ticket. Lindsey had been invited to go skiing in Colorado on the break, but the image of flailing down a snowy mountainside made her shiver. She chose to travel south, where the March weather would be balmy, the flowers in bloom. And she could visit Nathan's grave on his birthday, the Ides of March.

The week before she was to leave, sitting at her desk in the office of the *Latina,* Lindsey filled out a degree-check work-sheet. She was on track to graduate at the end of summer school, nearly a year ahead of the classmates who'd started when she did. While they spent another year of their lives cloistered on campus preparing for their futures, Lindsey would be out there living hers.

The closer she came to graduation, the more she thought about Nathan. If he'd lived, they might be married by now, planning the future together. She wondered if her career would have seemed so important to her then.

At five o'clock, Lindsey struck out across campus toward her apartment. The first signs of spring greened the trees, and pansies rioted in the flower beds. Thank God winter was nearly over. Lindsey was tired, but she kept her spine straight against the thump of her book-filled backpack. Her black mules clicked efficiently on the sidewalk. She'd stopped wearing sneakers and jeans to class when she got the editor's job at the *Latina,* after the scandal that resulted in Cord Thayer's preemptive resignation and the firing of three college administrators.

She wasn't surprised at the resentment from some of her professors after she broke the story. They were mostly Cord's friends, and faculty tended to stick together like the AMA when an inferior physician was under siege. What did surprise her was the suspicion she encountered from other J-school students. Didn't they understand that it was a journalist's job to expose corruption, whatever the cost? If not, they would be media peons forever.

In response to this coolness from her professors and peers, Lindsey had started dressing more professionally. She no longer hung around the staff rooms where she used to take part in the bitching and banter. She held herself to a higher standard.

She'd also moved out of the dorm. Her roommate had dropped out to get married the previous semester, and Lindsey felt too old for the dorm atmosphere. Making the rent on an apartment was difficult, but the privacy was worth it. The editor's job came with a small salary and a tuition waiver, and when Cord had vacated his apartment and moved back to Virginia, he'd left a month's rent already paid. She'd moved in the day he left.

Cord wrote to her every week, but she'd answered only twice. Today, in the bank of mailboxes at the apartment complex, the single envelope angled inside her box showed his familiar handwriting. Lindsey sighed. It wasn't the letter she was hoping for.

At a job fair on campus, she had interviewed with representatives from the *Dallas Morning News,* the *Arizona Republic* and the *Los Angeles Times.* She already had an offer from the *KC Star*—her ace in the hole. But she wanted to get away from the Midwest and its frigid winters. The *L.A. Times* was a long shot for a rookie, but it never hurt to aim high and she had the Hispanic factor in her favor. The reps from Dallas and Phoenix had been encouraging. It was too soon to hear from any of them, really, but every day she checked the mailbox just in case.

Carrying the letter from Cord, she unlocked the door to her apartment and was welcomed by an avian shriek. "*Si,* Eduardo. I'm home."

The parrot's cage hung on a hook in one corner of the living room, close to the window so he could look out through the sheer curtain while she was gone all day. She opened the cage door, transferred his thorny feet from her finger to the top of the cage, and dug a parrot treat from the box.

*"Por favor,"* Eduardo warbled.

*"Muy bien."* She rewarded him with the treat and stroked his head. She'd brought Eduardo back from San Antonio at Christmas break. The parrot was a comfort on the long evenings when she studied past midnight and had no one to call on the phone. On those nights, she missed Cord. But most of the time she was relieved that he was gone.

In the aftermath of the scandal, she'd seen a different Cord Thayer. Most likely he hadn't changed, but her perspective had. Weaknesses hidden by the clandestine nature of their relationship became apparent in this new light. Always slight of build, Cord suddenly looked frail to her. The confidence she'd found so appealing in him began to seem superficial, even misguided. And when that mystique cracked, so did his sex appeal. Lindsey realized the secrecy of their affair had been the better part of its allure, at least for her.

She dumped her textbooks on the table she used for a desk. Her laptop and printer sat there, too, the cables kinking like entrails over the table's edge. She kicked off her shoes and picked up the letter, examining the small, tight handwriting on the front before she slit it open.

Cord's old friends at the *Washington Post* had helped him wangle a job there. He'd wanted her to come with him to D.C., finish her degree at Georgetown or one of half a dozen other universities peppered around the nation's capital. In fact, he'd begged. But it made no sense to change schools two terms before she was to graduate. She was bound to lose credits and set herself back at least one semester.

Cord's neediness repelled her. Nathan would have had more dignity.

In today's letter, he was trying a new tack, hinting that he might be able to get her on staff at the *Washington Post* after she graduated. But she wasn't naive enough to think the *Post* would take on a rookie without hard experience someplace else. And she doubted whether Cord's recommendation counted for much.

Lindsey tossed the letter onto a stack of returned assignments on the table. Her stomach rumbled. She'd skipped lunch that day, but she was too tired to go out. Time to rummage through the fridge, then hit the books. She had a hundred pages of *Law and the Courts* to review before tomorrow's exam.

At 1:00 a.m., Lindsay awoke slumped over the table face-down, drooling on Constitutional Freedoms. Eduardo had already sought out his cage. She covered him up and went to bed, setting her alarm for six so she could finish studying in the morning.

The next day Lindsey left the classroom feeling anxious about the test. That usually meant she'd made a B instead of an A; she never made anything less. But she wanted an A in this class, particularly. She'd set her sights on law school and if she couldn't ace the J-school version of a law class, it didn't bode well for the LSAT.

She didn't want to practice law, but the degree would set her résumé above the others and be invaluable in the field of investigative reporting. Law school with a full-time job would be tough and leave no time for a social life, but she didn't have much of one now. Except for Hunter McDonald.

Hunter was a graduate assistant in the zoology department. She'd met him a few weeks after Cord left. She was doing a story on the growing number of successful women in research, and the entrenched obstacles they had to face in getting research grants compared to their male counterparts. Hunter had put her in touch with several good interview subjects, and she'd offered to buy him lunch as a way of saying thanks.

Hunter had smiled at her invitation. "I'm sort of engaged," he said. His brown eyes and athletic build reminded her of Nathan.

"So that means you don't eat? I didn't offer to date you, just buy you a burger."

Even his laugh was a little like Nathan's. "Point taken. I accept."

At lunch, she'd questioned him about his background, his goals. Hunter was like any other guy; those were his favorite subjects. Those and genetic research. By the end of lunch he'd invited her to come by the lab and see the fascinating project they were doing with fruit flies.

"You have got to be kidding," she said. "I'd rather sit through a foreign film with no subtitles."

He shrugged. "Okay. We can do that."

And that's how they started dating. Hunter turned out not to be as engaged as he thought. Or as good a lover. But at least he was intelligent and he read the newspaper. And he didn't whine when she turned down his invitation for a ski trip on spring break.

On Saturday morning, Lindsey caught a bus to the airport. The caretaker's wife at the apartment complex was thrilled to babysit Eduardo. Lindsey's mom met her at the

San Antonio airport just outside the security checkpoint, her face a wreath of welcome. When they hugged, Lindsey noticed a new softness in her mother's body, a few more lines in the beloved face. It hurt her to think of her mother growing old. Thank goodness she had Carlos, who loved her and treated her well.

Lindsey had always believed you could tell how a man would treat his wife by the way he treated his mother. That was one of the things she'd admired about Nathan; he and his mom were friends, like Lindsey and Maria were. Hunter had said he avoided visiting his mother because she was a nag. At that moment, Lindsey stopped taking him seriously.

On a day full of warm sunshine and Gulf moisture, Lindsey borrowed her mom's car and drove to a cemetery outside the city limits, a peaceful plot of ground away from traffic noise and air pollution. The first year, Maria had come with her, but after that she'd told her mom she wanted to come alone.

Already the grass here was green. Dandelions scattered the hillside like chips of the sun. Wild bluebonnets danced in the adjoining field, and the smell of Confederate jasmine perfumed the breeze. Standing at Nathan's grave with the spring wind blowing her hair, Lindsey pictured his smile as clearly as if he were standing beside her. Funny how his face had never faded in her memory. She remembered his athletic body, the scent of his skin, the dark eyes that held no deceit.

In the granite vase atop his tombstone, she placed a bouquet of white calla lilies, the kind she always brought. Pure white, like the ones she'd sent to him every year on the anniversary of his death.

Today, it didn't seem enough.

Lindsey knelt in the grass and used her fingers to dig a small cavity next to the headstone. She kept working until the hole was several inches deep. Then she twisted her high school ring from her finger. The ring's weight felt surprisingly substantial in her palm. She looked at it for a moment, the red stone and gold initials. Its absence left a white mark on her finger, like a scar. She placed the ring inside the hole and covered it up, tamping down the displaced grass.

Lindsey stood and gazed down at the carved tombstone. This would likely be the last spring that she came to his grave. There was no telling where she might be a year from now.

A train whistle echoed in the distance, and Lindsey had a sudden vision of all the men she would meet in her life, passing by like a regiment, changing like the seasons. Kent Woolery was damaged goods; Hunter McDonald, a minor diversion. Cord had enthralled her for a time, but in the end he was a disappointment. She saw other faces, men she had yet to meet. Some would be significant for a while, but most were inconsequential.

From her shoulder bag she pulled a T-shirt with the number thirteen on the front. She lifted it to her face and inhaled its fading scent one more time. Then hung the tattered shirt across the gravestone and said goodbye.

A regiment of men might come and go, but for Lindsey there would never be anyone like Nathan O'Neal.

## MORE ABOUT THIS BOOK

## MORE ABOUT THE AUTHOR

## WE RECOMMEND

MIRA

Read all about it...

## QUESTIONS FOR YOUR READING GROUP

1. Mason suffers from survivor's guilt—but he isn't the only one. Which other characters experience this emotion, and why?

2. How would you feel about allowing your spouse/child's organs to be removed and donated? Would you then want to meet the recipients?

3. Do you know someone who is an organ recipient? Have you notified your family that you'd want to donate any usable organs in case of accidental death?

4. Do you believe that "cell memory" can really exist? What evidence do you see for it, or against it?

5. A major theme in the story is Claire's loss of faith, both in life and in a higher power. When did this disillusionment begin for Claire? Are there signs later in the story that she will regain her faith in life?

6. How does the contrast in climate between San Antonio and Santa Fe reflect Claire's changing state of mind?

7. Lindsey says part of her attraction to Cord Thayer lay in the forbidden nature of the relationship. If Mason and Claire had met under other circumstances, without the link of Nathan's heart, do you think they'd still have been attracted to each other?

8. What do you think was the turning point for Mason: playing the violin again? The letter from Julia's mother (as Claire supposes)? The night she stayed with him? Or some other incident?

9.  Was there a turning point for Claire, or was the change more gradual?

10. Why does Mason tell Claire she needs to talk to her father?

11. The author has said this is a story with no villains—just ordinary, flawed people with lessons to learn. What does each principal character need to learn?

12. Do you believe Claire's "mirages" were caused by her arrhythmia, or were they actual visitations of Nathan's spirit?

*Read all about it…*

## INSPIRATION FOR *The Story of Us*

A year or so ago, a local television station aired a commercial about a woman whose son was killed in a car crash, and his heart was donated to a man dying of heart disease. The commercial showed the mother laying her hand on the man's chest, where her son's heart still beat. Every time I saw it, I cried—and the story started from there.

*The Story of Us* is about a mother who after three years has not coped with the sudden loss of her teenage son. She sets out, without going through approved channels, to find the recipient of her son's heart, and finds him smoking, drinking, and wasting his life. In trying to save his life against his will, she eventually saves her own. In a larger context, the novel is about the ripple effects of a heart transplant on the families of both the donor and the recipient.

*"…In trying to save his life against his will, she eventually saves her own…"*

## MARCIA PRESTON ON WRITING

**What do you love most about being a writer?**

I like the idea of leaving some kind of record that I once lived on this planet.

Then, too, in real life I rarely can think of what I really want to say, or should have said, until the moment has passed. But in writing, I get time to think of it. And then edit.

**Where do you go for inspiration?**

*"...thunder-storms are inspiring and so is the ocean..."*

Outdoors. Writing keeps one hovering over a computer screen for long hours, and I try to get outdoors a bit every day, at least for a walk. Sailing on water, planting things in the soil, feeling the wind on my face—any kind of contact with nature centres me and fills me up again. Thunderstorms are inspiring, and so is the ocean.

**Where do your characters come from, and do they ever surprise you as you write?**

They surprise me constantly as I get deeper and deeper into the story, and if they don't, we're in trouble. As to where they come from, I'm not quite sure. Some of them are amalgams of certain characteristics from people I've met, but after I've cold-bloodedly assigned them a few primary traits or motivations, the rest grows organically from what the character wants, and from the story.

**When did you start writing?**

I wrote fictional stories when I was in high school, but in that time and place I had no concept that a girl could grow up to be a writer. But as a young mother who spent quite a bit of time with no adult companionship, I took up fiction again and began sending out my stories. They were ghastly. But I kept at it, and over the years the stories got better.

**What one piece of advice would you give a writer wanting to start a career?**

Write a million words, study craft, and never, never, never give up.

**What are you currently working on?**

I'm working now on a novel set in Berlin during the early years of the Berlin Wall, 1962-63, and also in the US during the Kennedy years. It's the story of a mother who is separated from her baby son by the Wall, and what she's willing to risk to be with him again.

## TOP TEN BOOKS

Naming twenty-five favourite books would be easier than naming ten. I narrowed it down by choosing only contemporary works that I admire so much (for different reasons) I wish I had written them. They are listed in random order.

*The Blind Assassin,* by Margaret Atwood

*The Poisonwood Bible*, by Barbara Kingsolver

*Pigs in Heaven,* by Barbara Kingsolver

*A Prayer for Owen Meany,* by John Irving

*Sometimes a Great Notion,* by Ken Kesey

*Pilgrim at Tinker Creek,* by Annie Dillard

*All the Pretty Horses,* by Cormac McCarthy

*Eats, Shoots and Leaves: The Zero Tolerance Approach to Punctuation,* by Lynne Truss

*Let Evening Come,* poems by Jane Kenyon

*A River Runs Through It,* by Norman Maclean

"...I write
for three to
five hours
and mostly
it's agony,
except
when it's
ecstasy..."

## A DAY IN THE LIFE OF
## MARCIA PRESTON

I usually get up about 6:30 a.m., if the cat doesn't wake me first. I try to leave the bed without waking my husband and noodle my way downstairs to the coffee pot, which I've set to brew before I get up. I gather two mugs of coffee and a muffin or bagel and go back upstairs to my office. I turn on the computer and let the hum warm my fingers and my brain. In winter, I sit inside a sleeping bag to keep my feet warm. I turn on only one small light, so the room is quite dim and I can fall into the fictional world of my characters before I'm fully awake, before the day's ordinary tasks start to fill up my mind.

I write for three to five hours, and mostly it's agony. Except when it's ecstasy. Then I stop and get dressed, check my e-mail and talk to Paul about what's going on that day. He's semi-retired, so he's usually there at mid-morning. If the weather is decent, we go out for a two-mile hike through an adjoining neighbourhood.

Our house is not in the neighbourhood. We live on three acres, which used to be on the south edge of town and surrounded by pastureland. Now it's surrounded by other houses and office buildings, but at least they are tasteful and quiet. Our house is a two-storey split-level, stone and cedar, thirty years old. We built it ourselves with the help of hired contractors. We have several flower gardens and a huge vegetable garden. There's a creek behind the house. Before the buildings moved in around us, we had foxes, bobcats, raccoons and coyotes that came through the back yard, but they're scarce now. My office has four windows that overlook the front and side yard, which is mostly trees.

After my morning walk, I usually have a short time to do some correspondence or laundry or whatever needs doing, then make a light lunch. In the afternoon I change hats and become editor of *ByLine*, a small-press magazine for freelance writers. I've owned the magazine for twenty years; it's my day job. I run the magazine from a home office, which is popular nowadays in the States. I started working from a home office long before it was cool, though. I have a small staff who also work part-time from their own home offices, and my husband pitches in, too. I generally put in four to five hours on the magazine, depending on where we are in the publication cycle. I may have to make trips to the printer, or post office or mailing service. Then it's time for a nice glass of wine before dinner. Saturdays are pretty much the same, unless we go to a football game (I don't mean soccer), or work on some home maintenance project. We travel quite a bit, too, mostly to writers' conferences where I've been asked to speak.

*"...Once you read like a writer it's hard to stop..."*

When my sons were teenagers, I cooked a lot, and the thrill is gone. I tell my husband that our next house will have no kitchen. But most evenings I cook anyway, because he likes my cooking. After that, he settles in to watch something on TV, and this is my reading time. Often I'm reading research material for my next book, and even when I read for pleasure, I'm learning from my reading. Once you read like a writer, it's hard to stop. I read one word at a time, and I often go back and review sentences to see why I liked them so much.

I don't watch much TV. It's pretty bad stuff, mostly, and I always have something else that needs to be done—if not reading, then more work on the magazine. I do like the original

*CSI* programme, though (that's my mystery-writing roots cropping up), and I used to like *Judging Amy*, but I'm not sure if that's still on. And I like *Three and a Half Men*, because it makes me laugh.

I spent thirteen years teaching in public high schools, and every day that I don't have to go back there I am a lucky woman. One day I will sell my magazine and spend more time in my gardens and watching the birds. (I keep a life list.) We own a small cabin near a lake in southern Oklahoma, and I'd enjoy spending more time there. My husband is an avid fisherman, and I like riding around in the boat with him and zoning out. I always take a pad and pen to write with.

## ABOUT THE AUTHOR

*Photograph by Paul A Preston*

**Marcia Preston** grew up in Oklahoma. From her father, she learned the art of storytelling; from her mother, a reverence for books. Marcia was a teacher for more than a decade, and then worked as PR and publications director. She lives with her childhood sweetheart and first husband (it's the same guy) beside a creek in central Oklahoma, where she gardens and dodges tornadoes.

## MARCIA'S DEBUT UK NOVEL,
### *The Butterfly House*

Roberta and Cynthia are destined to be best friends forever. Unable to cope with her alcoholic mother, Roberta finds Cynthia's house the perfect carefree refuge. Cynthia's mother keeps beautiful, rare butterflies and she's everything Roberta wishes her own mother could be. But just like the delicate creatures they nurture, the women are living in a hothouse.

Years later, a hauntingly familiar stranger knocks on Roberta Dutreau's door, forcing her to begin a journey back to childhood. But is she ready to know the truth about what happened to her, her best friend Cynthia and their mothers that tragic night ten years ago?

**"A tragic tale that will stay with you long after you've finished it. 5 stars."**
**—*Cosmopolitan***

*The Butterfly House*
is available now from all good bookshops.

*Turn the page to read an excerpt...*

# CHAPTER 1

*Alberta, Canada, March 1990*

From the window of my husband's house, I see the stranger stop beside our gate at the bottom of the snow-covered hill. He steps from his black Chevy Blazer, leaving the door open, and peers at the name on our mailbox. His down jacket hangs unzipped despite the cold overcast of the morning, and he's wearing cowboy boots. Even from this distance I am struck by the contrast of his black hair against the snow.

"You have the wrong house," I whisper, hoping he'll turn around and go back the way he came. Instead he gets back in the car and drives slowly up the slope. *Damn.*

I switch off the single lamp on the sunporch and lay aside the pillowtop I'm embroidering, a gift for someone I love. This one is a yellow-and-black anise swallowtail, scientifically correct. A dozen other pairs of silent wings lie stacked on a closet shelf—my butterfly collection, David calls it. Each time he says the words I feel the wings inside my chest. He has no idea.

From the cool shadows of the house, I watch the stranger park his car and walk up the snow-packed sidewalk to the front door. He is surefooted and somber. I guess him to be about fifty, nearly twice my age, and for some reason this makes me even more uneasy. I stand motionless, holding my breath as he rings the bell and waits.

*Go away. It's the wrong house.*

He rings again. He doesn't look like a robber or rapist, but I'm too tired to open the door and pretend to be amiable while I give him directions to whatever he's seeking. I need my solitude, especially today. I realize I'm pressing one palm flat against my abdomen and jerk the hand away, clenching my fist. My breathing clots in my chest.

The bell chimes again, and I jump when the doorjamb rattles under his knock.

*Go away, for heaven's sake! Nobody's home. Whoever you're looking for isn't here.*

And then the stranger calls my name.

Not Roberta Dutreau, my married name, but my childhood name.

"Roberta Lee? Bobbie?"

His voice sounds deep and somehow muffled. "I saw your light. Please open the door."

My heart pounds. I don't know this man; how does he know me? David is at work—I don't know what to do.

"Please," he calls out. "It's about Lenora."

My breath sucks in. I hurry to the door and jerk it open, sending small tufts of snow onto the hallway floor. No one ever uses this door.

The stranger stands bareheaded, his weight on one leg with both knees bowing outward like a cowboy's. But he isn't a cowboy. He's Indian. His dark eyes meet mine and there's something familiar there—something I cannot name. He's stocky and muscular, a full head taller than I am.

I haven't spoken aloud all morning and my voice sounds hoarse. "Is something wrong with Lenora?"

The stranger keeps one hand in his jacket pocket and the other hooked by the thumb through the belt loop of his jeans. When he finally speaks, his bass voice is flat and expressionless. "You mean besides ten years of prison life?"

I grip the edge of the door with both hands. "Who *are* you?"

He meets my eyes again. "I'm Harley Jaines."

The name echoes in my head, bounces through the empty rooms. *Harley Jaines Harley Jaines Harley Jaines...*

"You *bastard*." I grip the door tighter. "Harley Jaines is dead."

"Sorry to contradict you, but I'm not." A muscle in his jaw twitches.

I remember a photograph from years ago, a young man in uniform with the same black eyes—my best friend's missing father. How I envied Cynthia the heroic status of that photo.

And now he stands at my door.

When my knees sag, the stranger reaches a hand toward my elbow, but I shrink away. He drops his hand to his side. "You'd better sit down. May I come in?"

I turn without answering and weave my way back to the sunporch, my hands touching each chair back and door frame as if I'm walking on a moving train. I hear the door close behind me and his quiet footsteps as he follows.

Sinking into the flowered chair beside the lamp, I pull the afghan over my legs and hug my knees tightly to my chest. He stands in the center of the room, waiting, and finally sits on the sofa without being invited.

His voice is so low-pitched it's hard to distinguish the words above the buzzing in my ears. "I'm sorry to surprise you like this. I need to talk to you about Lenora."

"Have you been to see her?" I ask.

He nods. "Regularly, for several months. Ever since I found out where she was."

"How is she?"

"She says she's all right, but she isn't. I can see it in her eyes."

"We thought…she said you were killed in Vietnam."

His eyes look away. "It's a long story."

He leans back, gazing out the wide windows toward the end-less vista of snow-covered pines. "What I came about," Harley Jaines says finally. "Lenora needs your help."

He looks at me as if waiting for a reaction. But my mind has flown a dozen years away from here, to a house called Rockhaven that overlooks the Columbia River. I'm seeing Lenora the way she was then.

"I talked to the lawyer who represented her, if you can call it that," the stranger says. "He's convinced there was more to what happened than Lenora told him."

The wings rise to the back of my mouth. I wonder if he can see them beating behind my eyes as I regard him blankly. "And what does Lenora say?"

"She's told me about most of her life, a little at a time. She talks about you a lot. But she won't talk about that night."

He waits. A patient man. But my heart is like the permafrost beneath the northern Canadian soil. Resistant, enduring. I face him with silence.

"The attorney thinks you know the whole story. Says that when you were in the hospital, you told him Lenora was innocent."

My mouth twists. "Which hospital? Which time?" But I know exactly what he means.

"Lenora has a parole hearing in two weeks. I want you to come and testify. I've hired an attorney, a good one this time, and we're going to ask for more than parole. We're going to try for a pardon."

Harley Jaines watches my face. "She shouldn't have gone to prison," he says. "You know that, and I know it. I believe you have the power to set her free, if you come to the hearing and tell the truth."

I shake my head. "You're wrong. I have no power."

Outside, it has begun to snow again. I watch the air thicken. From the windows of our sunporch the world is a Christmas card, the pines stacked deep with snow. Despite the warmth of the house, I feel winter in my limbs.

"She's dying in that prison," he says. "When the spirit dies, the body follows."

*Wrong again. I'm living proof.* How can he be so naive? He's twice my age, a war veteran, a Cherokee, as I remember. But I don't bother to contradict him.

"Bobbie," says this man I've never met before, using the nickname he has no right to use, the nickname his daughter gave me. "Do you know where Cynthia is?"

The question catches me unprepared. I stammer. "I hear from her now and then."

"Why hasn't she visited her mother?"

My eyes cloud and I tighten my mouth to keep my face blank. "You'd have to ask her that."

"I'd like to," he says. "I'd like to see my daughter. She doesn't even know I'm alive."

Cynthia Jaines's husky, anguished voice on the phone six months ago echoes in my head. I picture the thin ghost who came to see me at Green Gables—a euphemism for the mental health facility where I lived for five years before I married David. Would seeing Harley Jaines save Cynthia, or push her, too, over the edge?

"She never gives me an address. I have the impression she moves around a lot. I don't know where she is." This is all true, so I meet his eyes when I say it. I've never been a good liar.

He nods, his face impassive. I can't tell if he believes me. *Where were you all those years,* I wonder. *Why did you let Lenora think you were dead?*

But I don't want to know his secrets. I don't even want to know mine.

My mind flutters to the appointment I've made at the women's clinic tomorrow morning and my stomach contracts. Will I be able to drive myself home afterward? What if I'm ill, or bleeding? What can I tell David that he will believe?

If Cynthia were here, she'd go with me. She'd take care of me, lie for me. Or talk me out of the decision I've made. I pull the afghan around my arms and take a deep breath. When Harley Jaines stands up, it startles me.

"I'll let you know when the hearing is scheduled," he says. "May I have your phone number?"

Perhaps if he can call me, he won't come here again. I rise slowly, untangling myself from the afghan, and scribble the number on a pad by the phone. I hand him the paper without meeting his eyes. "Please don't call in the evenings."

He accepts it with cigar-shaped fingers that bear no rings. "Lenora doesn't know I'm here," he says, and pauses. "You tried to tell the truth once, but no one would listen. I'm asking you to try again."

Suddenly I'm weary of his childish assumptions. My voice tightens. "Truth doesn't set people free. Didn't you learn that in the war? You have no idea what you're asking."

This time his dark eyes register some emotion, and I see them take note of the scars that snake down my jawline and flood my throat. He has no right to come here and ask me to rake those scars raw again.

A thought comes to me that his sudden appearance might be some cosmic punishment for the procedure I've consented to tomorrow.

But no. That decision is merciful. I'm sane enough, at least, to know that. If I never know another thing for certain, I know I have neither the right nor the skills to mother a child.

I lead Harley Jaines to the door, close and lock it behind him. But with my back pressed against the door, my eyes closed, I see a vision of Lenora as a young woman—Lenora, with the ocean-colored eyes, the person I've loved most in all my life.

*This isn't fair.*

Then I remember Lenora seven years ago, in a cold room floored in cheap tile. Her face looked ashen against the orange prison garb, her long chestnut hair already dulled and streaked with gray. And I hear the prison guard's comment behind my back as I stepped into the visiting room: "Ain't *she* something? Come to visit her mother's killer."

Outside, the black Blazer's engine bursts into life. I lean against the door until I hear the SUV drive away, then make my way back to the sunporch. Without turning on the lamp, I stand at the window and watch the snow.

Harley Jaines is wrong.

No one knows the truth about Lenora and Cynthia Jaines, Ruth and Bobbie Lee. Least of all me.

*Read all about it...*

## MARCIA PRESTON'S NEW NOVEL

### *West of the Wall*

The Wall built around East Berlin in 1961, cutting it off from the West, heralds the end of Trudy Von Hulst's safe existence. Her husband, Rolf, becomes embroiled in the political fight, helping desperate Germans escape to the West. But Rolf is betrayed, and his flight from East Berlin has fatal consequences.

The wife of a defector, Trudy's life is at risk, but help comes from an unlikely source—Wolfgang Kruge, an ardent Communist. He arranges for her escape through the Wall, telling her it's the only way she'll live to raise her baby son, Johann; but little does she know that Rolf is already dead.

Desolate and alone in the West, Trudy is wretched with grief at being tricked into leaving Johann and her desperation to be reunited with him knows no bounds. But when Trudy receives word from Wolfgang that her mother-in-law has died, leaving Johann in his care, Trudy faces a horrific dilemma: her son is now with the man she believes betrayed her husband—just what is she prepared to sacrifice to get him back?

**Marcia Preston's stunning new novel, *West of the Wall*, will be available in January 2008 from all good booksellers.**

*Read all about it...*

**If you enjoyed *The Story of Us,* we know you'll love...**

### *Everything Must Go* by Elizabeth Flock

To those on the outside, the Powells are a happy family, but then a devastating accident destroys their fragile façade. When seven-year-old Henry is blamed for the tragedy, he tries desperately to make his parents happy again. As Henry grows up, he is full of potential, but soon he questions if the guilt his parents have burdened him with has left him unable to escape his anguished family or their painful past.

### *Angel's Rest* by Charles Davies

It's 1967, and eleven-year-old Charlie York lives in Angel's Rest. His town is a poor boy's paradise —until a shotgun blast kills Charlie's father and puts his mother on trial for murder. When reclusive veteran Hollis Thrasher is also linked to the death, Charlie must embark on a dangerous midnight journey so that the truth about what he witnessed that fateful day can finally be revealed.

### *The Lovers' Room* by Steven Carroll

As the Allied forces occupy Japan at the end of World War II, an intense love affair develops between Allen "Spin" Bowler, an interpreter in the British army, and Japanese Momoko. In the quiet sanctuary of Momoko's room, Spin gradually sheds his shy bookish self and their love blossoms. However, the betrayal that follows has devastating consequences, forever changing the course of both their lives.